JFK &
the Muckers
of Choate

bancroft
press

SCOTT BADLER

Bancroft Press' Other Fine YA Books

Cover Design: Janet Perr Design
Interior Design: TracyCopesCreative.com

978-161088-566-9 (HC)
978-161088-567-6 (PB)
978-161088-568-3 (Ebook)
978-161088-569-0 (Audio)

bancroft
press

Published by Bancroft Press
"Books that Enlighten"
410-358-0658
P.O. Box 65360,
Baltimore, MD 21209
www.bancroftpress.com

Printed in the United States of America

Based mostly on real events and actual people.

AUTHOR'S NOTE

Why write an entire book about a famous person while he was in prep school?

Because I am interested in beginnings. And I think the beginning for John F. Kennedy was at the Choate School in Wallingford, Connecticut. It was here he began to define himself as a leader, to figure out his place within a large and competitive family, and to confront his seemingly perpetual health issues.

If he were alive today, he'd tell you he wasn't happy attending that strict boarding school. But perhaps that adversity helped him find his footing, realize his potential, and discover his strength and courage.

Thousands of books have been written about JFK and the Kennedys—sometimes called America's Royal Family. But while a few of them deal with his early years, the great majority focus either on his presidency or assassination, or go forward only from the saga of the PT-109 during WW II. But much of what happened at Choate informed the rest of his life. Hence, *JFK & the Muckers of Choate*.

This story is a work of fiction, but what I have written is based on real events and actual people.

While the book centers around the major events in young Kennedy's life between January 1934 and June 1935, I have taken a liberty usually granted to writers of historical fiction. While the Muckers Club existed for only a couple of months in 1935, I have expanded that period, and placed its start at the beginning of the book—namely 1934. I believe this helps create a more cohesive and interesting narrative,

Occasionally, I have created scenes and events to portray Kennedy's possible mindset and what he might have done. An example of this is his collaboration with the local high school in Wallingford, Connecticut.

A few secondary characters have been rounded out or given fictional names. For example, I have given an identity to Sergeant, one of the laborers Kennedy picks up on the road and later socializes with at the roadhouse. And though Choate did have a Campus Cops organization, I gave the leader a name and a personality.

I also advanced in time Kennedy's effort to rescind his and his club mates' expulsions. And I added a story line ... that he sought assistance from Queenie, the headmaster's' wife, Clara, the wife of the assistant headmaster, and Mr. Pratt, his Public Speaking teacher. But I think they would have helped the Muckers' cause, and indeed, might well have assisted JFK had he asked. And although there was certainly a madam at the brothel, Miss T is a character I created.

Kennedy was a writer himself, the author of several non-fiction books, including *Profiles in Courage*, for which he won a Pulitzer Prize for biography. (In fact, in 1990, the Kennedy family created the Profile in Courage Award to honor individuals who have acted with courage in the same vein as those profiled in the book).

Fortunately, he was also a prolific letter writer, and many of his more colorful letters and notes were to his best friend for life, Lem Billings. That correspondence was an invaluable resource for me, because it sheds light on this rebellious yet charming character—quite a contrast to the suave, sophisticated fellow who many of us knew as the adult JFK.

The oral histories of Billings and his Mucker friends, all available at the JFK Presidential Library in Boston, MA, were greatly beneficial to me in the writing.

I first became swept up in my Kennedy journey during the presidential campaign of 1960. My family were Democrats, and we were for Kennedy.

I recall facing off against Nixon supporters at Stagg Street School in Los Angeles on Election Day. "Nix on Nixon" we yelled at the top of our lungs. Perhaps we had the unconscious belief that if we shouted louder than the Nixon kids, Kennedy would win, maybe not enough to win California, which he lost narrowly (it was Nixon's home state), but so enough voters heard us across the nation to enable Kennedy to become our 35th president.

The next big Kennedy event I can recall was November 1963, when I saw television images of his alleged assassin, Lee Harvey Oswald, Oswald's own subsequent murder on live TV, and the somber JFK funeral procession. For four days, there was only one program on all the broadcast networks, and no commercial breaks.

But it was when his younger brother Bobby (who had served as JFK's attorney general) ran for the Senate in New York in 1966 and then the Presidency in 1968 that I became captivated by this remarkable family. Bobby touched me with his moral courage, toughness, and evolution as champion of the poor and the oppressed.

And those eyes. After his brother's death, I saw in them equal parts sadness and wisdom. Even today, I still get choked up thinking about him.

Memorably, my father and I attended a Kennedy rally at a local community college in Los Angeles, or at least tried to.

Because my father got home late that day from work, we weren't able to get inside the packed auditorium to hear his speech. But that turned out to be a blessing. Before the event began, we waited outside for an hour. Then suddenly, a motorcade, flashing lights, roaring motorcycle engines, and pandemonium. Out came Bobby. I charged towards him just as he left his limousine, offered my hand, and was rewarded with a brief touch.

Less than two months later, he was assassinated in Los Angeles after winning the California presidential primary.

His younger brother Ted took the family mantle, and became known as the "Lion of the Senate" for his long tenure and considerable influence. He was unsuccessful in his attempt to wrest the Democratic nomination from the incumbent president, Jimmy Carter, in 1980.

As the years went by, I widened my gaze to see what other members of the family were up to. There was plenty—both accomplishments and tragedies. But that's another story.

For many years, I lived in the Greater Boston area, perhaps drawn there by the Kennedys. While living in the same Congressional District in which Kennedy won his first election in 1946, I attended numerous lectures and programs at the JFK Library and Harvard University that involved the family.

But it wasn't until I moved back to the San Francisco Bay Area that I began to consider writing a book about the youthful JFK. After re-reading *A Catcher in the Rye*, I was struck by the similarities between the rebellious Holden Caulfield and what little I knew of Jack's turbulent prep school years.

I returned to the East Coast to examine the vast materials at the JFK Library, make side trips to Hyannis in Cape Cod, and visit the Choate School to get a sense of his life there. What a wonderful excuse to go back.

JFK & the Muckers of Choate is the story of Jack Kennedy and his lively and eventful teen years. And although it's been more than sixty years since Kennedy was elected to the White House, his life and family name endure in our collective consciousness.

If he hadn't faced up to his many Choate School challenges and matured in the process, his place in history might well have been very different.

Scott Badler

September 2021

CHAPTER ONE

Winter 1934
The Choate School
Wallingford, CT

"Kennedy, what are you doing?" housemaster J.J. Maher bellowed from the top of the stairs. Maher placed his hands on his hips as if he were the Italian dictator Benito Mussolini.

Clutching my large wooden trunk, I stopped in my tracks, teetering on a stair.

"Taking my luggage down to the basement, sir. Nothing in it."

"I don't care whether it's empty or full. You're disturbing others on your wing tending to their studies. They're being productive." He paused. "Unlike you."

"But school hasn't started yet, sir." It was the first day back from break. "Nobody's studying."

Maher shook his head. "You know better than that, Kennedy. Or should. Your brother Joseph would have." Pointing to my trunk, he said, "Take that back up to your room. Store it in the morning."

I stared, stone-faced. "Can I leave it here and bring it the rest of the way tomorrow morning?" Worth a try.

"No."

My muscles quivering, I glared up at him, then turned and hauled the trunk back to my room, slamming the door behind me.

Splayed on the bed was my roommate Kirk LeMoyne Billings —most of the time, he went by "Lem."

I grabbed my Physics book off my desk and hurled it at the wall separating our room from Maher's, then dropped into my chair and crossed my arms.

One minute ago, I'd been in a good mood, even if I was back at school. It was great to reconnect with Lem, whom I hadn't seen since the Christmas holidays, and I was looking forward to a few fun days before school started. Now all the good feelings had vanished.

"Johnny, that's the first time I've seen you touch that book all year," Lem cracked.

It was true. I didn't like Physics, so I didn't study. The same for French. I was perfectly content just getting by.

"Three years here have taken their toll on me," I said.

Lem sat up, his bulk taking up the entire bed. At six-feet-two, he was several inches taller than me and outweighed me by more than twenty pounds. He was also a year older and, unlike me, a sixth-former. He'd graduate in June.

"I don't know how much more I can take, Lemmer. And it's only been a few hours."

I'd met Lem while working on *The Brief*, the school's yearbook. We clicked almost immediately after discovering we both had enjoyed the *Billy Whiskers* children's books about a mischievous goat. Lem and I laughed at the same things and always had a good time together. And if I became discouraged about school, he cheered me up. As best friends, we were constantly inventing crazy nicknames for each other. He called me Ken, Kenadosus, Ratface, and Johnny, and for him I came up with LeMoan, DeLemma, Leem, Lemmer, Moines, and Moynie to name a few. Last year, we began rooming together.

Using my penknife, I began scratching my "JFK" initials into one of my desk legs. If I didn't finish school, at least there'd be a lasting memory of me.

"Your father would flip his lid if you don't graduate," Lem said. "Things will get better."

"He'd get over it. Besides, Joe's the one he expects big things from. He's got the most ambitious plans for him: Kennedy for President. That means Joe. Some shit, eh?"

"Really?" Lem said, wide-eyed. "That's a lot of pressure."

I looked at my trunk and scowled, thinking about what had just happened. I had to do something. Would revenge make me feel better?

"Maher is quite a problem. I'll be damned if I'm going to let him get away with this."

"What're you going to do?" Lem asked. Maher was Lem's football coach.

I jerked to my feet so swiftly my hair quivered. Sometimes the best solution is the most obvious. "I'll do exactly what he says. Bring the trunk down tomorrow morning."

"I don't get it," Lem said, stroking his chin.

"Maher said to take it down in the morning. I will. *Very* early in the morning. Our beloved housemaster will thank me for starting his day long before the crack of dawn." I smirked.

Lem grinned back at me. "I admire how you're always trying to help people. May I say you set an excellent example for all mankind?"

"Don't need to, Lemmer. I already know that."

Several hours before daybreak, I grabbed my trunk and dragged it downstairs, hitting each step with a thunderous *da-dump*. I even gave one stair a second helping—back up and then right back down again. Doors opened. "What's going on?" I heard somebody ask.

I was halfway down the stairs when Maher, clad in striped pajamas, stormed out of his room, a wisp of hair standing Mohawk-style atop his head. "Kennedy, have you lost your mind?!" he roared.

"You told me to take my trunk down in the morning. It is morning, isn't it?"

Silence reigned, except for the rattle and hiss from a near-by radiator. Maher's lips locked as if they'd been sewn together. Speechless. That's how I liked him. I finished the job, clattering the trunk the rest of the way down the stairs to the cellar. *Da-dump. Da-dump. Da-dump!*

———◆———

Later that morning, I trudged downstairs for breakfast. No need to hurry; I was already late. The familiar din of hundreds of guys chattering, the clink of silverware, and the smell of bacon greeted me as I entered the dining hall. Sun streamed through the large arched windows, and students were crammed into groups of eight at round oak tables.

At Choate, we were required to sit with our housemasters for all meals so they could keep an eye on us. The housemasters were on our backs even at dining hall, and Maher had to be the worst. "Kennedy, eat your vegetables." "Billings, you've got a speck of roast beef lodged between your teeth."

Maher had had it in for me from the start. And now there was no way to avoid him because he was everywhere: housemaster, teacher, and even football coach. My first year, he tried me out on the offensive line—the worst place for a scrawny guy like me. I longed to catch passes as an offensive end or toss them as quarterback. He cut me. Joe made the sting of not making the team worse by reminding me he had played on Choate's undefeated 1932 team. After that, I was relegated to the intramural squad for a couple of years and junior varsity last year. To make matters worse, I also had Maher for English. He always sneered when disclosing my punctuation and spelling mistakes to the entire class.

For my belated breakfast, I slid into an empty chair next to Rip Horton, a good friend. Rip was the serious sort, a bookend to Lem's boisterousness.

"Bow heads. Morning Prayer."

Student servers brought out separate platters of boiled eggs, bacon, and creamed codfish toast, placing everything in front of Maher, who sat at the head of our table. Grabbing the first platter, he placed the creamed codfish in the center of his toast and surrounded it with an egg on the left and two strips of bacon on the right. He took his own sweet time about passing the platters. I was the last to get them.

"Thanks for the early wake-up call, Jack," a guy next to me said. "I never got back to sleep."

Well, sorry he hadn't gotten his beauty sleep, but it had been worth it. At least to me.

Nibbling on a strip of bacon, Rip whispered, "Jack, I think you got the better of him."

"Cheers," I said, raising my orange juice to clink glasses. "He deserved it."

Immediately spotting our impromptu celebration, Maher glared at me as if I'd just committed a serious crime...

CHAPTER TWO

"How about a little music before chapel, Lem?"

The floorboards creaked as we entered room 215, West Wing. The overhead light barely illuminated our two beds, two desks with lamps, and well-worn wooden chests. Our closets were draped by a worn cloth. The dark brown walls made the space seem smaller than it was. I often found myself looking out the window, aching to be outside.

But there was a new addition to my desk that would make staying in more tolerable. On my return from winter break, I'd brought along my portable RCA Victrola turntable and some nifty records.

"Kenadosus," Lem said, "music would be most appropriate." Lem removed his thick glasses, fully revealing a massive forehead—probably enough room there to write a good limerick.

I opened the case and put big-band leader Benny Goodman's "Blue Skies" on the turntable, cranked the Victrola's handle, and the record's first bars blared out.

When the clarinet kicked in, I clapped my hands, Lem whooped, and the two of us sang loudly.

"Bringing down the Victrola was a great idea!" Lem said. "Got a feeling about this year. We're going to have plenty of good times, even if it kills us."

Rip poked his head into the room. "What you guys got going on in here?"

I waved him in. "We got entertainment, sir, and I order you to join us!"

"Hey, there's music in Kennedy's room!" Rip yelled down the hall.

In minutes, the room was packed with guys sitting on our desks and beds or splayed out on the floor. I put on "Anything Goes" by Cole Porter.

I pretended to play the clarinet as I strutted across the room. Lem, grin splashed across his face, shouted out the lyrics as Rip pseudo-drummed away on a desk. One guy swayed and another mimed a trumpeter. "I'm dancing with Mae West!" a buddy chirped while pretending to twirl the bawdy blond actress about. I was almost jealous.

Room 215 was jumping. I don't think I'd had a better time since coming to Choate.

We belted out that line: *Anything goes!* Indeed, that's what I wanted in my life at Choate. Nobody telling me what to do. No more "Kennedy, you're late!" or "Kennedy, your sloppy schoolwork is inexcusable." Or "Kennedy, your room is a disgusting mess." Had enough of all that. As far as I was concerned, *nothing* goes at Choate. I itched to get out. To see if anything somewhere else did go.

Caught up in the melody and the moment, we forgot about time. A smack at the door interrupted the fun. "Chapel!"

Shit.

I stopped the Victrola. Instantly, the mood changed from joy to gloom. Shoulders slumped as we shuffled to the door, lumbered down the stairs to the main floor, poured through the four white columns of Hill House fronting the quad, and veered rightward to the chapel.

Just as we approached, the last chime of the carillon rang out in the bell tower. *Late again.*

We straggled into the last pew on the left. The hardwood creaked as we settled in. I stared at the dim lights of the double-layered chandelier centered above the aisle and between the balconies.

Here we go again.

Headmaster George St. John surveyed his flock. I'd rather study terribly uninteresting French than listen to a St. John sermon. I'd seen that stern, balding, humorless figure at the pulpit almost every day for three years—except when I cut chapel. What would he regale us with tonight? Kindness to your fellow classmates? Politeness? Respect and deference to elders? Cleanliness next to Godliness? Whatever it was, after a few minutes, I'd be eager to get back to my not-so-great room.

But tonight, something was different

Was it my imagination or was the Head, an ordained Episcopal priest, staring directly at me with high holy fever? We were all late. So why was he glowering only in my direction? The hair on the back of my neck stiffened, and a sheen of sweat quickly developed on my forehead.

This seemed like a perfect time to check out—go into daydream mode. I picture myself at my favorite diner as a pretty waitress serves me a milkshake and tops it off with a winning smile.

Next daydream scene: Queenie, the wife of the assistant headmaster and, we heard, a onetime Miss Southern Alabama, takes center stage. She is lush and girlish, her hair notable for its finger waves. Whenever she strolls the campus, we furtively eyeball Queenie, who seems to like the attention. She responds with a cute smile and maybe a wink. In my fantasy, I am escorting her across campus. "Thank you, Jack," she says sweetly when we arrive at her house. Queenie moves closer, preparing to kiss me on the cheek…

"Ten percent of the boys at Choate are muckers!" St. John bellowed, his words reverberating through the chapel.

Daydream interruptus. Leave it to the Head to ruin everything.

My attention was drawn to the pulpit, where the Head's arms flapped, bird-like, and his face turned redder than the school's brick buildings. This sermon was going to be different; like a cat is different from a rhinoceros.

Lem elbowed me. "Think he's talking about us?"

"Hope so," I said with a snicker.

I wasn't sure what a mucker was. I'd heard the word before. Was it back in Boston?

A mucker, he bellowed, was a "bad apple in a basket."

So it wasn't good.

"He's talking about you, Ken." Lem elbowed me again.

"No, you're the bad apple. I may be a rotten orange, but I'm no bad apple."

We ducked below the pew so nobody could see us laughing. If any of the masters caught us, we'd be in big trouble—if we weren't already.

I also didn't want to be seen by the Campus Cops. The cops, organized in 1924 by a math teacher, were composed of a dozen or so sixth-formers—a grade above me—and recruited and supervised by a couple of Choate graduates. The cops assisted with traffic congestion during football games and patrolled off-limit areas during festival weekends. And maybe more.

Several guys pointed fingers at each other. "Mucker," they mouthed.

"The mucker," the headmaster continued, "spits in our sea."

What's wrong with spitting in the sea? I spit in the ocean quite often. But the Head didn't mean it that way.

St. John's voice was so loud now it probably echoed beyond the chapel. I imagined the school's neighbors complaining: "What the hell is going on over at Choate, Margaret? Can't hear my radio program, goddammit!"

St. John had a bug up his arse. That was for sure. He said muckers joked in class and were sloppy and lazy in their studies. What's more, these muckers—whoever they were—were embarrassing themselves and the school. God himself wasn't pleased with the muckers!

"At Choate, there will be no tolerance for muckers!"

I expected the headmaster to name the damned. Would I be one of those he'd shame in front of the entire school? Make us stand up like criminals? Confess to our crimes? Ask for forgiveness?

"These muckers have no place here. When, and if, they are identified, I promise you they will be expelled."

Wait. *If* they are identified? Ten percent of students, about fifty guys, were muckers, but he didn't know who they were? St. John had pulled a slipperoo. It was like saying a cell of spies was embedded somewhere at Choate, when in fact not a single one ever set foot on school grounds.

Was the Head creating a false crisis? Trying to scare us from *becoming* muckers? Or if we were muckers, warning us we'd better straighten up or get run out of school?

The Head rambled on about this and that—something about responsibility and our moral code. He closed with: "It's not what Choate does for you, but what you can do for Choate."

After that last line, I ground my teeth. The Head had raked these so-called muckers for their crimes, but now these scoundrels and everybody else were being asked to lend a hand to aid their beloved school?

I was *not* inspired. But weirdly, I got to thinking about what I could do for Choate. And, it turned out, it was a lot different from what the Head had in mind. Maybe I could help Choate by bucking the system. Help make it a better place. Sure, I wanted to trash the Choate rule book, eliminate Latin, and allow girls on campus. All were unrealistic possibilities. But there had to be something I could do. I sensed an opportunity to make my mark, to accomplish something significant.

On our way back to West Wing, we hunched our chins into our jackets, trying to survive the cold, fierce wind in the darkness of night. "What is a mucker anyway?" I asked Lem.

"I'm not sure."

"Maybe the warden—I mean Head—is making it all up. How these muckers are so awful. That a bunch of them are running around school like crazy idiots. You know what gets me? He says he doesn't know who the muckers are." I raised my voice. "That doesn't make sense. Sounds like he's just trying to scare us."

We hustled up the stairs.

Inside our room, I grabbed the dictionary. "Let's see what old Webster's got to say about a mucker."

"Webster's," I said, "defines a mucker as someone who 'takes things too lightly.'"

Lem was reading over my shoulder. "Mucks around. Says the mucker is 'ill-bred.'"

"Ill-bred? That's you, Lemster. I'm well-bred, although I do get ill."

"And you're vulgar, Johnny. Says a mucker is vulgar."

"I'm all right with that. Nothing wrong with a little vulgarity from time to time."

Mucker.

I stood up and paced the room. Suddenly, it came to me. "Leem, now I know where I've heard that word before. Webster's is missing something. That's what they call us Irish in Boston. Aimed at the Irish who clean up the muck in the streets. Guess what the muck is?"

"Horse shit?"

"Exactly."

"You never told me you had a talent for shoveling horse crap, Jack. Daresay, I have new respect for you. And now I know why you stink." Lem laughed his unforgettable screech, easily heard at the far end of West Wing.

"In addition to all that other stuff, St. John's calling me a shit-shoveler. He was looking at me when he said it." I pounded the desk. "I don't think that was a coincidence."

"I see your point."

Once again, I felt an overwhelming urge to respond. I fixed my eyes on Lem. "Maybe it's time for action."

"To do what?"

"I'm not sure, but I'll come up with something."

CHAPTER THREE

The more I thought about what the Head had said, the madder I got. Especially when I saw the horses' "road apples" littering the street outside Choate.

St. John had insulted my Irish ancestors by labeling them shit-shovelers. There weren't many Irish at Choate, but I knew Dad hadn't sent me here to be belittled. He himself had been the victim of discrimination against the Irish. So incensed was he at "No Irish Need Apply" signs that he moved the family from Boston to New York.

Not that there was anything wrong with cleaning the streets. It had to be done. But if that's all St. John thought the Irish were good for, he needed to be taught a lesson.

The next day, I picked up another bit of mucker history at the school library. After *Tarzan of the Apes,* Edgar Rice Burroughs wrote *The Mucker.* This mucker mugged and robbed, but he also fought off headhunters—"He towered above his pygmy antagonists, his gray eyes gleaming, a half-smile upon his strong lips"—romanced a millionaire's daughter, and escaped the hangman's noose.

I couldn't imagine fending off savages or enemies of the United States in hand-to-hand combat. I wasn't the strongest guy in the world. When I got sick, which was pretty often, I'd lose weight and my pants and shirts sagged. "Hey, Kennedy, you look like a scarecrow!" hollered Campus Cop Butterworth—we called him Butter. "Not much left of you. At this rate, you'll disappear, and we'll have one less stinkin' Irish at school. Tell me, why is it you Micks always smell like potatoes?"

Butter had graduated, wasn't going to college, and hadn't found a job. So, St. John had him and a few other recent graduates proctor exams, tutor, and act as teacher assistants. Of course, being older, they lorded it over the student Campus Cops, telling them what to do and when to do it. In return for doing the Head's bidding, Butter got a free room in West Wing and no-cost food and meals.

"And why do you always smell like you just came out of the crapper?" I shouted back. *Bastard!*

Inspired by *The Mucker*, I became further riled by the Head's threat.

St. John had been headmaster for more than a quarter century. He ran Choate like it was his kingdom. Maybe it was time to put a dent in his armor. Or at least raise a little hell.

To be honest with myself, I hadn't done much since starting here. But now, realizing I was scheduled to graduate next year and didn't have much to show for it, I felt the urge to accomplish something before leaving this place. For the rest of the day, I ruminated on what I'd do.

I found myself smiling in the middle of Physics class. A warmth radiated throughout my body. A plan was formulating.

In our room later that night, I clapped my book shut, declared a "study break," and leaned back in my chair. "I have an announcement," I said.

Sitting at his desk, Lem closed his book and looked up. A smile spread across his face. "Let's hear it."

"I'm starting a club."

"A club? What kind of club?"

I lowered my voice. The walls were thin, and several times I'd pictured Maher, an ear to our wall, straining to hear us. The enemy next door.

"A *Muckers'* club."

Recalling the headmaster's words, a grin spread slowly across Lem's face and his huge forehead expanded.

"Remember when the Head asked us to consider what we could do for Choate?"

"Yes, but—"

"This will be our contribution. The club will enliven the school, and this place could use a little enlivening."

Lem nodded slowly.

"We'll call ourselves The Muckers," I continued. "After all, that's what our beloved headmaster thinks we are."

"The Muckers Club," Lem said, rolling the words off his tongue. "I like it. It's good. Very good." He stood up. "We're muckers!" His laugh morphed into a series of guffaws—"Haw! Haw! Haw!"—that annoyed many, but not me, and certainly not now.

"Should we invite the Head to join?" Lem asked. "He did supply us the name for the club."

"Nah," I said. "He wouldn't be any fun."

"What would the club do?"

"Bust out in the middle of the night. Go into town and, uh, well, I don't know what. We'll think of something."

"Sneaking out is a good idea," he agreed. "This place closes in on you. Sort of like being in jail, although I've never been in one. Of course, we've got to play jokes on those who deserve it."

"Naturally. What's a club without pranks?"

We discussed whether we should have officers, regular meetings, and insignia that proudly announced we were Muckers.

"Do you think others would be interested?" I asked. Wouldn't be much of a club without members.

Lem's face sagged. "Maybe this should be our club, Ratface. Just you and me."

"DeLemma, a club has to have more than two people. Let's see if others want to get in on the action. The more the muckier."

"All right. When do we start?"

"Tomorrow. At our regularly scheduled meeting before chapel. Can you make it?"

"I've cleared my calendar."

I'd conveniently forgotten that forming a club was against school rules, but I reasoned that the Head was the one responsible for founding the club. He'd said we already belonged to this group. We were just making it official.

"Our brothers never started a club when they were here. We'll be remembered twenty years from now. John Fitzgerald Kennedy and Kirk LeMoyne Billings. Founders of the Muckers Club."

That was something else Lem and I had in common: excruciatingly successful older brothers who checked all the boxes. They were excellent athletes, good students, and good-looking, popular guys. Administrators and masters never failed to remind us how we didn't measure up to them. "Best boy ever," one teacher said of Joe while speaking directly to me.

Last year, Lem and I had been on the crew team along with Joe. I liked having somebody to hang around with when Joe was nearby. He could be a pain in the ass. I'm glad he graduated, although sometimes it seems like he's still here.

"You bet they will remember us," Lem said. "People will forget about Joe and Josh. We'll be the ones everybody will remember. As it should be." He held up a finger. "In the meantime, we should hit the books."

"I suppose. French is killing me. But I could use a shower. Feeling, ah, all mucky."

"Get all the muck off." Lem laughed. "Stinks in here."

"Muck you."

CHAPTER FOUR

In the corridor the next morning, I whispered to Rip in case Maher was lurking, "You are a member of a club—the Muckers Club."

"The Head's tirade gave you an idea, eh, Jack?" Rip said. "Don't know what you've got in mind, but count me in."

"To be discussed tonight after dinner. Gotta go."

I also recruited Blambo because he was a crazy guy and we needed somebody like him. We could always count on Blambo to do something unintentionally funny. Once, when a teacher asked him why he didn't have his textbook, he said, "I left it in the crapper."

I saw Moe coming out of the library. "Hey, Moe, want to be a Mucker?"

After I gave him a brief description, he said, "Moe the Mucker—I like how it sounds. Queenie will be impressed. Did you see her today? Oh, man, she looked good. Did I tell you I had tea at her house yesterday? Special invitation from Queenie herself."

Envious of the attention Moe was getting from Queenie, I forced a smile. "I'll keep an eye out for her. Better yet, two eyes."

Back in our room for rest break, I told Lem about our new members. Lem said Boogie and Shink were on board, too.

"Great," he said. "On our way. Though to where, I have no idea."

Neither did I, but I had a feeling I was about to make a name for myself, and although I hadn't done anything yet, I felt rejuvenated. My hands tingled and I felt almost weightless. Here was my chance to cut my teeth on something big. And I was ready.

CHAPTER FIVE

I spread out the day's *New York Times* on my desk.

"Any news about the Muckers in *The Times?*" Lem asked.

"Not yet." I grinned.

"You must be the only student here to get *The Times* delivered."

"How else are you going to find out what's going on in the world?" I said, then returned to reading how Nazi Germany had abolished states' rights. I was astounded to learn the Nazis had taken all of three minutes to ram that big change through. All power was now unified under Adolf Hitler. Could that same thing happen in the U.S.?

Lem mumbled something. I continued reading. More mutterings.

"God damn it, Jack, you put your nose in a book or newspaper and you're in another world. Didn't hear a word I said, did you? I might as well not be here."

I looked up at Lem's red face. It was rare to see him angry. What had gotten into him all of a sudden? "Did you say something?"

He shook his head. "When you're reading, I could call you the worst names in the history of civilization and you wouldn't hear me. It's irritating."

"You're probably right," I admitted. "What names might that be, Lemmer? They better be good."

"Ahhh," Lem said, waving me away good-naturedly.

We kidded each other frequently, though most of my barbs were aimed at him. Lem never seemed to mind. What's more, he laughed at my jokes—even the bad ones. Who doesn't appreciate somebody like that?

We got along so well that Maher didn't want us rooming together. Not only did I have a reputation as a happy-go-lucky rule-breaker, but I was also anything but punctual and neat. Perhaps that was why he thought the two of us together would be doubly disruptive. The headmaster believed I had a gland problem and suggested I see a specialist to overcome my childishness. To my way of thinking, the headmaster needed a specialist—a surgeon to remove the stick up his ass.

At the beginning of the school year the previous September, the headmaster decided Maher would take the room next to us so he could keep us in line. Of course, it was awful from the beginning. I wrote my father that we were practically rooming with him, which was a lot more than we'd bargained for.

I stopped reading my paper and jotted down a few rhyming words about Moe and Queenie. What did Moe have that I didn't?

Lem was putting on his skivvies when we heard a pounding at our door.

"I'm coming in!" Maher barked. But he was already inside. Maher's presence immediately sucked all the air out of the room.

Lem became tangled in his underwear, tripped, and collapsed in a heap on the floor. Under other circumstances, I would have howled gleefully.

Maher had the authority to inspect our rooms anytime he pleased. And he damn well did. Once, I was returning from the library and, like a rat, he slithered in behind me before I closed the door. Another time, I'd returned unexpectedly to my room and discovered him checking under my mattress. Hoping to find giggle juice or cigs, I guess. I didn't have either.

Maher sniffed, then scanned the room from left to right, his lip curled in disgust. The room obviously wasn't up to either the school's standards or his. *Maher's Rules.* I wouldn't have been surprised to see him go through my clothes drawers to look for mismatched socks. *Write it up, you silly bastard.*

"Neatness counts," Maher growled. "At school and in life. If you want to make something of yourself. But I don't think you two do." He pointed to my vertically striped boxers, which I had dropped on the floor. "Kennedy, are those yours?"

I picked up the garment and gave it a long sniff, inhaling the scent as if it was a sweet flower. "I believe it is. These skivvies have the undeniable and extremely pleasant fragrance of Jack Kennedy." Holding out my skivvies, I added, "Care to take it in?"

Maher shook his head in disgust.

"Billings, can you explain why your desk is a junk pile?!" Maher shouted, making certain the entire corridor could hear.

Lem opened his mouth, but he never had a chance.

By now, I was fuming, my heart was pounding wildly, and something fierce inside was threatening to erupt. This inspection was an invasion. Maher was doing anything he could to get under my skin. But I kept my cool, staring blankly at him.

"Think your little game the other morning was funny, Kennedy? It wasn't. I informed the headmaster. We'd hoped you'd begin to show a kernel of maturity. That appears not to be the case."

Maher pointed his finger at us. "Therefore, the headmaster and I have decided you two shall be designated."

Lem and I looked at each other in bewilderment. This had to be related to the Head's mucker rant.

Was he here to tell us that officially we were muckers? Stamp our notebooks "mucker." Tack a *mucker* sign on our door to shame us. Or, better yet, require us to wear a letter *M* around school like that gal in *The Scarlet Letter*.

Were we the only ones being targeted? Or were other masters at this moment marching on St. John's orders and notifying the fifty or so students of their mucker status?

"Designated?" I asked. "As what?"

"Public enemies."

My skivvies slipped from my hand. Lem gaped at Maher.

"Public enemies?" I asked.

I knew J. Edgar Hoover, who headed the Federal Bureau of Investigation, had designated notorious criminals on the loose as public enemies. Were schools now using a similar designation to crack down on their troublemakers? Had the Head come up with the idea and ordered Maher to carry it out? Or was this Maher's idea? It was the craziest thing I'd ever heard. Either way, the Head and Maher were trying to scare the hell out of us.

"You're kidding," Lem said. But Maher didn't kid.

"Bastard," I said, under my breath.

Pointing at me, he said, "That's right. Kennedy, you're Public Enemy Number One. That makes you Number Two, Billings. You're now associated with the worst criminals in American history. John Dillinger and Al Capone started off the same as you, goofing off in school, flouting the rules on their way to a life of law breaking. Both are Public Enemies. Dillinger is on the run and Capone is in prison."

Maher raised his voice. "If you're not careful, that could be you. You two will be watched very closely. We'll not allow you to bring down the entire school. We'd sooner not have you here. Understood?"

"Yes sir," we said in unison. Anything to get Maher to leave.

When Maher closed the door behind him, I exhaled deeply, and my anger instantly evaporated. "This has been quite a week, Lemmer. First, we start the Muckers' Club, and now we're public enemies one and two. We've come a long way We're famous!"

"Don't you think putting us in the same league as Capone and Dillinger is a bit much?" Lem said. "They're killers. Our wrongdoings have been harmless pranks, misinterpreting a few rules, and the occasional escape to town."

"Lemmer, you got it all wrong," I said, shaking my head. "They're honoring us. Remember that movie *The Public Enemy*, where Jimmy Cagney plays a gangster? Maybe Maher and St. John watched it. They believe we should be movie stars."

Lem laughed. "A compliment then. It's all how you look at it."

"And the way I look at it, if Maher's going to call me a public enemy, I need to give him a pet name. Only fair." I stared at my crotch. "How about the Prick? Why? Because he is one. Not only that, I hereby name my dick *JJ* in honor of our esteemed housemaster, Jack J. Maher."

"Seconded," Lem said.

"Will you excuse me, LeMoyne?" I said, heading for the bathroom. "My JJ needs relief."

Ten p.m. Lights out. "Good night, Public Enemy Number Two."

"Good night, Public Enemy Number One."

———◆———

Word got around. Our designation as public enemies was an honor, if a dubious one, but I embraced it, even if I felt what

Maher and St. John had done was ridiculous. I strutted around school, enjoying the notoriety. But I was conflicted. I hadn't done anything to be proud of. I hadn't accomplished anything other than getting under the skin of the Head and Master Maher.

"Haven't committed any crimes this week, Lem," I said, searching for a clean shirt in my bureau. Ties, socks, and underwear littered the floor. "Getting worried they'll take us off the Public Enemies list. We can't have that."

Later that day, while I waited in line at the tuck shop to buy a snack, somebody behind me said, "Hey, Public Enemy Number One, you considering a heist of the shop's loot?"

I turned around but didn't recognize the speaker. "No, can't be bothered. Small potatoes. Can't be but a few dollars. But maybe I'll bag a case of chips and share the wealth." I laughed.

As Lem and I walked that afternoon to the Winter Exercise Building, several members of the Student Council cornered us. One of them said, "Here come the public enemies. We better be careful. Might take over the school."

"We might," I said. "Best to watch out." But I didn't mean it. I wasn't interested in student government or politics. It was Maher and St. John I wanted to vex.

<hr>

Because of the Victrola, our room became the place to be after dinner. Guys had to get there early too. Our room overflowed as a dozen fellows crowded in. Latecomers had to stand outside. Room 215 was where the action was.

The music brought us together. Singing and snapping our fingers to Goodman, Duke Ellington, Count Basie, and others. Having that Victrola changed everything. Put us in a different world. We forgot about school and exams and Maher and all the other crap that made life grim for Choate students. That half hour before chapel was the happiest time of the day. I found myself grinning in Physics as I thought ahead to our pre-chapel session. Fortunately, Maher had other duties before chapel, so we had the wing to ourselves.

That Sunday, the Victrola blasted away until the bells signaled it was time for chapel. *But the song wasn't over.* I wanted to hear the rest of it. The Head could wait. When the song finished, we began filing out.

I grimaced when a sudden, familiar stab of pain ripped through my stomach.

"You go ahead," I said to Lem, who waited for me. I needed to stay close to the john.

"Stomach bothering you again, Ken?"

"If anybody asks, just tell them I got a case of the blues." It was true. I did have the blues, and the reason: my gut ache had returned.

"May God go with you, my son—because I'm not," Lem said, Hearing another of the Head's sermons might make my stomach problems worse. I pushed Lem gently out the door.

Mandatory chapel was one of the many Choate things that drove me nuts. Anybody enrolled in public school had to be happier than I was attending this harsh, unpleasant boarding school. Here, every hour of the day was scheduled, there were no girls, and there were so many rules they had to print a thick handbook to keep us all updated. I did my best to ignore or break as many of those rules as possible.

My day usually began with Mister Morning Alarm, J.J. Maher, pounding on my door. "Wake up! Get out of bed! Now!"

Jackets and ties required for all meals and classes.

After breakfast, I endured two and a half hours of "recitations," which was a fancy word for classes. The teachers recited and I listened. I did the bare minimum to prepare. They called it "boarding" school. Mostly, I was bored *of* school.

That's probably how and why I came up with the idea for my speech. It wasn't going to be boring.

CHAPTER SIX

"**G**otta go," I said to Lem, bolting for the door. "Presentation."

I'd been having trouble coming up with a topic for Public Speaking. For a few days, I considered discussing whether England was prepared if war broke out with Germany. Or Louisiana Senator Huey Long's *Share the Wealth* platform. But I decided on a timelier, more relevant topic.

Public Speaking was held in the Speech Room beneath the chapel. The Lord was above, and I might raise a little hell below.

I considered myself a confident and reasonably effective public speaker. Dad had given me a few tips that had proved helpful, and Joe had plenty of advice I ignored.

"Kennedy, you're next," Mr. Pratt, the Public Speaking teacher, said. His method of teaching was to instill fear. Lose your train of thought while you practiced a speech and he'd bang on his chair and open and shut windows. He was fond of saying, "You may be nervous speaking in public later on, but you will be terrified speaking in public here."

As I strode to the front of the room, I felt a fluttering in my stomach. I realized my speech might be considered provocative. And maybe it was.

The audience was a mix of students from all grades and various school personnel. The administration believed students should present before a variety of people. While waiting for his signal, I placed my right hand in my jacket pocket, then switched it to my inside pocket. I never knew what to do with my hands in these kinds of situations.

Pratt nodded. The Head stood to my right, ramrod straight. Maher was seated about five rows back to my left.

I spied Moe and Rip at the rear. I hadn't expected to see them. Nor had I expected them to put their fingers in their noses and make demonic clown faces at me. A vein in my neck pulsed. I let it go. Their distraction clearly was a challenge. I had to concentrate and stay calm, or I'd be embarrassed. Glancing down, I composed myself, then looked up and directed my attention at the middle of the room.

"Ladies and gentlemen, today I am going to talk to you about an important subject and a very important document. That document is the Declaration of Independence. I'll read from the beginning." I unfolded my note. "'When in the course of human events, it becomes necessary for one people to dissolve the political bands which have connected them with another, and to assume among the powers of the earth, the separate and equal station to which the Laws of Nature and of Nature's God entitle them, a decent respect to the opinions of mankind requires that they should declare the causes which impel them to the separation.'"

I put the paper back in my pocket.

"The document says political bands, but I say that the words need not apply only to political bands but also to organizations and groups of people, among them Negroes, Chinese, Jews, and others who suffer under the shackles of injustice." I paused for effect as Mr. Pratt had taught us. "That could include fellows, staff, and administrators here at Choate."

Feet shuffling. An uneasy cough. Somebody whispered, "What's Kennedy up to?"

The Head had asked us to consider what we could do for Choate. The Muckers' Club was my first contribution. Hinting at a shake-up or reform was another.

"I'm not advocating that fellow students, staff, or administrators should, ah, muck things up at this great institution." I paused, leveling my gaze at Moe and Rip. "But I do believe that all of us, as the Declaration of Independence states, have 'certain inalienable rights such as life, liberty, and the pursuit of happiness.' Who among us can argue against that?"

I glanced at the Head, stone-faced St. John.

I continued by discussing despotism and repression, then referred to Hitler and Mussolini by name. My voice soaring, I ended with, "Freedom, as our forefathers proved, cannot be bought. It must be earned. Thank you."

Students applauded and cheered. Rip and Moe stood, pounding their hands on the chairs in front of them. I beamed, surprised at the reaction.

Pratt and Maher, still standing, were largely expressionless, though the Head slowly shook his head.

"I'd be happy to answer any questions."

The Head stepped away from the wall, moving closer to me. "Jack, your reference to Choate is curious. I hope you're not suggesting that an upheaval would benefit this great institution."

"Not at all, Headmaster St. John. I only ask each person to consider their inalienable rights. If they are being deprived of those rights, then speaking out, organizing, and proposing new tools to obtain those rights are in order. Consider those who argued against King George's policy of taxation without representation. The final result was the American Revolution and the formation of the United States. I doubt anybody here wishes the colonists had failed to instigate the revolt."

"Jack, I'm sure you are aware there are consequences for those who advocate radical change."

"I am. Our forefathers understood such risks. They chose to go forward. 'Give me liberty or give me death,' said Patrick Henry. Fortunately, he got liberty. As did this country."

After receiving another ovation, I tingled from head to toe, and acknowledged the response with a crisp nod.

I took a few more questions from students, then walked to my seat, suppressing my smile because I didn't want to incite the Head any more than I had, But inside, a deep warmth of satisfaction came over me.

The Head stomped out, or so I'd describe his unhappy departure.

CHAPTER SEVEN

"**H**i, Mucker," I said, greeting each club member at the door with a firm hand shake.

Lem and I had limited membership to thirteen and put others on a waiting list because our room, the Muckers' Clubhouse, couldn't hold any more. Several wait-list guys were on athletic teams, including four varsity captains.

While I didn't have any specific ideas, my general plan was to "put over festivities in our own little way and to buck the system." That's what I'd written in the oversized, hardcover scrapbook the school gave us the first year. I wasn't sure what that meant, but it seemed like a good framework. Most of all, it should be a club without rules. There were enough of those at Choate to choke a pig.

"Quite a speech, Mr. Declaration of Independence," Moe said when I offered him my hand. "Planning a revolution, Jack?"

"No." I laughed, although it wasn't a bad idea.

"Welcome to the first meeting of the Muckers' Club," I said, standing in the middle of the room surrounded by Muckers. "We've got the best and the brightest here. The Head might differ. He's branded some of us as lowly muckers. Might be a few in this room, too, but we won't name them."

"Why should we?" Shink said. "He didn't."

Shink was a big, out-of-shape guy who came from a wealthy family in St. Louis.

"I'm pleased to inform you that 'mucker' has another meaning," I continued. "Lem and I looked it up. It's what they called the

Irish who cleaned the streets of horse shit. A mucker is an Irish shit-shoveler. I'm not the only guy of good Irish stock here, but everybody should be offended. The Head believes we're lazy, sloppy shit-shovelers. Anyway, let's get down to business."

"What shall we do first?" Boogie asked. Boogie was a thin, angular guy from Scarsdale, New York. He played most sports at Choate, and still found time to be a cheerleader, a member of the choir, the dramatic club, and the dance committee. Now he was a Mucker.

"Elect officers," I said.

The Muckers murmured approval.

"Okay, then. Who wants to be president of the Muckers' Club?"

Several hands shot up.

"Yes, you should be president," I said, pointing to a raised hand. "And so should you. And you." I continued until I had pointed to everybody.

"We can't all be president," Moe said.

"Why not?" I asked.

Silence.

Shink and Moe looked at each other as if they and I were from different planets. Others stared dumbfounded at me.

A club where everybody was president? Nobody had heard of such a thing. That would be *anarchy*, a subject discussed in my history class. A club with nobody in charge. Or since everybody was president, everybody was in charge. Depended on how you looked at it. I was putting what I'd learned at Choate into action.

"Let's vote," I said. "I move that each person in this room be elected president of the Muckers' Club."

"Wait," said Rip. "Somebody has to take notes. Keep the Muckers organized. I'll be the secretary."

"Thank you, Rip. Do I hear a second?"

"Second!" all the Muckers shouted.

"All those in favor?"

Thirteen hands went up in the air. A roomful of presidents. And one secretary.

Thirteen Muckers slapped each other on the back and shook hands.

"Congratulations, Mr. President," Boogie said to Moe.

"And congratulations to you, Mr. President," Moe responded.

"Let the word go forth," I said extemporaneously, "from this time and place, that, uh, the torch has been passed, uh, to a new generation of Muckers!"

Boogie got us going, waving his hands, shouting, "Muckers, Muckers, Muckers!" Everybody joined in. Then we got to our feet and pranced around the room bellowing our club name. I swelled with pride, reveling in the group's excitement.

While I figured the Muckers might help me make a name for myself, I wondered later that night if forming any new, non-approved school club might be too risky. I wasn't sure how far the Muckers thing would go because this was new territory. Previously, I'd been on my own, with some assistance from Lem, in challenging the Head, Maher, masters, and the Campus Cops, but now others were involved. I had no idea what schemes the Muckers might undertake. While there was strength in numbers, there was also the potential for trouble. But I didn't want to think too much about that now. We were just getting started.

For the next few meetings, we rejoiced in being Muckers, although we still didn't have a plan for what we were going to do. We tossed around ideas: Get rid of the school mascot and replace him with a Mucker shoveling shit? Sure to scare the crap out of our athletic rivals. Publish our own newspaper, *The Muck?* Change the school sign to *The School of Muckers?* Challenge the Campus Cops to a fight? The application to attend Choate asked, "Is the boy any part *Hebraic?*" Should we cross off "*Hebraic*" on all such applications and replace it with "Mucker?"

Most of what we talked about involved pranks, but we also discussed our dissatisfaction with school policies that squashed our spirit. We were damn tired of being told what to do and when to do it. Another topic was the Student Council, which we considered useless and run by a bunch of snots.

"Maybe we should consider running our own slate of candidates," Boogie said. "Take over the Council."

We needed something that told the world we were Muckers. And ourselves.

"Let's wear hats that say 'Choate Muckers Club,'" Moe said.

Butch, a terrific athlete from Oshkosh, Wisconsin, suggested we print stationery. "At the top goes *The Muckers' Club.* Putting our name on paper makes us an organization. We could send out letters to everybody about all the stuff we're going to do."

"What if we got a pin that said 'Mucker'?" Boogie suggested.

The Muckers howled agreeably at the idea because you could show off the pin everywhere.

I'd written some verse. "You wanna hear my little ditty about the club?" I didn't wait for an answer. "Well, you don't have any choice."

The Head labeled us Muckers
Said we were out-of-luckers
So we started a club
Should have called it—

I let them finish, roaring the similar-sounding and rhyming four-letter word.

———◆———

On the way back from chapel that night, still giddy about plans to produce a club emblem, we roughhoused a bit, gently pushing and shoving each other. Didn't matter that it was dark and cold out there.

Lem balanced himself on his knees and hands. "Hey, Ratface, crawl through." There was room to spare. Others joined in taking turns crawling in and out of one another.

I thought we could do better. Reach for the sky. "Human tower!" I shouted.

Everybody stared at me. There were thirteen of us. We'd constructed a few smaller towers in the past, but this would be a challenge. Maybe dangerous. I'd have to be on top because I was the lightest. And it was my idea.

The big guys, Lem and Shink and three more, got on their hands and knees. Four more formed the second row, and three managed to climb atop them. When the formation was set, I scampered to the top. When I got there, I knelt on Moe and Boogie, one knee on each back. We'd done it.

"I hope my boney knees aren't causing you discomfort," I said. "But it's all for a good cause."

"What's that?" Moe asked.

"When I find out, you'll be the first to know."

"Jack, tell us what you see up there," Shink said.

"I see a great future for the Muckers!" I chortled. "Now, on three, we yell, 'Muckers!'"

But we never got the chance.

"This behavior is unacceptable," said a voice behind me.

Campus Cop Butterworth. Behind him were several of his fellow enforcers.

"Kennedy, get down from there."

Who the hell did Butter think he was? He'd been a nuisance before, but now he was acting as if he had increased authority. Had the Head given him new powers? Had he told him to crack down specifically on us? I didn't want to do anything Butter told us to do. Would set a bad precedent.

Butter and his cops walked around to the front of our pyramid.

"But I just got here, and I like the view," I said. "Besides, it's a study session for Physics class. Can't you see we're testing the laws of physics?"

"Hey, Butter, don't you have anything better to do?" Boogie chided. "Like improving your technique for kissing the Head's ass."

"Why don't you take your brigade and teach them the ins and outs of proper lavatory cleaning," Shink said, then hooted.

"Your stupid activity is against school rules."

"I don't recall the construction of a human pyramid being mentioned in the handbook," I retorted.

"Shall I get Mr. Maher to intervene? He'll report your mischief to the Headmaster. Make it worse for you."

He didn't follow through on his threat because the Prick himself had suddenly entered the scene.

"You heard Mr. Butterworth," Maher said. "What you are doing is considered roughhousing and therefore prohibited. Athletic period is the time to obey your animal spirits. Now break this up. Go back to your rooms."

Descending from the pyramid, I said "Okay, animals, back to being human beings."

Our pyramid dissolved. Once again, any attempt at a little harmless fun had been quashed. I ground my teeth and pounded my fist against my thigh. We then scattered, anxious to get away from Butter, the campus clods, and Maher.

Now I had somebody else on my case—Butter and his lemmings. Butter was on a power trip. Had to think about how to let him know he shouldn't try bossing us around any longer.

CHAPTER EIGHT

One Saturday morning, five Muckers and I poured into the town's lone jewelry store like ants scouting for food, then scurried from case to case, dazzled by the glittery items.

The jeweler spilled his coffee, startled by so many unlikely customers at once. "What can I do for you boys?"

"Hey, fancy stuff here," Rip said, peering at a case of diamonds.

"Lots of sparkle," Boogie added. He gaped at a display of rhinestones.

The six of us assembled at the jeweler's counter.

"We're from Choate," I said.

"I gathered that," he said dryly. "So was I at one time."

"We want a pin," said Rip. "For our new club."

"Okay. What kind of club is it?"

"It's called the Muckers' Club," I said proudly, thrusting out my chest. It was the first time I'd mentioned our club name outside of school.

"And we're Muckers," Lem said, putting his arms around Rip and me. "All of us."

"Muckers, eh?" the jeweler responded. "And you go to Choate. Tell me, how did you become muckers?" He leaned toward us. "The word has a familiar ring to it."

"What do you mean?" Rip asked.

"By any chance," the jeweler said, "did Headmaster St. John call you out as muckers during chapel?"

We stared at one another. Was this a St. John tradition? Bring out the mucker sermon, scare the hell out of students to keep them in line? My shoulders dropped. I thought we were special—the first muckers. Guess not. *Wait.* I straightened up. "But I bet we're the first Muckers Club." That was what was important.

The jeweler stood up and smiled knowingly. "You're not the first students he has antagonized. That's what he does. Hauls out that tired mucker sermon whenever he's got boys who want to do things their way, not his." He frowned. "I know. Twenty years ago, I was one of them. As I recall, one definition of a mucker is a guy who shovels the muck—the horse crap. Is that your intended avocation?"

"No, not that kind of mucker," I said. "But we do intend to muck things up a bit."

The jeweler pointed to a small gold pin shaped like a shovel. "This might work for you. A sarcastic swipe at the headmaster. Put the club's name on the back." He took out the pin and handed it to me.

I rubbed my thumb and forefinger over the smooth, shiny surface. "Can't shovel a lot of you-know-what with it, but what do you think, fellas?" I said, handing it off for examination and approval.

We ended up ordering pins engraved *C.M.C.* for Choate Muckers Club on one side, and *Pres.* and each member's initials on the other.

"I'm tempted to have one made for myself, for old time's sake," the jeweler said softly. "The pins cost twelve dollars each. I require a deposit before I can start making them."

"Whew! That's a lot for those little things," Rip said.

"Last you forever," the jeweler responded. "They're gold. Twenty-two karats."

"That's a lot of karats," Boogie said.

"The more karats the better," Butch said. "We need our karats."

The Muckers dug into their pockets for bills and loose change.

I came up short, which surprised neither me nor any of my fellow Muckers. I never carried much money with me and often didn't have any at all. The Old Man had accounts everywhere. I was used to just saying my last name and having the bill put on his tab. "Could you pitch in for me?" I asked Lem. "Remind me to pay you back." I often needed a reminder. Sometimes two.

"Bumming again," Lem said. "What a surprise. Got a new nickname for you. Cashless Ken."

After we scraped together the deposit, I said, "Let's celebrate. Go get a milkshake." Didn't matter that it was a blustery cold day and the sidewalks were crusty with dirty snow. "Maybe we can get Mr. Foote to name a drink after us—The Mucker," I said, holding up an imaginary glass. "Sure to be a top seller."

The six of us crammed into a booth at Oliver D. Foote's soda shop on Center Street. Moe, Rip, and Boogie on one side, Lem, Butch, and me on the other. Mr. Foote, a tiny mustachioed man, asked for our order. "Mr. Foote," I said, "I have a business proposition for you. A chance to improve your bottom line."

"Really?" Mr. Foote said, offering a tight little smile. "Make it quick. I'm busy."

After briefing him on our new club, I suggested he create a drink using our name. "Call it 'The Mucker,' Mr. Foote. When we're famous, you'll make a lot of money from it. Everybody will order it." I paused. "Including Headmaster George St. John." I snickered. "After all, it was his idea."

"Well, when you're famous, let me know, kid, and I'll think about it. Right now, what are you guys having?"

We made it easy, ordering his specialty: a drink blending house -made vanilla ice cream, chocolate syrup, and whipped cream topped with chocolate sprinkles.

I borrowed a few cents from Butch, and we slurped our milkshakes, basking in the good cheer of our new club. "This is great, but I think a Mucker milkshake would taste better," I said.

"To the Muckers!" Boogie shouted, raising his goblet. A white and black mustache decorated his upper lip. We clinked glasses.

Ordering the pins was huge. Once we had them, we could do anything. We'd swagger around school, proudly wearing them. Couldn't be any rule against wearing a pin, could there?

I glanced out the soda shop's window and noticed Butter and one of his crew across the street. A coincidence? Were they spying on us?

"Now that we've got a club and pins, what are we going to do?" I asked, although an idea was close to forming.

Several of us had already gotten under the skin of our beloved headmaster and housemaster. But after Butter called me out for being Irish, coupled with the pyramid confrontation, I thought he and the cops might be perfect marks for our first prank.

Most of the cops were losers. Pimply and clumsy with poor manners and worse attitudes. Nobody wanted to be around them. But when Butter appointed them Campus Cops, they behaved as if they were transformed. Strutting and swaggering around campus, showing off their Campus Cops armbands, like they were real cops. Urged on by Butter and the other graduate cops, they went after the first-year guys especially hard, belittling and ordering them around, for no reason other than to flex their egos.

We called them "the Campus Flops."

I was beginning to think they were the eyes and ears of the school, and not in a good way.

"The flops are like spies." I jabbed the air with my spoon. "Watching, guarding, informing."

Rip agreed, recounting how one Campus Flop had been hiding behind a tree, creepily watching him play on Choate's golf course. "He wasn't there to help me with my putting. Maybe he was watching to see if I was going to smoke or drink."

"I've seen them in town," Boogie said. "Not doing a thing. Just lurking. I had the feeling that if I did anything remotely wrong, they'd inform on me."

"Yeah, like Butter and his lackey over there," I said, my chest tightening in anger. As I pointed out the window, we could see Butter staring back at us. "I'd like to nominate myself to be the first mucker to do something, er, muck-worthy," I said. "But I'll need your help."

⟫•⟪

We could hear Butter's footsteps coming up the stairs.

The Muckers had carried dozens of pillows and several mattresses from our rooms. While Butter tutored a student in the student's room, we went upstairs and piled the heavy cotton pillows and mattresses ceiling-high against the door of Butter's room. Lem and I pushed the dresser, bed, and desk against the wall of pillows to keep them in place and climbed out the window. Then we scrambled back inside and waited in the corridor for Butter's return.

"Hallo there, Butter," I said when he came into view.

He was all smiles until he saw us.

"Afternoon," Rip said.

"How'd it go today?" Lem asked.

"Quite well." He hesitated, his hand on the doorknob.

We didn't move or breathe.

As soon as Butter yanked the door toward him, an avalanche of pillows and mattresses rained down on him, much as he'd caused our pyramid to come crashing down.

"Aaaah!" he screamed, now sprawled on his back. Only his feet were visible.

We walked over to where we figured his head was and surrounded him. Butter seemed to be in shock. He said nothing, and he blinked rapidly.

"Look at this, will ya?" I said. "One of Choate's finest sleeping on the job. And in the corridor no less. The Head won't be happy about this. As we Irish say, 'Top of the morning to you.'" He stared at me blankly. "Gone silent on me, Butter boy? I suggest you kiss the Blarney Stone if you ever get to Ireland. According to legend, it gives the kisser the gift of gab." I fingered my chin. "Come to think of it, I hope you don't go. I like you better when you don't talk. Let's get our stuff, boys. All this excitement makes me sleepy. Could use a nap " We began plucking pillows off Butter.

Back in our room, Lem said, "That went well. I deem the first Mucker operation an unqualified success."

I beamed. "Seconded."

Chapter Nine

A week later, our pins were ready for pickup. We sprinted to the jeweler, arriving breathless and excited. It was nine-thirty. The store didn't open until ten, so we shivered outside. Seeing our discomfort, the jeweler opened early.

"Here you go," the jeweler said, spreading the pins out on the counter.

The gleaming gold shovels were small but elegant. Most of all, they basically said: "Now our club is official." After paying and proudly affixing the shiny pins to our winter coats, we bolted out of the store. Strutting around town, we thrust our chests forward like five-star generals, shouting, "We're Muckers!" Most people kept their distance, thinking us hooligans.

"We're the Muckers and we want a booth!" Lem shouted as we entered a restaurant. Everybody laughed, except the older hostess, who looked as if she'd been there since Teddy Roosevelt was president.

It felt great to be part of something all our own. Still, we had to give the Head credit. Without him, there'd be no Muckers Club. He's the one who got us all riled up in the first place.

We practically pranced back to Choate, laughing and shouting "We are the Muckers!" every few seconds. Life at Choate was definitely on the upswing.

Still feeling jazzed about our outing, I rang up my younger sister Kathleen, or Kick, as most everybody called her. Kick was lively, and my favorite sister. Even cheered me up when I got into it with Joe. And we shared the same mischievous sense of humor. During the recent holidays, we'd stayed up late into the night, trading stories about everybody who'd been to the parties we'd attended. If I ever got one, my girlfriend would need to get along with Kick or else I'd have to break up with her.

Kick was a student at the Noroton School, Convent of the Sacred Heart, which was not far from Choate. The school was run by the nuns of the Sacred Heart, and they were very strict. Like Choate, Noroton looked nice from the outside, but Kick complained there wasn't much freedom. The girls woke at six every morning and were forced to attend Mass wearing black veils. Lights out at nine. When she complained of being lonely during her first week there, Lem and I snuck out to visit her and cheer her up.

"Kick, I'm a Mucker!" I shouted into the telephone.

"A what?"

"A Mucker. We've formed a club. A mucker cleans up muck and doesn't do what Headmaster St. John and his gang want us to do. Lem and I and the other Muckers are planning some mischief. We've got thirteen members!"

"Don't get into too much trouble, Jack."

"I'll try not to, although I have pleasant dreams about getting kicked out." I laughed. "I'm really tired of this place."

I told her about our Mucker pins and the pillow prank. "We want to have a little fun. Promise you won't tell Dad."

"I won't."

I trusted Kick.

CHAPTER TEN

"Sore throat coming on," I said to Lem after breakfast. "Again?" he said, suspiciously.

"If my calculations are correct, my throat will become exceedingly irritated shortly before Physics. I regret having to miss that class. It's an utter joy. On my way to the wonderful Archbold Infirmary."

"They might suspect others of making up an illness," Lem said, "but you get laid up at Archbold so frequently you can get away with it."

"I might as well use my poor health to my advantage." I smirked.

After I had my throat sprayed and was awarded a tardy slip, I doctored it so it was now an absent slip. Stepping lightly, I hummed while I walked to the administration building, where I'd place it on the clipboard. After all, it was important to follow school rules while I was breaking them.

But the Head was waiting for me.

"Come into my office, Jack." He held out his hand. "I'll take that." He scanned it, shook his head, then crumpled it up and dropped it in the wastebasket. I swallowed several times. A sour taste filled my mouth.

The office was dark and heavy. A sliver of sunlight slipped through the thick red brocade curtains. St. John sat behind a massive wooden desk and lit his pipe. Soon, his face was shrouded by a cloud of sweet-smelling pipe smoke. After he put his pipe aside and the smoke cleared, his pursed thin lips, slightly up-turned nose, and gleaming forehead came into view.

He glowered. Obviously, he hadn't invited me in to praise my schoolwork. Not that there was much to praise. Was he going to interrogate me about my fake sore throat? Double down on the Public Enemies designation?

"Sit down," he said, pointing to the chair in front of his desk. He spun the tin desk globe while I fidgeted. When it stopped, he pointed to my pin. "Let me get straight to the point. I've been made aware that you and some of your friends are wearing some sort of charm or emblem."

Blame it on Butter and the flops.

True enough. We the Muckers had been proudly wearing our pins everywhere on campus for the last few days. Boogie had stuck his on his basketball uniform. Moe had attached his to his hat.

On campus, I'd heard people say, "When's the next meeting of the Choate Masturbation Club?" Or "All the way with the CMC!" And "Hey, Jack, what's the CMC?"

For us to know and you to find out.

Our new club ornaments got plenty of stares as we strode around Choate. I liked the attention. But now I was getting attention from the wrong person—the school headmaster.

"Yes," I said, looking down at the pin on my jacket. "Do you like it? I think it's quite attractive."

"Why are you wearing it?" he said sternly.

"It's just a pin. A friend pin." I was making it up as I went along. Was smart of us not to inscribe "muckers" on it.

"Tell me, what does"—St. John peered intently at the emblem—"CMC stand for?"

"Choate Men's Class," I said. It didn't make sense, but it was the best I could do in the moment.

"Choate Men's Class? What is that?"

"We're proud to be men of Choate. So we had a pin made."

"Interesting shape. What is it supposed to be?"

"A shovel."

"Why a shovel?"

"Because Choate men dig deep," I said, using my hand in a downward motion. "Go below the surface."

St. John clasped his hands. "Jack, without permission, it's against school rules for any student to form a club or organization, even one such as yours, assuming it's what you say it is. There's a reason for this rule. First and foremost, students must attend to their studies. That is why you are here. That and nothing else. To do otherwise is a waste of time. Do you understand?"

"Yes."

"Were you aware of this rule?"

"Well, I uh…"

Maybe I was, maybe I wasn't. Or maybe I'd forgotten.

"You are now."

I shifted in my chair.

The Head's voice deepened. "In addition to what should be the shame of being on the school's Public Enemies list, I'm concerned that you are becoming the leader of students who may be, shall we say, taking the wrong path. Your path. Poor study habits. Lazy. Sloppy. This kind of behavior is unacceptable. I'm sure you recall my words regarding this group at a recent sermon, do you not?" He practically shouted the last couple of words.

"I do." I tensed up and crossed my legs.

St. John suddenly softened. "Jack, do you consider yourself one of the muckers I spoke about?"

"No, sir, I don't." I offered a fake smile. True, I'd been labeled a public enemy, so I'm sure the Head also considered me a mucker. But not in my view. I was a full-fledged member of the Muckers' Club, but I wasn't one of *his* muckers.

"That's good, Jack. You don't want to be. And let's keep it that way."

"Yes, sir."

"Good. I'm glad we understand each other. One more thing."

Uh-oh.

"Remove your pin. You may keep it, but I forbid it to be seen on campus. Is that clear?"

I unpinned the pin from my jacket and put it in my pocket.

"Make sure your friends do the same. Remember, the rules are for your own good. I won't tolerate efforts to undermine the school. Do I make myself clear?"

I nodded.

"Now go to Physics class."

I walked there disconsolately. In mere minutes, my mood had changed from high spirits to a creeping melancholia. I wondered if the doctors at Archbold had a spray to alleviate that. But by the time I walked into Physics, I'd convinced myself I'd done a pretty good job of standing up to the Head's interrogation and stonewalling his inquiry about the club. The Muckers might have to operate under the radar, and our activities might have to become more secretive, but operate we would.

"Guys, I had a meeting with the Head," I said at our pre-chapel assembly. "Called me into his office."

"What did he want, Jack?" Boogie asked, eyes wide.

"I was hoping he was going to offer me a slice of his wife's apple pie." I chortled. "But he didn't. He was curious about the pins. Wanted to know what CMC stood for. Told him it was Choate Men's Class." I shrugged. "Had to come up with something fast."

"What did he say?" Rip asked.

"Thinks we're up to something. Said the pins couldn't be seen on campus."

"What!?" Smoky said. "The old stick in the mud!" He visibly slumped.

"The Head knows how to ruin a good time," Shink said.

"I have a solution." I pulled down my pants. The emblem was now attached to my skivvies. "Can't be seen. So we're in the clear."

After the shock of seeing me half naked with the pin on my skivvies, everybody broke up, hooting and hollering.

"What are we waiting for?" Moe said, removing his pin from his shirt. He dropped his trousers and attached it.

The remaining Muckers lowered their pants and did the same thing.

"But I don't see any reason not to wear them at Muckers meetings," I said. "Make sure we keep the door closed so nobody sees us."

I looked at twelve Muckers in their underwear, their bunch-up pants atop their shoes, and I started to laugh. "If I didn't know better, I'd say we were about to have our yearly physical examinations. You know, everybody's favorite part, when the doc grabs hold of your boys and says, 'Turn your head and cough.' " A couple of the guys grabbed their crotches in mock agony.

"Oh, one more thing," I said.

"What's that, Jack?" Moe asked.

"Before we go to chapel, don't forget to pull up your pants."

CHAPTER ELEVEN

I lay on my bed in Archbold Infirmary and picked at the creamed spinach. I wasn't hungry, nor was I in the mood to tackle a Physics worksheet.

I'd gotten the chills a few days earlier. My stomach acted up and I lost several pounds, so they'd thrown me in the school's hospital. Choate didn't fool around. Worried about tuberculosis spreading, they quarantined anybody with symptoms. The nurses even wore masks when they came into my room.

I stared at the ceiling and sighed, wondering if I was going to have a long life, and if I did, would I always be laid up like this? The anguish of missing games as a member of the basketball team, of being unable to attend English or History class, was almost as bad as the physical pain. I didn't complain. Kennedys didn't complain. The Old Man wouldn't tolerate it.

My ill health began at age three, when I came down with scarlet fever. Two months in the hospital, then shipped off to a sanatorium in Maine. Almost kicked the bucket, they told me later. After that, I had a long series of illnesses, and I never seemed to stay better for long.

Then stomach problems began, along with backaches, blurry vision, and unexplained symptoms such as fainting spells, overall weakness, and weight loss. Mother kept a card file on all our illnesses, and I'm embarrassed to say I had the most cards by far. What made it worse was the doctors often didn't know what was wrong with me.

In fact, I had two residences at Choate: my room and Archbold Infirmary. I'd just started attending classes in 1931 when I found myself doubled over in pain. When walking, I was so weak I could barely carry my books, so they sent me straight to Archbold. I was back in the infirmary again in January of '32 for a bad cough. Then to the hospital in April for swollen glands. Last year, I had what the doctors called "flu-like symptoms" that I couldn't kick. Later, they treated me for hepatitis. Maybe it was something worse.

Would I graduate to a life spent mostly in hospitals? The prospect filled me with dread. That was no life. Was time already running out for me? Might the Grim Reaper be heading my way so soon?

So I figured I'd better take care of business. I'd push ahead with the Muckers Club, but there was something else I needed to do.

That *something else* had to do with women. I vowed that I wouldn't kick the bucket without first having been with a woman. Hell, I'd never even seen a gal undressed except in a magazine. Once, I came home and was shocked to find a nudie magazine on my bed. Courtesy of the Old Man.

"Lemmer," I said walking back from chapel the same day of my discharge from Archbold, "the way things are going, I don't think your good friend Jack Kennedy is getting laid anytime soon." I'd never had a girlfriend. Filched a few kisses. That was it. Going to an all-boys school made it that much more difficult to meet girls.

"He's not?"

"No, and unless a plan of action is undertaken, the situation is not likely to improve. Let's look at the options." I held up a finger. "One, we could go to Pennsylvania."

"Why would we do that?" Lem looked at me like I was crazy.

"Intercourse."

"Intercourse?"

"Intercourse, Pennsylvania. I saw it on the map. Our first intercourse in Intercourse, Pennsylvania. How memorable would that be?"

Lem snorted. "Yeah, sure. Any other ideas?"

"Brothels—houses of ill repute. Ladies of the night. Hookers. Call girls. I'm almost seventeen, and you're more than a year older than me. You're graduating in a few months, right?"

Lem cleared his throat and gave a hesitant nod. "I suppose."

"And I'm guessing you don't have any more sexual experience than me. Correct me if I'm wrong, but we're not getting any younger."

"We certainly aren't. Soon we'll be old men."

"Is that a gray hair I see, Moines?"

"No, you're seeing things. You're the one showing your age. You've got a permanent room at Archbold. Soon you'll be ready for a rocking chair."

"Need to do something. Soon."

"I guess. If you want to."

Evidently, Lem didn't share my enthusiasm, but I knew I'd have the pleasure of his company wherever we went.

"A lady of the night, huh?" said Lem. "Suppose that's one way to take care of the matter."

"Know another way?" I asked.

"Mmmm. No. Not offhand," he said.

"If you do think of an alternative, let me know. Any time. Wake me up in the middle of the night, barge into Math class, yank me out of the john, I don't care. We're not going to learn anything about it here. There's nothing in the Choate Handbook about the art and skills necessary to achieve congress with a person of the opposite sex. It's an important topic in my view, and I hope in yours."

"Yes, Senator," Lem said, mocking my formality.

Females were in short supply at Choate. In fact, there were only a couple of women and no girls here at the time—the office staff, the dining hall ladies, and the women who cleaned our rooms. Girls of our age were allowed in only for the occasional tea dances and the annual Spring Festival.

Wasn't it strange that the more interested in girls I became, the fewer of them were around? I'd gone to a public school, then been sent off to two all-boys schools before Choate. Who came up with the idea of schools without girls? Some guy who wanted to drive us insane?

<hr />

I had planned to go to a brothel soon, but after I fell in love with Mae West, I couldn't wait any longer.

Rip, Lem, and I went to see her in the movie *I'm No Angel*. She was the most popular actress in America. In the lobby was a cardboard cut-out of her in a sexy red dress. Blond and nice and full in all the right places. What would it be like to be with a woman built like that? Exciting and probably a little scary.

"Hey, Rip, do you think Mae and I would make a good couple?" I asked, putting my arm around her cardboard shoulders.

"No, she's not your type," Lem kidded. "Too stiff."

"I might ask her out. Maybe the Old Man knows her. Dad's got connections in the movie business, you know." For several years, my father had been a movie producer in Hollywood.

"C'mon, Jack," Rip said, leading the way into the theater. "You might not want to take her out after you see her in the movie."

During *I'm No Angel*, Mae West sang, danced, quipped, and otherwise mesmerized guys while her partner picked pockets. The trick would have worked on me. While I watched her star in the movie, my mind drifted to the colorful cut-out of her in the lobby.

I wanted her. Had to have her.

"Still want to go out on the town with Mae?" Lem asked as we began to walk out.

"Yes," I said, "and that's what I'm going to do." I grabbed the cut-out and raced away, jostling other folks leaving the theater.

"Come back here!" the theater manager shouted.

Lem, Moe, and I laughed as we raced down the street, Mae West bouncing along in my arms.

Back in Room 215, I placed Mae by my desk.

"Meet our new roommate, Mae West."

In the morning, I placed Mae underneath my covers. Figured I'd give the cleaning lady a jolt. That way I could say I'd had Mae West in my bed.

When I ran into the cleaning lady later that day, she said, "You are bad, Mr. Kennedy. Very bad."

The cut-out of Mae West was gone when I returned to my room, but I couldn't get her and women out of my mind. I wondered if any of the brothel ladies were as sexy as Mae West. Probably not, but only one way to find out.

CHAPTER TWELVE

Lem and I got all slicked up in suits for our big day in Harlem. Lem sported a bowler—a hard felt hat with a rounded crown just like the one film star Charlie Chaplin wore.

We signed out, scribbling "New York City, Lady Liberty" as our destination. Well, that was accurate. We *were* on our way to visit gals who'd liberate us—of our virginity.

Lem and I hopped aboard the train. I looked forward to the escapade, but once we found seats, Lem stared straight ahead, his legs beginning to shake.

"Going to have a good time, right?" I said. "No need to be a jitterbug."

Lem offered a tense smile.

The train lurched, then picked up pace as it sped south to New York City.

Across the aisle, a lady wearing a large-brimmed hat said, "Don't you boys look nice? Going to the big city? What are you going to do?"

"Uh, see the sights," I stammered. We were going to see the sights all right, but not your everyday tourist attractions.

"Enjoy yourself," she said.

"Thank you, ma'am," Lem answered. "We'll try."

We didn't talk at all for the next half hour until Lem whispered, "Let's do it with the same girl."

I looked at him as if he was an alien. "The same girl? Why? To save money?"

"No," Lem said, biting his lip. "See if she's different with you than she is with me."

I didn't get his logic, but it didn't matter to me. "All right," I said. "But I'm going first."

"Be my guest, Ratface," he said, waving his hand like a restaurant maître d'.

At the train station, we hopped a cab. The neighborhoods were noticeably poorer the closer we got to Harlem. I felt the desperation of people queuing up in long lines behind steaming cauldrons at a soup kitchen. Competition was stiff among apple sellers too. I counted six people selling apples only a few yards apart, their fruit piled high on wooden cartons. In front of the Hippodrome, Atlantic, and Empire State employment agencies, a large cluster of people jostled to see the job listings on a bulletin board.

Couldn't the government do something about helping these people? It wasn't their fault that the stock market had collapsed and they'd been thrown out of work.

These neighborhoods were nothing like Bronxville, where we lived. Bronxville was only a dozen miles from here but it might have been a million.

"Area not so good," Lem whispered so the Negro hackie couldn't hear. "Are places like where we're going always in poor neighborhoods?"

"Couldn't tell you. If there's nothing else, guess being a prosty is the only kind of work for some. In any event, we'll be doing our part to help the local economy."

I pressed my face to the cab window. Most of the people we passed were Negroes, and many sections of the neighborhood were run down. Skid row. Houses peeling like they had a bad sunburn, many with broken windows or no windows at all. Empty storefronts. A man wearing only a T-shirt shivered. The sidewalks were strewn with used tires and mounds of trash.

But amid the poverty, I saw vitality. Street corner preachers spoke from soapboxes and stepladders. Knife sharpeners and ice vendors hawked their wares from wagons on the avenues. Others crowded around dice games. Kids played leapfrog. There was an energy to the streets.

In white letters, a restaurant advertised its entire menu of about thirty items. "3 LARGE PORKCHOPS 30c YANKEE POT ROAST 20c ROAST LEG OF VEAL 20c." My stomach rumbled. Better to wait. Didn't want a nervous gut at the wrong time.

As we drove through Harlem's entertainment district, the fashion changed. Women donned fancy hats. Men wore colorful suits featuring wide lapels and padded shoulders.

"Hey, there's the Cotton Club," Lem said, pointing to the famous Harlem jazz club at Lenox Avenue and 142nd Street—Rip had told us about it. Jazz great Duke Ellington and others were regulars there, and tonight Cab Calloway, famous for "Minnie the Moocher," was headlining. The busy marquee proclaimed: Three Shows Nightly 7-12-2. $1.50 Dinners. Never a Cover Charge. 50 Sepian Stars. 50 Copper Colored Gals.

"Yeah," snorted the hackie, "that's where the great music is. And Negroes playing it. Only problem is we ain't allowed in. Only whites."

"Why not?" Lem and I said simultaneously.

The hack stopped at a light and turned to face us. His eyes burned angrily.

"You tell me. Every Christmas, the club hands out baskets of food so they don't feel guilty about keeping us out. Still don't make it right."

I shook my head at the unfairness.

"Used to be Negroes ran the numbers in Harlem, but no more," he continued.

"What's the numbers?" I asked.

Players, he told us, selected numbers between 0 and 999 and placed bets on numbers slips. You could play for as little as a penny. Number runners collected players' betting slips and delivered them to the number banker. "Nobody going to stop buying the numbers just 'cause it's going to make white gangsters rich instead of Negro ones."

"Guess not," I said.

"And that ain't the worst of it. White people calling for Negroes to be fired if a white person out of a job needs one. Ain't that a kick in the head! Shit."

On my way to acquiring sexual experience, I was getting a different kind of education. Inequality. Discrimination. Segregation. Racism. Negroes weren't allowed to share the same rights as white people.

It was nearly dark when the cab stopped at a row house.

"You going to spend your jack in there, might as well give it to me!" shouted a guy across the street as we exited the cab.

Lem took out a handkerchief and mopped his glistening forehead.

After we paid, the hackie hollered, "You boys have a good time!" and roared away.

"I don't know about this, Johnny," Lem said, his voice soft.

"LeMoan, we've come this far. No backing out now. It'll be fun," I said with false bravado. I was nervous too. My stomach had knotted up.

"Yeah, sure."

I opened the door and a bell jangled. Places like this want to know when company arrives. I gave Lem the best phony smile I could. "Here we go." The staircase was gritty and dusty. I stumbled on a missing step.

Lem frowned and put his hand on the wall for support.

Doors squeaked. There was a *clack* of high heels and mutterings.

"Finally got us some business."

"Couple of young white boys on the way up. All dressed up to see us!"

Guess they had a lookout. Alerted the house when customers pulled up.

When we reached the top of the stairs, seven or eight women in skimpy, see-through outfits formed a line. My eyes stung from the sickly smell of perfume. Mostly white women, and a few Negroes. Hands on hips. Staring. Flirting.

A Negro woman, older and heavier than the other gals, said, "Hi, boys. I'm Miss T. Welcome. Three dollars each, if you please." She held out her hand. We didn't move. I thought we'd pay afterwards, like we did after having a milkshake at the diner. Different rules here, evidently.

She frowned. "Pony up, boys, or git back the way you came."

Several gals shifted their weight on their high heels. Sighs of irritation. Miss T wagged her finger. "No credit. Ain't the way the business works. Uh-uh."

After we handed over our three dollars, Miss T said, "Give the boys a thrill, ladies."

The girls pirouetted slowly and slips were raised. Brief glimpses of naked parts. One gal winked at me.

"Looking for a good time?"

"You look like you'd be a lot of fun."

"I like big fellas."

The show ended when Miss T waved her hand. "Time to make your choices, boys."

"You pick," Lem said.

I pointed to a white gal in a black lace slip. She had a good chassis and a winning smile.

"It's your turn, big boy," Miss T said to Lem. "Choose."

"I'll take her too," Lem said.

"What kind of crap is that?" Miss T said sourly. "All my years, that ain't never happened. Same gal. Shiiit!"

"That ain't right," complained one. Another gal said, "What she got that I don't? Three titties?" Angry because they had been left out. No work, no dough.

The girl grabbed my hand, and Lem followed along. She pulled me into a room, closing the door in Lem's face.

The musty smell of dirty sheets, stale perfume, and who knows what else was overwhelming. Tucked in a corner on the floor was a narrow mattress. How many guys had laid here before me? A hundred? A thousand?

I stared at the girl. The black lace slip extended only inches beyond that place I'd soon find myself.

"What's your name, honey?"

I didn't want to use my real name. "Saint John," I blurted.

"Saint John?" she said, raising her eyebrows. "What? You think you're some kind of saint?"

"No. George. George Saint John. What's yours?"

"Call me, ah, Eunice."

"Eunice! That's my sister's name."

"Uh-huh." She lit a cigarette. "First time?"

"Sort of. I mean, yeah…"

Eunice exhaled and laughed. "Young virgies. I like 'em. Don't worry. You'll get your jack's worth. Make yourself comfortable."

"Huh?"

"I suggest you take off your clothes. Works better that way."

Eunice stubbed out her cigarette. While I stripped, I snuck a look at her as she removed her barely-there undergarment.

There was something on my mind. I had named my dick after our beloved housemaster, but now I worried that Prick/Maher wouldn't cooperate—that Maher's ghost would haunt me at the worst possible time.

Solution. I temporarily renamed my wanger *Roosevelt*. Couldn't go wrong naming my dick after somebody as powerful as the President of the United States.

Roosevelt stood at full attention. Ready for action. *God bless the President of the United States!*

Eunice laid down and parted her legs. "Any time you're ready, Mr. Sainjon."

I explored her body, especially her bubs, but Eunice was bored. Her attention was fixed on the ceiling like it was the Sistine Chapel.

She grabbed my butt with both hands, pulled me in, and began to rock and roll. Felt like I was back on the roller coaster at Revere Beach in Massachusetts. Eunice kicked into overdrive, bucking and bouncing. I held on for dear life.

The bed squeaked, I gasped—and then I was done.

Eunice pushed me off and scrambled from the bed. She put on her slip, mumbling, "Not sure why I have to put my clothes on again, but rules is rules. Tell your friend it's his turn."

I dressed quickly.

Lem hadn't moved. "The dirty deed is done," I said. "You're on, boy."

He slumped. "Sort of not in the mood."

"What?" I said, annoyed at his resistance. "Mr. Billings, we dressed up, rode the train for an hour, took a cab, and now you're not in the mood?"

"But—"

"Get in the mood, my friend. I'll tell you, it's not great. But it's not like anything else you've ever experienced. That's for sure."

"Hmmm." Looking down, Lem fiddled with his hands.

"You ever been on a roller coaster?" I asked.

"Yeah."

"What goes on in there," I said, pointing to the door, "is like that. Fast. Kind of scary. But fun."

"So it's not that bad?"

"No, and you don't have to do very much. Our gal Eunice takes care of most everything."

"Okay," he said like a man about to be executed. "Get it over with."

I clapped him on the back, guiding him toward the door. "Here he comes," I said.

His shoulders trembling, Lem handed me his bowler hat. He exhaled several times, then stared vacantly past me. I'd never seen Lem so scared, like he was expecting Eunice to paddle his butt raw.

How long had I been in there? Five minutes? Fifteen minutes? Half an hour? The sex part lasted about five seconds.

Muddled voices came from the room, but I couldn't make out what was being said. Was Lem following through? I took out my penknife and marked the banister with my initials.

Not long after, Lem bolted out of the room, avoiding eye contact with me. "Let's go!" he screamed. For once, I followed.

We scampered down the stairs, two at a time. "Come back soon," one of the gals hollered. "But next time, pick your own girl. Shit! White people! Don't they know a gal gotta make a living?"

It was cold and dark as we made our way outside. Many of the houses and apartments were black. No electricity, apparently.

"Did Eunice treat you all right?" I asked "Enjoy yourself?"

"Let's get the hell out of here," he said.

CHAPTER THIRTEEN

To get back from the brothel, we hailed a taxi and directed it to Rip's family's apartment on Park Avenue, in a posh area of the city. Lem stared straight ahead. He didn't want to talk. I'd hoped Lem and I would walk out of there whooping and hollering and swapping stories on the way back. Lem was absolutely silent.

Going to the brothel was something I had to do, but would I do it again? I hoped there'd come a time—and soon—where I didn't have to fork over money to be with a woman. Not that I couldn't afford it but...

Opening the door, Rip said, "Well, boys, how was it?"

"The best I ever had," I said, grinning.

"It was okay," Lem said, staring at his feet.

We chatted for a few more minutes when suddenly I broke out in a cold sweat. I stood up and paced the room, my hands clasped to my cheeks. My shirt stuck to my back like I'd gone swimming in it. I was worried sick. Or worried that I might be sick.

"What's wrong, Jack?" Rip asked.

"I didn't use a safer, Lem. Did you?" I rubbed the back of my neck.

"No."

My voice wavering, I said, "We have to do something so we don't get the clap. Otherwise, we might suffer the consequences... whatever they are."

Rip took us to a nearby hospital, and the nurse gave us kits consisting of a tube, some creamy medication, and a hand-sized plunger. She instructed us to fill the tube with the cream, and shove the creamy stuff up our penises using the plunger. If we were diseased, the nurse said, the medicine would kill the germs. "Good luck," she said, closing the door.

Like boxers between rounds, Lem and I went to our separate corners.

"Hope I'm doing this right," I said. Not sure how deep to stick the tube in, I put it in as far as I could stand. "Oww!" I immediately felt great pain. Burned like hell.

"Jack, now do you see why this whole thing was a bad idea? Look at us!" Lem inhaled deeply. "Here goes. Aaaaaah! Man alive! Goddamn that hurts! Better work."

"Agreed."

Although I didn't have any symptoms, I couldn't sleep that night, doubting that the cure was going to be successful.

In the middle of the night, I shook Rip awake. "We have to see a doctor. Maybe that other thing didn't work."

Rip made a call, and at about four a.m., the three of us dashed to the doctor's house.

The doctor opened the door, wearing his bathrobe. Guiding us to his office, he said, "So, you boys availed yourself of some local gals and you're worried you're infected? Is that correct?"

"Yes, sir," I said.

"All right." The doctor reached into a steel case and took out a hypodermic with a long needle and a bottle of fluid. "This will cure whatever you got—if you got it. Who's first?"

"I went first with Eunice," I said. "Your turn, LeMoyne."

"Drop your shorts and bend over, please," the doctor said.

Lem stripped down and turned his back. The doctor prepared the needle.

"Big arse you got, Moines. Makes it easy for the doc. No way he can miss."

"Zip it, Jack."

"Going to sting a little," the doctor said, plunging the needle into Lem's ample buttocks.

"Yow! You said a little."

The doctor extracted the needle. "Next."

The doctor prepared a new needle, and Lem and I traded places.

No big deal for me. I was used to having needles jammed in my butt and practically everywhere else.

The doctor thrust the needle into my backside and held it. "Is that as deep as you can go, Doctor?" I said, grinning at Lem.

Hardly bothered me. Kennedy, the Human Pincushion.

Lem shook his head.

Butt sore, both of us limped out of the office like a couple of wounded Great War veterans.

Chapter Fourteen

We returned to Wallingford Sunday afternoon, disheveled and tired. Lem's bowler hat was smudged and battered. Our shirts were wrinkled and stained; we didn't bother tucking them in. As we approached Choate, a figure emerged from behind a tree.

Maher!

"Kennedy and Billings." He looked us over from top to bottom. "I'm sure you had quite the weekend. Judging from your slovenly appearance, you've made fools of yourselves. Remember that as students here, you are expected to act with a sense of decorum. You represent Choate wherever you go. Get yourselves cleaned up."

When he was out of earshot, I said, "Nice to see you too, Master Prick—I mean Master. Darn, I didn't get a chance to ask him about his weekend. Probably spent it spying."

Lem mocked him, sticking his tongue out while putting his fingers in his ears. Maher turned around at exactly that moment, charged back to us, and got in Lem's face. "Billings, I saw that."

"Saw what?" Lem protested, backing up a step. "I didn't do anything."

Maher was red-faced, fuming that Lem wasn't going to admit his offense.

"Apologize to me."

Lem trembled.

I couldn't let Lem down when he'd been there for me so many times before. But what could I do? Maher saw him make the face and was going to pry an apology from him if it was the last thing he did.

I took a step forward. "Mr. Maher, Lem was only—"

"Shut up, Kennedy."

Maher shoved Lem up against the tree. When Lem's hat fell to the ground, Maher kicked it away.

"I'm sorry," Lem mumbled.

Poking him hard in the chest, Maher said, "That's not good enough, Billings. Sorry for what?"

"I'm sorry for making a face at you."

But Maher wasn't going to let him off that easily. "I assume you're also sorry for disrespecting me and the entire school?"

"Yes," Lem said.

"Okay," Maher said. He was within inches of Lem's face. "Then let's hear your entire apology. And make it good."

"I'm sorry for making a face at you, and for disrespecting you and the entire school."

"One more time," Maher said. "And say it like you mean it."

After Lem repeated the apology, Maher said, "That's better." He glared at Lem. "And if you ever do something like that again, I'll have you expelled so fast you won't even have time to pack your trunk."

"Yes, sir."

"Now get out of my sight. Prepare your studies for the week." He walked away.

"You okay?" I asked.

Lem's face was white. He gripped his hat and took deep breaths. "I will be," he said.

I patted him on the back. "I bet you're glad to be done with football. Won't have Maher on your ass anymore."

"Hmmm. Uh, yeah."

I looked curiously at Lem. Maher had just berated and bullied him, but he didn't seem relieved not to be under his control anymore. I'd be happy never to play for that guy again. Well, maybe Lem was in shock.

He smiled sheepishly. "Oh, I have some news about that. Seems that I'm not, er, graduating—this year, that is."

I halted. "What the hell are you talking about? How can you not graduate?"

"Sticking around another year. Couple more classes to take. We'll graduate together." He kicked a rock. "Besides, somebody needs to watch over you."

I heard but wasn't sure what to make of this development. I thought when you completed four years at Choate, you graduated, unless you failed a bunch of subjects, and that certainly wasn't the case for Lem. Unless he was lying. But Lem wouldn't lie to me. His family wasn't well off, and money had become even tighter after his father died last year, but evidently there was enough. Well, it was his decision, and I was fine with it. My last year at Choate would be a lot better with him around.

I could confide in Lem, tell him important things. Bitch about Joe or the Old Man or Choate or my lack of success with girls. Lem didn't judge or criticize or tell me what to do like Joe and the Old Man did. Lem was encouraging and upbeat. "We'll get through this, Johnny," he'd say. He helped keep my spirits up on the many occasions when I was sick.

"So," I said, "I'll be stuck looking at Mr. Unattractive for yet another year?"

"I'm afraid so," Lem said.

"Welcome aboard." I clapped him on the back. "Or should I say, glad you're staying aboard. Anyway, bad idea for you to leave right when the Muckers are getting started."

"Exactly," Lem said.

———>•<———

Monday morning, I walked to one of my least favorite classes. Plane Geometry. But when I entered the building, the corridor echoed with an unexpected chant.

Maury Shea, Maury Shea,
Drinking tea every day.
Maury Shea, what's your appeal?
Queenie, we want a new deal!

I'd told Lem and Rip what I'd written about Moe and Queenie. Word had gotten around, but it didn't appear the singers knew I was the author because nobody looked at me. Just as well.

I smiled to myself as I sat down, but after that night in Harlem and everything that happened afterward, my mind wasn't on Plane Geometry. Not that it ever was. Or French, for that matter. Both subjects were too precise for my taste. No room to imagine, to wonder.

I gazed out the window, picturing myself sailing on Cape Cod. The wind in my hair, sun on my face, and not a care in the world. The open sea was calling to me.

"Mr. Kennedy, tell me the properties of a rhombus," Mr. Collins said. He had a bad habit of interrupting my daydreams.

"Rhombus?" I stammered.

Whap!

A wad of wet paper struck my cheek. I turned in the direction of the jerk who'd tossed the wad—the president of the Student Council or, as I called it, the *Stooge Council*. The head stooge sneered.

Naturally, the Head and Maher believed these Council twonks to be superior beings. To me, they were only best when fabricating stupid ideas. Like when the Council proposed that Choate students be required to shovel Wallingford streets as part of their school service. *Shovel the shit*. Horse-drawn carriages had made a comeback during the hard times. Folks who couldn't find a job relinquished their cars because they were too expensive to run. An abundance of muck resulted.

However, the Council made one exception: all Council members! Because they considered their community service to be devising stupid ideas like that one.

Fortunately, the school administration recognized the fraud. Unless Council members also agreed to shovel the muck, they couldn't expect everybody else to gather road apples. The Council withdrew the proposal.

Mr. Collins rapped on his desk, clearly not a witness to the spitball. "Your brother set an exemplary record here, Mr. Kennedy. Perhaps you might learn a thing or two from his model. If I recall, he was awarded the Harvard Trophy. Doesn't appear that you'll be in the running for that or anything else next year."

Joe again.

Joe liked to boast about the award. And the Old Man did, too, hoping his accomplishment would cause me to apply myself at Choate. It hadn't, at least so far.

Joe was good at everything, and I wasn't.

After class, the head stooge said to me, "Hey, Catholic boy, go back to where you came from. Too many of you in this country. Especially at this school. If you Catholics had your way, the Pope would rule the country. A Catholic president would be his puppet. But it ain't going to happen. Smith found that out. Got his ass kicked. We don't want a Catholic President." Al Smith, a Catholic who'd been the Democratic nominee for president in 1928, had been soundly defeated by Republican Herbert Hoover.

"The Pope running the country?" I said. "Are you out of your mind?" I walked away. It was startling that people feared the Catholic Church taking over the country. But a lot of people did, including the Ku Klux Klan, which, I'd read, made it a point to physically threaten or attack Catholics in the U.S.

After the spitball assault and the vilifying of my religion, I had something besides Joe on my mind. *Payback.*

Was this getting to be a habit?

I resolved to pull a prank on the Stooge Council president. But first I'd talk it over with Lem and Rip, preferably in a private place, away from prying eyes. The masters and the cops were everywhere, and you couldn't go anywhere without being watched.

A hideout. An escape for when Choate made me a nutcase, which was pretty damn often.

Later that day, I slipped out of Assembly and explored the rural countryside, searching for an abandoned barn or cave.

I came upon an old shack that locked like it hadn't been used since the Great War. The rusty door squeaked when I pulled it open. I peeked inside and walked around. Room enough for a dozen people. Perfect. Nobody would bother us here.

Except the owner.

When I came out, I faced a grizzled farmer. He was a mean-looking old coot in muddy overalls and a torn flat cap. A shotgun in hand, he spat at my shoes.

"What you doing in there, boy?" he growled through gapped yellow teeth. "Private property. *My* private property. Now git!"

My muscles quivered and my pulse raced. "All right," I said, but I didn't like his manners. Sure, I was kind of trespassing, but he didn't have to go all crazy on me. Did he think I was going to steal his empty barn? Could have said something polite like, "May I help you?"

I looked at him straight on. "I'm on my way, you old goat."

His nostrils flared. "What you call me, you little shit?" He gripped my wrist tightly. "I'm going to teach you a lesson—one you won't get in that uppity Choate school."

"Got nothing to learn from you, bastard."

I kicked him in the knee, yanked myself free, and sprinted toward a wooded area. Fortunately, I was quick and agile. No way he could catch me. But he didn't need to.

Blam! Blam!

Bullets chunked into a tree to my right.

Holy shit! Was he trying to kill me? Or just scare me?

I zigged and zagged, racing back to school. For the first time in my life, I was glad to be at Choate.

I scrambled up the stairs two at a time and burst into my room, startling Lem, who was sitting at his desk.

"You all right, Jack? Copperhead on your tail?"

I recounted the incident.

"Ornery fella," Lem said. "Shoots his gun off for that? Crazy. Good thing you're thin as a rail. Less of a target. Hell, you could sleep in a shotgun. Why were you poking around there?"

I told him my idea about having a secret place.

"A hideout. Is that what you're thinking, Ken?"

"Yeah. You can't get away with anything here. They're watching us everywhere, both in town and here." I lowered my voice and cocked my head toward the wall separating us from Maher. "And there."

"I don't think Shotgun Sam is going to reconsider," Lem said. "Need to find someplace else."

"Care to look around Sunday? I'll skip church."

"What a coincidence. Believe Mother is coming to town that day." Lem winked. "I too will take a pass on chapel. Rude to stand up Ma."

In my scrapbook that night, I wrote, "Got shot at today for calling an old farmer a bad name. Almost got hit."

Sunday, I steered Lem in a different direction than my earlier exploration. After we'd walked about a mile, I heard the snort of animals coming from a barn, but next to it was a rickety shack. No door. A couple of hay bales and a few crates. That was all we needed.

CHAPTER FIFTEEN

The next weekend, Rip, Lem, and I convened a club meeting at our new hideout. "Here we are, Public Enemies One and Two," I said. "And the Ripper." Sprawled on hay bales, we bitched about Choate and talked about girls and sports.

I chewed on a piece of straw. After I recounted the spitball incident, I said, "Action is required. A retaliatory response. Anybody have any ideas for getting back at that asshole?"

We discussed several options before an idea occurred to me.

Passing the rube's room the other day, I noticed his radio, a fancy Crosley Tombstone, a few feet from the door. "Maybe he could use a wake-up call," I said. I ran the plan by my fellow Muckers.

"Ken, after waking up Maher and now this, I firmly believe rousing people from slumber is your emerging talent," Lem said. "This skill could be a big part of your future success."

"What I was put on earth for, Lemmer." I laughed. "To wake people up."

"But, Jack," Lem cautioned, "won't everybody else on the wing be woken up too?"

I pondered Lem's statement. "That's a risk I'm willing to take."

"Courageous," Rip said in a mocking tone.

———⟶◆⟵———

Three a.m. and I was ready. When the stooge wasn't in, I'd practiced silently opening his door. And once he was asleep, I could have farted in his face and he wouldn't have woken up.

I pictured myself a saboteur on a secret mission. Quietly turning the doorknob, I tiptoed in. The big lunk snored like a congested pig. I spun the radio's big knob, cranking the volume up all the way. It would be twenty seconds before the Crosley tubes warmed up. Closing the door, I scampered back to my room.

Lem and I waited, suppressing laughs. When the radio blasted Benny Goodman's "Stompin' at the Savoy," our Stooge Council president yelped like he'd been jolted with electricity. We bolted to the corridor and pounded on his door. Rip joined us, and soon the entire West Wing had come out to see what the noise was about.

The dope opened his door. His eyes bulged. "*Whaat?*" he stammered.

"Turn that goddamn radio off, you idiot!" I yelled. "Trying to sleep!"

"Hey, where are your manners?" Lem quipped. "Up your arse!"

"What a jerk!" Rip taunted.

Maher stood in plaid pajamas outside his door, hair askew. "What's going on? What boy has their radio on at this hour?"

We pointed to our beloved school officer.

"Sir," I said, "if this kind of behavior continues, we must consider removing him from office."

Maher was speechless again. I returned to my room and closed the door in his face.

⇒•◦•⇐

The radio prank was a complete success. The school officer never suspected he'd been pranked. And we reminded him often about his mistake. "You wake us up again with your radio, we'll have to start impeachment proceedings," Len warned.

But I still had the problem of dealing with his anti-Catholicism. What could I do? Probably he'd always be suspicious of the Catholic Church and afraid the Pope might try to control any Catholic ever elected president, but if I could change his mind about me, I would have made progress. I decided the best way was to joke with him, see if I could use my wit to find common ground.

After a Friday fish dinner, I muttered to him, "Man, that fish was so bad, I'm thinking of converting to Protestantism."

He laughed and said, "What makes you think we'd take you, Kennedy?"

I smiled and nodded obligingly. "Good one."

I also knew that, like me, he was a Boston Red Sox fan. When he happened by one day after I'd gotten off the phone, I said, "Just talking to the Pope." He stopped in his tracks and smiled. "Guy's a Yankees fan," I said, "and thinks they'll win it all this year. I told him I wouldn't bet on it."

"Yeah, the Pope doesn't know what he's talking about. It's the Red Sox' year."

"I'm with you."

After that, we got along pretty well.

CHAPTER SIXTEEN

S hortly after the radio caper, I was engulfed by a fierce fever and the sweats.

Walking from the dining hall after breakfast, my head seemed to float above my body, an absolute silence surrounded me, and my legs went watery. I reached out for something with which to steady myself, but there wasn't anything to hold onto. I collapsed in a heap.

I was sent to Archbold and stayed a week. Because this was shortly after Lem and I had returned from Harlem, I pondered whether my illness was related to our expedition. Lem was fine, but I wasn't convinced he'd done the "dirty deed," even though he made himself endure the "thing-up-your-prick" and bared his backside for the anti-hooker shot. But my problem this time had nothing to do with that. My knee got infected after I'd skinned it playing tennis, and it had swelled up to twice its normal size.

As I sat beneath the large glass window, relaxing on the Archbold solarium daybed, the sun barely warmed me. The solarium was supposed to help heal you, but so far it hadn't worked its magic on me. But it was better than being in my room all the time.

Sometimes, if I couldn't sleep, I'd visit the solarium at night and gaze at the stars. Then I'd come back to earth and wonder if I'd ever stop feeling terrible. Just when it seemed like I was okay, something bad always happened. I'd faint, or my gut hurt, or I got skinnier and skinnier. Was I going to fade away? *Where's Kennedy? He was here a minute ago.*

"Are you sick of me?" I said to the nurse stationed at the reception desk one day. I had dropped a few more pounds and ghastly red blotches covered my body—hives.

The nurse chuckled at my wordplay. "We're always glad to see you, Jack."

"Hello, Jack." The Head's wife, Clara, had swept in. This time she had ice cream for me. Sometimes it was soup. She smiled, softening her long face, and placed the ice cream on the table. She put her hand on my shoulder. Mrs. St. John smoothed out her lengthy, flowing Victorian-style dress before seating herself on the wicker chair. Besides providing a motherly touch for the Choate boys, she taught several courses in Greek and Latin.

While I disliked her husband, I had only warm feelings for Mrs. St. John. She checked on me regularly whenever I was sick. Sometimes, I wished I had a mother more like her—warm and affectionate, and who cared enough to visit. My heart ached because Mother and Dad never stopped by to see how I was doing. Well, Mother had a large household to manage, and the Old Man was busy with his new liquor-importing business.

Mrs. St. John said gently, "Jack, we had hoped you'd be feeling better by now."

"Well, I'm not feeling worse," I said, forcing a laugh.

She touched my shoulder. "The doctors aren't sure what the cause of your sickness is. It's important that you get the best care." She hesitated. "Because your condition hasn't improved, we believe it best to send you to the hospital in New Haven. They have specialists and your family agrees. Arrangements have been made for you to leave tomorrow, Jack."

My head dropped to my chest. Here I go again. This time I was going to a real hospital. *Oh God, will this ever stop?*

But I didn't have to wait until tomorrow. Later that day, I started to feel really terrible, and they didn't know whether it was the knee infection, my gut, or something else. I was rushed in a meat wagon (ambulance) to New Haven Hospital.

For the next few days, the doctors put me on a special diet of nothing while they probed and tested. Might be leukemia, they said.

During the next several days, I read several books and wrote a bunch of letters, most of them to Lem. "It seems that I was sicker than I thought I was, and because I'm supposed to be dead, I'm developing a limp and a hollow cough."

I was enjoying my first decent hospital meal in days when Mrs. St. John stopped in.

"Jack, how are you feeling?" she said, drawing a chair close to my bed. She'd brought my Victrola and books.

"Okay, except they've been starving me." I took a bite of toast. "It was good they decided to give me breakfast. If they hadn't, I think the nurse would have come in pretty soon, looked in my bed, and not been able to see me at all."

"I see you haven't lost your sense of humor, Jack."

No, but I wanted to lose the hospital. Didn't need to be here any longer—I was feeling better, and they still had no idea what was wrong. "If this had happened fifty years ago, they would have said, 'Well, the boy has had a case of hives, but now he's over it.' Now, instead, they've got to take my blood count every little while and keep me here until test results corresponded with what the doctors diagnose it to be."

A week later, when it was clear I was feeling better, they sent me to recuperate at our winter home in Palm Beach, Florida. I spent the remainder of the semester there and finally returned to Choate after Easter.

———⊷◦⊷———

I trudged up the stairs to my room, my mood brightening when I remembered Spring Festival was coming up soon.

Surprise. The Prick was waiting for me.

"Don't think I'll be easing up on you just because you were ill," he said, sneering. He'd come back from school break meaner than ever. "The opposite is true. Since you're behind on your studies, I'll make sure you put your nose to the grindstone. And you'll now have plenty of time. Because of health concerns, we think it best you not participate at all in spring sports."

Great. No crew team for me.

"Have a good holiday, Mr. Maher?" I said, going into my room and closing the door behind me.

"Welcome back, Jack," Lem said. Cracking a big smile, he came over to shake hands. "It's good to see you. For a while, we weren't sure you were going to make it. The Head made us pray for your recovery."

"You're not going to get rid of me that easily." I frowned. "But Maher just told me they won't allow me to play spring sports. You'll have to crew without me, Lemmer."

"Sorry to hear about that, Ken. But you've still got next year."

I asked if the Muckers had continued to meet while I was laid up.

"Sometimes we did, sometimes we didn't. Not as many guys showed up." He pointed to the Victrola. "The Head's wife brought back your Victrola, but it started acting up, so we didn't have any music."

I nodded. "Have to get that thing fixed," I said.

Final exams were coming up. But the Spring Festival and summer vacation were just around the corner.

CHAPTER SEVENTEEN

The weekend of the Spring Festival, Choate came alive. *With girls.*

The school put them up on campus—one of the few times they were allowed on school grounds. The weekend included a fancy dinner, the school production of a Gilbert and Sullivan musical, and a gala dance.

"Hey, Lem, let's go to the tuck shop. Need something sweet." I picked up my rumpled khakis from the floor and put them on, then rolled up the cuffs. "After that, I've got to pick up a gal named Cawley at the train station." I was taking Ruth Moffett to the dance. They printed who you were going with in *The Choate News.* You had to get approval before your date was allowed on campus. But now I had added responsibilities.

At the tuck shop, Lem got a double-dipped chocolate Oh Henry! candy bar. I chose a Zagnut peanut brittle bar. Between bites, I said, "Smoky is sick. He asked me to take care of this Cawley girl for the weekend. She goes to the Kimberley School in Montclair. Somewhere in New Jersey. I'm obligated to dance with her, but I'll ditch her if she's a drag."

Lem went back to our room, and I took North Main, passing the bustling Caplan's Market. Then came the smell of freshly baked bread wafting from Heliman's Bakery. I walked by Marx's Pharmacy and the sign advertising Kemp's Salted Nuts "Right off the Fire," then took a right at Center Street and past the First Congregational Church.

I glanced at my watch. Late! I dashed the last few downhill blocks to the Wallingford railroad station.

I scanned the people waiting around. Smoky had described her as pretty, with short, dark, curly hair. Slim and a sharp dresser.

A matronly woman. Guy with a briefcase. Mother with two children. A young gal, stylishly dressed, arms crossed. Had to be her. "Are you Olive Cawley?"

She nodded, narrowing her eyes. "Yes. Who are you? Where's James Wilde?"

"I'm Jack Kennedy," I said. "Smoky—I mean Jim—is sick so I have to take care of you for the weekend." I should have left it at that, but I added, "I'm in love with Ruth Moffett, so don't fall in love with me."

What? Did I just say that? I immediately wished I could take back those words. What a crazy thing to say. That I was in love with Ruth Moffett. I wasn't. Didn't know what love was. Hell, I'd only danced with Ruth a few times at tea dances, and we'd gone out for ice cream just once. But I wanted Olive to understand the situation. I wasn't happy about having to be her escort. I'd help out a friend, but one gal at a time was enough for me, at least for now.

"Fall in love with you?" Olive said, backing up. "With somebody who doesn't have the decency to be on time and who thinks a gal will fall in love with him in the blink of an eye?" She surveyed my casual attire of worn khakis and beat-up sneakers. "A boy who doesn't have the sense to make a good first impression by the clothes he wears?"

"Well—"

"I guess this Ruth Moffett you're so in love with doesn't mind a sloppy dresser and inconsiderate boy. And you needn't worry about me falling in love with the likes of you. What a thing to say when first meeting someone. I don't think I like you, Jack Kennedy."

"That's what they all say at the beginning, then—"

"Please show me the way to your school," Olive said, shaking her head. "It's the least you can do. Then leave me alone and go back to your Little Miss Moffett."

I laughed. "All right, no need to get your skirt all twisted up."

We walked to Choate in silence. Olive stared straight ahead, not responding to my feeble attempts at conversation. It was a short walk, but it felt like one of the longest of my life.

"I'll see ya later tonight," I said.

"Don't bother," she said.

I walked away, stung by her remark and chastened by what had happened. I'd tried to help out a sick buddy by pinch-hitting for him. But I'd been rejected by his date, who'd rather go to the dance alone than have me escort her. What had I done wrong?

That night, after a few dances with Ruth, I sidled up to Olive. Although I had a date, we were expected to dance with other girls. Figured I'd give Olive a second chance. I didn't like being rebuffed by somebody who didn't know me. Besides, she was pretty.

"Hey, remember me?"

Olive put her finger to her chin. "No, I don't recall seeing anybody who looked like you. Some guy picked me up at the train station, but he was pretty full of himself and dressed like a country boy."

"Yeah, don't know who that was. Anyway, guess I'm obligated to dance with you. Have to take care of you and all."

Olive put her hands on her hips. "Oh, now you're going to do me a favor by taking me for a spin? Why don't you go back to your Ruth Moffett and leave me alone?" She walked away.

I'd done it again.

After dancing and refreshments, I noticed Olive wearing a much fancier dress. Odd. Maybe she'd brought two dresses and gone back to her room to change.

I danced with Ruth and a variety of other girls. When I danced near Olive, she looked the other way. Hips swinging, Olive was graceful and light on her feet. Guys seemed to enjoy dancing with her—they left her company reluctantly. Olive was in high demand.

I decided I just had to dance with her. Find out what all the fuss was about.

"Hey, Olive, I've been told I'll be kicked out of school if I don't dance with the gal I'm supposed to take care of. You don't want that on your conscience, do you? Responsible for getting me thrown out on my ear?"

She stared at me. "I couldn't care less."

"Neither do I."

Her eyebrows raised. "You don't?"

"No, but let's dance anyway." I surprised her by taking her in my arms to start the waltz.

There was no doubt she was the best partner I'd danced with all night. Lithe but firm, she responded to my lead, and moved with more elegance than any of the other girls. She had a way of throwing a sideways glance and tilting her head that had my pulse racing and my mouth dry as a desert.

There was something different about her. She wasn't like the other girls. "Couldn't help but notice you're wearing a different dress than the one I saw you in an hour ago. Brought another?" Figured she'd be pleased I'd noticed.

"Not exactly," she said, blushing. "Promise you won't tell anybody how I got it?'

"Promise."

"Well, I felt dowdy in that other one. When I went to the lavatory, I saw a girl with the perfect dress. I asked if I could try it on, and it fit. I just had to have it. So, I ran out with her dress on. I've been avoiding her the whole evening."

I scratched my jaw. I admired Olive's pluck, although it did come at somebody else's expense. Turned out she was a prankster, just like me.

"I'm sure you look better in it than she did."

Olive brightened. "That's the first nice thing you've said to me all day."

"I hope you'll forgive me for my past remarks. That's not the real Jack Kennedy."

"No?" She pulled away. "Then who is the real Jack Kennedy?"

"He's kind and generous and fun and—"

"Hmmm. So far, I haven't seen any evidence of that."

"You will. We still have the rest of the weekend."

I was starting to like Olive. She was witty, adventurous, and prideful. Nice-looking too.

"Oh no," Olive said, her eyes flashing. "Here she comes. I have a feeling she wants her dress back."

"I don't know why." I smirked. An angry girl was striding toward us. "I'll take care of this, Olive." I motioned to Moe, who was sitting the dance out. "Moe, give Olive a spin," I said.

"With pleasure," he said, eagerly taking over.

I intercepted the gal coming our way. Offering her my best fake smile, I said, "May I say you look stunning in that dress? I'd be honored to have a dance with you."

Her anger promptly dissipated and she entirely forgot about her mission. "Well, of course," she said.

Steering her away to the other side of the dining hall, we danced several numbers before I turned her over to another Mucker with instructions to keep her so occupied she couldn't get near Olive. Before the evening was over, every Mucker had taken a turn with her, always dancing far from Olive.

At the end of the evening, Olive was back in her original dress. "Well, Mr. Jack Kennedy, I must say you redeemed yourself." She hesitated. "Where do you plan to escort me tomorrow?" she said, running her hands through her hair.

Spring Festival events kept me busy the next day, with me squiring two gals. But I spent most of the time with Olive. We'd taken a liking to each other.

At the end of the weekend, I announced, "Lemmer, I'm done with Ruth Moffett. Got a thing for Olive."

He smiled weakly. "Couldn't happen to a nicer guy." But it didn't look like he meant it. Normally, I could count on Lem for encouragement. Not today. Was he jealous I might have a girlfriend? Concerned I'd be spending more time with Olive and less with him?

"Thanks," I said. "I'm sure a fine-featured gal will soon recognize the wonderful qualities of Kirk LeMoyne Billings, even if he does resemble a good-looking ape man."

"I'm in no hurry," Lem said, looking away. "Prefer to play the field."

Several more dates with Olive followed. Besides her mischievous streak, she was also a good athlete. She played on her school's basketball and field hockey teams. I liked that about her. My sisters were athletic. This relationship, I decided, might turn into something.

CHAPTER EIGHTEEN
Summer 1934
Hyannis Port, MA

When school ended, we Kennedys caravanned from New York to Hyannis Port, Massachusetts, and our summer home on Cape Cod. Even before going inside, we ran down to the break wall and stuck out our tongues, tasting the faint salt on the breeze and waving to the waters of Nantucket Sound. That was our way of ensuring good luck.

Of all my brothers and sisters, I had the most fun with Kick. "Hey, Kick!" I yelled a few days after arriving. "Bet you can't tumble all the way down the hill!" We stood at the top of the slope leading to the beach. Kick was always ready to take a dare.

"Don't think I can do it?" she retorted with a broad grin. "I'll show you!"

Somersaulting from the top of the hill, Kick continued to tumble until the lawn flattened out. She stood up, her arms spread triumphantly. "I did it!" Then she collapsed, dizzy from all the rolling.

I clapped. "Now, tumble back up the hill!"

Kick dropped to the ground, ready to give it a try until she realized I was kidding.

My younger sister was an excellent athlete and the best of the girls at touch football, which was a Kennedy tradition. Agile and elusive, Kick caught any football thrown her way. She could take a joke and didn't mind if you pranked her. Like when I called her "Bigfoot" after I stuffed toilet paper in her shoes and she couldn't squeeze her feet in.

Try something like that on Joe and, because of his temper, he'd blow up. He was big and broad-shouldered and sometimes he'd mix it up with you over the slightest thing. Sometimes his target was me. But I wasn't a brawler. I used my wits to escape punch-outs.

When I was in my first year at Choate, an older kid cornered me, itching for a fight. "I only fight smart guys," I said, and challenged him to name every U.S. President. When he couldn't, I rattled them all off, in order, to his amazement. "When *you* can do that," I said, "let me know. I'll be around." As I walked away, he looked as if he'd been sucker-punched.

Kick was still breathless when we entered the living room of our big white house in Hyannis Port. It was actually three houses that sat on a hill together, only a few hundred yards from Nantucket Sound and the beach. Inside, Dad had installed a motion-picture theater where we could watch the talkies. There, sitting alone on the couch was my sister Rosemary, a year younger than me. Rosemary was different, but her condition wasn't discussed. There had been a problem when she was born because a doctor wasn't instantly available. All physicians were attending the sick and dying, victims of the Spanish flu that swept the nation in 1918. The doctor had been delayed and her birth had been botched. As a result, Rosemary had trouble learning the basics, like addition and subtraction, and was easily frustrated.

Our younger sister Eunice—wiry, direct, and matter of fact—joined Rosemary on the couch. Over the years, she had made it a point to look out for Rosemary. "Hey, Rose, want to get some ice cream?" she asked.

Eunice was thirteen but already a skilled sailor and excellent tennis player—we had our own backyard court.

"Sure, let's go," Rosemary said, and off they went to the Cape Cod Creamery in Hyannis for a double-dip of homemade ice cream.

A loud squeak came from the stairs, and I looked up to see Lem on his way down. He was joining us for a couple of weeks.

"Ready to sail the ocean blue, Lemmer?" I asked, extra friendly. I had yelled at him the night before because of his snoring, and I was now feeling bad about having done so.

We were taking out the *Victura*. Later today, Joe and I would race it in a local competition.

I named the boat the *Victura* because the name suggested victory. The Old Man instilled the idea in all of us that winning was everything.

"As long as you don't put us in the drink, Ken."

"Have I ever let you down?" I said.

"Let me begin with the time—"

"Let's go. Time's a-wastin'."

Lem had become a regular at our family gatherings. Having him with us made the summer more fun, partly because I spent less time with and around Joe.

Joe, a know-it-all, had returned from a year of studying and traveling in Europe. He'd been to Germany and was impressed with the changes Chancellor Adolf Hitler was making, including the Hitler Youth, which made me think of the Campus Cops for some reason.

In one of his letters, Joe wrote: "Hitler is building a spirit in his men that could be envied in any country. This spirit could be very quickly turned into a war, but Hitler has things under control. The only danger would be if something happened to Hitler and one of his crazy ministers came into power."

From what I'd read in *The Times*, I had my doubts. "Maybe Hitler is the crazy one," I said.

"Nah." He dismissed me with a wave of his hand. "You don't know what you're talking about. I've been there."

"Guess you know everything then," I said.

Like Hitler, Joe didn't think people who had physical or mental disabilities should be able to have children. "Another thing I like about Hitler," he wrote, "is he passed a sterilization law, which I think is a good thing. It will do away with one of the many disgusting specimens of people who inhabit the earth."

Okay, Joe. Did he realize Rosemary had mental disabilities and would be covered by his law if we lived in Germany? Hell, I had my own share of physical problems. Joe and I looked at the world very differently.

As we readied for our sail, my much younger brothers and sisters now came screaming through the house, running between Lem and me.

"I'm first!" eight-year-old Bobby yelled. Although he was painfully shy with strangers, looking away if somebody he didn't know asked him a question, he had no problem speaking up at home.

Mother shouted from the kitchen, "Quiet down, children! Your father is trying to work!" She stomped into the living room.

Mother was tiny, and already dwarfed by four daughters. But it was her, not Dad, who handled the spanking, and he would use a ruler or a coat hanger. Behind Mother, two-year-old Teddy wobbled in. Would he be the last, or would the number of Kennedy children reach double figures? Nine kids were enough if you asked me. (Nobody did.)

Small squares of paper were pinned to Mother's blouse and skirt. Written on each were reminder notes: *Shoes, Bobby. Sweep basement. Milk.* It was Mother's system for managing the large household whenever she was home; she sometimes traveled and stayed away for weeks at a time. Once, she went on a road trip to the West Coast with her sister Agnes, and several times traveled to Europe, leaving us in the hands of household staff.

Behind her was our black-clad maid, whom Mother had pinned with additional child-related or household tasks to do.

A door opened and the Old Man appeared. He removed his round, tortoise-shell glasses, and the room quieted, except for the stock ticker clacking away in the background. President Roosevelt had recently nominated him as chairman of something called the Securities and Exchange Commission. His job was to increase public trust in the financial markets.

"Rose, I need peace and quiet in the morning. Work to do. That won't be a problem, will it?"

"I'll see that you aren't disturbed."

"Please do." Turning to me, he said, "Jack, good luck in the race today. I'm expecting you and Joe to finish first."

"We'll do our best."

"If you do, you'll win. Don't let me down."

That was Dad. Second place was for losers, so summer vacations weren't all fun and games. While other families relaxed during these breaks, the Kennedys didn't. There was a schedule and plenty of planned activities. Sometimes it didn't seem that different from Choate.

At seven o'clock in the morning, we'd be on the lawn doing calisthenics. Then there was golf, swimming, tennis, and sailing lessons.

On our way out, Mother said, "LeMoyne?"

"Yes, Mrs. Kennedy."

"In the future, please refrain from putting your shoes on the piano." Mother pointed to his sneakers.

"But—" Lem protested, snatching his shoes.

"Lem is sorry, Mother," I said. "He promises it won't happen again. C'mon, Lemmer."

He knew I was the culprit. "Thanks for making me look bad in front of your mother," he said.

"Guess you'll have to make it up to her," I said. "Maybe you could offer to clean the storeroom."

"That's not funny."

"Well, all right. Let's go for a sail."

Lem brightened instantly. He never stayed mad for long. "Okay," he said.

After grabbing a handful of Katie Lynch butter crunch candy, we walked along a path lined with scrubby beach pine trees to the Hyannis Port Yacht Club.

"I've always wondered about your fascination with the ocean, Jack. I'm a landlubber myself. Pittsburgh has three rivers, but it's not the same as the ocean."

I popped a butter crunch into my mouth. "I need to be near the water. Another reason why being at Choate is tough on me. People—and I'm one of them if you haven't noticed—are committed to the sea." I stopped mid-stride. "Maybe it's because we all came from the sea."

"Evolution? Darwin?"

"Yes. I read an interesting biological fact that all of us have the exact same percentage of salt in our blood that exists in the ocean. We have salt in our blood, in our sweat, in our tears."

"Really?"

"Yes, so we're sort of tied to the ocean. When you think about it, when we return to the sea—whether it is to sail or to observe—we're going back to where we originated."

"Never thought of that," Lem said.

"Neither did I." I laughed. "Until now. That's what I like about you. You get me thinking. But enough beating one's gums. Let's get to work."

Lem saluted. "Aye, aye, Captain Kennedy."

We boarded the twenty-five-foot *Victura*. Its hull was gold, the sides painted blue, and the deck buff colored. It was a family sailboat, but nobody had taken to it as I had. Despite Mother's objections, I kept its cotton sail in my room.

I gave directions to Lem, who aided me in checking the rudder and tiller. After raising and cleating the mainsail, we were ready to go.

I liked being in command of the boat. When Joe and I sailed, he usually had the upper hand, although we were equally capable.

Taking the tiller, I steered the *Victura* into open water. Would I ever command a different kind of ship—perhaps a fighting ship? Never know what might happen with people like Hitler and Mussolini around. If there was a war, I decided, I'd join the navy. Better to be out on the water than stuck in the trenches like the soldiers of the Great War.

"Full speed ahead," Lem said.

"Whatever you say," I said.

Joe and I stood on the veranda while dinner was being prepared, gazing out over Nantucket Sound. Dad read the newspaper. It was a rare shorts-and-shirtsleeve summer evening on the Cape.

Joe and I usually did well, winning more than our share of races, but that afternoon we had finished toward the back.

I swatted a mosquito off my arm, but he'd already bit me.

"That mosquito took quite a risk biting you," Joe said with a laugh. "After a sip of your blood, he's bound to die quickly."

"Funny," I said sarcastically. His jokes about my health were tiresome to me.

Dad put down the newspaper and motioned for the two of us to come over.

"I watched the race today, and I have to tell you that I was disgusted with both of you," he said. "There is no sense in going into a race unless you do your damnedest to win. In that regard, you failed miserably. Don't let it happen again."

Joe and I kept silent. We recognized when the Old Man was on a rant.

"I'm expecting a lot of you, boys. You know that. Both of you are smart and capable, but it takes more than that to succeed in this world. There are a lot of sharp people out there, but unless they work hard and have goals, they end up barely scraping by. Make hardly enough to feed their families. These days, what with the terrible economy and high unemployment, many can't do even that."

Joe and I nodded.

"It's what you do with your talent that's important. I can only help you so much. Like you, Jack, Joe started off slow at Choate.

But then he stepped it up." He gave Joe a proud smile. Turning to me, he said, "I haven't seen that from you so far."

Joe snickered.

The Old Man stood. "I believe the Kennedy family has a big part to play in the future of this country. I don't know how long I'll stay as SEC chairman, but it won't be forever. And Roosevelt won't be re-elected if he can't get this country's economy going in the right direction. I'm for him, but people in breadlines without jobs don't have much patience. They want food and work. Maybe the time will be ripe for a businessman, not a politician, to get this country back on track—someone who's been successful at managing a company, at making money. People want to see a track record."

"Are you thinking of running?" Joe asked.

"I'm not saying I would or wouldn't run for president. But if the circumstances were right, I might."

I'd never heard the Old Man talk openly about the possibility.

"One problem, should I consider running, is that we are Catholic. Some people don't like Catholics. Have had to fight that my entire life. When I graduated from Harvard, I couldn't get a job. Companies didn't want to hire a Catholic from Boston. But , my friends, who were Protestant but not as good with numbers as me, had no problem getting hired. Then, after I became successful, they wouldn't let me join their country clubs." Dad tightened his fists. "But I showed them," he said, waving his hand at the vast property.

He paused. "There's never been a Catholic president, and I'm not sure the country is ready for one quite yet. But if not me, another Kennedy has to come forward. That's you, Joseph."

Joe smiled broadly.

Joe could have it. Made it easy for me. I could go on having a good old time while Dad put the screws to Joe to make the Kennedy name famous.

"Joseph, leave us for a few minutes. I need to talk with Jack."

Joe gave me a nasty smirk before going inside.

I gulped. This wasn't going to be good. If he planned on praising me, he would have done it in front of Joe. "Sit down, Jack." I took a seat and prepared for the worst. Dad gazed out at the water for a few seconds. I crossed my arms.

Turning to face me, he said, "Jack, I'm going to level with you. The latest reports from school were extremely disappointing." His voice rising, he continued, "I had hoped when you got back to school after your illness, you'd buckle down and give it your best for the next few months. But you didn't. The headmaster and your housemaster have nothing good to say about you. Besides all the horsing around, your grades are clear evidence you're working way below your potential. I'm very disappointed."

I sighed. I was going to have to take it.

"Do you have any explanation for yourself?"

I didn't. Or I did, but I wasn't going to tell him the truth— that I was bored at school, didn't care about getting good grades, found the school's restrictions maddening, and considered Maher's interventions intolerable. Why would I try my darndest to be successful at a place I detested?

Sure, I'd enjoyed competing on the football, basketball, and baseball teams, even if I hadn't made varsity. But when I'd come back to school that spring after my illness, I'd been forbidden from resuming athletic competition. I was jealous when Lem regaled me with highlights of the crew team's races—a team that I'd been on last year.

And there was no way I was going to tell him about the Muckers. That the club had become my greatest source of pride and accomplishment since I'd been at Choate. He wouldn't understand. It wasn't what the Old Man wanted me to focus my attention on. But to me, the comradery was special. I was learning things about myself. I was respected by the guys and had taken a leadership role. That was something to be proud of, in my opinion. At some point, Dad might find out what I had going, but I wasn't going to worry about that now.

I'd just have to put him off. "No. I could do better." Not *I will*.

He told me I better shape up or there would be severe consequences. "Don't make me lose confidence in you again because you'll find it nearly impossible to get it restored."

He abruptly went inside.

I gasped and had trouble swallowing. A sudden coldness enveloped me, and I began to shiver. The Old Man's warning was clear: If I didn't shape up, he'd forget about me, and his threats were never idle. I'd lose his trust forever. Probably ignore me at the dinner table. Ask Bobby for his opinions about the world. I'd be an outsider.

Last chance. What should I do?

I didn't want to lose Dad's good opinion of me, but I wasn't motivated to toe the line and study my ass off. Besides, if I did hit the books, there wouldn't be enough time for the Muckers. I'd have to disband them or bail. Then they'd view me as a fly-by-night kind of guy—a guy who didn't keep his promises, who started something, then checked out. How could I live with that?

I decided I wouldn't worry until school resumed. That was a couple of months away. For now, I'd try to enjoy the summer.

But it wasn't to be. The summer turned sour a few days later.

———➤◆◄———

Joe barged into my room. "Heard your marks weren't that good this year, Johnny boy. What's the matter with you?"

Lem continued making his bed.

"I'm doing fine," I said, but a slow burn crept up my neck.

"You're going to have to do better if you think Harvard is going to take a chance on you. They aren't looking for lazy boys."

"What makes you think I want to go to Harvard? I've got my own plan."

"Yeah, sure. What? Serving up ice cream at the creamery?" He practically cackled.

That was enough. "You son of a bitch!" I lunged at him, but Joe was ready. He laughed in my face, easily holding me at bay. I flapped helplessly. That crooked smile of his made matters even worse.

Pushing me away, he taunted, "Get away, flea!" and left.

I dropped on my bed, put my head in my hands, and was about to sob. I was ashamed that Lem had to see me like this.

Sensing I wanted to be alone, Lem said, "I promised Teddy I'd help him build a sandcastle. I'll see you later, Jack."

A few days later, I doubled over in pain, as if I'd been punched in the gut. My stomach ached so badly I spent the day in bed. When I got up, all I could do was bend over like an old man.

"LeMoyne, will you excuse us?" Dad said, entering the room later that day. I was back in bed, hoping for a few minutes of relief from the incessant throbbing. When Lem left, the Old Man pulled up a chair. "Jack, my boy, you're white in the face. We've got to find out the cause of your ailment.'

"I'm for that."

"Nobody has been able to figure out what's wrong with you. You're not getting the help you need. You can't live like this the rest of your life."

Dad had a plan.

"Arrangements have been made to send you to the Mayo Clinic."

I sat up, crossing my arms. "The Mayo Clinic?" I cleared my throat. "What's that?"

"A hospital with the best doctors in the world. They'll be able to help you. Unfortunately, it's in Minnesota. You have a long trip ahead of you. But it'll be worth it."

"Minnesota!" I sunk into my bed, turning my head away.

Dad spread his hands and said firmly, "You're leaving in a few days."

I didn't want to go all the way out there and miss any summer fun, but I didn't have any choice. There was no stopping the Old Man when he made up his mind.

CHAPTER NINETEEN

"Here you go," said the nurse, showing me to my room at the Mayo Clinic.

Another bland hospital room, only this time in Rochester, Minnesota. The usual medicinal smells. The familiar aromas of bleach and ammonia. I put my hand on the cold steel bed frame.

A few days later, while still in the stark white room, I began to get lonesome because the only people to gab with were nurses or doctors or orderlies. But they were busy, rushing in and out after bringing my meals or preparing me for what medical process was to come. I started talking to myself, which was better than talking to nobody.

While I was a patient at the New Haven hospital, people had stopped by. Nobody was going to visit me all the way out here.

I was used to having a lot of people around. With eight brothers and sisters, friends, and relatives who intermittently stayed with us, plus the live-in hired help, our homes always crackled with activity and talk. I missed my family. I got a lump in my throat thinking about them.

The same was true at school. Wherever I was—the West Wing, dining hall, class, athletic fields, Winter Exercise Building—people were always coming and going, chattering away.

I yearned to see the Muckers again, missing the fun and commotion of our daily meetings. Since forming the club, I felt a stronger bond with the dozen other members (and fellow presidents). We'd become tight, sharing what our lives were like outside of school. Some were from the South or Midwest. Everybody had a different take on politics, customs, and even food. Now we had a special bond. Thanks to the Muckers.

Jumping out of bed, I retrieved my Mucker pin from my trunk, pinned it to my hospital gown, and smiled, probably for the first time since arriving. As I pondered the future of the Muckers, I suddenly felt less homesick. Some momentum had been lost when I'd gotten sick. Maybe some guys would lose interest over the summer. Would the club drop by the wayside in the fall?

I didn't want that to happen. I'd do everything I could to keep the club alive and intact, expand it, and try new things. Maybe pranking wasn't the only thing we could do. Was there something more meaningful we could devote our energies to— something that had a better, higher purpose? I wasn't sure, but I had plenty of time to think about it.

And while I pondered that question, there was one image I couldn't get out of my mind: everybody else enjoying the summer, wherever they were, while I was stuck, alone, in hot, and humid Minnesota. That burned me up.

Lem was normally the one who complained that I didn't write to him often enough when we were away from school for the summer. There wasn't much to do here, so for once I wrote to him more than he wrote to me. "I am suffering terribly out here," I said. "I now have a gut ache all the time. I feel very sorry for my family being billeted with you for 2 or 3 weeks, but I am burdened with you for 9 months." After I sent the letter, I regretted that last phrase about him being a burden. That was harsh, and it wasn't true. I'd written after receiving the first enema of the day, when I wasn't in the best of moods.

Never had I been so humiliated in my life. I was on display, my bum often exposed while I lay on my side. I did my best to close off all thoughts of what was happening, hoping to send my mind somewhere else.

The enema contraption had a canister filled with liquid. Attached to that was a rubber tube. When they jammed the rubber part in where the sun didn't shine, I wanted to hide. Then they shot me up with warm liquid. Blew me up until I felt uncomfortably full, like I'd made ten passes at the all-you-can-eat buffet.

And then I didn't feel that way.

In minutes, I was shitting pretty.

I was lonely as hell, and now they were blowing the heck out of me. So I blew things up when I wrote Lem, making light of my dismal existence. Since he was enjoying himself on Cape Cod, I wanted him to believe I had some excitement going on here too, even if I had to stretch the truth. "Had an enema given me by a beautiful blonde nurse. That is the height of cheap thrills." She was blonde, alright, but calling her beautiful was a wild exaggeration.

To keep my sanity, I plowed through books and read the local newspapers. I made the best of it, lying on my ass most of the day. One memorable book was *The World Crisis* by Winston Churchill. Churchill was Great Britain's minister for air and war during The Great War. He had tried to stop the war, but once it began, he did everything to assure victory to Great Britain and its allies. I wondered if the leaders of important countries would work things out without having to go to war the next time there was trouble. "Will our children bleed and gasp again in devastated lands?" asked Churchill. I was haunted by the image of toddlers and young people, bloody and breathless, wandering the streets like zombies.

I read everything I could get my hands on. For variety, I read several old copies of *Captain Billy's Whiz Bang,* a magazine full of racy jokes and naughty stories.

I browsed a copy of *The New Movie Magazine* and read about a controversial film called *Tomorrow's Children.* It tells the fictional story of a 17-year-old girl who is going to be sterilized based on her family's history of alcoholism, mental illness, and physical disabilities. I thought of Joe's comments supporting sterilization after he'd returned from Germany.

I was reading the sports section of the *Rochester Post-Bulletin* when the Negro orderly came in to take my food tray. He began rolling out the trolley, then abruptly stopped at the door. "You're from New York, aren't you?" he asked.

I looked up from the newspaper to see a large man, graying at the temples. "Yes, by way of Boston."

"Don't think the Yankees are going to make the series this year," he said. "Babe Ruth on his last go-round. Past his prime."

"Yeah, I think you're right."

"Now, if they had Satchel Paige, they'd win it all."

I knew the name. Paige was a phenomenal pitcher who dominated the Negro Leagues.

"Best pitcher in the world, and he can barely make a living for himself," he said, pointing his finger at me. "That seem right to you? He'd have no trouble with Ruth. Strike him out like he was a little boy. I saw Satch when he played with the Pittsburgh Crawfords. Would have sat Ruth's ass right down. That's how good he is. White people won't let him play." He wound up like he was going to throw a pitch. "Maybe they're afraid he'll make them look bad." He finished throwing the imaginary pitch. "Strike three! Grab a seat, Babe." He grinned.

"Hmmm." I didn't know what to say.

"Want to hear a little secret?" He abandoned the trolley cart and came closer.

"Sure, why not?"

"Now, I don't know if you know it, but this place is pretty special in a lot of ways. Them Mayo brothers aren't out to make money. In fact, this hospital ain't for profi . And they're known for taking on difficult cases. People who other doctors can't cure. I'm guessing you're one of them."

I blinked hard. "Maybe I am." So far, a diagnosis had been elusive.

"Uh-huh. And maybe your family got money and maybe it don't." He rubbed his thumb across his fingers. "But if I'm a betting man, which I am, I bet your family ain't in the poor house. But, like I said, the brothers aren't in it for the money."

"Okay." He was driving at something.

"But that doesn't mean they always let everybody in. No, sir." He arched his eyebrows. "Tell you a little secret. Fact is, not long ago, they wouldn't admit Jews, Negroes, and Greeks unless they come up with a hundred-dollar deposit. A hundred dollars! Lots of people without money these days with this Depression thing. Some folks arriving from other countries. They don't have that kind of cash. Now, what you think about that?"

"Well—"

"It wasn't until a few years ago that a Jew protested and others got involved and they got rid of that ridiculous rule. That's all I got to say." He nodded and wheeled the trolley out the door.

I was reminded of the cab driver in Harlem who'd complained of discrimination against Negroes. Of how Choate made it difficult for Jews to enroll. And how my father had been passed over for jobs because he was Catholic. This guy had told me about others who, at one point, also weren't receiving fair treatment. Discrimination was everywhere.

———✦———

"How are you, Jack?" Dad was on the line.

"I'm getting by. They're pretty rough on me."

"Yes, hopefully it will all work out in the end."

There was a long silence.

I sighed. "How much longer do I have to stay here?"

"That's hard to say. They still don't know what's wrong with you."

I lowered my head.

"Jack, are you there?"

"Yes," I said softly.

"I hope it won't be for much longer. They're sure to find the cause of your problems soon. Oh, I have some news for you. You're not the only one in the hospital. So is LeMoyne."

"What?" I gasped, jerking upright. "What happened? Is he all right?"

"Yes, he's okay."

I breathed a sigh of relief.

According to Dad, Lem had been taking a shower when he mistakenly blasted the hot water. He fell on his back while the scorching water gushed all over him. Mother heard him scream and hauled him out of the tub. He was taken to Cape Cod Hospital.

"Mother hauled him out? What a sight that must have been!"

Little Mother and Big Lem. When I pictured Mother pulling buck naked Lem out of the tub, I laughed heartily. Best laugh since I'd been here.

Lem was hospitalized for three weeks with third-degree burns. He sent a picture of himself sporting that goofy grin while he relaxed in a wheelchair on the hospital's porch. A pretty nurse stood behind him. "Having Fun. Wish You Were Here!"

Lem said that my mother and his mother visited him, and that all the Kennedys in Hyannis Port came by at one time or another. Sure, I was glad he had company, but I had trouble swallowing for a moment because of a thick throat. Made me feel even more alone.

I didn't feel any better when they transferred me to nearby St. Mary's Hospital, where they hoped the anal connoisseurs there might have better luck.

"What's in that thing?" I said to one doctor preparing to poke me.

"The serum comes from horses. We hope it will help alleviate your stomach problems."

"You're putting stuff from horses inside me? If I start neighing, I'll know why."

One sweltering night, I couldn't sleep so I got out pen and paper and wrote to Lem. "I'm a shell of my former self," I confided, "and my penis looks as if it has been run through a wringer. I have not experienced orgasm for six days, so I feel kind of horny, which has been increased by reading one of the dirtiest books I've ever seen."

I added a line about no luck with the nurses.

Lem's reply arrived a week or so later. I opened the envelope. There was a letter, but there was also something else and not what I expected. *At all.*

Bum rag. *Toilet paper.* Folded in a tight square. What the hell was this? Why was Lem sending me toilet paper?

There was writing on it. Lem's idea of a joke?

I read it. Then I read it again to make sure he wasn't joking. He wasn't.

Lem was offering to do something for me. Something that some boys did with and to each other at Choate.

Guys wrote on toilet paper what they wanted to do with somebody else. Use their hand. Or something else. Wrote it on toilet paper so it could be eaten or thrown in the crapper and not discovered by the wrong person. Evidence destroyed.

Goddamn it, Lem!

Where did he get the crazy idea I'd want him to do something like that to me?

I brooded for a few minutes, then tore up the toilet paper, flushed the scraps down the john, and began to pace the room. Didn't want Lem or any other guy around my prick. Besides, only a few months ago in Harlem, we'd shared the same gal. Or I thought we had.

Now I thought about whether I'd be uncomfortable rooming with Lem. Sleeping next to a guy who wanted to do that to me? Maybe I wouldn't be able to sleep.

Maybe it was best to go our separate ways. For both of us. The Head and Maher would be happy to split us up. That's for sure.

Or was there a way to handle the situation so it didn't get out of control?

Bottom line, I didn't want to lose Lem He was my best friend. We had a helluva good time together, goofing off, pranking others, and joking. With the Old Man on my back, Joe giving me a hard time, and the Head and Prickmaster Maher putting the screws to me, I needed a guy like Lem around. I could count on him. He didn't judge me. Always had my back. You can't choose your brother, but I wish I had a brother more like Lem and a lot less like Joe. Lem had become the brother that Joe never was.

If this thing got out of hand, however, we might never be friends again.

I wasn't sure how to respond. It was tricky. I could simply ignore his proposition. Pretend it never happened. But then there'd always be this tension between us. Or he might make another overture. I didn't want that.

Another possibility was to make a joke out of it. Write back and say something like, "I don't want your ape hand around my dick, but thanks for the offer."

No. That wasn't the answer. This wasn't something to joke about.

I decided I'd respond firmly, letting him know I wasn't interested in anything like that. To avoid embarrassing him, I had to be careful what I wrote back.

I started out lightheartedly. "Dear Pithecanthropus Erectus," I scribbled, and then told him about "the most harassing experience of my life. They gave me five enemas until I was white as snow inside. My poor bedraggled rectum is looking at me very reproachfully these days."

When I wrote the last sentence, I hooted so loudly the night nurse burst in to see if I was okay.

"I'm fine. I was imagining something looking at me very reproachfully."

"I see," she said, "and what was that something?"

"You don't want to know." She left me alone to finish the letter.

"Please don't write to me on toilet paper anymore," I continued. "I'm not that kind of boy." Short and sweet. Move on.

I ended the letter with a personal story so the last thing Lem read wouldn't have anything to do with his proposition and my rebuke. I told him I slipped out to see a movie, and a couple sat next to me. Her perfume was so strong I had to move. When she whispered to her date, he got up to challenge me, pissed off because I didn't like his gal's scent. But she grabbed his arm and he sat down. "It was a lucky thing for him because he was only about 6'3" and I could have heaved him right into the aisle on his ass."

Yeah, sure I could.

By the middle of July, I'd been in Minnesota for nearly a month. Recovered from his burns, Lem was back home with his family in Pittsburgh.

CHAPTER TWENTY

To keep my sanity, I did my best to constantly joke with the nurses. One of them had immigrated with her parents to the U.S. from Denmark.

Blonde and slim, she was about five years older than me, and very pretty. The drab nurse's uniform couldn't cover that up. At mealtime, I hoped Ingrid brought my tray. It was one of the few things I looked forward to that wretched month.

"What do you do in Rochester for fun?" I asked.

Ingrid laughed. "The lakes. I love the water, so that's where you'll find me."

"I hope I get the chance," I said, trying my best to flirt.

Ingrid's visits saved the day while I was in that lousy hole.

Noticing the mountain of books on my bed, she said, "I see you read a lot of history, but do you know anything about my country?"

I didn't know much about Denmark and thought Scandinavia was a country, not a region. Over the next few days, Ingrid provided me a history of Denmark, talking about the Vikings and how Denmark had been neutral during the Great War.

One day, Ingrid entered my room, carrying my food tray and two books. She had neglected to clasp a few buttons on her blouse. On purpose? After she put the food tray down, she pulled a chair up to my bedside.

"I brought you a few presents. Both are by a famous Danish author, Jens Peter Jacobsen." Holding up the first book, she said, "This one, *Niels Lyhne,* is about a man who doesn't believe in God."

"I don't know if Mother would want me to read that. So I will."

"This next one is called *Marie Grubbe*." Ingrid blushed.

"Hey, you're red in the face!" I said.

She averted my eyes. "It's a little, how can I say, emblemishing?"

"I think you mean embarrassing. Why?"

"It's about a woman who enjoys a variety of partners. In the intimate way."

I thought about Harlem. The gals there certainly had many partners. "So she's a prostitute, or what we call here a lady of the night?"

Ingrid laughed. "No, no. You Americans are so—what's the word?—old-fashioned when it comes to sexual relations. Don't suppose you've ever heard of sexual freedom."

"Sexual freedom? What's that?"

I didn't know what to expect when I came to Minnesota, but the goal of obtaining additional sexual experiences was never far from my mind. Maybe I'd have better luck in this part of the country. While I was affectionate with Olive, my sex life hadn't existed since Harlem.

"*Marie Grubbe* is about a Danish noblewoman in the seventeenth century who, shall we say, wants to pursue an, ah, erotic life." Ingrid looked at her shoes.

When Ingrid said "erotic," I felt the welcoming onrush of blood to my penis.

I sat up. "She does? Well, more power to her!"

"Would you like me to read you from the book?"

"Yes, but only the good parts."

"Good parts? I don't understand. It's all very good."

"By good parts, I mean the sections where Miss Grubbe appreciates the virtues of, ah, the erotic life." I winked.

Ingrid smiled and ran her fingers through her hair. "Ah, now I see where your interests are." She flipped through the pages.

"Here's a section where she and Sti Hogh, ah, do what comes naturally between a man and a woman." Ingrid read. "'He kissed and fondled her wildly, immoderately. At last, she tore herself away and ran into the next room, her cheeks flushed, her bosom heaving.'" Ingrid stopped abruptly. "Is that what you mean?"

"Yes. Please read on. I want to learn more about the erotic life."

Ingrid continued, but the lovemaking scene—over in a single sentence—was disappointing.

"There's not much to see," I said. "In my opinion, the author did a bit more telling than showing. That's what my English teacher, Mr. Tinker, taught us. Show, don't tell. More specifics. You know, what her body was like. How he and Marie got together. What went on while they were doing it."

"Jack," she said, smiling sweetly, "you sound like a man who has some experience in the art of lovemaking."

I didn't realize lovemaking was an art.

"No more than most." I hesitated. "To be honest, I'm feeling a bit like Sti Hogh at the moment."

Ingrid turned as red as the brick buildings at Choate. "I see."

I glanced up. We stared into each other's eyes. "I have a suggestion," she said.

"What's that?"

"Perhaps exercise would benefit your health."

"Exercise?" What did Ingrid mean by exercise? I wasn't in the mood for pushups.

"A workout. That's what we call it in Denmark."

Oh. That kind of workout.

I tingled from head to foot. I yearned to touch and kiss Ingrid. "Yes, I'd like a workout," I stammered.

Maybe something good might come of what so far had been the worst summer of my life. Was I going to have some fun with Ingrid? Possibly have sex with a woman for the first time without having to pay for it?

"I'm working the overnight shift. May I stop by at, say, midnight?"

"Of course the good doctors have scheduled a surprise late-night enema for me."

She hesitated. "And you think a workout would be beneficial to your health?"

"I'm, uh, certain that it, uh, would."

"I'll see you tonight," Ingrid said. She stood up, gave me a kiss on the cheek, waved, and exited the room.

I got out of bed, trying to walk off my pent-up sexual energy. My hands were moist and my breath quickened. Now I had to wait, and waiting is the hardest part of life for me.

Reflecting on my so-far awful stay in Minnesota, I concluded that a summertime romance with Ingrid would more than make up for all the humiliation and physical pain I'd suffered here. I could handle all future probing and poking and everything else if I had a special time with Ingrid.

For the next few hours, I imagined my "workout" with Ingrid.

We'd start off standing up, kissing and caressing. Or maybe I'd offer her a back rub. A massage. Hadn't I read something about Swedish massage? How it was supposed to be so great? Well, Denmark was pretty close to Sweden. Shouldn't be too different. Next, I'd slowly remove her blouse, button by button. I'd ask her if she'd mind helping me out of my hospital gown. I'd caress her breasts through her bra before removing it, which, to be honest, I wasn't sure how to do. I hoped I didn't need to ask for her help, having hinted I had experience with such things. Or I could always say, "Why don't you take off your bra and make yourself comfortable?" Then I'd take her by the hand and lead her to my bed, where we'd climb over each other. Let the workout begin.

While I waited, I read *Marie Grubbe,* but I couldn't concentrate on the book for more than a minute. Every few seconds, I was interrupted by an image of Ingrid half-clothed. I got up and paced the room, then I walked the hallway several times.

Midnight came and went. Ingrid didn't arrive. Maybe another patient needed assistance.

I began to have doubts. I clasped my hands in prayer and pleaded softly, "Please come, Ingrid."

One a.m. and still no Ingrid.

There would be no workout.

I lay on my bed, the light still on. I teared up. My chin trembling and my shoulders quaking, I stared at the ceiling. Nothing good was going to happen in Minnesota. I sighed and turned off the table lamp.

The next morning, breakfast tray in hand, Ingrid told me she later recognized our rendezvous wasn't a good idea. "You're young, Jack. I'm a lot older. It wouldn't be right. And I'm a nurse. Nurses shouldn't do such things with patients."

"But you said a workout would be benefical to my health."

"Yes, I did. I'm sorry." Ingrid looked at her feet. "Don't worry. There will be plenty of other girls for you."

———◦———

I was dying.

Didn't feel any worse or better, but after the terrible beating of the last month, I got it in my head that I wouldn't live to a ripe old age.

"They have found something wrong with me at last," I wrote to Lem. "I've got something wrong with my intestines—in other words, I shit blood. I don't know what, but it's probably something revolting like piles or a disease of my vital organ. What will I say when someone asks me what I've got?"

Luckily, I didn't have to worry about that.

After a few more weeks of all the old routines, the doctor paid me a visit. He looked down at his feet. I half expected to get my death warrant to hear him say: "It doesn't look good for you, Jack. We're going to keep trying, and while you still have some time left, there is no cure."

Instead, he said, "Jack, we're discharging you. We're sending you home."

I sprang out of bed like I'd been catapulted. The news was totally unexpected. "That's great!" I shouted. "Not that I haven't enjoyed my stay here. Because I haven't."

The doctor clasped his hands. "The other news is, uh, not bad news. It seems that we haven't been able to pinpoint the source of your discomfort. Your case is quite puzzling."

The doctor told me that after perfecting the art of the enema on me, cleaning me out like a plumber unclogging the crap from the john, and injecting me with horse serum, he still had no idea what was wrong. Incredible.

"Don't know what the problem is?" I asked.

"That's right."

Again? No different than the New Haven hospital. No diagnosis. "So it was all for nothing."

"Well…" the doctor trailed off. "We can certainly say you have digestive problems."

I rolled my eyes. I think I knew that.

When the doctor left, I danced gleefully, waltzing around the room.

When my euphoria finally died down, I collapsed on the bed. Reality set in—the stark realization that apparently nobody could help me. Not even the best doctors in the world. I'd always be plagued by terrible stomach pains and other ailments that would come and (hopefully) go, probably replaced by new diseases for which there was also no cure.

What a life that would be.

I had to make the best of it.

CHAPTER TWENTY-ONE

When I got back to Hyannis Port, my gut ache mercifully disappeared. Poof. No more stabbing pain. I don't know how or why. Nobody did. Wasn't anything the Mayo doctors could take credit for. Sometimes I wondered if it had all been in my head. But for the moment, enjoying a pain-free life, I didn't care if I was a little crazy.

It wasn't until I had been away that I realized how much I had missed my family and how I'd taken them for granted, even my brother Joe. I'd never been that far away from them all for so long a stretch.

When I arrived home, Kick shouted, "Jack's home!" I got a lump in my throat when Mother and Dad, my eight siblings, and a few of our staff poured out of the house to greet me. First, Kick bounded out of the house and down the steps. Then Eunice and Rosemary. Bobby sprinted past our sisters and reached me first. Then Teddy waddled down the stairs, followed by my younger sisters. Finally, Mother and Dad and Joe made their way toward me. Soon I was embraced in a family hug.

A hero's welcome, but I wasn't a hero. All I'd done was get sick. Embarrassed at all the attention, I smiled sheepishly. I didn't deserve all the attention. Still, I was gratified. An inner glow filled me, and I had a deeper appreciation for my family.

I prayed I'd remain pain-free so I could enjoy what was left of the summer. Energized by my newfound vitality, I spent the next month scampering from one activity to another, cramming in as much fun as I could because I didn't know when Mr. Gut

Ache or somebody else would pay a visit. I woke up earlier than I ever did, rousing Eunice to play tennis. After that, I dashed into Nantucket Sound for a bracing swim. Then I took the *Victura* out for a quick sail. But I wasn't done yet. Bobby and Kick and I threw the football around. All that before noon.

"Jack," Kick said, "you haven't stopped since you came back."

"That's right," I said, throwing her a pass. "I'm afraid if I do, I might get sick again." I gulped, holding back tears.

After being confined to the hospital, I longed for the open sea, and so I sailed twice a day, and raced as often as possible.

My competitive spirits had been reawakened after an unenergetic month in Minnesota. In what seemed like forever, I hadn't so much as thrown a ball or done anything physical.

So when we caught a good wind on a day when a sailing race was scheduled, I was so excited I couldn't sit down, standing up while I ate.

"Hey, old boy, good time to have you crew the *Victura* for the big race," I said to Tom Bilodeau, Joe's Harvard classmate, at breakfast. Tom stayed with us for part of the summer.

"Oh, why's that?" Tom asked, although he knew the answer.

"You're kind of not that good-looking, so when we collect first prize, I'll be the center of attention."

"That, and I weigh a ton."

"Really? I hadn't noticed. Have some more pancakes, Tom." I cheerfully dumped several large ones on his plate. "Don't want Mrs. Bilodeau thinking the Kennedys are starving you."

Since we had a heavy wind, having Bilodeau crew was an advantage. He was an able crewman, but most of all he was heavy. When the winds were strong, you needed ballast. At more than

200 pounds, Tom was the guy. When the wind was light, there was no way I'd even think about having Bilodeau on board.

"You stay here. Eat a few more pancakes."

Bobby helped me get the *Victura* ready. At nine years old, he was sandwiched in age between our sisters. Three of them were older, yet they became his daily companions. I'd been spending more time with him lately, sensing his desire to be with the guys. Bobby was already a good sailor. He learned quickly, grasping the basic procedures for preparing a boat and how best to navigate the tricky waters of Nantucket Sound.

As I bent the jib, Bobby pummeled me with questions. "How fast can the *Victura* go? Who's a better sailor, you or Joe? Are you going to win?"

The *Victura* was ready to go, and Bobby and another guy hopped aboard. For racing, the *Victura* required four crewmen.

When the race began, I maneuvered the *Victura* to a substantial lead, helped by Tom's weight. Heavy gusts arrived and we were on a run. The finish line was in sight. Victory seemed assured.

Until it wasn't.

Suddenly, the wind got light. *Very light.* The sail slackened like wet laundry. The *Victura* slowed down. We were going nowhere. Drifting.

You never knew what might happen out on the water. There could be enormous wind shifts in seconds. A race could appear to be lost, and then the wind would return, sweeping around the course. Instantly, the winds would favor the boats that went their own course and hadn't followed the leader.

My lead vanished as two boats passed me. *The reason?* Weight.

I made some quick calculations and considered the risks. If I didn't act now, I'd lose unless the winds picked up again, and I couldn't count on that.

Put Bilodeau in the drink? After the disaster of the last race, I badly wanted to win. I didn't want to face another tongue-lashing from the Old Man.

The *Victura* would speed up without Tom's bulk, but I'd lose a crew member.

Then again, what happened if the wind picked up? I'd be dead in the water without Tom's considerable ballast and assistance.

I shouted up to Tom, "Over the side, boy. We've got to relieve ourselves of some weight."

Tom stared, not comprehending my order. We were far from shore, and the water was chilly. I pointed to the water. The race crew would pick him up.

"Go! Now!"

Bobby pointed at Tom and then the water.

Resigned to his fate, Tom unhappily splashed into the cold water.

Instantly, we sped up like we'd been given an energy boost, and I guided the *Victura* back to a comfortable lead and victory.

I had done what I needed to do to win.

Back on shore, I greeted my wet crewman. "Thank you for your sacrifice, Tom. However, if you could lay off the pancakes during your stay here, next time I won't be obliged to send you overboard."

"I'll try," he said, shaking his head and laughing.

<hr />

"C'mon, everybody!" Joe called. "Let's play!"

About a dozen of us dashed out to the well-worn lawn, the scene of countless touch football games. *Game time.*

There's nothing really "touchy" about Kennedy touch football games. In fact, you could hardly call it "touch football" because it was pretty rough. Somewhere between touch and tackle. Plenty of physical contact, blocking, and roughhousing. It wasn't a real game if there weren't scrapes, bruises, and blood by the time it was over.

Sometimes, we were united as a family against friends, and Bobby would lead us out to the field, screaming, "Let's go, Kennedys!"

But today I quarterbacked one team and Joe the other. Joe played football at Harvard and had a few of his teammates on his side. My team was at a disadvantage. Usually, I had Lem blocking for me, keeping Joe away. But Lem was in Pittsburgh.

We huddled up. A guy about Joe's age who lived in the neighborhood and played football at college said, "Jack, give me a handoff and I'll run to the right. The rest of you block for me. It's always worked. Can't fail."

His buddy agreed. "It's a sure thing."

I eyed them dubiously.

But they seemed to know what they were talking about—they had college football experience, and were older.

"Okay. Let's give it a try."

The play was stopped cold when Joe knifed in and made the tag. A second, similar attempt resulted in similar failure.

I was angry with myself for caving in. I hadn't trusted my instincts and my own skills. I was nimble, could throw accurately, and devised imaginative, deceptive plays.

We couldn't outmuscle Joe's team, so we'd have to outsmart them. The way I looked at it, tricking the other team was like conducting a prank, except you were doing it on the football field. Fool the other guy, make him feel like a chump. use plenty of fakes and laterals. I created unorthodox formations and borrowed plays I'd seen work.

So now I took control. "After the next play, Kick, you stroll over to the porch like you're taking a break. I'll take the snap. Everybody else run to the other side of the field. Joe's team will follow you. When they do, yell, 'Throw it to me, Jack' or something like that. I'll run in your direction and then stop. They'll forget about Kick, and I'll throw a long one to her on the other side of the field." Kick's eyes gleamed, excited at her unique role.

Sure enough, Joe's team lost track of Kick. I threw a wobbly pass, but it didn't matter. Kick caught it. *Touchdown!* I embraced Kick at midfield.

Joe glared. "You can't do that!" he screamed.

"Tell your sweet sister, Joe, that you forgot about Kick? Ain't that a *kick* in the pants?"

The next time we got the ball, I set up the *rumblerooski*. When I got the snap, I put the ball on the ground in front of me. I told my team to keep their hands in the face of the defenders for a couple of seconds so they couldn't see the trickery.

"Bobby," I said, "are you ready to score a touchdown?"

He clapped his hands excitedly. "Ready, Jack."

My team scooted to the left. Except little Bobby. While Joe's team prepared to stop our false thrust, Bobby scooped up the ball and sped to the right—all the way to the end zone!

Was that steam coming out of Joe's ears? Add his beet-red face, and he resembled a funny-page character.

"What's the matter?" he complained. "Afraid to play normal football?"

"Aw, c'mon, Joe," Eunice said. "Give 'em credit. They made a good play."

We couldn't stop Joe's team from scoring, and they couldn't stop us, except one time. I rushed Joe, tipped his pass, and Kick intercepted. A touchdown now and we'd win.

I had one last trick play up my sleeve, or in this case, the Statue of Liberty sleeve. That's the name of the play.

"Sounds crazy but fun," Kick said. "Let's do it!"

I took the snap from center and cocked my arm, ball in hand, similar to our gal holding the torch of liberty. Joe's team froze, waiting for me to throw a pass. But I didn't have the ball. Kick, hidden behind me, snatched the ball from my hand and sped away. By the time Joe's team realized my hand was empty, Kick was off to the races. Touchdown. Game over.

Joe kicked a divot of grass. Kick squealed and did a somersault. Bobby screamed, "We did it! We did it!"

As I climbed the steps to our house, I noticed the Old Man off to the side on the veranda. He nodded but didn't smile. "Nice job, Jack."

"Thanks."

He walked into the house.

Maybe my father wasn't that happy my team had beaten Joe's team. After all, Joe was the family's Golden Boy and I'd taken him down a notch. No, it wasn't tackle football, or a high school game, but still, I'd done a pretty good job of leading my team. I devised a creative, winning strategy despite the fact that we were outmuscled by the competition. Best of all, I'd had the confidence of my teammates. We'd won. And the Old Man had noticed.

CHAPTER TWENTY-TWO

"What would you do as president?" Dad asked at dinner that night after grace. He looked at Joe and then me. Our dinner discussions revolved around world events. Dad didn't have much patience for small talk.

More than a dozen of us, including the guests, sat around the table crowded with various courses. At the center, steam rose from the large beef roast.

"I'd see what could be done to help people in places that aren't well off," I said. "Like Harlem."

"Oh," Dad said, his eyebrows raised. "Didn't know you knew much about Harlem. Have you been there?"

I flushed. "I, uh, passed through. Once."

"What else?" Dad persisted, impatiently tapping his knife on the table.

"I was reading about something called the Communications Act," I said. "Establishes the Federal Communications Commission. It will regulate telephone, telegraph, and radio communications."

"That's right, Jack," Dad said. "President Roosevelt signed it into law earlier this year."

"The Republicans didn't like it," I said. "I read where this senator, I think from Iowa, said the law would Hitlerize the press of the nation. Say goodbye to a free press."

"What do you think, Joe?" Dad asked. "Will it?"

Joe pointed with his fork. "No, I don't think so. Besides, some of what Hitler is doing isn't all that bad."

"You may be right, or you may be wrong," Dad said. "In any event, let them do what they want over there. We shouldn't get involved in Germany's affairs."

"That's right," Joe echoed. "At least Hitler is helping the Germans get back on their feet. We've still got high unemployment in this country. Maybe we need somebody more like him, at least in some ways."

"I don't know," I said. "Hitler has outlawed all political parties except the Nazi Party. Is that what you want?"

"It's temporary—until Germany gets its house in order," Joe said.

"Not my kind of house," I retorted.

That night, I wrote in my scrapbook calendar: "Summer is fast coming to an end. School starts soon. Oh, God."

"Jack, there are a few things I want to discuss with you before you go back to school," Dad said later that night as we sat out on the veranda. "I know you had a difficult experience at the Mayo Clinic, and I'm relieved to see you in good health now. Hopefully, you'll stay that way so you can do well in your final year. I hope you understand why it was in your best interests not to participate in spring sports when you went back to school last semester ... after your illness."

I disagreed. Although I'd lost a few pounds and felt weak, I still could have played. Normally, I crewed and played baseball during the spring.

But now, I felt better—at full strength. I had moved up to JV football last year, and I believed I'd make varsity this year.

I shifted in my seat. Something was coming. I could sense it in the way Dad looked away and then back at me.

"Jack, I'm sorry to tell you this because I know how much you enjoy being part of the teams at Choate, but the school and I believe it would be unwise for you to compete on any athletic teams. Frankly, we're worried you might get hurt."

I could feel my face redden and my body tense. "You saw me play against Joe's team today. Did I look weak or sick?"

"That's touch football, Jack. Big difference. I'm sorry."

The way my father pursed his lips, I knew the matter was closed.

I sagged and my heart sank. Guess I wasn't going to win the Harvard Trophy like Joe had. Yeah, fat chance of that even if I could play. Still, athletics were one of the few activities at Choate I enjoyed. The comradery, the bus trips to play other schools, and the chance to "obey my animal spirits," as Maher put it. All that was over. Now what was I going to do while everybody else was having fun on the field? Play tiddlywinks?

Dad went on to say there was a benefit to foregoing team sports. I could spend more time concentrating on my studies. That didn't seem like an upside to me. I sat there in silence.

"There's something else I want to discuss with you."

Oh no. More to come. It couldn't be good.

"Jack, I've always encouraged my sons and daughters to seek out new experiences. That's why I wanted you to have something different than the Catholic education you were getting at the Canterbury School. And why I sent Joe to study with Professor Laski at the London School of Economics. Laski is a socialist, while I am nothing of the sort. But it's important to hear the other side and then make up your own mind. Joe has found the experience quite valuable."

I tried to figure out where this was going. Was he going to split up Lem and me because the headmaster had told him it would be better for the both of us? I recalled the tension and acrimony during my first year when rooming with Godfrey Kaufman. He liked a neat room. I was beyond indifferent about such things. We survived a very unpleasant year only by dividing the room in half.

Or maybe Dad was going to send me to a different school altogether. Spending that last year trying to find my place in a new school—that wouldn't be fun. And it would spell the end of the Muckers.

Dad leaned forward. "I've made an appointment for you to see a person in the Psychology Department at Columbia. You can meet with him before you go back to school. His name is Prescott Lecky."

"What?" I said. A psychologist? I didn't know anybody who had seen a psychologist, but from what I gathered, only crazy people saw one of these head doctors. Did the Old Man think I was loony?

"He's highly regarded in his field."

"But why?" Did Dad think psychology might be a career goal for me? Did the Old Man think I was nuts? Or did he want to prevent me from going nuts?

"So you can learn about yourself, Jack" he said, pointing to me, then clasping his hands together. "Discover what you want from life. How you can succeed after talking with Lecky. I expect you'll learn things about yourself you never knew. St. John thinks so too."

Hmmm. St. John was also in on this. Double-teamed. Now I was doubly suspicious.

"Oh, he does, does he?" I offered a fake smile.

The Old Man got up. "Time for bed." He went inside.

I slumped over and put my head in my hands, reeling from the two body blows. First, no sports because I was thought to be too frail. Then, as a know-nothing weakling, I was being forced to see a head doctor because my father and St. John thought I had a screw loose. They weren't saying that. Not in those words.

But it got me wondering, again, if maybe I was off my rocker a little bit. Well, who wouldn't go nutty with guys like the Head and Maher on your case, along with all the other restrictions at Choate? Starting the Muckers was my way of preventing myself from going completely insane. The way I looked at it, something was wrong if you didn't go a little sideways given the situation. Maybe the doc would have some good ideas about that. Guess I was going to find out.

CHAPTER TWENTY-THREE

Columbia University, New York City
Psychology Department

I bit my lip and stared at the door. I didn't want to go in. I wasn't sure what was going to happen behind that door, but I didn't think it was going to be good. I expected there'd be plenty of questioning, maybe even grilling. Not a lot of fun. But I was here. I knocked. Lightly. I hoped Lecky wouldn't be in and I could leave. After all, I wasn't sure what I was doing here.

No luck. The door opened and the man said, "Welcome. I'm Prescott Lecky. Please come in."

I almost laughed in his face because what I thought I heard was "Prescott Icky."

"I hope you didn't have too much trouble finding my office," he said warmly.

"No, I didn't."

Lecky himself wasn't icky. A normal-looking guy, really. Kind of heavy, round metal glasses, and most of his hair was gone. Early forties, I guessed, but something about him seemed sad and older.

We shook hands, and he held mine slightly longer than most people did. Did that mean anything? Did all psychologists do that? If so, why? I was buzzing with questions.

First surprise. I had expected to sit in a stiff wooden chair while he interrogated me. But Lecky's place of work was both an office and living room. An armchair, a desk, a couch, bookshelves.

Pictures and several framed, official-looking documents adorning the walls. Nice room.

"Jack, make yourself comfortable," he said, inviting me to sit on the couch. I balanced on the edge like I was expecting a court summons.

Lecky sat in the armchair. "Would you like some water?" He pointed to a pitcher on a table, next to which was a box of Kleenex.

I shook my head.

"Let me introduce myself, Jack. Briefly, I was born in Virginia. I was a newspaper reporter before finding my true calling." Since I thoroughly enjoyed reading the newspaper, I was pleased to learn of his former career and intrigued that he'd switched to teaching and psychology. "I've been with the psychology department, lecturing here, since 1924. I also talk with people such as yourself. Young, old, and in-between."

"That's about everybody, isn't it?" I joked.

"Yes, it is," he said, chuckling. "Jack, tell me a little about yourself."

After I covered the basics about where I'd grown up and what I liked to do for fun, he said, "Before we go any further, I'd be interested in your knowledge and thoughts about psychology. It's a relatively new field."

I didn't know very much. I'd heard the term psychology, but that was about it. "I know of Freud. Read about him in *The Times*."

"I'm impressed," Lecky said. "That's more than most people your age know. Or adults for that matter. I'm curious what you remember reading about him. Anything stand out? No pressure."

"Let's see," I said, trying to recall. "Oh, yeah. Something about the unconscious mind. Affects how we act in life."

"Good memory."

"And how almost everything is related to sex," I added with a lopsided grin.

"What do you think about that, Jack?"

"I don't know," I said, doubtfully. "Could be right, I suppose." Since I didn't have much experience with sex other than a night in Harlem—and with myself, if that counted—I wasn't sure what to say. So I changed the subject. "Do you have a specialty? Like Freud did?"

Lecky nodded appreciatively. "I do. My research and expertise are in self-consistency and self-help."

I didn't know if I needed help, but I liked the idea of self-help. Of helping myself.

"In a few words," he continued, "it's a theory of personality. Each person defines who he is or who he will become." Lecky paused and spread his hands. "But I don't think we want to spend a lot of time talking about theories and constructs and so forth. Too much like being at school." He laughed. "And I'm sure you get enough of that there."

I smiled in agreement.

"May I ask why you decided to come?"

I sighed. "My father insisted, Dr. Lecky. And I'm not happy about being forced to see another doctor. I've wasted too much time seeing people who stuck me with needles, gave me pills, or jammed tubes up my behind."

Lecky chuckled. "Believe me, nothing like that will happen here."

I cracked my knuckles. "Then I'm forced to see a doctor who wants to get inside my head."

"Well, first of all, I'm not a doctor. No need to call me Dr. Lecky."

"Oh," I said. That was a surprise.

"Our sessions may involve some interesting discussions," Lecky said, "but I will not be interrogating you. I won't be telling you what to do either."

"No?" I let out a huge breath. I already had the Old Man, the Head, and Maher on my case. And Butter too.

"Do you have any idea what might happen in our sessions?"

"No. I'm only here because my father told me I had to. The headmaster suggested it to him. Dad said I might learn something about myself. St. John probably told you to knock some sense into me."

I broke eye contact and gazed at one of the pictures on the wall.

"I can understand your hesitance, even resistance. After all, people your age frequently flout authority. It's part of growing up. In fact, I did so myself."

"Really?" I said, looking back at him. I was surprised because he didn't look like a guy who'd get into mischief. I tried to picture him as a young person. But I couldn't.

"I assure you your father or Headmaster St. John never made any suggestions about how or what I should do in our sessions." Lecky paused. "And if they had, I'd have ignored them. After all, I wouldn't tell your father how to run the SEC. Nor would I tell the headmaster how to run his school. I'm just a psychologist."

I wished he would give the Head advice on running the school because I already liked Lecky a lot more than St. John. Relieved to hear he wasn't a St. John toady, I relaxed my hands, both of which I'd tightened.

Lecky spread his hands in a friendly manner. "Let me tell you a little about our sessions. First, I want you to know that nobody will know what we talk about. Everything we discuss in this room is between you and me. That's my professional responsibility. Plus, you have my word on that. So feel free to say anything you want."

That Lecky wasn't going to tell my father or St. John what we talked about instantly put me at ease. I believed him.

"Well," he said, "let's get started."

I gripped the couch arm.

"The way I work is pretty simple. You talk and I listen."

That was a surprise. I expected mostly to be lectured to by the psychologist.

"There will be times when I'll offer a comment about something you've said. Or I may not understand what you're trying to say, and I'll ask you to go a bit further, to talk a little more."

"Okay." I relaxed my grip on the couch's arm. This didn't sound too bad.

"Most importantly, I'm not going to give you answers. I'm here to help you come up with your own."

Okay, but I wasn't here looking for answers. So that might be a problem. Not that I knew everything. But I didn't have any questions, so I wondered where this would go. An hour or more of silence? What would I talk about?

I scanned the bookshelf and zeroed in on two by Freud. *The Interpretation of Dreams* and *Jokes and Their Relation to the Unconscious*. Hmmm. I was fond of joking around and pranks. What would Freud say about me?

"I noticed you looking at the books. Do you enjoy reading?"

"Yes."

"What do you enjoy reading?"

"Mostly history. I recently read a book by Winston Churchill."

"What is it about Churchill or what he wrote about that interests you?"

"The Great War. What he did during the war. And how terrible it was."

"Other kinds of books, or reading?"

"I read *The Times* every day." Lecky nodded. He seemed impressed. "I read *Uncle Tom's Cabin*. It's about the injustice of slavery. I enjoyed *The Story of a Bad Boy*. He's not that bad. A few pranks, that's all. Like me."

"Sounds entertaining."

"It is."

"Do you have something in common with this bad boy? Do you consider yourself a bad boy, Jack?"

I gulped. The question caught me by surprise. I'd never hurt anybody or broken any law. Except for speeding. And ridiculous school rules. I certainly wasn't a bad boy for starting the Muckers.

"No. I don't think so. What is a bad boy, anyway?"

"Well, you tell me. What does being a bad boy mean to you?" Lecky countered.

"Somebody can say a person is a bad boy and maybe he is, and maybe he isn't. Because my room isn't clean, I don't study as hard as I should, and I start a club that the school doesn't like— does that make me a bad boy? I don't think so."

"Okay, I see your point. You mentioned school. How is school going for you?"

"Between you and me, this time next year, I'll be happy not to be at Choate."

Lecky nodded. "Many young people find school difficult. And schools like Choate, with their high standards and discipline, can be quite challenging. Why did you attend Choate?"

"I went to the Canterbury School in Connecticut first. My mother wanted me to go there because it's a Catholic school."

"What was your experience there?"

I recalled the cold, drafty school perched on a hill. Not being able to leave except for the Harvard-Yale and Yale-Army football games. A whole lot of religion. And being sick. "Not very good. I wasn't there long. They had to take my appendix out. It took me a while to recover, so I did my final exams at home."

"And after that?"

"My father wanted me to go to Choate. Mix with non-Catholics. Help me in the long run, he said. I don't know if it has. But that's where I've been." I sighed. "It's been three tense years."

"Tense? That's a strong word. What about your experience at Choate has made it tense?"

I stomped my foot. "The place is strict. Very little freedom. I feel like I'm always being watched."

"Some find the discipline helpful, but others do not. You obviously do not."

"No, I don't," I said firmly.

"Are there any subjects you have enjoyed, or at least obtained some useful knowledge or ideas from?"

"English and History, except for one teacher, have been okay. My marks have been pretty good in those two subjects. Would be better except for my spelling. I'm a poor speller."

Lecky perked up as if he'd gotten a jolt of electricity. "That's interesting. The spelling. So you consider yourself a poor speller?"

"Yes," I said matter-of-factly. No doubt about that. Plenty of evidence. My essays and letters home were littered with misspellings.

"I see. Has the school made any effort to help you improve?"

"Yes. I've gotten extra instruction. Doesn't seem to help."

"Let's go back a bit, Jack. When did you become aware of this spelling problem?"

"Hmmm." I looked away, trying to remember when I'd first become aware of my lousy spelling. I snapped my fingers. I had it. "A teacher in public school told me my spelling was terrible. She really let me have it. I was about ten. Dad and Mother and my brother said stuff too."

Lecky sat back in his chair, crossed his legs, and looked at me intently. "From what I gather, other people have said you are a poor speller. That's their opinion. But what matters most is your opinion. Let me ask you again: Do you consider yourself a poor speller?"

"Well…" I shrugged. "I make a lot of mistakes, so I guess I am."

He looked at me intently. "And are you aware of your mistakes?"

"Sometimes."

"Would you mind giving me an example?"

I told him about an essay I'd written. My English teacher had praised it but circled my spelling errors. "I misspelled the words 'weighed,' 'luxury,' and 'ability.'"

"Those are not easy words, but they are commonly used. I'm sure you've seen them when reading *The Times* and your books. Do you think you've ever spelled those words correctly?"

I wasn't certain. Did I know how to spell them correctly? Or were they words I wasn't sure about but didn't bother to look up?

My brow furrowed. "I don't know. I didn't think about the words that much. Went with what seemed right at the time."

"I see."

"And I mix up 'then' and 'than.'"

"Hmmm. And do you know the difference?"

"Yes," I admitted sheepishly.

"But you don't go back and make the corrections? Is that sometimes the case?"

"Yes."

Lecky stroked his chin. "Let me propose something, Jack. Perhaps this deficiency is not due to lack of ability."

"It's not? Well, that's good." But what other reason could there be? Did I have some sort of spelling disease? Sort of like my sister Rosemary, who couldn't do certain things.

"Rather, it might be due to an active resistance," he continued. "A resistance that prevents you from learning how to spell in spite of your natural ability and despite getting additional help."

"Active resistance?" Sounded like I was some sort of violent warrior in the spelling wars.

"Well, the resistance may arise from the fact that, at some time in the past, you accepted someone's suggestion that you were a poor speller and incorporated that into your definition of yourself. Simply put: They said it, you believed it, and you kept right on making spelling mistakes."

I leaned forward and clasped my hands. "You're saying I was told I was a bad speller, and I believed it, whether it was true or not. I became 'Jack Kennedy, bad speller?'"

My brain went into in a tizzy. Was all of this true?

I'd received plenty of criticism about my spelling. Strangely, it hadn't bothered me. Maybe because that's what I was. A bad speller. I'd been given a free pass to screw up words. And I'd used it.

"There are very bright people—of which I can tell you are one—who do well, or have the ability to do well in school, but for some reason have atrocious spelling," Lecky said. "On the surface, it doesn't make sense."

I nodded. What was he getting at?

Lecky tapped his lips with his index finger. "The problem is they define themselves as deficient spellers. The misspelling of a certain proportion of words becomes normal. Because that is who they are—or told themselves who they are."

"They're doing it on purpose?" I gasped.

"Strange as it may seem, it is the correct thing for them to do. It is perfectly fine to misspell words. Because that is how they see themselves in the world. As misspellers."

"They do?" Did I know people like that?

"Consider it from a different point of view. This person misspells words for the same reason he refuses to be a thief. He's never been told he's a thief. He doesn't steal. He hasn't accepted the idea that he is a thief. I trust you do not define yourself as a thief."

"No, I do not." I chuckled.

"Good." He grinned. "I needn't worry about turning my back."

I liked his sense of humor.

"People's virtues and defects," Lecky continued, "are a matter of how they define themselves. The kind of self-concept they have."

My head continued to spin. What kind of self-concept did I have of myself? How much of it was true? "So, a person becomes what he thinks he is because of what others have told him he is?"

"If," he emphasized, "he accepts the belief."

"So maybe my self-concept is that I'm a lousy speller?"

Lecky leaned back in his chair. He wasn't going to answer. I had to come up with my own.

"My spelling is bad," I said, "because others have told me it's bad and I've bought into it."

"Perhaps," he said, placing a hand on his chin. "Why you are deficient in this area may be something for you to think about. For you to determine. I'm simply presenting the idea to you that your difficulties with spelling may be self-imposed."

"You're not going to *spell* it out for me, are you?" I said.

"Well done." Lecky appreciated my wordplay. "No, I won't. As I said, I'm only here to guide you. To help you find answers. And perhaps your self-concept affects you in other areas, which we may want to explore, but right now tell me about the rest of your subjects."

"French and Physics I could do without. Thank God I don't have to take Latin anymore. Public Speaking is all right."

"What about your marks? As you look back, are you satisfied with the effort you've put in?"

My attitude was, I liked to learn what I wanted to learn. Not what they wanted me to learn. So I pretty much did as little as possible when it came to subjects I didn't like. I failed Latin and French my first year. My grades were mostly low seventies. "I could have done better. Maybe I will. Try to finish strong."

Lecky nodded. "Is that something you want to do?"

I gulped. I was on the spot. He wasn't going to let me get away with saying things if I didn't mean them. Did I really believe that I'd get serious about school? Or was I just saying it to make myself feel better? Or to get approval from Lecky?

"I'm not sure." That was the best I could do.

"That's okay, Jack. Sometimes we make promises we don't keep."

Did Lecky just wince?

He continued. "It may be because it sounds good. Maybe we want to impress others. Perhaps fool ourselves. It might be helpful for you to think about that. Your approach to school. We can delve into that more at our next meeting. I'm looking forward to getting together again."

Believe it or not, so was I.

CHAPTER TWENTY-FOUR

Back at school, Lem and I silently made our beds. We hadn't talked much since returning Things weren't right between us.

"Writing on toilet paper?" I blurted out at one point. "Geez, Lem."

Lem tucked in a sheet corner. "Huh? Uh, yeah. Mistake." In a low voice, he said, "Thought you were asking for, you know, some relaxation. Just wanted to make you feel good. Sorry." He shuffled to the other side of the bed.

"Relaxation? Where did you ever get the idea that I wanted that kind of relaxation?"

"Your letters."

"What about them?"

"The nurses. No luck with them."

"Uh-huh."

"And other stuff."

"Other stuff?"

"About your prick withering away."

"Uh-huh. Felt like it."

I stopped making my bed. "Well, you were having a great time at our house, laying out in the sun, playing football, enjoying a round of roast beef at Sunday supper with the Kennedys, while I was laid up in Nowhere, Minnesota. So I wrote crap. I was bored. Some of what I wrote was true. But I exaggerated. And when I wasn't bored, the doctors and nurses were quite happy to stick up my ass whatever was handy. Maybe I wanted some sympathy. Wasn't getting much of it there."

"Had me going. Believed everything you wrote."

"Don't believe everything I say."

"I'll remember that."

"Okay."

"All right."

We were done with the subject, although I still felt some residual tension, which I hoped would be gone soon. I wanted things back to normal if it was possible.

"Hey, Lem?" We faced each other in what felt like the first time since the new school year.

"Yeah?"

I paused. "I've got a new perspective since coming back. Sort of a new way of looking at things. Been thinking a lot about this. Can I run it by you?"

"Sure. I'm all ears," he said.

Asking his opinion was a good strategy. I sensed that the trust, the joking, the ease of being together—all was coming back already.

"Okay. I was sent to one of the best hospitals, if not the best in the country. The Mayo Clinic. They couldn't figure out what's wrong with me. Maybe nobody can. But that's not the point. The point is that others in the United States and elsewhere don't have that opportunity. Like those folks in Harlem. You remember what we saw? The hardship. Poverty. What do you think about that? Is that fair?"

Lem took a deep breath. "Difficult circumstances. No, I don't think it's fair. The luck of the draw."

"Yeah, so I guess there's always inequity in life. Some people die because they can't get medical help, some people suffer from lack of care, some people aren't sick a day of their lives. And some, like me, are born to rich parents, while others grow up without enough food to eat."

"I guess that's right."

"I never thought about it before. But now I realize it. Life is unfair, Lem. And it's kind of a relief."

"Really?"

"Yeah. Just knowing that life is unfair is going to help me deal with it. Whatever happens."

"They may not have found out what's wrong with you at the Mayo Clinic," Lem said, "but you came back with some knowledge, if not a cure."

When he said "knowledge," I thought about telling him about my visit with Lecky and what I'd learned about myself. Not now. Perhaps another day.

"What about you? Did you think that when your father died? You know, why is this happening to me?"

"Yes. And I thought, why did this have to happen to my family?" Lem looked away. I thought he was going to cry, which I'd never seen him do. He turned back to me. "It certainly didn't seem fair. But it's what happens."

We resumed making our beds.

"Subject change." I laughed. "Remember when I wrote 'My bedraggled rectum is looking at me very reproachfully' after my enema episode?"

"Unforgettable."

"One of the few times I laughed in that hell-hole," I said. "The nurse barged in. She thought I'd gone crazy."

Finished making my bed, I sat down at my desk. Lem laid on his bed, arms behind his head.

"We were both cooped up in hospitals," I continued, trying to find common ground. "You were burned, and they were probing me like I was a damn puppet."

"Sounded like non-stop enemas."

"Felt like it, too. But, as I said, I may have embellished the circumstances a bit."

"I understand now."

Maher's voice echoed from the corridor. "Should you continue your descent into further decrepitude, I shall be forced to take extreme measures. You've been warned!"

Our eyes met. We scowled. Our enemy in common.

———

Rip and I walked to the Winter Exercise Building, where we planned to meet Lem. All of a sudden, Mrs. St. John and Queenie, my two favorite women at school, came toward us.

"Hello, boys," Mrs. St. John said. On school days, they habitually walked this route following tea at the headmaster's house.

After Mrs. St. John excused herself, saying she needed to attend to a student, Queenie narrowed her gaze at me. "I've heard you've got a way with words. Written a ditty. And I'm in it."

I looked away.

"Sing it to me." She smiled sweetly.

A flush crept up my cheeks. I hoped to put her off, but Queenie wouldn't have it.

"Now, please."

Rip and I looked at each other. This was going to be more nerve-wracking than my speech about inalienable rights. "Well, all right," I said, and together we croaked out the rhyme.

Queenie smiled and my heart thumped. "Much better to hear it from the author," she said. "It's an honor." She put her hand to her heart. "That meant a lot to me."

"Thank you," I said, looking at the ground.

"Tell me, how are you boys doing? Between you and me, I suppose it must be hard for sixth-formers like you not having any girls around."

"Well, uh, yeah," I stuttered.

"Used to it by now," Rip said.

"Speak for yourself," I countered.

Queenie sighed. "Do you boys have any steady dates?"

"I kind of do," I said. Olive and I had picked up where we'd left off, and I had a steady for the first time. "But she's all the way out in New Jersey, so we don't see each other much. I met her at last year's Spring Festival."

"Still looking," Rip said.

"It's too bad," Queenie said with a deep sigh. "There are all those girls over at the public high school in town. Just a few blocks away. But the Headmaster doesn't approve of fraternizing with them. Thinks they're almost second-class citizens. I've been trying to change the mind of my husband, then get him to convert the headmaster's viewpoint. No luck so far. But I'll keep trying."

"That's very nice of you," I said. Her husband was the assistant headmaster.

Fingering her curls, she said, "Well, I should be going, but if I can ever do you boys a favor to thank you for including me in your song, please feel free to ask." She waved. "Bye, boys."

That Queenie was something else. Beautiful *and* nice.

Rip and I looked at each other. "I wonder what she meant by doing us a favor?" Rip asked, as we continued walking.

I didn't know either, but it couldn't hurt to keep the offer in mind.

Lem, Rip, and I shot baskets for about fifteen minutes before taking a break. I wiped the sweat off my brow.

"I've been wondering about the Muckers' Club," I said. "Where's it going? What's next? Have you guys given it any thought?"

"Not really," Lem said. "A few guys asked about it. I didn't know what to say. Figured we'd wait until you got back. And you're back."

I wanted to discuss my thoughts about taking the Muckers into new territory. It was important that I had Lem and Rip's support for my idea, though I'd go it alone if nobody else was interested. If I wanted to make my mark, to do something substantial, it had to involve something more than a bunch of simple pranks. What we did should have a good purpose. I hoped the Muckers would agree to take the club to the next level.

"Up till now," I said, "the pranks have been about getting even. Making somebody the butt of a joke. It's been great and a lot of fun." I paused. "But I'm wondering if the club could do something more meaningful."

Lem cocked his head. "Not sure what you're getting at. The radio wake-up call and the pillow avalanche were quite meaningful. Especially for them."

"Yes." I smiled at the memory of Butter hidden beneath all the pillows. But a new school year called for something fresh and different. I didn't want to continue doing the same old things.

"What if we could buck the system, but do it in a way that helps others?" I paused. "A prank with a higher purpose, inother words."

Mother and Dad frequently challenged us, quoting the Bible passage, that "to whom much has been given, much is expected." We were expected to give back, to make a contribution to society. I didn't know if the Old Man or Mother would consider my plan for a new Muckers agenda a contribution to society. Probably not. But I did.

Rip's eyes widened. "So you're saying we continue to plan jokes, but we should do more than that?"

"Yes. So far, it's been getting back at people who've been jerks. Nothing wrong with that. They deserved it. But couldn't we do something that's fun, serves a good purpose, and helps makes Choate a better place? At least in our opinion?"

I narrowed my gaze. "I think we can do better." Lem and Rip's eyes were glued to me. That was a powerful phrase.

"I'll be damned, Kenadosus." Lem whooped. "I'm not sure what it is, but I think you've got something here. You're right. We *can* do better."

"Maybe," Rip said, his forehead wrinkling. "Still not sure exactly what we'd do, though."

"Since they are serious pranks, I'm thinking of calling them spranks. Get it?"

Rip laughed. "Spranks. Okay, then. Let the spranking begin."

"Sprankenstein," Lem added. "We'll be like that good old boy Dr. Frankenstein. He didn't mean any harm. He was only trying to learn the secret of life when he created the beast. So are we. Maybe the secret of life is spranking."

"I hadn't thought of that, Lemmer." I sized him up, with my hands forming a picture frame. I couldn't resist. "But looking at you, I'm reminded of Big Frank."

"Jack," Rip said. "What are you thinking of? Any ideas for spranks?"

"I have a few, but let's bring them before the Muckers. See what they say."

<hr />

Thirteen of us crowded into the hideout on a Sunday afternoon. I decided it would be helpful to start the school year in a new location. I'd taken the trouble to bring along my portable Victrola. When we walked in, I was pleased to see the hideout looked exactly the same as when we left it. I didn't think anybody had set foot in there since our last visit. Good! It was ours!

The Muckers were spread out on hay bales and crates while I addressed them.

We'd lost several members due to graduation, and a few had dropped out, worried that membership might lead to trouble with the administration. I'd recruited some new guys from the waiting list. One of them was A. J. Lerner, an associate editor for *The Brief*. A. J. was short and wiry, had a wide smile, and wore large spectacles. He'd written the football marching song for Choate.

During the first few minutes, we snacked on potato chips and corn chips, and guzzled colas.

"Jack, great idea to have our meeting here," Boogie said, sitting on a crate. "Away from school."

Though nobody was around when we caroused in Room 215 before chapel, you never knew who might be spying. Maybe our room was bugged. Or Maher had somebody stay behind and listen in. Out here, we could say and do anything we wanted.

And there wasn't a time constraint. We didn't have to go to chapel immediately afterward.

Standing on a hay bale, I plucked a piece of straw and put it in my mouth. "Okay, all you farmers," I said in mock seriousness. "Glad you could make it. The reason I brought you here is to talk about crops. And animals. And muck." I paused. "My advice is, Don't step in the muck, even if we are Muckers."

"You can say that again!" Boogie shouted.

"Even if we are Muckers!" Smoky bellowed.

When they calmed down, I brought up the idea of stepping up our game, of committing ourselves to more meaningful acts. Pranks with a purpose. Remembering how Lem and Rip had reacted to the phrase, I repeated it, my voice soaring, "I think we can do better." The Muckers also seemed positively affected by the phrase. They liked being challenged.

Several Muckers nodded in agreement. Moe, Boogie, and Butch smiled.

"You're right, Jack," Smoky said. "We can do better."

"Since these are serious pranks," I said, "I call them spranks."

Other Muckers mouthed "spranks," getting a feel for the word.

"Spranks, eh?" Smoky said. "Sounds interesting. Tell us more."

"Let's go back in time a little bit," I said. "Do you remember when the Head asked students to think about what we could do for Choate? And when he also called out unnamed students as Muckers?"

Heads nodded.

"Who could forget?" Blambo said.

"I've been thinking about what we could do that might benefit Choate, but not in the way the Head thinks."

I looked out over befuddled faces. Shink gave me a blank stare. Moe rubbed his chin. Butch frowned.

"What are you suggesting?" Butch asked. "That we become spranksters?"

"Something like that, Butch. I think we can agree that certain practices here make Choate, if not intolerable, then difficult. Some aren't fair or equitable. And some discriminate. There are rules or restrictions about who gets in, for example." I mentioned that applicants to Choate had to answer if they were of *Hebraic* descent. "Why should that matter? Or Negro descent or Mexican descent? It's not right. It's an injustice. I'd like to see it eliminated. Perhaps a sprank might be the answer."

"I didn't know they did that," A.J. said. "Lucky I got in. Guess there's a quota." He paused. "That's assuming my parents are Jewish. To be quite honest, they don't look Jewish," he joked.

"Neither do you, A.J.," Boogie said. "You faking it?"

"This sprank idea sounds like a mitzvah," A.J. said.

"A *what?*" I asked.

"In the Jewish tradition, a mitzvah is a good deed. I'm all for it."

"Another injustice is that there are no girls at this school," Smoky said. "Not that I don't like you guys"—he laughed—"but it just doesn't seem normal. I don't get it. That's what it's like in jail, or so they tell me—just guys. Okay, they're being punished. But why are they punishing us? We didn't do anything wrong."

Several Muckers shouted, "We want girls!"

"Maybe we should present the idea to the Head," Smoky said. "Demand that girls be allowed to attend Choate with us. If he doesn't like it, we dress up and go to class as girls."

"Yeah," Blambo said, pulling up his shirt. "I've always wanted to wear a bra."

I held up the thick Choate rule book. "Everything in here concerns what we have to do or what we can't do," I said. "Do we have any rights here as students?"

"The right to be held captive," Rip said.

"We got the right to be free of girls, and I'd gladly give that up," Smoky said, turning his back and wrapping his arms over his shoulders like he was kissing somebody.

"Student rights," I said. "They are in short supply at Choate."

"They are," Blambo said. "I can't name a single one."

"Maybe we should tell the administration which things we don't like," I said. "How would we go about doing that?"

"Talk to the Head," Butch offered. "Barge into his office with a list of demands."

"I don't think he'd like that," Lem said. "Too confrontational."

"How about a march through campus or a rally?" Smoky suggested. "We could get other classmates to join us. Maybe the whole school."

"Maybe there should be an alternative to the rule book. Maybe anarchy. A rule book for anarchists. That's what the club stands for, right?" Leave it to Blambo to come up with something original and wacky.

"A rule book for anarchists." Boogie said. "But what would be in it?"

"Nothing," Blambo said.

I looked out over a barn full of confused faces.

"*Nothing?*" several Muckers asked in unison.

"A rule book with nothing in it?" Shink said.

"Nothing," Blambo said, straight-faced.

Dead silence.

"Every student gets one and makes up their own rules," Blambo said. "Or leaves it blank. No rules."

"A rule book with no rules?" Shink chewed the idea over in his mind. "So, what you're saying is, this new rule book has no rules."

"Exactly." Blambo stood, puffing himself up.

"I think you've got something there," Shink said.

"Yeah," Blambo continued. "Sell these blank rulebooks for a nickel. We'll make a fortune. And we should also sell our Mucker pins. We're becoming pretty famous. Everybody will want one."

Some of the Muckers cheered and several clapped Blambo on the back, but others grumbled at the idea of others wearing the pins if they weren't members.

I didn't think Blambo's ideas were spranks, nor did I think they would come to fruition, but the last thing I wanted to do was to discourage enthusiasm.

"Brilliant suggestion, Blambo," I said, reaching for a phonographic record. "And I've got the perfect song." I placed it on the Victrola and the hit, "We're in the Money," blared out. Instantly, the Muckers pranced and danced around the barn, shouting the irresistible refrain.

After a few more tunes, I concluded the meeting, saying, "We've come up with some great ideas. Let's think about them and then decide what to do."

A comfortable warmth enveloped my face. I beamed, pleased that the guys embraced the idea of serious-minded pranks. As far as I was concerned, the club was on the way to accomplishing something important. And perhaps I was on the way to making a name for myself after all, even becoming my own man. Joe had never done anything like this at Choate. Perhaps, in some way, the Old Man might approve. After all, I was taking charge and contributing to society. Best of all, I'd have help in this collective endeavor.

With smiles and a skip in our step, we all headed back to school.

CHAPTER TWENTY-FIVE

Besides being excited about the Muckers, I'd become entranced with Olive. Other than my sisters, she was more fun to be with than any other girl I'd known, and we laughed and enjoyed ourselves while wandering around town, seeing a movie, or shooting baskets. She was the first girl I could put my arm around and kiss spontaneously, though she had her limits when it came to that kind of thing. She was an accomplished tease, often reminding me of my boorish behavior on our first meeting at the train station. I didn't mind.

"Jack, what have you been doing?" Olive asked as I slid into the booth at Moran's Drug Store. She'd taken the morning train from New Jersey. "Besides keeping me waiting." Olive toyed with the folded silk handkerchief in her jacket breast pocket.

"Sorry. Late again." Late to class, late to chapel, and late to meet Olive.

We ordered chocolate marshmallow ice cream sundaes. It was late fall, and we were bundled up in sweaters and coats.

I told her about the Muckers and how we were upping our game to serious pranks.

Olive slumped. "Jack, I don't think that's a good idea. You might get kicked out of school."

"Might turn into something good," I said. "Then maybe we could hit the road together." I smiled slyly.

"Hit the road?"

"Go to California. When Dad was in the movie business, he spent long stretches in Hollywood. We'll use his connections. You'll be a movie star, and I'll be a writer."

"Maybe we should finish school first." Olive's brow furrowed. "Promise me you won't do anything too stupid."

"If I do, it won't be stupid. In fact, it'll be entertaining and pretty damn interesting."

Olive narrowed her eyes at me. "But, Jack, you graduate next spring. Don't throw it all away. Stick it out."

"Don't know that I can." I clenched my fist. "Choate is driving me crazy. The headmaster, the masters, and the Campus Cops are all on my case. And all the rules."

Olive sipped her milkshake.

"If I stay here any longer," I added, "I might lose my magnificent sense of humor. You wouldn't want that, would you, O? Isn't that what brought you to me? The Kennedy wit."

"Wit*less* if you get thrown out!" Olive said.

"I suppose." I recalled what my father had said about losing faith in me if I didn't buckle down.

It didn't seem right to bitch to Olive and ruin our date. "Enough about my problems."

"I hope being with me cheers you up," she said, kicking me under the table.

"Sure. It's always great being with you." I paused. "But we could have a better time." I winked.

"Jack!"

Our physical relationship hadn't progressed as far as I would have liked.

"Let's take a walk. See what's happening on Center Street."

We finished our sundaes and headed outside. Olive put her arm in the crook of mine. I wasn't a hand holder. If your hand got clammy, or if you got tired of holding hands, you risked offending the girl when you pulled away, so it worked out better this way.

Out on Center Street, Fords, Chevrolets, and Buicks competed for space with horse-drawn buggies. A horse stopped to drop a load. "More muck on the streets these days," I said. "The Head believes us Irish have a special talent for cleaning it up. Maybe another reason why he called us muckers."

After passing a market and the local Post Office, I stopped in front of a tobacco shop. "Let's get cigars," I said.

"Cigars! What for?"

"For smoking. What else?"

"Didn't know you smoked."

"Had my first cigar when I was six years old. Sort of."

"Oh, come on," Olive said. "That can't be true."

"It is. I have a picture of me with a big fat cigar, sitting with my grandfather, P. J. Kennedy. He gave the cigar to me. I'll show it to you."

"Please do, so I know you aren't making up this story."

"Coming?" I opened the door for her.

Olive drew back. "I've never smoked a cigar in my life! What will people think?"

"They'll think you're smoking a cigar." I laughed. "Remember the gangsters Bonnie and Clyde?" They terrorized the Midwest, robbing banks and killing innocent people, until they were gunned down by the police only a few months earlier.

"Yes." Olive rubbed her eyebrows. Clearly she had no idea where this was going.

"Remember that picture of her smoking a cigar?" I said.

"It was in every newspaper. Couldn't miss it if you tried."

Olive looked at me as if I was insane. "I don't know why I'm doing this. Are you going to have me robbing banks next?"

The strong aroma of pipe, cigar, and cigarette tobacco greeted us as we entered the store. So did a layer of bluish-gray haze. It came from a burly, bespectacled man smoking a pipe behind the counter.

"Good afternoon," he said. "How may I help you young people?"

"Two cigars, sir. Of medium length and mild flavor. What do you recommend?"

"For you?"

Some tobacconists sold their products to youth, but most refused. "One for my grandfather. The other for his associate. They enjoy discussing the affairs of the day over a good cigar. The troubles in Europe. Germany and Hitler...and so forth."

The proprietor smiled. He plucked two cigars from a case. "Your grandfather and his associate will enjoy these. They're Cuban. *Upmanns.* In my opinion, the best cigars in the world. Two cigars. Five cents each, please."

Outside the store, Olive said, "Wait a minute. Didn't you tell me your grandfather is dead?"

"Yes. I'll enjoy this cigar in his memory. Olive, strike a pose like Bonnie Parker out on the lam. Pretend you're a movie star!"

When I said "movie star," Olive lit up. She became somebody else. Grabbing a cigar from my hand, she strutted to the front of a Ford Tudor sedan. "Lights! Camera! Action!" Olive put the cigar in her mouth, propped her left leg on the fender, and adjusted her beret. I'd never seen her like this. Like a champ, she'd taken on the role of Bonnie Parker.

"How's this, Jack?" she said, settling into position.

Before I could answer, the tobacco shop guy came out.

"Do it right. Take this," he said, handing Olive a handgun. "Authenticity. And don't worry. It's not loaded."

Olive cautiously took the gun, then reverted to being Bonnie Parker.

"Since Lem and I are public enemies one and two at Choate, you can be our mobster gal. just like Bonnie!"

The tobacconist said, "She's good. Your gal could play Bonnie if they ever make a movie about them."

People stopped and stared at Olive, and she took it all in, glowing immodestly at the attention.

"Olive, you've found your true calling."

"When I graduate next year, I'm going to pursue modeling. Maybe movies after that."

We strolled in a direction away from town. Olive, still flush from our pretend photo session, danced a jig. "Jack, it's always a fun time with you. I never know what'll happen."

I guided Olive to a bench near St. Xavier's Catholic Church, where I went to services on Sundays.

"Let's give these a try." I took out my cigar and put it in my mouth.

"Jack!"

"Sorry. Where are my manners? Let me light one for you. Don't inhale."

"Oh, what the hay," she said.

She slowly put the cigar in her mouth. I got Olive's started, then lit my own.

In a few minutes, Olive began enjoying her smoke, smiling as she reclined on the bench. "Best cigar I ever had. I could get used to this. But I won't. Not very ladylike."

We smoked in silence.

But then I got the urge to do something else. I took Olive's cigar from her hand. "Let's take a break." I put our cigars on the bench.

"What kind of break did you have in mind?" she said. Olive wiggled her eyebrows and parted her lips.

I moved in and kissed her full on the lips while my hands circled her waist. "You've made quite an impression Miss Bonnie Parker. Hope you won't leave me for Hollywood too soon."

She placed her arms around my neck. "Not until I finish school, so you're stuck with me for the next year."

Slowly, I raised my hands from her waist until they were close to her breasts, which I had never touched. Twice before, Olive had firmly restricted my hands from going north.

"Jack, that's enough. It's cold out here. I need to catch the train. It's a long trip back to school."

Disappointed, I walked her to the train stop. "See you soon," she said, then kissed me on the cheek and boarded the train. "And, in the meantime, don't rob any banks." She laughed, waving goodbye as the train pulled away.

I'd keep trying to take things a step further, but I suspected Olive, like most girls, was the kind you had to marry before you had sex. She may have drawn a line, but I always found her to be a lot of fun, ready to join in if there was an opportunity for amusement or mischief. We were good together.

Nevertheless, I wondered: Was it possible to have two gals at the same time? One who didn't want to have sex but that you could hang with and enjoy talking to. And another you weren't that crazy about, but was willing to go all the way.

After Olive departed, I felt frustrated and wound up. Unsure what to do, I wandered aimlessly around town, in no hurry to get back to school. I returned to the bench where Olive and I had been sitting. I bounced my knees, staring vacantly at the sky.

"Hey, haven't I seen you in church?"

Startled, I looked up to see a girl sitting on a bench across from me. Her short hair was parted on the side, and she wore saddle shoes, a big shirt, and a baggy sweater.

"You might have," I said.

"Since I've never seen you in school, I'm guessing you're one of those Choate boys who think they're too good for us. I go to Lyman Hall."

The public high school was only a few blocks from Choate, but it might as well have been in a different country. In addition, it was one big cinder block, unlike Choate, whose buildings were scattered throughout the campus. We didn't have anything to do with the kids at Lyman, and they had nothing to do with us. That's just the way it was. Different worlds.

"Maybe *we're* not good enough," I countered, smirking.

After a moment of silence, she said, "You know, it's too bad there's no exchange between the schools. Our teams don't play yours. We're not invited to your tea dances, and you're not invited to ours. You might learn something from us, and we could learn something from you. I'm in my last year at Lyman, and you're the first person I've ever met from Choate—probably the last, too."

I told her how Choate wasn't that great, and I wished I had gone to a public school. She laughed and said she wished her parents had been able to afford a boarding school like Choate.

"You've got one advantage over us," I said.

"What's that?"

"You have girls at your school."

"Yes." She smiled. "And I'm one of them. You should invite us over sometime. I'd love to see the campus, and I know a lot of other girls would too." She cocked her head flirtatiously.

I shook my head. "Our headmaster wouldn't allow it."

"Even if it's for a good reason?" she said, raising her eyebrows and offering a questioning gaze.

I sat up. "And what might that be?"

"I don't know, but maybe we can come up with something."

A spark ignited. A future sprank started to appear on the horizon.

After we exchanged names, she said, "I'm here every Sunday after church. Maybe I'll run into you again.'

The chance encounter with the Lyman girl had gotten me out of my funk. And who knew? Maybe we could figure out a way to get Lyman girls on campus that fell more or less within school rules—probably less.

When I got back to school, Butter was waiting for me.

"Hold it there, Kennedy," he said, motioning for me to stop. We stood face to face in the West Wing corridor.

"Something on your mind?" I asked. "If so, make it quick. Got to hit the books." I wasn't going to study, but I needed an excuse to get away from him.

"You should be ashamed of yourself."

"Should I? I'm not."

He pointed his finger. "Buying cigars, forcing a young woman to smoke one, and then smoking one yourself. Flagrant abuse of school rules."

Even smoking outside school was prohibited. The bastard had seen us, or somebody had reported us. Moles everywhere.

"Can't a guy enjoy a good Cuban cigar with his steady without being hassled? Don't you have something better to do than spy on people?"

Choate Cops like Butter reminded me of double-agents in the Great War. Like Mata Hari, the exotic dancer who allegedly spied for warring opponents Germany and France. Some of the cops were your classmates, but they also snooped on you and guarded the campus, making it difficult to sneak out as well as get back in. I half-expected them to barge in while I was in the crapper.

"Making sure students adhere to the rules is part of a Campus Cop's responsibility," he said. Butter thrust his shoulders back, chest out and chin up. "I have no choice but to inform the headmaster."

"And I have no choice but to ignore you," I said, brushing right past him.

CHAPTER TWENTY-SIX

Intrigued with the possibility of combining efforts with the Lyman gal, I met with her after church the next couple of Sundays.

This particular Sunday, she'd brought along two friends, both of them females, both from Lyman. All three Lyman girls were active in school activities and assured me they'd have no problem getting other Lyman girls to come over to Choate. To cover ourselves, we'd meet in the quad and call it a study session. The girls would each bring a textbook, as would we. Students could talk about their studies or anything else they wanted.

Wanting to lay low and not risk further confrontation with the Head, I made them promise I wouldn't be identified as a co-organizer. "If anybody asks, say the guy was, uh, I don't know, Sphink," I said, making up a name. "Of course you'll never see him at the study session."

"Okay." One of them grinned. "Let's get a few more details. First name?"

"Richard. Or Dick. Same thing."

She brightened, enjoying the activity of creating a character. "And let's say he was a dick because he wanted a nickel from each girl to come. That's a lot of money. Trying to get rich off the event."

"Right. So you came on your own. Our headmaster may try to identify him, but there's no Sphink at Choate. He doesn't go to Choate. He's a trickster. A con man."

Another girl said, "Exactly. Now, let's flesh him out a lit-tle more. What does he look like? How does he act? Let's see," she said, stroking her chin. "He has wavy black hair, combed straight back. Needs a shave. Never smiles. Shifty eyes. Says he came from South Carolina—Coward, South Carolina." It was a real town.

"That makes sense. What a jerk he was." One of the girls laughed. "He tried to pick me up. Said he'd only charge me a penny. What a guy."

"Okay, I think we're covered," my co-organizer said. "We got conned by this tricky Dick Sphink."

"Yes, you did." I chuckled. "And don't let it happen again."

———⟫•⟪———

Everything was set. I just had to run the plan by the Muckers.

It would be great to have girls on campus, even if only for a short time. Who knew what might come of it? Olive was great, but I wouldn't mind having a steady who lived in the same state, or at least closer. Olive's school was a hundred miles from Wallingford. Maybe I'd meet a gal who'd like to go further than Olive would.

But I had another ulterior motive. I wanted to hang out with the Wallingford kids. I was curious about their lives. No doubt their lives were a lot different from those of Choate students, the vast majority of whom came from well-to-do-families. On my explorations around Wallingford, it wasn't uncommon to see houses that were more like shacks. I'd seen more than a few children outside them, so I knew they had to be pretty cramped inside.

As a group, we barely acknowledged the Lyman students in town, and I wasn't proud of that. Most of us didn't know anybody at the high school. Fraternization was discouraged by the Choate administration. They frequently derided the public school as inferior and poorly managed. "Your life is here at Choate," we were told. "They are doing the best they can over there, but it is not in your best interests to associate with them," one of my teachers said.

All our athletic contests were against private schools like Deerfield and Groton. And the gals who attended the tea dances and Spring Festival came from private girl schools like Olive's Kimberley School or Miss Porter's School.

We needed to break down social barriers. Make new friends. Make new girlfriends. Definitely a worthy sprank.

"The Head needn't know," I said, after telling the Muckers of my contacts at Lyman and going over the plan. "He'll be enjoying his Sunday drive with the Missus. And Mater will be away for the weekend. Only Butter and a few of his cops will be on campus." Like the cops, I was now a sixth-former. I wasn't going to let them bother me. Queenie's husband would be in charge, and I had a plan to take care of him.

"Intriguing idea, Jack," Moe said. "Even if they are public school kids."

"Didn't you use to be one, Moe?" I asked.

"I was. When I was young," he said

I laughed. "I attended a public school in Brookline, Massachusetts, through third grade," I said. "But if I hadn't come to Choate, I never would have met you guys, and there wouldn't have been a reason to start the Muckers." My voice cracked.

Regaining my composure, I said, "Anyway, that's neither here nor there."

"One problem," Rip said. "Girls aren't allowed on campus without permission."

"But they would have permission, Ripper," I said, waving my hand dismissively. "In fact, the Head has already invited them. He just doesn't know it yet."

"He has?" Shink said.

"Sure. He's always saying to take charge of your studies, right?" The Muckers nodded.

"And haven't we all heard him encourage us to have *anybody* join us for a study session? Well"—I grinned—"that's what we'll be doing. In this case, the 'anybodies' are the Lyman girls. We're covered," I said, giving a half-shrug. "And we'll do it on a Sunday—this Sunday—when girls are allowed."

You'd see an occasional girl on campus during the weekend, but they were watched carefully. And their number was limited. Girls had to be visible, and they couldn't be anywhere near a residence hall. But if the Lyman girls' assurances were good, plenty of them would be visible come Sunday.

Moe slapped his thigh. "Hot damn, Jack."

"This is going to be my favorite study session of all time," Boogie said. "Yeah, but what are we going to study?"

"We'll study them, and they'll study us," I said. "But make sure to bring a book with you. Remember, this *is* a study session. Spread the word among friends."

We ended our meeting just in time to file out for chapel. "Lem," I said, "speaking of gals on campus, Gertrude Stein is speaking on campus tonight. The writer. Hung out with Hemingway,

Fitzgerald, and other artists in Paris a few years back. Heard of The Lost Generation?"

"No. How did they get lost?"

"Stein coined the phrase to describe people after the Great War. Lost, wandering, confused. Guess that's what war can do to you. She's going to talk about writing. Might be a writer when I grow up."

"*If* you grow up," Lem deadpanned. "Well, at least she was born in Pittsburgh."

"Won't hold that against her, DeLemma."

CHAPTER TWENTY-SEVEN

A crowd of students and administrators had come to hear Stein at Choate's Andrew Mellon Library. Andrew Mellon, a wealthy businessman from Lem's hometown, had donated the funds for the library.

Stein stood at the podium. She was old and thick and about the same height as Mother. Her hair was cropped short, shaped like a helmet, and she dressed like a man. Mother would have been appalled.

The administrators were happy to have a famous Jewish writer speak on campus. Good publicity. But they didn't want many Jewish students at Choate.

"A novel is what you dream in your night sleep," Stein said. "A novel is not waking thoughts, although it is full of waking thoughts."

I'd never considered writing a novel, but if I did, I'd pay attention to my dreams.

Stein had become world famous after writing *The Autobiography of Alice B. Toklas*, which was about writers and artists living in Paris. It had been written in the voice of her friend Alice B. Toklas but was about Stein's life. Stein was part of the Modernist literary movement that questioned ways to make sense of the world after the destruction of the Great War. She challenged what was normal or accepted. Well, the Muckers were also challenging the status quo, so we had something in common.

Maybe I'd go to Paris someday and become famous like Stein or Hemingway. Perhaps my letters to Lem had the makings of a book. *Down and Out in the Mayo Clinic?* I wondered where this Muckers thing might go. A novel? *Jack and the Muckers?* Another idea I had was to write about gutsy statesmen making unpopular but courageous decisions. Profile them. *Profiles in Bravery?* Or *Courage?*

Stein spoke contemporaneously, and without notes. "The English language has been thrust upon Americans," she continued, "and it is wrong. As static and immobile as are the English, just so ever-moving are Americans… Our problem is to adapt the English language to American needs. To make it move with us Americans. That is the problem—to write things as they are, not as they seem."

That there was a difference in how the English and Americans wrote made sense. Americans did move around, and my own family was an example. We'd moved from one house to another in Brookline, then to New York. We also had summer and winter homes in Hyannis Port and Palm Beach respectively. The Kennedys were mobile. More so than most Americans.

"Let's get her signature," I said after the talk. The crowd had thinned out and Stein was by herself, ladling her cup in the punch bowl.

We thrust scraps of paper forward and got her autograph.

"I'm thinking about being a writer like you and traveling the world and writing about interesting places," I said. "My English teacher said I had a flair for writing, that I should think of pursuing it after graduation. Any advice?"

Stein gave me a fierce stare that dissolved into a warm, crinkly smile. "That's what you ought to do. See the world."

After Lem wandered off, I said to Stein, "You've been all over. Any suggestions? What about London?"

"Yes, and Paris, of course. Here in the United States, I suggest California. Visit San Francisco."

"And what about that city across the bay from San Francisco?" I said.

"Oakland," she said. "I grew up there. I went back recently after living abroad for thirty years. My old Oakland neighborhood had been torn down and replaced by a bunch of factories. For me, there's no there." Stein paused. "There."

Interesting way to put it, but I got it. "I see."

She looked at me fiercely. "Young man, if you were going to write about something this very moment, what would it be?"

I was taken aback but honored. A famous person like Gertrude Stein cared enough to ask me what I wanted to write. "I'd write about famous people, probably statesmen, who showed considerable integrity under difficult circumstances."

"Like whom?"

"There was a senator named Ross. He voted to acquit President Andrew Johnson when the Republicans tried to kick him out of office after the Civil War. His own party put the squeeze on Ross. But he didn't buckle. Did what was right. Took guts. And another senator, Lucius Lamar from Mississippi, helped bring the North and South together during Reconstruction. Those kinds of people."

"Worth looking into," she responded.

I walked to the West Wing.

Lem was reading in bed. "You hitting on Gertie?" he said. "Not your type."

"She's quite something, Leem. We talked about writing, about seeing the world. She said visit Paris, London, San Francisco. But not Oakland."

"Why not?"

"She said, 'There's no there, there.'"

"What? No there, there?" Lem shrugged.

"Not there. We should go."

"What for?"

"See for ourselves if there's no there, there," I chuckled. "Make up our own minds."

"Yeah, you're right. Make up our own minds if there's a there, there. Might be a there, there, and she missed it." Lem broke out in his trademark loud guffaw.

I sat down at my desk. "Time to send a newsy letter to Dad." I needed to head off the reports he'd be getting concerning my low grades, general sloppiness, and chronic lateness. Try to stay on the Old Man's good side, or at least not get on his bad side. Once again, I recalled his warning about losing his confidence.

"LeMoyne and I have been talking about how poorly we have done this quarter and we have definitely decided to stop fooling around. I really do realize how important it is that I do a good job this year."

I almost believed what I wrote.

I ended the letter: "P.S. Gertrude Stein lectured here. LeMoyne + Moi rushed up and got her autograph and had a nice old conversation."

———✥———

Before we could pull off our co-ed study session, I needed to call in a favor. When I saw Queenie and Mrs. St. John head in opposite directions after their afternoon tea, I intercepted Queenie. I told her about our Sunday plan and that we were only following the Head's suggestion to study with anybody.

"Clever, Jack," she said.

I hesitated, not sure if I was pushing things too far. I didn't want to get Queenie in trouble. "Do you remember, after Rip and I sang our little song, that you said to feel free to ask for a favor if I ever needed one. Remember?"

"Yes," Queenie said, tilting her head forward a bit. "What did you have in mind?"

"I wonder if you could, uh, keep your husband occupied for a few hours on Sunday. You know, while we study. Take him for a walk away from campus. Or whatever."

"Aah," Queenie said. "Keep him busy."

"That's right."

"Good idea, Jack. He's been working too hard lately. He deserves some real rest and relaxation. I'll do my best to give him some, so your study session won't be disturbed."

CHAPTER TWENTY-EIGHT

A few minutes before two o'clock, the Muckers huddled outside the West Wing, jittery with excitement. In a few moments, the campus was going to be sweetly invaded by the Lyman gals.

Blambo bounced on his toes. Boogie dropped his textbook. Shink licked his lips. Moe and Rip traded friendly punches. Only Lem seemed detached, indifferent. With a lightness in my chest, I smiled broadly, enjoying the communal energy.

"Well, I guess it's time to hit the books," I said, pointing to my text. "To your stations, everyone." Since the girls lived in the community, they'd enter campus from several different directions. Boogie positioned himself at North Main, me at the North Elm entrance, while the others dispersed to other intersections.

We heard them before we saw them. The high-pitched sound of young women pierced the afternoon wind. A group of about fifteen smiling gals approached. One of them winked and said, "We're here for the study session." I pointed in the direction of the quad. Not far behind them was another large squadron of Lyman students.

When I looked behind me, I saw more gals entering on North Elm. In minutes, I estimated more than two hundred gals had now been joined in the quad by Choate boys, who came pouring out of their rooms to greet them. The noise from the excited chatter reverberated like some sort of political rally.

"This is really something," Boogie said, awed at the developing scene of hundreds of Choate boys coming together with hundreds of Lyman girls. The quad wasn't big enough for the gathering, which seemed to be growing exponentially by the minute. I had expected a couple of hundred students, but this was twice that number—at least.

"I bet Choate has never seen anything like this!" I shouted above the din.

For the next half hour, we "studied," mingled, flirted, talked about school, and traded stories about our lives. I chatted with several Lyman gals, one of whom told me her younger sister's school had been closed due to the Depression.

Seeing one of the Lyman coordinators, I yelled, "You did a great job! Must be half the school's girls here."

"Well"—she beamed—"a girl's gotta study, doesn't she? Even if it is Sunday. Say, have you seen Sphink?"

"Not so far. And I don't think we will. What a dick!"

Out of the corner of my eye, I saw Butter charging toward the quad. As I expected, he came at me, his face red with rage. "Is this assembly your idea, Kennedy?"

"No, Butter boy," I said, because technically it was the Lyman gal's idea. "I was told to come to a study session. As you can see, everybody has their books. The credit goes to the headmaster."

"What?" Butter said. "What are you talking about?"

"His idea. You know how he's always encouraging us to ask our fellow students to join us for a study session. Help each other out. Certainly that includes students from Lyman Hall. Somebody took him up on his suggestion. My congratulations to the organizer, whoever that was. I've learned a lot so far." Holding up my book, I said, "Definitely going to help me in Physics. And from chatting with people from the community, I'm learning about different points of view. Expanding my world."

"But—"

"Now if you'll excuse me," I said, turning away, "got to get back to the books." Returning my attention to the Lyman girl, I said, "Now, as you were saying before we were so rudely interrupted, your mother supports your family since your father lost his job?"

We continued talking, and I learned about what happened to families when the father became unemployed about how difficult life was. Dad had never been unemployed—in fact, he had been his own boss most of the time. Currently, Roosevelt was.

A couple of Campus Cops came over to try to break things up. They pointed to their armbands but they were outnumbered. Several girls surrounded one of the Campus Cops and shamed him. "We were invited by a guy named Sphink for a study session. And that's what we're doing. Now, will you please go back to your cave and let us study in peace?" she scolded, holding up her book.

Butter and his cops slinked away.

We "hit the books" for another hour or so before the girls left. St. John would be back soon.

Later, at our Muckers' meeting, everybody was still exuberant because of the event. One thing was certain. It had been a successful sprank.

"I've got a date for next weekend." Blambo whooped.

"A gal told me about a swimming hole nearby," Shink said. "All this time and I never knew about it. The locals know where to go."

"It was great fun," I said, "and I don't know how much any of us studied, but I learned some important lessons. One serious note for the day: I didn't realize how difficult it is for some people around here to get by. Fathers out of work. Doing what they can to survive. Most of us don't feel the effects of the Depression. A lot of the families these girls come from do. Opened my eyes, anyway. Maybe some of yours also."

The Muckers seemed sober for a few moments. "Yeah, we've got it pretty good," Rip said. "I don't think anybody here has to worry about where they'll get the money to buy food or clothes."

"Some of them had clothes that looked pretty worn," Boogie added.

"Do you think we could get away with another study session?" A. J. asked hopefully. I'd seen him animatedly talking with several girls. He never got an answer. Chapel bells interrupted.

Afterward, the administration undertook a brief investigation of the study session, but all they could come up with was a name, Richard Sphink. They never found him. He seemed to have disappeared. A warning was circulated reiterating Choate policy prohibiting "unauthorized gatherings."

Chapter Twenty-Nine

"Jack, during our last session, we talked about your approach to school," Lecky said, peering over his glasses. "Have you thought more about that?"

I slumped. "About knuckling down? Applying myself to my studies? Haven't decided." That was the truth. Also true was I didn't have a great urge to become the hard-working, nose-to-the-grindstone student that the Head and my father wanted me to be. Not yet. Maybe never.

"That's honest, Jack. It's hard work. Choate demands a lot. And I'm guessing you don't like it when people or institutions put pressure on you."

"Not so far."

"Fair enough. We'll get back to school later, but for now I'd like to find out more about you. I'd like to hear about your family."

Good. I didn't want to talk about school anyway.

I gave him a summary of the large Kennedy family. "Always somebody to play with. And plenty of players for touch football and to crew our boats. Only two parents, though." I laughed.

Lecky nodded and smiled. "Some civilizations—Samoa, for example—have done quite well with whole villages parenting the children."

"Really?" I tried to picture what that would look like. All these people in your life, telling you what to do. Could be confusing. What if one guy tells you to do something but the other guy tells you to do something different? "One mother and one father are enough for me," I said.

"I understand. Parents can be challenging. I'm one myself. I've got three young children. Maybe I'll ask them if they'd like an additional father," he said, a twinkle in his eye. He motioned with his hand. "Continue."

"My father wants the best for us. He's always on me to do better at school. To win. He doesn't like losers. Won't tolerate them. We Kennedys have to win at everything. He'll go on a rant if we don't win our sailboat races. Really lay into us." I grimaced. "He's pretty rough sometimes."

"I can imagine."

"And you better be prepared at suppertime."

"Prepared at suppertime? I'm not following you."

"I don't think it's like this with other families. We don't talk about what we did that day. My father asks my older brother Joe and me about what's going on in the country and the world. And we better have opinions. He'll question us. You have to be ready. If you're not, he'll let you have it."

"I see. More than normal dinnertime conversation." Lecky stroked his chin. "And how about your mother? With nine kids, I imagine she's very busy."

"I suppose so," I said. I felt my neck redden. I kicked at a crumb on the floor. "Always—"

"Always what, Jack?"

I rocked back and forth. "In four years, she's been too busy to come to Choate even once," I said. "Not even for Mother's Day, when the school holds a big celebration. But she's been to Europe a bunch of times since I've been here! I'd be damn surprised if she even came down for my graduation. But she did for Joe."

"I hope she does," Lecky said softly. "You might want to tell her that it's important to you."

"Well, I doubt that would matter. She never took me to school when I was young. Ever. When I was five years old and she was getting ready to go on one of her trips to Europe, I said 'You're a great Mother to go away and leave your children.' Like she didn't want to be our mother." I trembled with anger, and my foot shook uncontrollably. "No, she'd never come."

"Most of the time," said Lecky, "we worry about disappointing our parents. But sometimes our parents disappoint us. I'm sure I've disappointed my children, and it hurts me to think about that." He grimaced.

I'd never thought about my parents letting me down. Only the other way around.

"Jack, apart from your studies, are there other parts of school life you've found enjoyable?"

"I enjoyed playing sports. I played basketball, football, baseball, and rowed crew the first couple of years." I sighed. "But the school said I couldn't play on any teams after I got sick last year. Not even golf." I rolled my eyes. "I like working on the school yearbook."

I brightened when I thought of the Muckers and our daily meeting, but I wasn't sure I wanted to mention the club. "And our room has become a meeting place. Every night before chapel, we play records."

"That must be a lot of fun. So you have a roommate?"

"Yes, but Lem's more than a roommate. He's my best friend." I suddenly welled up and got a lump in my throat. "Lem joins us in Hyannis Port during the summer and in Florida in the winter."

"It's important to have good friends. Tell me, what is it about Lem that brought you together?"

"Well, we laugh at the same things. He keeps my spirits up when school becomes difficult. My brother Joe can be quite a bother, so things are better when Lem's around. I've spent a few days more than most in hospitals and the school infirmary. Lem has, well, been a great help then, too."

"I can tell you treasure that friendship. And I hope your illnesses are a thing of the past. What about girls? Have you met anyone you enjoy spending time with?"

I told him about Olive.

"Jack, you mentioned an older brother."

"Joe. He's at Harvard now."

"There was an overlap. You were both at Choate for a time?"

"Yes," I said. My throat tightened and my whole body tensed.

"What comes to mind when you think of Joe? Perhaps an early experience in your life."

I recalled seeing my leg scar when dressing for our session that morning. "It was about ten years ago. We were riding our bicycles and Joe threw out a dare. We'd ride in different directions around the block. When we came back round, we'd head straight for each other. The first one to yield would be a chicken."

Lecky focused his eyes on me. He seemed sincerely absorbed by my story.

I stood up and began recreating the memory, waving my arms wildly.

"So here I come, pedaling as fast as I can. And there's Joe." I pointed to an imaginary figure. "We go right at each other. Full speed. As we get closer, I see Joe's face. Man's smiling like a crazy person. And I want to wipe that smile off his face. Get the better of him. He figures I'll swerve away but I don't. Go straight at him. Head on. We smash into each other," I said, knocking my fists together. "I fly off my bike and crash into the pavement. Blood everywhere. All mine. I'm on the ground and Joe walks up to me and says, 'You should have gotten out of the way, little brother.' Twenty-eight stitches for me! Joe didn't have a scratch."

"That's quite an event," Lecky said, shaking his head. "Why do you think you chose that incident to talk about?"

"Hmmm. I think it's because I didn't back down," I said proudly. "But Joe expected me to." I paused. "Still, I ended up second best. And that's the way it's always been. Always getting the worst of it. Always following Joe."

I sat down.

"Yes, I can understand you feeling that way. What else comes to mind regarding your brother?"

I sighed. "Joe gets the most attention in the family," I said, "and my father wants him to become president someday. Also, he's better at everything than me. Joe plays football better. Joe dances better. Joe gets better grades. I'm glad he isn't around now," I said. "He graduated in 1933."

"I sense some conflict there."

"Yes. Joe had a habit of barging into my room at school and telling me what to do." I mocked Joe's voice, "'Better get those grades up, Johnny boy, or you'll end up holding a tin cup.' Or he'd make fun of me when I got sick and lost weight. 'You're nothing but skin and bones. If you're not careful, you might disappear.' That kind of crap."

"I can understand you feeling more comfortable at school without him."

"We'd fight at home too," I added. "I always end up on the short end."

"Have you felt bullied?"

"Yes. And the Old Man—I mean Dad—warned everybody in the family to stay away when Joe and I get into it."

"How did that make you feel?"

I looked at the floor. "Well, kind of lonely."

"Not a good feeling, I'm sure. Jack, I'm going to say something you may find peculiar."

I held my breath.

"A certain amount of competition between family members is normal and may even be healthy. As strange as it may seem, rivalries between brothers and between sisters can be beneficial."

I had never thought of my battles with Joe as benefiting anybody except him. Especially since I was always on the losing side. "Healthy? How?" I crossed my arms.

Lecky spread his hands outward while he explained. "Quite often, the younger brother increases his efforts to try to measure up to the older one. Take the example of a brother who excels in sports and academics. The younger brother may strive to meet that standard. He may not succeed, but the competition forces him to up his game. And there can be different outcomes."

"Like what?"

"There are plenty of examples of when the youngest surpasses the oldest. Without the competition, that something to shoot for, he probably wouldn't have leapt over his older brother."

I thought of Joe and me. Where did we fit into Lecky's analysis? Did I want to emulate Joe's success? Sure. Had I? No.

"If the other brother is deficient in, say, athletics or school," said Lecky, "the younger brother won't try to emulate him. What's to gain?" He gave me a pointed look. "Unless he finds it natural to take on his older brother's poor example or misguided ways. Like the younger brother of Al Capone did. He also became a gangster. I don't think we need to worry about that with you."

"No," I said, though I didn't tell him that both Capone and I were Public Enemies.

"Do you feel the school has placed impossible expectations on you? Expecting you to be like Joe?"

"Yes."

"I'd like to hear more about that."

"My first day at Choate, one teacher said I have a lot to live up to. Said Joe was a credit to the school. Told me I couldn't have a better model. Joe was pretty well-known and popular. He won the Harvard Trophy."

"What did he do to win the award?"

"It's given to the student who best combines high scholarship and outstanding sportsmanship."

"Okay. He set the bar pretty high. And I suppose the school also looks at additional activities when deciding who to give it to. Was Joe involved in other facets of the school?"

I nodded. "He was on the Student Council. And he was vice-president of the St. Andrews Society."

"I've heard of them. They help out people in need, don't they?"

"Yes. I think so."

"Now tell me what activities you have participated in besides academics. Have you served on the Student Council or contributed in another way? The St. Andrews Society? Something else?"

"My first year I ran for the Student Council. Didn't come close to winning. Never bothered after that."

"Why not? Didn't want to lose again?"

"Maybe."

"Anything else you're doing or been involved in at school?"

I again told him about playing sports until they wouldn't let me, and how I hadn't put much effort into my job as business manager of *The Brief*.

Lecky nodded. He didn't have to say what he was thinking: I was a deadbeat.

"Now you say he got better grades. Better marks don't always mean one person is smarter than another. There could be a variety of factors. One factor might be the energy the student puts into his studies. Would you agree that an average student might do better than a brighter student who decides not to work hard?"

"I suppose that's true."

"Smarter doesn't mean more productive. It doesn't mean better grades, though it could. History is strewn with smart people who led unproductive lives."

"Guess I don't want to be one of them."

"Good. If you wish, we can talk more about this next time."

CHAPTER THIRTY

My English teacher, Mr. Tinker, announced our next class assignment: write an essay on "justice." First, though, he tried to convey what the word meant. Reading aloud from a book, he said: "Justice is the legal or philosophical theory by which fairness is administered. Fairness in protection of rights and punishment of wrongs. Justice is one of the most important moral and political concepts. The word comes from the Latin *jus*, meaning right or law."

He looked up. "What comes to your mind when you hear the word *justice*? Is it the American flag flapping in the wind? A bald eagle flying over the Grand Canyon? Or is it something less symbolic, like the sweet taste of redemption. Getting back what you once lost? What exactly is justice?"

"Maher relocating—out of the country," I whispered to Rip.

Mr. Tinker asked us to think beyond our own limited world. "Some of you have traveled outside the United States or read about the lives of others perhaps less fortunate than us. Or seen events that you consider unjust or just. Consider your own experiences." He wrote the essay question on the board.

My mind whirled around the events of the last couple of years. I considered my luck at being born to a wealthy family, but I was becoming increasingly aware that the country was having a hard time. More and more people were hungry and without jobs.

I'd had many illnesses. That didn't seem fair, but I'd been sent to the best hospitals. I hadn't seen any Negro patients at the Mayo Clinic. I'd had a difficult time here at Choate, but it was obvious the schools in Harlem didn't have a big, modern library and athletic facilities like we did. Also, Choate didn't enroll Negroes and had restrictions against admitting Jews. Was that justice?

———❖———

Emboldened by the success of the study session and thinking about the justice assignment, I decided to take the spranks idea up a notch. First, I'd conduct my own investigation.

"Good morning," I said to the woman who handled admissions. I needed to find out where the school kept the applications. When we broke in, I didn't want to be fumbling around looking for them. "I'm here on behalf of a friend back home. He's heard good things about Choate and has his heart set on coming here. He's an excellent student, great athlete, and all-around good guy. He'd fit right in."

"He certainly sounds like a worthy candidate." She brightened. "Would you like an application to share with him?"

"May I? He's very eager to get the ball rolling."

I watched as she got up and went to a cabinet, extracted an application, and handed it to me.

"Yes, thank you." I browsed the application. There it was: *Is the boy any part Hebraic?* "Hmmm. That's interesting."

I decided to play the naïve fool.

"Is something wrong?"

"No, I'm just a little perplexed about this question asking if the boy is any part *Hebraic*. So I take it there's an advantage if a guy is any part Jewish. Even a little bit. Like one-thirty-second Jewish. That would be an advantage? It would help him get in?" I shrugged. "In a way, it doesn't seem fair. Why does being Jewish put you ahead of Protestants or even Catholics like me who might want to enroll?"

"You misunder—"

"Didn't know Choate was looking for more Jews," I interrupted. "Between you and me," I said lowering my voice conspiratorially, "I'm not sure my buddy is Jewish. It's never come up. But now that you've made me aware of the Choate policy," I said, using air quotes, "if he isn't any part Jewish, I'll suggest he discover some long-lost *Hebraic* relatives somewhere in his family's past. You know, like his great-great uncle on his mother's side. That should be enough Jewishness, right?"

The woman frowned. "No, I'm afraid you don't understand. The headmaster believes having too many boys of the *Hebraic* faith might, uh, not be best for the school. Might be a negative influence."

"Oh, I see," I said, covering my mouth in mock embarrassment. "What was I thinking? I obviously wasn't. Well, we certainly don't want any more negative influences here, whatever those negative influences might be. We've got enough of that with all those muckers, whoever they are, running around." Placing my hand on my chest, I said, "Thank you for straightening me out. I had it all wrong. It's a disadvantage to be Jewish. Not a benefit. The opposite. Well, now, that's good to know." Holding up the form, I said, "I thank you for the application. I'll get it to him as soon as possible." Crossing my fingers, I said, "And let's pray he's not Jewish."

⇒•⇐

"I understand you're a word man," I said to A. J. in *The Brief* offices.

"Yes, but words and music are best when they go together," he said.

"Even better," I said, "though words sometimes need to be eliminated."

A. J. cocked his brow. "What do you mean, Jack?"

I reminded him about the application. "That's not right," A.J. said, stroking his throat and grimacing.

"You might be interested to know what's happening in Germany," I said.

"What?"

"Did you know that Hitler has restricted the numbers of Jews allowed in schools? I think it's going to get worse."

"No, I didn't." A. J. frowned.

I suggested we do the school a favor and make it easier for Jews and others to get in after we left Choate.

"That's going to take a long time. People don't change overnight. Especially St. John and his gang."

"True, but I think we can help speed up the process. It involves undercover activities, though. Still interested?" I leaned forward and pulled my chair closer.

"Perhaps."

"When you wrote the football marching song for Choate, I'm sure you made a lot of changes before you got it the way you wanted. Cutting words, right?"

A. J. nodded emphatically. "You don't know how many hours I spent on that song."

"Suppose you could cut out one word or phrase that would eliminate an unfair restriction. Could you do it?"

He smiled. "What do you have in mind?"

I told him about my idea to sneak into the school offices and put a line through *Hebraic* on the application for admission.

"You'd still be able to see *Hebraic*. But above it, we'll write another word. *Mucker*. And we'll do it just before graduation, so by the time they discover what we've done, we'll be gone. History."

A. J. cracked up. "Yeah, they'll catch it eventually, but by that time, perhaps more Jews will be applying here. Or more Muckers. Or both. Anyway, gotta go, but how about we hit a few golf balls later in the week?"

"Well, all right," I said.

I considered mentioning the plan at our next Mucker meeting but decided that the caper should be a smaller side operation. Only one or two other people involved. I didn't want to risk word getting out.

This certainly wasn't something my father would have approved of. During his stint as a movie producer in Hollywood, the Old Man often railed against Jews, complaining that they were unethical. Joe had taken up the same line of criticism, calling Jews "unscrupulous." For a while, I questioned Joe but gave up. Couldn't change his opinion. It always ended up in an argument.

Rip, the captain of the golf team, and I met A. J. for a round of golf.

We told A. J. about our performance for Queenie. "Great." He beamed. "If you want me to write additional lyrics and add some music, let me know."

A. J. made a nice putt for par. He took out a cigarette and lit up. Jauntily, he leaned on his putter. "Smoke?" he said, offering his pack to us.

Rip and I declined.

Before he took a second puff, a figure emerged from behind a tree—Butter.

"Come with me," he said, taking A. J. by the arm. "You guys got lucky. Had you taken his offer, you'd be joining our meeting with the headmaster."

Rip and I shook our heads. Damn campus cops. Exchanging my putter for a driver, I slammed the ball as far as I could toward the Head's house on North Elm.

I was reading *The Choate News* in *The Brief*'s offices when Charles Hoyt, the *Brief*'s editor-in-chief, said to the staff, "I require your attention. I have some important news."

I didn't like Hoyt much because he was pretty full of himself. He had the annoying habit of always flexing his muscles. He was a big, blond football player, and because of his physique, had acquired two nicknames—Chesty and Mr. Atlas, after the popular bodybuilder. Hoyt was also sixth-form class president and on the Student Council.

Hoyt didn't like A. J. With a smirk, he happily told us A. J. had been expelled for smoking on school property.

I bared my teeth, angry at Hoyt for finding joy in A. J.'s dismissal, and at St. John, who'd carried it out.

They'd put A. J. on a train back to New York, Hoyt added. My shoulders drooped. I didn't even have a chance to say goodbye.

I rolled my eyes and shook my head. Now what was I going to do? I'd lost my partner for the application caper. Would I do it on my own or recruit somebody else to take A. J.'s place?

I turned the page and continued reading. The sunlight illuminated a three-quarter page ad for Chesterfield cigarettes.

Hypocrites!

———◦———

Lem blew through our door. "We did it, Jack." Lem had been celebrating with his teammates.

"Congratulations," I said, shaking his hand. Lem played tackle on the Choate football team. They had defeated Kent by a score of 35-0, capping an undefeated season. I winced, realizing I would have been on the team if they'd let me play.

"I'm going to go into town tonight," I said to Lem. "Their kicking A.J. out has put me in the dumps. Want to come?"

"Sure," Lem said.

At night, you had two ways to bust out of Choate—go below ground or put yourself closer to the stars. A subterranean passage connected the school's main buildings and The West Wing. You could take the tunnel, then sneak out through Hill House. But under the cover of darkness, we chose to climb out the window and scamper along the rooftops before descending at the rear. We celebrated the biting cold, exhaling the condensation in each other's face.

Once beyond school boundaries, I whooped. "Freedom!"

"You can say that again," Lem said.

"Freedom!" I repeated.

"Okay, that's enough."

We ran into town.

Since it was Saturday night, places stayed open late. We poked our heads in a few taverns that had opened after Prohibition's end in December 1933. I wanted to see what was going on. In one tavern, several people were singing. In another, men crowded around a pool table. In a third, we saw a fight break out.

After a milkshake at Moran's, we headed back to Choate. It was after midnight. We took off our shoes before creeping up to our room. Maher's snoring gave us cover as we opened our door.

———————

On the way back from chapel the next night, a fellow Mucker drew me aside. "Talk to you a minute, Jack?"

"Sure. What about?"

"A. J. told me about your plan before the Head put the kibosh to his Choate career. I want to help. I'm Jewish."

I didn't know he was Jewish, and I didn't think anybody else did either. His last name sounded Irish.

"Jewish on my mother's side. My dad's Catholic, like you. According to Jewish tradition, your identity is determined by your mother's religion. If your mother's Jewish, you're considered a Jew. Maybe that's why they let me in, because the Head considered me only half-Jewish."

"Or half Catholic." I laughed.

We shook on it. I was excited about the plan, though carrying it out would be challenging—we'd have to do it at night. I looked forward to the satisfaction of pulling off a prank that would bring attention to a wrong and, if not right it, at least make it more apparent to others. A lightness enveloped me as I walked back to West Wing.

CHAPTER THIRTY-ONE

Winter 1935

For the next few weeks, I didn't think much, if at all, about school. I was in Palm Beach enjoying the holidays and the balmy weather with my family. But the moment I stepped back on campus in early January, I scowled.

I trudged through the heavy snow, my hands buried in my pockets. Several feet had accumulated in the last couple of days. Lem wasn't in the room, but I noticed a crate of oranges Mother had sent.

I didn't feel like staying in my room alone, so I took a walk.

Shink and Boogie intercepted me. "Jack, you don't look so happy," Boogie said.

"I was thinking about the Head and Maher."

"Maybe a little extra money in your pocket might lift your spirits," Shink said.

"Yeah. What did you have in mind?"

"All you have to do is tilt your head back, put this dime on your forehead, and drop it in here," Boogie said, displaying a large funnel. "Do it, and the dime's yours."

Ten cents was enough to buy a couple of Zagnut candy bars. Why not give it a try?

"I'd be happy to take your money," I said.

"All right, here's your dime," Boogie said, handing me the coin, then inserting the funnel in the front of my pants.

The instant I tilted my head back and put the dime on my forehead, Shink dumped a cup of icy water into the funnel. The dime flew off. My crotch was soaked and cold.

"Better luck next time, Jack," Shink said, picking up the dime and gleefully departing.

I couldn't help but laugh. Most of the time I was the one who played jokes on others.

I turned to head to my room so I could change before class, but Queenie and Mrs. St. John approached on their customary walk.

"Jack, are you ill?" Mrs. St. John asked, glancing at my wet trousers. "Shall I take you over to Archbold? If you're losing control of… Well, that can't be good."

"No," I said, "not sick. Just a little wet behind the ears. And somewhere else. I'm sure the condition will cure itself."

Mrs. St. John and Queenie exchanged puzzled looks.

"A couple of guys got me good," I explained.

"Just make sure to look your best for our special guest tonight. Mr. Ledbetter is a very accomplished musician."

"I'm looking forward to it, ma'am. In the meantime, I better get out of these wet pants. Have a nice walk." I scurried away before my JJ froze off.

I'd broken a few rules, and the Head had strongly hinted that one more offense and I'd be on my way out, but if what we'd heard was true, a *real* lawbreaker was coming to campus. Ledbetter was a folk and blues musician who'd spent time in prison, and the rumor was he went there because he killed somebody.

"Hey, Lem," I said, walking into my room. "I'm back."

"Yes, you are. Get a little excited coming back to school, Jack?" Lem pointed to my wet pants.

"No, that wasn't it." I explained how I got tricked.

After changing clothes, I pointed to the crate of oranges "Mother sent these. Let's see how they taste," I said, tossing one to Lem.

I peeled one and took a bite. "Awful," I said. I spat it out in the trash can. "Sour as Maher. Like drinking lemonade without sugar."

"Throw 'em out," Lem agreed.

I pointed my finger in the air. "Wait. There may be a good use for this wretched fruit."

"What?"

"In my humble opinion, our fellow Choate prisoners of war haven't been getting enough fruit in their diet. Come on."

Grabbing the orange crate, I carried it up to the ledge on the top floor. Our vantage point overlooked a pathway. "Spring training and the baseball season are just around the corner. Let's warm up. I'll be Dizzy Dean of the Cards and you be Carl Hubbell of the Giants."

Several fellows were going about their business below us. Two of them were Shink and Boogie.

"Time for payback. I think Boogie and Shink, courtesy of Mother, could use an infusion of Florida oranges, sour as they may be. Don't want them getting scurvy."

"Somebody might get hurt," Lem cautioned.

"I think it's worth the risk. We've got to make sure our friends receive all the great benefits of vitamin C! I'll take Shink. You aim for Boogie."

My first throw missed but my second nailed Shink in the back.

"Yow!" shrieked Shink.

"Oh, why not?" Lem said, throwing up his hands in mock exasperation. He had a strong and accurate arm. His orange hit Boogie on the leg.

"These oranges are from my mother!" I shouted. "She wanted to make sure you got your vitamin C!"

"All right, we're even Jack," Boogie said.

Scurrying to the other side of the wing, we searched for more targets.

"Hey, there's Butter," I said, pointing at a figure below.

"Let's give him a double dose," Lem said. "He's been a tad lethargic lately."

"Hey there!" I called out. When Butter looked up, I showed him an orange and shouted, "Want to play catch?"

Butter, a former baseball player at Choate, was shocked, but he smiled and said, "Sure," so we let loose a barrage of oranges. One hit him on the head, another on his backside. We snickered, watching him flee like a scared rabbit.

We scurried downstairs to pick up the oranges. Later that night, we dumped the remaining citrus outside of school.

———⊰•⊱———

The gap-toothed Negro man adjusted his floral bow tie and fiddled with the strings on his twelve-string guitar.

This dark-skinned guy was allowed to entertain us white guys at Choate, but nobody of his race could attend the school. Was that justice?

A guy in my class, Morton Davis, was so dark we called him "Blackie." But he wasn't Negro. Or didn't identify himself that way.

Alan Lomax, who graduated from Choate a few years ago, introduced Ledbetter to the audience in the Speech Room. He had met him while collecting the songs sung by Negro chain gangs serving time in penitentiaries in the South. He'd heard Ledbetter sing at Louisiana State Prison at Angola.

"My name is Huddie Ledbetter, but everybody calls me Lead Belly." He stomped his feet and clapped his hands, playing a kind of music I'd never heard before. Rhythmic, spiritual songs that were sung by prisoners to help alleviate the boredom of hoeing and chopping. One song called "Sheriff Tom Hughes" was about the man who had arrested him. Two others, he said, had been sung by his grandfather when he was a slave.

After the performance, Ledbetter set aside his guitar and came down from the stage. Where was he going? He strode over to St. John, looked him in the eye, took off his hat, and held it out and open.

"St. John didn't pay him," I whispered to Lem. "Lead Belly wants to make a few bucks. Why shouldn't he? He worked for it."

The Head cringed and rubbed the back of his neck. I'd never seen him embarrassed and nervous like that. Made the school and him look bad to have a guest ask for money. Well, that was his fault. It was fun to watch the Head humiliated after all the times he made me feel uncomfortable. And he deserved it.

The Head didn't know what to do. Maybe he'd never seen anybody pass the hat. Didn't know what it meant. Thought Lead Belly was bowing to him.

"Mister John, do you know what the greatest nation in the world is?" Lead Belly asked.

St. John puffed up. "Of course, I do. We all do. It's the—"

"Naw, you're wrong," Lead Belly interrupted. "The greatest nation in the world," he said, pausing for effect, "is the DOnation." Lead Belly gave his hat a hard shake.

The Head's red face was visible to all. He dug into his pocket, pulled out some coins, and began counting them.

"Chump change," I said to Lem. "Give him a bill. At least a dollar."

His hands shaking, St. John dropped the change on the ground.

Nobody moved. St. John expected Lead Belly to pick it up, gesturing with his hand.

Lead Belly never looked down. He just stood there, still holding his hat open.

The Head buckled and fell to his knee. He picked up a quarter, a nickel, a dime, and a penny and threw them in the hat.

Lead Belly nodded.

I shot to my feet and waved a dollar bill. "Here, Mr. Lead Belly. You earned it." Lead Belly smiled and said, "Much appreciated," as I put the dollar in his hat. Soon, with a rush, others threw in change and dollar bills. Lead Belly's grin grew broader and broader the more his hat filled up. By the time he left, his hat was overflowing, and he had to carry it with two hands. Probably weighed ten pounds.

As we filed out, Lem said, "Looks like Lead Belly got paid after all."

Energized by the music and happy about helping out Lead Belly, I was in no hurry to go back to my room to study. I scampered along a shoveled snow path and got on my knees as I faced forward, my head just above the snowbank. Lem sat on a bank of snow behind me and put his legs over my shoulders so it looked like I was carrying him. I commanded, "Wave to our fellow Muckers."

We got plenty of laughs, and Boogie said, "Billings is either a lightweight, or Kennedy is stronger than I thought.'

Maher passed by and stopped in front of us. "Haven't you got something more worthwhile to do than climb over each other? Your grades are barely mediocre, Kennedy."

"You're right, Mr. Maher," I said. "I'm tired of carrying this lunk around. Billings has got to stand on his own two feet from now on. That's the reason my schoolwork has suffered."

I removed Lem's legs. "Glad to get that load off. Thanks for the suggestion, Mr. Maher." Lem and I strolled arm in arm away from Maher.

"A question for you, Lem. Is anybody better equipped to spoil fun than the Prick?"

"He's the bombastic best."

"And a bastard."

"He's a bombastard!" we shouted simultaneously.

Lem and I had only been in our room for a few minutes when we heard, "Inspection." Maher came charging through the door. He stopped and sniffed. "This room smells terrible. It's a disgrace." The aroma of clammy boys was not to his liking.

"Nice evening, Mr. Maher," I said while reclining on my bed. "Did you enjoy tonight's show?" Lem sat at his desk.

Maher bent down, got on his knees, and peeked under my bed, displaying his butt crack. Lem and I looked at each other, smirking in disgust. Lem held his nose. Not only did we have to endure the Prick's presence but also the sight of his keister.

"Anal slice," I whispered.

"Intergluteal cleft," murmured Lem.

"For crying out loud," I said in a monotone, pointing to Maher's butt.

"What are you crying out loud about, Kennedy?"

"The weather. Awful, isn't it, sir?"

"But you just said it was a nice evening."

"Did I? Oh, well. You know how quickly the weather can change in New England."

Next, like a madman, he opened our closets and pawed through our belongings.

"Help you find something?" I asked. "If you tell us what you're looking for, Billings and I would be more than happy to assist."

"Two offenders committed an assault involving dangerous weapons on school personnel," Maher said. "Trust me, we'll find out who committed this heinous act."

"Yes, your *heinous*, I mean, Mr. Maher," I said straight-faced.

Had students brought a knife or firearm to school? Were the perps still at large?

"I suspect the two of you were involved." He leered at us.

"And what was the dangerous weapon?" I asked. "A crowbar? A knife?"

Maher cleared his throat. "The criminals, ah, used fruit."

Oh. Maher was searching for evidence of the oranges we'd used to pelt Butter. But we'd gotten rid of them. We were totally in the clear.

Lem and I did a no-effect thing, our faces as blank as a new chalkboard.

"Fruit?" I said, stroking my chin. "Interesting choice of weapon. Did the bastards force-feed the victims grapes? Slap them crazy with banana peels? What did they use?"

"Oranges."

"Oranges?" I said, pretending to be shocked. "Valencia or Navel? My choice, if you're interested, would have been a coconut. Don't you agree, Lem?"

"Yes. Or an apple. That is, a road apple a cow had left behind."

Maher shook his head at the clutter. Because our room was now the headquarters for the Muckers, it had become messier and dirtier. There were plenty of forgotten items—books, sweaters, jackets, socks, hats, shoes without mates, toothbrushes, stolen food scraps from the dining hall, a tennis racquet, a baseball glove.

Maher made notes, then announced the violations.

"Skivvies on floor, southeast corner."

"One sock and two sweaters under Billings' desk."

"Scraps of paper, candy wrapper, pencil, paper clips next to trash can."

The more violations Maher found, the louder he announced them. And the redder he got.

"Used handkerchiefs by Kennedy's bed."

"Pants and shirt on floor next to Billings' desk."

"That shirt isn't mine," Lem said.

"Mine either," I said.

"Books on floor," Maher continued. "Billings' closet."

"This room is a pigsty," he grumbled. "Guess what that makes you?"

"Rabbits?" I quipped. "Because the detritus keeps multiplying?" *Detritus* was a word I'd recently learned. More fun to say than rubbish. But it didn't impress my old English teacher.

We watched in amazement as Maher scurried around like the rat he was, compiling the entries and piling all the offending articles in a mound in the middle of the room.

"That's quite an art project you've got going, Mr. Maher," I said. "Need any help?"

"No," Maher snapped.

Grabbing my skivvies from under my pillow, I placed it under my bed, where Maher had already inspected.

Thinking he was finished, Maher mopped his brow.

"Sir," I said, pointing to the skivvies. "I think you missed one."

"Get it, Kennedy," he sneered, "and put it on this disgusting pile."

"Like I said, glad to help." I picked it up and pretended I couldn't find the proper place for it. "Billings is the more artistic public enemy, but I'll do my the best." I inserted the skivvies inside a shoe. Surveying the pile, I said, "This would make a great centerpiece for the dining hall."

"Make sure this mess is cleaned up by tomorrow night. I'll be back."

"We'll be here," I said. "What time can we expect you?"

"I don't think my report will please Headmaster St. John. Or your father, Kennedy, for that matter. Haven't you boys learned anything about hygiene and neatness in all the time you two have graced us with your presence at Choate? What will it take for you two to grow up?"

He didn't wait for an answer, slamming the door on his way out.

"That was fun," Lem said, rolling his eyes. "But he brings up a good question. What will it take for us to grow up, Ken?"

"For us to get the hell out of here. That's the only way we'll grow up. So we don't have that prick breathing down our necks and barging into our room like he's King Kong!"

Lem did his best ape imitation, gibbering and jumping up and down, which pulled me out of my foul mood. Hard to be unhappy for long around Lem. That ludicrous grin and flamboyant laugh always snapped me out of my funks.

CHAPTER THIRTY-TWO

Lem and I stood before the Head.

St. John, sitting stiffly behind his big wooden desk, got right to the point. "You two are suspected of attacking Mr. Butterworth with these," he said. He took an orange from a desk drawer and placed it on his desk. "Is this the weapon you used?"

Was the Head manufacturing evidence, or had we missed one? I thought we'd gotten them all.

"I couldn't say for certain, sir," I said, "until I tasted it. They were godawful. But don't tell Mother. She sent them."

"What I'm concerned about—"

"They were sour, sir. Worthless. We played catch. That's all. And I can tell you this: Mr. Butterworth needs to work on his fielding. Even if he has graduated. Can't catch worth a darn. Charged him with three errors."

The Head threw up his hands in exasperation. "You're telling me you were playing catch? Using oranges?"

"That's right. If he was an honest chap, he would have told you we invited him to play. He said sure."

The Head flinched, leaned backward in his chair, and ran his hands through his non-existent hair. "He did?" he said.

"Yes, Lem wanted to warm up his arm. Get ready for baseball season. Right, Lem?" I was taking a chance. Lem wasn't on the baseball team. I hoped the Head didn't know that. I looked at Lem bug-eyed, hoping he'd catch on and play along.

"Great chance to win the conference title this year." Lem beamed.

"But LeMoyne has never been on the baseball team," he said, dryly.

"I've developed quite a curve ball during the summer," Lem said. "Think I could help the team."

St. John put down the orange. "We'll see about that. I'm inclined to believe your actions are a continuation of your efforts to undermine the school." He huffed. "But I'll admit I don't have proof. Other than this orange. Which you say you used for athletic purposes." He paused. "Listen carefully."

He got up and stood in front of us.

"It's my understanding that there was an unauthorized assembly on the quad."

"A study session, sir," I said.

"So you say, Jack. Was that your idea?"

"No." Technically, that was true. It had been the Lyman girl's idea. Or I could have said it was the Head's idea because he encouraged us to study with whomever was around and willing, but I decided to keep my mouth shut.

"Hard to believe. But it doesn't matter." He pointed at us. "Because I'm giving the both of you a final warning.' He was nearly shouting. "I've reached the end of the line with you two. What this means is, should you or your friends decide to partake in any activities that shame the school, or in any way violate school rules, there will be serious consequences."

Serious consequences? What did that mean? Confiscate the Victrola? Ground us from going into town? Or worse?

"It's up to you. Do you understand?"

We nodded.

He leaned forward. "I've had to expel quite a few boys over the years. Sent them packing. For a variety of reasons. They all had their excuses, but in the end, dismissal was best for them and best for the school. They didn't belong here. Couldn't cut it. I suggest you learn from the example of your departed friend, Mr. Lerner. He violated a school rule and paid the price."

The Head was laying it out for us. Toe the line or he'd expel us. Unless this was another scare tactic of his.

I wasn't afraid, but it saddened me that I had spent the last few years at a school where I definitely didn't want to be.

<hr />

"What should we do to liven up Spring Festival weekend?" Smoky asked the Muckers. "Remember," I said, "it should be something meaningful. However, what won't have any meaning for us is if we're subjected to more Gilbert and Sullivan." Every year the Head forced us to watch his choice of one of the duo's comic operas: *The Mikado, H.M.S Pinafore, Patience*. He had a thing for them. "After I get out of here, I'll never see another Gilly and Sully production for as long as I live."

"Hear! Hear!"

"Ban them!"

"Send Gilbert and Sullivan to detention! Permanently."

"The Muckers ought to do something," Shink said. He pointed to the gold shovel adorning his sweater. We wore them only during our Mucker meetings now. "Impress our dates with our Mucker pins." He paused. "Privately, of course."

One wild, impractical idea after another was introduced, but I kept my mouth shut. I didn't want to do anything that would disrupt the Spring Festival or put a damper on it for everybody else. There was nothing wrong with letting off a little steam, but the Spring Festival was no time for a sprank.

Boogie said, "Since we're the Muckers, we should do something with the muck. Use the shit from the stables."

"Bribe one of the cafeteria workers to serve the Head a pile of muck for his dinner entrée," Moe said.

"Add it to the Gilbert and Sullivan set," Butch said. "Might shorten the performance."

"Bring the muck to the dance," Boogie said. "Shovel it in." He removed his emblem and used it to make a scooping motion.

"Dump it on the dance floor," Moe said.

"Each of us brings a shovel," Boogie said. "We put our dates on the shovel. Take a picture. Then another picture of us holding our shovels next to the pile of muck. Wearing our Mucker pins, of course."

Several more silly, even ridiculous ideas were bandied about, but without any follow-ups. I didn't expect there would be, but it was a hoot to imagine the reaction we'd get to any of these spranks. Picturing the horror on the Head's face was half the fun.

We trudged to St. Andrews Chapel. Was it now necessary to repent for sins imagined but not committed? Didn't think so.

CHAPTER THIRTY-THREE

I had the last bite of my cottage cheese sandwich in my mouth when the lunchtime dining hall hum came to an abrupt halt. St. John stood up. Maher motioned for quiet, putting a finger to his lips.

What was this about? Announce a new spring menu? Eliminate Latin from the curriculum? Was Choate going co-ed? Or something bad? Probably. In my four years, I couldn't remember the Head interrupting a meal with anything positive.

"When your name is called, report immediately to my office," St. John intoned. He unfolded a paper. "Ralph Horton. Paul Chase. LeMoyne Billings." Low whistles and *oohs* and *aahs* accompanied each name.

"Jack Kennedy."

As soon as I heard my name, I lost my taste for cottage cheese. I took the white glob out of my mouth and put it in my napkin.

By the time St. John finished, thirteen names had been called. *Hmmm.* All Muckers.

Drawing up our collars, we put our hands in our jackets and plodded through the windy, cold New England day to St. John's office. That was fitting. I had a feeling we'd get an icy welcome in a couple of minutes.

This had to be about the Muckers. I tried to be hopeful because we hadn't done anything seriously terrible.

The Head hadn't been able to connect us to the study session. Besides, the event had been a fantastic success. Students were still talking about it a week later. I'd seen Choate boys sitting with Lyman girls at Moran's. Groups from the two schools congregated on street corners or strolled along Main Street. What was wrong with socializing with other kids in the area? Was there a law against that?

So, what could it be?

"What do you think this is about?" Smoky asked, his head down.

"Probably wants to put a stop to our pre-chapel meetings," I said without enthusiasm.

Smoky shook his head. "I don't think so. He wouldn't have made a big production of calling us out in front of the entire school. I don't have a good feeling about this."

I thought Smoky was right, but I tried to cover up my worry. "Naw," I kidded, "he wants us to expand the club, open it up to more members." No response. Wrong time for a joke.

We filed into the Head's office, standing in rows of threes and fours.

St. John regarded us solemnly from behind his desk. "Form a line. I want to see all of you." When we spread out, he gave us a tight, evil smile. "This won't take long. Then you can be on your way."

On our way? That was good. At least it would be quick. We wouldn't have to endure a long lecture.

St. John glared at us. "I've been headmaster at Choate for many years," he began calmly. "Since 1908." But then he raised his voice. "But never, and I mean *NEVER*, have I seen such immature behavior from a group of boys. You are a colossally selfish, pleasure-loving, unperceptive group that's quite the opposite of the hardworking, solid people here at this school, be it masters or boys." He paused. "Furthermore, you are an insult to this fine institution from which so many have gone on to great success. I don't see that happening for any of you. The pranks, the disrespect for others, the inattention to studies, the illicit activities. Sometimes I think I've been dealing with children, not young men. You should be ashamed of yourselves."

I wasn't. And I hated it when somebody told me I should be ashamed of myself. Strictly their opinion. In this case, why should I be ashamed? I thrust a fist into my pocket. If anything, I was proud of myself for not bending to the powers that be. The way I looked at it, the Head should be ashamed of himself for the way he ran the school. Like a prison.

St. John cleared his throat. "I'll go through the offenses, the rule breaking, and the disregard for Choate. First," he said, holding up a finger, "you have established an illegal club. As you know, it's against school rules to form a club on this campus. Yet you went ahead. What did you expect to achieve through this prohibited action?"

I was itching to respond, but I swallowed my words. I didn't think St. John was in a listening mood. I didn't like being quiet, and I wanted to say, "What's wrong with starting a club? Shows independence and strength. Initiative. But you don't want that here. Perhaps it's time to flush the goddamn rule book down the toilet. Start all over." But it wasn't the time and place for such a radical suggestion.

"You needn't answer. There is no satisfactory response."

St. John turned his gaze on me.

"Furthermore, the fact that you have appropriated a word that I used as the name for your so-called club is a further affront to Choate and all it stands for."

St. John stood up, walked around his desk, and faced us. I got an unpleasant whiff of stale tobacco breath.

"If you recall my sermon, I called out a certain kind of student who was on the road to ruin. I was trying to help you. It was a warning you ignored. Instead of using that knowledge to right your ship, to adjust your behavior and become boys worthy of this school, you chose to form a club, a prohibited organization as I have noted, and to expand your disreputable activities."

St. John let his words sink in. He scanned the eyes of all thirteen Muckers.

Several guys shifted on their feet. Out of the corner of my eye, I saw Butch grimace. Shink seemed to lock his jaw. Moe's hands trembled.

"Then you flaunted your club," he continued, "by producing ridiculous pins bearing your organization's name." Spittle projected from the Head's mouth. "To top it all off, you wore those pins on campus until I banned them. Such foolishness. Heavens, what good did you think could come from that?" He shook his head. "Need I remind you of the extraordinary opportunity you've been given here to become worthy scholars? Choate has given you so much the past four years. Rigorous studies, athletic competition, social engagement, extracurricular activities. And what do you do in return?" he said, waving his hands. "You throw it all away."

I couldn't hold back any longer. "But—"

"Quiet," he interrupted. "A good deal of the blame belongs squarely on your shoulders, Kennedy. Public Enemy Number One. I gave you that disreputable designation in the hope you'd wise up. Realize you were headed down the wrong path. But you ignored the warning. Not only that, but you decided to take your disobedience a step further. It's my understanding you are the leader of this effort to shame the school." St. John sneered. "Are you proud of yourself? You shouldn't be. Your childish behavior is an embarrassment. As sixth-formers, you've become troublemakers. I've been headmaster here since before you were born. I'll be here for years to come, God willing. I've seen your kind before. Let me tell you that it always ends badly for those who engage in delinquent behavior. As it will for you."

St. John clasped his hands. "The particulars. First, there is the matter of the toilet seat. Destroying school property. Did you think that was funny? What purpose did that serve?"

My muscles quivered and my blood began to heat up. That had happened several months ago on Halloween, and nowhere near West Wing. And there was no evidence we were involved in that prank. Because we weren't. Not my style. What was the point of blowing up a toilet? What kind of statement was made by destroying school property? None that I could see. Certainly not what I'd call a sprank.

"Sir, if you—"

St. John held up his hand.

"Now, the most damaging evidence. One of your classmates, a young man of high moral character, unlike any of you, came forward to tell me of your ghastly plan. I commend him. He told me of your involvement in a plot to destroy Spring Festival weekend by hauling manure onto the dance floor. That's a criminal act. Defacing property. Despicable in every sense of the word. Did you think it would be amusing to ruin the entire weekend for others with your immature prank? I've never heard of such selfishness."

He was asking a question, so I answered. "It was all in jest, sir. Never a thought given about actually doing it. Ask anyone here." I decided to do it for him because I knew he wouldn't. "Guys, were we planning to haul manure to the dance?"

The Muckers shook their heads.

St. John ignored my question to the Muckers. Maybe he never heard it.

"Did you expect me to wait to see if you would carry out your plot? Let you go ahead and ruin the dance for everybody else? I think not."

St. John scanned the entire lineup of Muckers one by one, from left to right. I swear he scrutinized me for a moment longer than he did the others.

"After a careful review of the facts…I have concluded that the punishment for these offenses is…" He paused, bobbing his head up and down.

The radiator hissed.

"Expulsion."

Several Muckers groaned.

No. Can't be.

He wouldn't expel all thirteen of us for doing nothing more than running our mouths, would he? What kind of justice would that be? He might as well expel the entire school. I'd heard plenty of boys whisper about what they'd like to do. Sneak a horse into the Head's office at night. Cover a hallway floor with cups of water so nobody could walk on it. Nobody did it. Just talk. Like us. They were never expelled.

But then a weird thing happened.

I felt relieved.

Because a part of me wanted to be expelled. Released from purgatory. I'd finally be out of here. I'd be able to breathe. Not have to look around to see if somebody was watching me, following me, or listening through the door.

But that feeling of relief vanished in a few seconds. Something else bubbled up in my consciousness. Thoughts of widening my scope. Rearranging my point of view.

Perhaps I should look beyond what *I* wanted. If I were being honest with myself, I'd been concerned mostly with myself up to then. The way I looked at it, I might not graduate from Choate if things got really nasty between the Head and me, but I had never thought I might drag down others. Now I had.

So I was having a major change of heart because St. John's action affected more than just me. Dismissal would be devastating to the other guys.

Most of them, if not all of them, were able to tolerate the school environment much better than I could. Some of them even liked it here. Found the discipline and regimentation helpful. They respected the masters and appreciated the excellent facilities. Nevertheless, they had wanted something more. Comradery. To be part of a lively club. Now they had been thrown under the bus. By me. That wasn't right. I had to make things right, at least for them.

St. John had rounded up the Muckers, and we were in this together. Or out of it together. Every one of us faced the same penalty. Even though some, like me, were more responsible than others. This wasn't like a crime where the murderer got a harsher sentence than the getaway driver. We were all going to get the same sentence.

If he was going through with it. Maybe he wouldn't. Another empty threat?

"And that is what I intend to do. I recommend you pack up. Once you've done that, I expect you to leave in due time. The train departs this afternoon. I suggest you be on it. Dismissed," he said, waving his hand toward the door.

Silently, we filed out of the office. I was surprised, but the others were in complete shock. Rip and Butch sobbed.

"What am I going to tell my father?" Butch cried. "He's going to kill me!"

"What did we do to deserve this?" Rip moaned.

As we trudged to our rooms, I thought about the consequences. Sure, most, if not all of us, would go to college, but without an honorable dismissal from Choate, the Muckers could forget about attending prestigious universities. We'd never get into Ivy League schools, which was where most of us expected to go.

We'd also face the wrath of our parents.

This wasn't the way it was supposed to happen. So I couldn't let it. I had to do everything I could to stop it. There had to be a way out of this mess.

But what, if anything, could be done? I didn't have any idea, but I knew I wasn't going down without a fight. After all, I was the leader of the Muckers, I started the club. I was responsible for getting us into this predicament. Now I had to get us out of it.

I looked back to see my friends dragging behind me. Blank faces. Boogie had the shakes. Shink stumbled into a tree. Moe tripped over his feet. I recalled reading stories about Great War soldiers who suffered combat's psychological effects.

I thought of the undead. I'd read about West African slaves who were brought in to work on Haiti's sugar cane plantations in the seventeenth century. The slaves longed for freedom and to escape their brutal conditions. The life—or rather, afterlife—of a zombie represented the horrific consequence of slavery.

But we weren't dead yet.

Remarkably, I felt calm and under control. I considered the options.

We could plead with our parents to intervene and talk to St. John. See if they could reason with him. Persuade him to give us another chance.

I wasn't sure what the Old Man would do, but begging him to bail me out wasn't appealing. He'd be disappointed and angry, having warned about permanently losing confidence in me if I continued to screw up. No way would I have it after this. He'd ignore me. He'd no longer ask for my opinions at dinner. If you can't handle your own affairs, he'd say, then I'm not interested in hearing your opinions about what's going on in the world.

Even worse, he might warn the rest of my brothers and sisters. *Don't be like Jack! He disgraced the family.*

Joe would have a field day. He'd get a kick out of sticking it to me. "You really mucked things up this time, Johnny boy!" I'd never hear the end of it from him.

And Bobby. He and I had been spending more time together recently. He looked up to me as his closest brother in age. After this, I'd be taken down a notch. He'd no longer ask me for advice, and he'd probably make excuses not to go sailing with me.

Kick? It wouldn't be the same between us. I'd no longer have a favorite sister because she'd keep her distance. Afraid she'd turn out like me. Well, she *had* warned me. Maybe I should have listened to my kid sister.

I'd lose the respect of the entire family.

Persona non grata—I didn't remember much from Latin class, but that's what I'd be in my own family. Unwelcome.

I'd go to the Old Man only as a last resort. But there had to be a better choice.

And suddenly it occurred to me, there was.

Sacrifice myself.

That was the answer. The simple solution. Give myself up. You can boot me out, but let the others stay.

It might prevent expulsion of the others. I'd take the blame and the fall. After all, the club was my idea from the beginning. I felt comfort and satisfaction that I'd come up with a way out. I smiled grimly.

Now, before I returned to the Head's office with my offer, I allowed myself to reflect on what the Muckers had meant to me. Because it was all going to be over in a few minutes and I'd be on my way back to New York.

Yeah, the Muckers had been a hell of a lot of fun, but the club stuff had also been rewarding.

Running the Muckers had given me confidence. When I spoke at our meetings, the guys listened. They looked to me for guidance on how to go forward. They had faith in me. I saw it in their eyes. Moe and Boogie and Shink and Rip and Smoky. And of course, Lem.

Before the Muckers, I wasn't a leader. Now I sensed that not only could I lead, but I might be good at it. What's more, I liked that others believed in me, valued my judgment, my leadership, and respected me.

But then I came back down to earth. The problem was I had guided everybody—all thirteen of us—into disaster. What kind of leadership was that? Well, I'd led us into this mess. By sacrificing myself, I could lead them out of it.

And sacrificing myself was the right thing to do. It was what I wanted to do. I didn't want them to go down with me. I'd finish school somewhere else, probably at Boston Latin, where the Old Man had gone. Then I'd attend college somewhere, unless he decided I wasn't worthy of a college education.

Of course, there was no guarantee I'd be successful if I gave myself up. There was the real possibility that St. John would reject my offer. Maybe he wanted us all out of here, and didn't care who was more responsible; if you were a Mucker, you were gone. Still, it was worth a try. I couldn't do nothing.

I'd apologize and take the blame. There was no other option. I had to give it my best shot. For the Muckers. Not for me.

I took one step and then slammed on the brakes.

Holy shit.

My friends kept going, passing me like they didn't see me. The undead.

Wait. Wait a goddamn minute. There might be another strategy. A weird, some would say crazy option. But the more I thought about it, the more I thought it was a reasonable option.

What about a strategy that was the opposite of action?

Play the waiting game. Delay. Defer. Postpone. As strange as it might seem, maybe the best tactic was to do absolutely nothing. How could it hurt?

See what the other side did when we made no move to leave.

Because maybe the ball wasn't in St. John's hands.

He'd given the ball to us.

Maybe he was waiting to see what we would do.

Maybe he didn't have enough proof to expel us. Heck, we weren't responsible at all for the toilet incident, and nothing we did had hurt anyone. I tried to get into the Head's head.

Could he be bluffing? He'd done it before.

If we left, all well and good. His problem was solved. He'd be rid of us. He'd have his school back. Wouldn't have to worry anymore about the Muckers wrecking Spring Festival. If he really believed we were going to bring havoc to the dance. Which I don't think he did. He'd been looking for an excuse to get rid of us. And he thought he'd found it. Even if it wasn't valid, or borne out by the facts.

He could say to anyone who asked that he gave us a choice and the boys thought it best to leave. We were troublemakers and weren't up to Choate standards. Better for everybody if we disappeared. Once we hauled our trunks aboard trains headed for New York, Massachusetts, Missouri, Pennsylvania, and wherever else, we'd never come back. We'd never know if he was bluffing. Or if we ever did, it would be too late.

But what if we didn't leave? Stayed put. Continued as though nothing had happened. As if we'd been given a choice, not an order. What then?

Because maybe the Head was testing us. Seeing if we'd take the easy way out and disappear. But I didn't want to take the easy way out.

Was I delirious? Gone nutso? Maybe I should stop by Archbold to see if I was crazy? "Hey, Doc, run some tests to check my sanity, will ya? I might be losing it." But I didn't think I was.

I needed to know if the Head was tricking us into leaving. If he wasn't, fine. I still had two options: sacrificing myself, or groveling before the Old Man. I didn't want to do either. Right now, I didn't need to.

What I did need to do was to make sure nobody packed up and left.

I did an about-face, ran past our bedraggled group, and stopped at the steps of Hill House.

Jumping to the second stair ahead of everybody else, I turned to face everybody. I put my hands up.

"Guys, hold on a moment. We aren't done yet."

"Jack, we're finished," Rip said.

"Rip, you may be right." I gave him an understanding nod. "But it can't hurt to see if there's some way of getting out of this mess. I've got some ideas. You want to hear them, don't ya?"

The Muckers looked at each other. Nobody knew what to do.

"Lem," I said, "let's get everybody up to our room." His eyes were vacant, as if he hadn't heard me. "LeMoan!" That woke him up.

"Uh, yeah, okay," Lem said. "Let's go, guys. Can't hurt to listen, right?"

CHAPTER THIRTY-FOUR

We gathered in Room 215. Would it be the last time? I looked out over the sorriest bunch of Muckers I'd ever seen. Shink huddled in the corner. Moe leaned his head on Boogie's shoulder for support. Butch sobbed, then wailed, "What am I going to do?" Rip sat on my bed, head in his hands. Lem slumped, standing next to me.

"I think we need to look at the situation carefully," I said.

"The situation is we've been kicked out of school, Jack," Boogie said. "Are you hard of hearing? The Head told us we've been expelled."

"Maybe I am hard of hearing, Boogie. I'll have it checked as soon as possible. But did he actually say we were expelled? I'm not so sure he did."

I had everybody's attention. "He did say the word *expulsion*. But," I said, pointing my finger at the Muckers, "he didn't say we, us, all of you, were expelled. He said the punishment for the offenses was expulsion. He said he *intended* to expel us. Not that we were expelled. There's a big difference. That's like saying to some guy who's charged with murder that the penalty is thirty years in prison. It is. But the problem is the guy didn't do it. Never convicted. Like us. We were never going to bring the muck to the dance, so how are we guilty? Why should we pay the price for something we didn't do?"

"Jack, you're off your rocker," Boogie said, shaking his head. "We're goners."

"Not yet," I said. "Hear me out. There's even more evidence he might be bluffing. He *recommended* we pack our trunks," I continued. "Didn't order us to do it. Big difference. I have my own recommendation. That we don't. Never liked packing anyway. All the folding, etc."

"You know what he meant, Jack," Moe said.

"I'm not sure I do," I continued, tilting my head back. "I clearly remember the Head saying he *expected* us to leave in due time. *Due time.* What the hell does that mean? A month from now? After we graduate?"

"Jack," Rip said, "you got another fever or something? Lost your mind?"

"Wait a minute," Smoky said. "Maybe Jack's onto something."

I gave Smoky a look of appreciation. I had an ally. One was a start. "Maybe I am, maybe I'm not. I don't know myself. But let me continue. The Head said there was a train leaving in the afternoon. *Suggested*—that was the word he used. *Suggested* we be on it. Well, I have a suggestion for all of you. I suggest we don't get on that train."

I stood tall, my body and feet pointing forward. "It's a bluff, guys. St. John's bluffing."

"I don't know," Moe said. "Didn't sound like a bluff to me."

"Maybe," I said. "But maybe we should go not on what it sounded like but more on what the Head actually said. Take him at his word. Literally. He's the one who used *intend, recommend, suggest.* Or look at it another way. Why didn't he say, 'All of you are expelled. Go to your room and pack up. Take the four p.m. train?' He didn't say any of those things, did he? I could be wrong, but it can't hurt to find out, can it? Remember, he has a history of bluffing, of trying to scare us. That's what he did last year when he said a bunch of muckers were shaming the school. Said if he could figure out who they were, he'd get rid of them. Never did identify them, did he? And the jeweler said he pulled the same thing on his class. A bluff. A scare tactic. Now he finds some flimsy reason he hopes will send us on our way." I paused. "I asked this question once in front of the Head, and I'll ask it again: Will you raise your hand if we were ever going to haul shit to the Spring Festival?"

No hands.

"Why should we be run out of town for something we were never going to do? Like confessing to a crime you didn't commit. By running away, we'd be admitting our guilt. And we are not guilty."

"But—" Moe said.

"I say the first thing we do," I said, holding my finger in the air, "is nothing."

My twelve friends stared at me like I'd lost my mind.

"Nothing?" Boogie said. "How can we do nothing?"

"Easy. We continue like nothing happened. Go on about our business. Go to class. Well, probably not. Maybe best to hang out in your room. If he's going to follow through, he'll have Maher and Butter come get us. Do his dirty work. But I don't think he will. My guess is the Head is a man of words, not action. And as we know, actions speak louder than words."

I was going to say we could always barricade ourselves in our rooms. Fight them off. *Remember the Muckers!* would be our battle cry. But I didn't. Bad time for a joke.

I saw plenty of grim smiles. "St. John is expecting us to leave quietly. Then he can say, 'They left on their own. Realized they weren't up to Choate's standards.' Wouldn't that be a slap in the ass? You get home and a week later you find out you didn't need to leave. Too late to come back at that point." I pointed at Shink. "I don't think Shink is going to go all the way back to St. Louis and then return to school. How would it feel knowing you'd been played by St. John?"

I let that sink in.

"But what it comes down to is this." I pointed a finger. "We haven't done anything wrong. We beat our gums. Mouthed off in what was supposed to be a private conversation. Freedom of Speech. It's in the Constitution. But we were never going to do it, and we all know it. So I'm not leaving. At least not yet."

The Muckers sighed, grumbled, swore, and shifted their bodies, not certain what to do. Butch walked in a circle. Moe bit his nails. Smoky threw a pencil against the wall.

"That's my suggestion, but if you want to pack up and leave, then go ahead. I'm not. What have you got to lose by waiting? See how it plays out?"

"Okay, but what if Maher knocks on our door?" Butch said. "Tells us to pack up? What then?"

I held up both my hands. "Stall him. Pretend to pack. Inform him the train doesn't come for several hours. Whatever you do, don't say *my* train because I don't think it will be. And don't say you're going to be on it."

I needed to inject another dose of optimism. "In the meantime, I know some people who might be able to help. We have allies."

"We do? Really?" Shink said.

His slight hopefulness was becoming contagious. I noticed glimmers of optimism from several Muckers. Boogie perked up, his gloom at least momentarily gone. Moe stood up straighter.

"Really," I said. "And if that doesn't work, we'll try something else." Important to keep everybody's spirits up.

"Like what?" Butch asked.

"For now, my plan has to be kept secret for it to succeed. You'll have to trust me."

But I hadn't convinced everybody. A few guys didn't see any hope, and they were going to pack. They said their goodbyes. "Pack slowly," I said to them.

Boogie lagged behind. "Jack, it's all my fault." His hands trembled, and he stared at his feet.

"Your fault? No, we're all in this together."

Boogie looked up but averted my eyes. "I'm the one to blame for all this. I told my roommate about us hauling crap to the dance." His roommate was on the Student Council.

"Did you tell him it was all a joke, that we were just mouthing off."

"I did."

"And he still went straight to the Head? Even though he knew that?"

"Yeah."

"What a bastard!"

"Yeah, but if I hadn't blabbed, this never would have happened."

I didn't want Boogie carrying the entire burden of our dismissal. Having that on your conscience could wreck a person's life. "Well, I don't know about that. I take responsibility. I should have told everybody that what's discussed at our meetings stays in the room. I didn't."

"Yeah, but—"

"Don't worry about it, Boogie. I have a feeling this matter will sort itself out." I patted him on the back and led him to the door. He gave me a distant stare before heading down the corridor.

The more I thought about it, the more I doubted the Head would go through with kicking us out.

One reason was there were too many of us. Expel thirteen students and the story would hit the Wallingford newspaper— I'd see to it. "Thirteen Choate Students Expelled for Idle Chatter."

Most of all, the school would lose money. Parents of expelled students would want their money back. Quite a scandal. A big stink.

Also, if he expelled me, he could say goodbye to the Old Man's financial support forever. Dad had arranged and paid for the installation of the school's film projection system, not to mention all the money spent for Joe and me to attend Choate. If I was booted out, there'd be no chance that Bobby and Teddy would follow in our footsteps.

Lem and I looked at each other. "Is this the end, Jack? What a way to go." I was surprised that Lem doubted my ability to lead us out of this fiasco.

"We'll see about that."

"It doesn't look good."

I forced a smile. "You didn't need to be here. You were supposed to have graduated last year. But you stayed another year. Now you think you might be thrown out of here. You'll have lost your chance to go to Princeton. Having second thoughts about your decision now?"

"No," he said, teary-eyed. "I don't. I guess I'm crazy, but I had a helluva time, Jack."

"You can say that again."

Lem laughed sadly. "No, once was enough." He had no regrets about staying an extra year even if it cost him a chance to go to Princeton. Remarkable.

Lem went to his closet and got out his trunk. "Best to be prepared."

"Moines, I'll let you do what you need to do. Got a rendezvous." I looked at my watch. Meeting with my allies. At least, I hoped they were allies.

"Rendezvous?" he said, scratching his jaw.

"Yeah. I'll stay out of your way. See you in a bit. In the meantime, do me a favor?" I didn't wait for his response. "Don't leave without saying goodbye. Promise?"

Lem nodded glumly.

"Good. Since you promised you wouldn't leave without saying goodbye, you can't leave if you don't see me."

"You got me, Jack," he said, shaking his head, realizing my wordplay had trapped him.

I hustled to the interception point. I had five minutes. Timing. It was all about timing.

On cue, Queenie and Mrs. St. John came walking up the path. Did they know what had happened? I would have thought St. John might have told his wife he was expelling thirteen senior boys. An important part of the school, she was active in all aspects. But when Mrs. St. John said, "Jack, what are you doing wandering around? You should be in class," I had my answer.

"I'd like to be," I said, "but there's a problem." I explained how we'd joked about dumping manure at the Spring Festival dance.

Mrs. St. John crossed her arms. "That's disappointing, Jack."

"Believe me, Mrs. St. John, we were never going to do it. Not in a million years. But the word got out, and somebody told the headmaster."

"Oh?" She touched her throat. "He never mentioned it to me."

Maybe that was a good sign. Maybe the expulsion wasn't going to happen. Otherwise, he would have told his wife. Or perhaps he was afraid to tell her because he knew he'd have a fight on his hands. Mrs. St. John was well-respected, and many of the Muckers, like me, had expressed our appreciation for her. But I'd appreciate her a lot more if she'd help us now.

"We just came from a meeting with him," I said. "He said the thirteen of us should leave Choate. Permanently."

"Expelled?" she gasped, clasping her hand to her heart. "He said that?"

"Yes. Made us all come to his office."

Mrs. St. John stomped her foot. "For letting off a little steam? I don't know what's gotten into George. I realize you and the headmaster have had your differences, but to send thirteen senior boys on their way for joking around is going way too far."

"It's just not right," said Queenie, chiming in.

I added my final points. "The headmaster also blamed us for blowing up a school toilet, but we had nothing to do with that. We may bend rules when we can, but we wouldn't destroy school property." I also brought up my father and how he'd talked about contributing beyond his donation of the movie projection equipment, but I suggested he'd probably reconsider. And I said he had high hopes that Bobby and Teddy would also attend Choate. If the expulsion went through, he'd probably send them to another school. Probably none of the other parents of the Muckers would send any of their younger children to Choate either. The school stood to lose a lot of money.

Mrs. St. John nodded and pursed her lips. "He can be so impulsive sometimes." She threw up her hands. "What am I going to do with that man?"

I had a few suggestions but I held my tongue. Heartened by her sympathetic response, I said, "If there's anything you could do on our behalf…"

"Jack, I'm going to have a talk with that husband of mine."

"And I'll do the same with mine," Queenie said.

"C'mon, Queenie." She grabbed her arm. "No time to waste," she said, striding to the headmaster's office.

Would the combined efforts of Mrs. St. John and Queenie be enough to change the Head's mind? After four years at the school, I knew him to be stubborn and inflexible, but I liked our chances.

I spied Mr. Tinker in the quad. He was headed toward the administration office. I cut him off and briefed him on the situation. "The headmaster told us to pack our trunks and take the afternoon train home. Mr. Tinker, I ask you: Is that justice?"

Mr. Tinker smiled warmly, acknowledging the assignment he'd given us on that topic. "Jack, it seems you're taking what you learn at school and applying it to your life."

I nodded.

"Now back to the matter at hand," he said. "The headmaster. What's the matter with him?" He shook his head. "Has he forgotten he was a boy at one time? Probably did something like that when he was your age. We all did. Jack, I'll talk to a few other masters. Strength in numbers. We'll do our best to appeal to his common sense."

After Mr. Tinker walked away, I considered what to do next. If Mrs. St. John, Queenie, and Mr. Tinker weren't successful in their appeals, I had to go to my other options. Sacrifice myself. If that didn't work, plead with the Old Man to intervene, though that was the last thing I wanted to do.

For the moment, there was nothing more I could do. Maybe it was better for everybody if I slipped away for a short time. Might exacerbate the situation if others knew who I'd ask to intervene on our behalf. But I didn't want to go back to my room.

Suddenly, I craved a chocolate marshmallow ice cream sundae. If I was leaving Choate for good, why not one more sundae? And if I wasn't, then savoring one more would be a great way to mark the occasion. Couldn't lose. It was against school rules to leave campus during school hours, but that's only if you were a student. I wasn't sure I was.

Butter confronted me at the school exit. That guy was everywhere. "Hey, Kennedy, where do you think you're going?"

"Moran's for a sundae. Want to come?"

"You know you can't leave school during the day. Turn around and get back to class."

Butter didn't know, but that wasn't surprising.

"But that rule is for students. Now, if you'll excuse me." I brushed past the dumbfounded cop.

Mostly older women populated Moran's, many of them enjoying a sweet before their children and husbands came home for dinner. I sat at the counter.

"Shouldn't you be in school?" the waitress asked.

"I agree with you, but the headmaster recommended that I not be in school." The waitress was confused. "You can ask him yourself. But for now, can you throw on an extra dollop of whipped cream please? It's been a tough day."

The waitress stared at me a few seconds, then scooped an extra-large portion.

I finished my sundae, told the waitress, "Thanks, I needed that," and wandered around town. Was this the last time I'd see

Wallingford? I preferred to say goodbye in a couple more months. It was funny—I'd been impatient to get out of Choate, but now I was desperate to stay.

As I headed back to campus. I checked my watch. One hour since I'd left school.

As I neared The West Wing, I saw Mr. Tinker. He walked toward me. I focused on his face. Was he smiling? Frowning? Glaring? That would give me a hint on the outcome of his meeting.

I was prepared if Mr. Tinker was going to tell me we'd been expelled. That's when I'd immediately march into St. John's office and sacrifice myself. Fall on the sword.

And if that didn't work, I'd say my father, the chairman of the Securities and Exchange Commission in President Roosevelt's administration and a friend of the President, would be in touch to see if there's something that could be done so thirteen students didn't leave school prematurely. If St. John still wouldn't budge, perhaps I'd say President Roosevelt himself would be giving him a jangle.

I didn't want to get my father involved, but if I had to, I would. And if I knew my father, he'd be outraged that St. John had ordered the expulsion. He'd let the Head have it. But I wouldn't come out unscathed.

Mr. Tinker's expression was blank.

"Jack, I've got something to tell you."

"Yes?" I held my breath.

Mr. Tinker broke into a limited smile. "I'll be brief. The expulsions have been rescinded. You can unpack your trunk."

I exhaled. "Shouldn't take long. What happened?"

"I told a few other masters, and we arranged a meeting with the headmaster. We didn't think your conversation, although inappropriate, deserved expulsion. Mrs. St. John also had a firm talk with him. We brought him to his senses."

"That's great."

"One more thing. Disband the Muckers. That is, if you want to stay in school."

"That's fine."

"Let the others know."

I charged up the stairs and barged into the room. Lem was fastening the clasp on his trunk.

"Lem, can you do me a favor before you leave?"

"What?"

"Would you mind taking your clothes out of your trunk and putting them back where they were?"

"But—"

"The Head backed down. Mr. Tinker told me. Nobody's expelled."

"No joke?"

"No joke."

Lem and I spread the word to the remaining Muckers. Everyone in our corridor was greatly relieved—with one exception.

"Kennedy, you and your gang got lucky this time," Maher said as I was about to enter my room later that day. "But if there's another incident or provocation, I assure you there will be no chance of reinstatement. Absolutely none."

"As it should be, Mr. Maher." *The Prick.*

CHAPTER THIRTY-FIVE

The guys grilled me at the pre-chapel meeting that night, eager to find out how our dismissal had been averted. Felt like a press conference.

"How'd you do it, Jack?" Boogie asked. "Thought we were done for."

"Did your old man pay him off?" Moe asked.

"No, but I sweet-talked Mrs. St. John and Queenie, and a few masters had a good old talk with the Head. Got him to change his mind. Convinced him the Muckers were a credit to the school." I cackled.

I looked out over the Muckers, or former Muckers. "However, the Muckers are disbanded. Effective immediately. The Muckers are history." I paused. "But I imagine we'll still raise a little hell." The ex-Muckers cheered.

When the guys left, I had at least one other thing on my mind. Should I continue on my own, with the plan to borrow and mark up the Choate applications? I didn't like the idea of not following through. We'd dodged a bullet, so there'd be no way I'd involve any of the former Muckers in the caper. That included the guy who'd volunteered his services after A. J. had been canned.

No, if I was going to do it, I'd go it alone.

I weighed the risks against my chances of success. I'd have to break in late at night without the benefit of a lookout. I'd grab a bunch of applications and return to my room. If Maher caught me, I'd be done. But if I was able to slip into my room without being noticed, I'd alter the applications with Lem. He'd probably help me cross off *Hebraic* and write in Mucker even if I tried to keep him from getting involved.

Another option was to bring a flashlight and take the applications to the subterranean passage and mark them up there, while hoping I wouldn't run into a master or a Campus Cop.

Another possibility was to mark them up right there in the office. Probably the best choice. In and out. Wouldn't take more than an hour to do a hundred. Risk versus reward. If I was going to do it, that was the best option.

Or so it seemed until I had the chance to think more about it.

CHAPTER THIRTY-SIX

Although St. John had rescinded his 'intended" dismissal of the Muckers, he didn't want any more trouble from us, so he dispatched telegrams to Dad at his address in both New York and Washington. Dad called and tersely told me of St. John's telegram message: It was vital that "he make every possible effort to come to Choate Saturday or Sunday for an essential conference with Jack."

The Old Man wasn't happy about having to change his plans. The family was planning to gather for the weekend in New York. Both Dad and I would be missing.

Lem's mother had also been summoned to meet with St. John. "Don't understand why he'd have my mother spend money she doesn't have to come all the way from Pittsburgh," Lem complained.

Lem and I crossed Christian Street on our way to classes at Paul Mellon Science Hall. A white Chevy, emblazoned with *Choate School* and the school insignia, slowed down to let us pass.

"He probably said something like, 'If you are unable to meet with me regarding your son's behavior, I may have to make a very difficult choice,' I said. "You know, threaten but not really mean it."

"That sounds like something he'd do," Lem said.

"Quite a hardship on your mother. Dad's coming this weekend."

The next day, I rang up Kick.

"Jack, how are you?"

"Good, Kick." I hesitated. "Overall." I told her about the Muckers and our war with the headmaster. "St. John demanded that Dad come down. The three of us are meeting Sunday."

"Wow. Must be important. Wouldn't want to be in your shoes right now." She promised to send a telegram before the meeting to buck me up.

"Looking forward to it, Kick."

———◆———

Lem pretended to read at his desk, but I felt his eyes on me as I paced the room. I was nervous about my meeting with Dad and the Head. The Old Man would be here any moment. The Head had brought in the Old Man to pressure me to fall in line for the remainder of the school year. I anticipated they'd grill, threaten, and humiliate me. Irritated at having to make a special trip, the Old Man would be on edge. Pressure from both sides. My gut already ached from what would be the big squeeze.

I was disappointed I hadn't received Kick's pre-meeting telegram. And it was strange, too. She always kept her promises. And I needed all the reassurance I could get.

"Let's see what this is all about," Dad said briskly as we walked up the steps to meet with St. John. "He sent me a cable saying there's a crisis in your life here at Wallingford and to come at once."

He halted before we entered the office.

"Jack, this better be worth my time to come here on a weekend and cancel family plans. He's a Republican like most of the students and people at Choate, and he doesn't like us Democrats. Maybe he doesn't like us Irish-Catholics all that much either. If you don't know, Jack, that's one reason I sent you and

Joseph here. Your mother preferred you continue at Canterbury. Get a good Catholic school education. But I thought it better for you to mix it up with the Protestants. Help you make it in the world. Break out of your own group."

Dad put a hand on my shoulder. "Jack, we won't take any shit from him."

I breathed a sigh of relief. Maybe the Old Man would have my back after all.

We sat at a circular table in St. John's office. After thanking Dad for coming, St. John said the school's objective was to "save a boy's soul at the same time we are saving his Algebra."

"Well, I'd suggest you focus more on the Algebra than the other," Dad said. He wasn't as pious as Mother.

"Be that as it may, I have two things to do. One is to run the school, and another has been to run Jack and his friends." Then he went through our illicit activities. I'd heard it all before, of course. The illegal Muckers club, the Muckers' pin and our disruptive behavior. But Dad didn't seem upset. That was a good sign. "When I was informed of a plan by Jack's group to haul manure to the dance at our Spring Festival, I was forced to act."

"Is that right, Jack?" Dad asked. "Is that something you and your friends were going to do? Bring a load of crap to the dance and spread it on the floor? That doesn't sound like you."

"No," I said. My nostrils flared. "One guy threw it out as a humorous suggestion. A couple of guys joked about it. But we weren't going to do a stupid thing like that. Why ruin the dance for everybody else, including ourselves? Can't dance on manure."

"Don't think you can either," Dad said, his gaze wandering. "Anyway, boys will be boys, won't they?" Dad smiled grimly.

"Blowing off steam, that's all. And like Jack said, they never were going to shovel crap to the dance. I believe him too."

St. John frowned. "Even to suggest such a thing—"

"A big to-do about nothing," Dad interrupted.

"Nevertheless, I can't take threats to the school lightly."

"Hardly a threat, to my mind," Dad said.

The Old Man was going toe-to-toe with St. John.

For the next few minutes, my father and St. John talked about my schoolwork.

Then the phone on St. John's desk began to ring.

He didn't move. It rang again. St. John squirmed in his seat, weighing the etiquette of interrupting an urgent meeting with the SEC chairman and his son. But the phone might ring a dozen more times before the caller gave up. My father tapped his fingers on the table.

What would St. John do? After the third double ring, he held his hands outward in apology and got up. He went to his desk and picked up the phone. "Yes?" he said. Turning to my father, he said, "Will you excuse me for a moment?"

Dad gave the headmaster a hard stare.

When St. John left the room, Dad's face reddened. "He should have told whoever was calling that he'd call them back. I suppose the Chairman of the Securities and Exchange Commission and his son can cool their heels for a few minutes while the esteemed Headmaster of Choate talks with his wife about table decorations. Or whatever it is that's more important than us. He better be goddamn quick."

I nodded.

"I'm not sure why he thought it important for me to come down here, but if he has a notion to expel you—"

"He won't. That's over."

"Good. Because so far, this has been a whole lot about nothing." He paused, then whispered, "My God, you sure didn't inherit your father's reputation for using bad language. If that crazy Mucker's Club had been mine, you can be sure it wouldn't have started with an M!"

I thought of my rhyme using the word he was alluding to. Like father, like son. Our eyes met. For a second, I saw my father as a young man about my age. Fun-loving, rowdy, and a cusser.

The Old Man and I were thinking along the same lines. He would have named the club using the same word I'd used in the ditty I'd read to the Muckers. Perhaps more significantly, was he saying he respected me for starting the club? For taking on St. John?

St. John returned. "Pardon the interruption. Very important matter that—"

"I'm sure it was," Dad cut in. "Don't think we have much more to talk about. Jack and I have discussed these, uh, trivial matters. I don't anticipate any additional problems, nor does Jack. He's already disbanded his club."

He paused and drummed his fingers on the table. "Now," Dad said, "there's something I'm going to ask of you. I've paid a lot of money for Joe and Jack to attend your school. I want to make sure I get the most bang for my buck. So I want your assurance that Jack has all the resources he needs to be successful in his final couple of months here. I'll be checking in to make sure that happens. Any problem with that?"

St. John's face reddened. The tables had turned. Now St. John was under the gun.

"Uh, well, uh, you can, uh, be sure, uh, he will," the Head stammered.

"Good."

My father stood up. "Now I want to have lunch with Jack before going back to Washington."

St. John extended a weak hand. "Thank you for taking time out of your busy schedule, Mr. Kennedy. I hope it's been beneficial."

"We'll see if it has. Now we're off to Pepe's Pizzeria in New Haven. Jack says it's the best pizza around. Oh, one more thing. I've heard the movie nights have been a great success."

"Yes, they have. The boys quite enjoy it."

"Good. Let's keep it that way. Would be a shame for that to end."

St. John sagged like a wet doll.

As we walked outside, Dad's mood darkened. "I think we have an understanding with St. John. He's going to give you all the help you need. To suggest removing you from school because of a bullshitting session you guys had... Well, that's absolute bullshit!" he said loudly.

"It certainly is," I said.

He halted and pointed his finger at me. "But you have to do your part, Jack. I realize Choate has been difficult for you in some ways. Your marks haven't been the best. Mine weren't the best at Boston Latin. Mediocre, actually. Much like yours."

"Really?" I always assumed Dad was at the top of his class.

"But I excelled once I got to Harvard. I got down to business. That's what I'm expecting of you."

I nodded.

"You could do much better. Agreed?"

"Yes."

He faced me and put his hands on my shoulders. I used to look up at him. Now we were the same height. "Jack, I want you to promise me you'll buckle down. You won't pursue any more nonsense. Do your schoolwork. No more mischief."

"I'll do my best."

"Oh, I also wanted to find out how it's going with Lecky? Have you been getting something out of your sessions with him? I don't want details. That's between you and him. I just want to hear from you whether you're finding it worthwhile. You know I don't like throwing money away."

"It's going well," I said, glad he didn't want to know what we'd talked about.

"Good. Because Roosevelt is putting a lot of pressure on me to help get this country turned around. We're still in terrible shape. I can't be coming down here again to deal with your problems."

"Okay."

"And when you graduate, you'll go to Harvard. I'm sure you'll be successful there. I was, and Joe is not only doing great work there, but having a fine time. You will also."

"Yes, well, I'm considering Princeton. Just because Harvard is good for Joe doesn't mean it's the right school for me." I was laying the groundwork for applying to Princeton. I preferred to be with Lem and Rip than with Joe.

Dad stared at me. "I suppose that's true. But I think Harvard is still the better choice."

"Let's get that pizza," I said. "Pepe's waiting for us."

Dad laughed. "I'm sure he is."

Chapter Thirty-Seven

As we strolled the Montclair, New Jersey shopping district, I began filling Olive in on the tumultuous events of the last few weeks.

"Jack, you've sure been busy. Quite the wild one with your Muckers gang. Almost ended in you getting kicked out. I do hope you'll grow up someday. Preferably soon. You'll be eighteen in May. Graduating the month after that."

"I think I am growing up. Learned a lot from the experience."

"Well, that's good. Any plans after you graduate?"

I frowned, thinking about the decision I'd have to make soon—whether I'd go against Dad's wishes. "The Old Man wants me to go to Harvard, but I might join Lem and Rip at Princeton. To be decided. What about you? Anything in the works?"

Olive smiled broadly. "I've got an appointment with the John Robert Powers Agency. It's a modeling school, and if they like you, they'll represent you in Hollywood. I want to be a model or an actress."

"That's fantastic, Olive."

"Your father has something to do with the movie business, doesn't he, Jack?"

"*Had*. He gave it up a while ago, but he did produce several movies, including a couple with Gloria Swanson."

"Maybe he still has some connections. Perhaps he could introduce me to a few of the right people."

"He's been out of the business for a while, but I'll ask him."

Olive stopped and put her hand on my chest. "But that's not something I want to do forever. Or for long. I'd like to find a man with means, a successful man. Then have a big family. Do you like big families, Jack?"

"I come from a big family, although Mom and Dad didn't consult with me about having another seven Kennedys after me." Was Olive gauging my long-term interest in her? My family had money, but I wasn't yet interested in marrying and having kids. In fact, I really didn't know what I wanted to do with my life.

———»•«———

When I got back to Choate, I called Kick to tell her about the sit-down with Dad and the Head.

Initially, her voice was flat.

"It went fine," I said. "But are you all right?"

"No. Daddy isn't happy with me." The Old Man had come down hard on her for sending me the cable before the meeting with St. John. "He wrote saying he doesn't think there was anything smart about it, and he hopes it won't be the cause of having you expelled from school. Oh, Jack, I'm sorry."

I squeezed the receiver. "How would Dad know that you sent me that cable? I only got it today. The meeting was last week."

I had the telegram with me. "All our prayers are united with you and the twelve other Muckers," it read.

"Really?" Kick said. "I sent it the day after we last talked."

I clenched my fist. I knew immediately what had happened. St. John had intercepted Kick's telegram and informed Dad of the contents. Then Dad gave Kick a kick in the pants. A week after our summit meeting, St. John finally put the cable in my box.

Intercepting correspondence from my sister. Or anybody. What gave St. John the right? Damn him.

After I hung up with Kick, I had an intense desire to get away from school. And I'd only been back a few minutes. I enlisted Lem to join me for a drive in the country.

I drove the station wagon Dad had lent me for the final months of school. Lem held tightly to his door handle.

I waved to people walking on the side of the road.

"Oh no!" I yelped, hearing the wail of a siren. The speck in my mirror was a police car.

"Now you've done it, Ken," Lem said. "Say goodbye to your license."

"We'll see about that," I said, easing off the gas.

If I didn't want to lose my license, I had to think fast. How to plead my case? "Mechanic told me to blow it out on the open road. Good for the carburetor." Or, "It's the Old Man's fault. Said he was going to fix the speedometer."

No, I needed something better. Those fabrications hadn't worked last time. I'd gotten written up. Why should they work this time?

The police car was quickly closing the gap. Had its Christmas lights on.

"Lem," I said, "you wouldn't mind taking one for old Kenadosus, would you? You owe me if my memory is correct."

I had a habit of pushing Lem to the limit. Once, I'd offered him a hundred dollars if he'd take off all his clothes and walk in on the Old Man, who sometimes liked to work in the nude. I also requested he belt out "I'm No Angel" from the Mae West movie. For a minute, I was sure Lem was going to do that. But he decided against it. To his credit.

"I owe you? For what?" Lem said, waving his hand.

"I don't know. I'll think of something."

"You got it ass backwards," Lem said. "If we're keeping count, you owe *me*."

"We'll sort that out later. Right now, we have to move quickly. Trade seats with me. When the cop pulls us over, you'll be in the driver's seat."

Lem looked at me like I belonged in an insane asylum. "How are we going to do that without stopping?" he asked.

"I'll slide under you while you climb over. Move!"

Using the steering wheel for support and to keep us on the road, Lem lifted himself over me. I slithered beneath him.

"Don't sit on my face, you big ape," I said.

"I'd like to," Lem retorted. "Turn you from Ratface to Flatface."

Our car swerved to the left, then to the right as we switched places. "Don't run us off the road," I said. "My father would not be pleased if you crashed his car."

"Damn you. Doing my best."

Lem righted the car after finally collapsing into the driver's seat.

Only a couple of hundred yards separated us from the police cruiser.

"What should I say?" Lem said, pulling the car to the side of the road.

"Don't worry. I'll take care of it. Even if it was your fault."

"My fault?" Lem lifted a single eyebrow. "You were driving."

"Well, your job was to make sure I didn't exceed the speed limit. You failed in that regard, LeMoan, so you'll have to take the fall. Because I'm a nice guy, I'll pay your ticket. But don't let it happen again."

"Mighty big of you," he said as the policeman approached the car.

"Next time you're on your own." He folded his arms over his stomach. "I can't keep covering for your mistakes."

"Afternoon," the policeman said.

Out of the corner of my eye, I saw it was the same cop who'd cited me last time. Small town. Not surprising.

"License and registration please."

Lem pulled out his driver's license while I dug out the registration. I stared straight ahead, hoping the cop wouldn't recognize me.

"Kennedy?" he said, looking at the registration. "I remember you. Caught you speeding a couple of weeks ago. See you've learned your lesson. Handed over the speed—I mean driving responsibilities—to your buddy here. Unfortunately, it seems he's adopted your bad habits."

"Former habits, sir. LeMoyne should know better."

The policeman stared at me and then Lem. "Strange."

"What's strange, sir?" I asked.

Stroking his chin, he said, "I could swear the driver was smaller."

"He tends to slump down when he's driving," I said. "Terrible posture, right, LeMoyne?"

"I guess," Lem mumbled.

"One more question, Kennedy. Did you authorize him to drive your car?"

"Yes, I did. I had complete faith in LeMoyne's ability to drive safely. Apparently, I was wrong."

"All right, sonny," he said to Lem, "I'm going to cite you for driving over the speed limit." He began writing out the ticket.

Lem slumped and stared at his lap.

"I trust this won't happen again," he said, handing Lem the citation.

"No," Lem said, staring coldly at me. "I assure you it won't."

Lem was still in a sour mood when we got back to school, so I wandered over to the Choate stables. Blambo was doing his best to stay mounted on his bucking horse, which seemed intent on throwing him off.

"What's the matter with this no-good horse?" Blambo yelped.

"Stay with it, Blambo!" I shouted, but the horse had had enough. He threw Blambo off and ran away. Blambo and I chased the horse for several minutes before corralling him.

"Blambo, I'm sorry you feel the need to blame the horse for your terrible horse-riding skills. Stick to riding the gentle horses at the Coney Island carousel. Much safer."

"Thanks, Jack."

"Fortunately, there's a football game going on now. Let's get in on the action."

We played for several hours until it was time for dinner.

I wasn't in the frame of mind to get cleaned up. Problem was, Sunday evening meals at Choate were formal occasions. Suits required. My pants were torn, my jacket muddy, and my hair coated with sweat, though I did manage to wipe some of the dirt from my forehead.

When I arrived at the dining hall, the very strict Mr. Shute, head of the Math Department, was at the door, standing between me and my table. "Jack," he said, seemingly intent on keeping me from eating, "explain yourself. You're required to look your best for Sunday dinner. You're a disgrace."

Breathing hard, I said earnestly, "Well, you see, sir, Blambo—I mean Ed Bland's horse threw him and ran away, and we had a heck of a time catching him. He ran us all over the grounds. He might have escaped to another school if we hadn't caught him." Of course, that was hours ago, but old Shute didn't know that. "I was only trying to help out a classmate. If I hadn't gone to Ed's aid, that horse might still be on the loose."

Shute gave me the stare-down. I didn't blink.

Shute blinked first. "All right," he said, waving me inside.

CHAPTER THIRTY-EIGHT

Spring 1935

I had been laying low since the expulsion debacle, studying more, and trying to avoid Maher and the Head.

Lem and I went to a screening of *Beau Geste* at school and sat at the back.

The movie was about three orphaned brothers who join the French Foreign Legion and find themselves in the Sahara fighting Arabs. The Legion was unique in that it was open to foreign recruits willing to serve in the French Army.

"The French Foreign Legion," I said as we walked back to our room, "looked exciting, didn't it, Lemmer?"

"What part?"

"Traveling the world. Fighting for good causes." I pictured myself in a unit liberating a village, the people showering us with bouquets of flowers. Pretty girls blowing us kisses. "Those brothers had an interesting time."

Lem shrugged. "A couple of them got killed."

"Only a movie," I said.

"Still."

I'll admit I was impressed with their uniforms—the dark blue overcoat and white kepi cap. "Sharp outfits too." I halted. "Hold on now, Lem. Got my best idea ever. Why don't we join the Foreign Legion after we're done here? That would be something we'd never forget." I wanted excitement after I got out of Choate. Maybe I'd put off college for a year or two. See the world.

"If we lived through it," Lem deadpanned.

"You might be interested to know that one of my favorite poets, Alan Seeger, joined the Legion. I'm sure it was quite an education for him—one that you wouldn't get in college. Joe took a year off to travel around Europe before going to Harvard. He enjoyed it. We ought to do something adventurous. Let's write to them. See what they say."

"Okay," Lem said, rubbing the back of his neck. "I guess it can't hurt to find out what the Legion is all about." He held up a finger. "But no promises."

I paced the room, organized my thoughts, and felt ready to dictate a letter to the Legion.

"Should we say we enjoyed *Beau Geste?*" Lem asked.

"No. Don't think telling them we saw a movie about the Foreign Legion would help. Like I said, it's only a movie."

A half hour later, we had a letter. "Okay, Lemmer, let's hear what we've got."

Dear French Foreign Legion Commander,

My name is John Fitzgerald Kennedy. It has come to my attention that you seek young men like us (my friend Kirk LeMoyne Billings also wants to join) to assist you in your efforts to make the world a better place. I can tell you we are for that and are willing to go anywhere you want to send us.

You may be interested to know that I have read many books about history, including Winston Churchill's The World Crisis. *I highly recommend it. I'm sure you agree we must do all we can do to avoid another world war.*

Let me tell you more about us. Kirk and I attend the Choate School in Wallingford, Connecticut. That's near New York City. For the most part, it is a good school. We will be graduating in a couple of months and are in great physical snape. Both of us have performed admirably for various Choate athletic teams.

If we have a choice, it is our wish to serve in the French Foreign Legion's navy, if you have one. I am an accomplished sailor and have had my own sailboat since I was very young. Kirk is a good sailor in his own right.

Since school is ending in a couple of months, it might be better to send the application materials to us at 151 Irving Avenue, Hyannis Port, Massachusetts. That's where we'll be this summer. Kirk and I look forward to hearing from you. It would be an honor to serve in the French Foreign Legion.

Viva la France!

Sincerely,

John Fitzgerald Kennedy
Kirk LeMoyne Billings

"Good work," I said, taking the letter. "I'll drop it off myself at the school office first thing tomorrow. Who knows? In a few months, we might be on a fighting ship off the coast of Africa!"

"Great. I think," Lem said, unenthusiastically.

At lunch the next day, St. John whispered to Maher. Maher nodded and gave Lem and me the stink eye.

"What did we do now?" Lem asked as the the devil-like Maher approached.

Other than attending one Sunday dinner in dirty clothes, I'd been a model of good behavior.

"The headmaster will see you two in his office immediately after lunch," Maher said.

"Mr. Kennedy and Mr. Billings," St. John said from behind his desk. We stood, waiting to hear about our latest transgression. "It has come to my attention that the two of you have expressed an interest in joining the French Foreign Legion." He held our letter and shook it. "It's obvious that last night's movie put this foolishness into your heads."

Lem and I looked at each other. The bastard had intercepted our letter! I knew the Head read incoming correspondence. After all, he'd delayed giving me Kick's telegram for nearly a week. But now it was clear he was sticking his nose into my outgoing mail as well.

"Mr. Kennedy, it is my job to know as much as possible about every student. Applying to the Foreign Legion? That's not something to concern yourself with. Not while you are enrolled here. After, or should I say, *if* you graduate from Choate, proceed as you wish. Until such time, however, this nonsense must stop."

"What's crazy about joining the Foreign Legion?" I asked. "Their ranks include soldiers from all over the world."

"They do, and most of them, if not all, are older and more mature than the two of you. While at Choate, your job is to focus on your studies and nothing else. Sending out applications to serve in the French Foreign Legion distracts you from your studies. And that, for you, Mr. Kennedy, is disastrous."

"But—"

"I'll not waste any more of your or my time on this matter," St. John interrupted. "If you pursue this ridiculous quest, I shall be forced to alter your diet. You'll be served only the gruel they serve in the Legion. Now go to class."

I immediately began to fume. My muscles quivered as I stomped down the path to class. "He opened our mail and read the letter before it went out! Nothing better to do than spy on us? From now on, I'll personally take my letters to the post office."

"Good idea. He shouldn't have done that."

"It's not the first time, Lem. Remember, he intercepted Kick's telegram to me." I kicked a rock. "Nothing's safe from St. John."

"No, it isn't. Well, so much for joining the Legion. Not that hot on the idea anyway. Did that poet guy you like have a jolly good time with them? What's your favorite poem by him?"

"Yes, I think he did. For a while. Anyway, my favorite poem of his is called 'I Have a Rendezvous with Death.'"

Lem jerked his head back. "Interesting title. By the way, whatever happened to him?"

I cleared my throat. "Well, uh, he didn't make it."

"Didn't make it? What happened?"

"It seems he, uh, died during the Great War at the Battle of the Somme. Apparently, Seeger had a desire to die gloriously at an early age. That's what the poem is about. Got his wish."

"Oh." Lem rolled his eyes. "Now you tell me."

"You could have asked."

We walked in silence for a few minutes.

"Class awards coming up," I said. "We want to get in on it. *The Brief* board has come up with several, shall we say, inventive categories." We'd mixed in serious awards like "Most Influential," "Most Optimistic," "Done Most for Choate" with several eccentric ones. "Should be some very competitive races."

Pulling out a crumpled piece of paper from my pocket, I said, "Let's hide out for a few minutes." We looked around, then slinked behind the chapel.

I scanned the categories. One caught my eye. "Least Appreciated."

"Lemmer, do you think I'm underappreciated? Would I have a chance at that?"

"Jack, if anything, you're overappreciated." Lem smirked. "Forget it. You'd never win. I certainly wouldn't vote for you."

"Thanks. Probably right. Doubt if I'd vote for myself." I pointed to another category. "Here's one you'd be certain to win—Class Caveman."

"No. I'd only get one vote," he said, enjoying the kidding and give and take. "Yours. Maybe you think I'm a recent descendant of our distinguished forefathers, but nobody else does. No, I'd lose. Let me see," he said, staring at the paper. "Here's one that might interest you. Biggest Drag on Faculty."

"No," I said. "Wouldn't want to win unless the faculty could vote."

"Good point."

"I see you being very competitive in a number of these categories, Lem. Remember, you can run for more than one. How about Biggest Roughhouser? Hey, why don't you cover your bets and also put your name in the hat for Daintiest. You're bound to win one. Or maybe both of those. If you did, you'd forever be known as the Dainty Roughhouser. I promise here and now your gravestone will read: 'Here lies the Dainty Roughouser.' Take me up on my generous offer?"

"I say no. But thank you."

"Well, all right. But since you keep finding fault with my suggestions, LeMoan, perhaps you ought to run for this one: Biggest Carper. If you really put your mind to it, and buckle down and improve your nitpicking and quibbling skills, you'd win in a landslide. I'd even tutor you."

"Thanks. But let me get back to you. I see two excellent choices for you: Class Snake or Class Politician."

"But aren't they the same thing?" I said with a laugh.

We agreed to think about our selections. "What about the faculty elections? Who do you think will win Most Human? Certainly not Master Maher. He's only one-fourth human."

"Right."

"But I think he's got a helluva shot to win Most Hard-Hearted. I'm going to offer my services to the Prick. Be his campaign manager. Hope he takes me up on it."

Mixing it up with Lem about the class awards had been fun. But was I going to run for something, or was I content just to joke about doing so? And if I did run, for which award? Whatever it was, I wanted St. John and Maher to take notice.

And I'd make sure I won.

CHAPTER THIRTY-NINE

Lem and Shink rode with me in the station wagon on our way back from New Haven. It was rainy and cold, and Lem sat in the front seat and Shink in the second section. The third compartment was empty.

We were discussing the class awards. Shink said Blackie shouldn't be allowed to run for a class award. "How did they ever let him in?" Shink asked. "That guy is as dark as the Black Sea." Shink was talking about Morton Davis.

Shink didn't like Negroes, and he wasn't shy about telling you. One time, he said to me, "If the school ever allows the coloreds to go to Choate, that's the day I'm out of here. No way am I going to be in a class with some darky."

Morton Davis had come to Choate as a fifth-former last year. He was a standout tennis player and easily the best player on the team. He competed in the Greater New York junior tennis championships.

He'd been given the nickname "Blackie" because he was so dark. Everybody else had white skin, so Morton stood out on campus. Black on white.

But how could he be Negro? Negroes couldn't enroll at Choate. So what was he? Half Negro? A quarter Negro? An eighth? At what point, or fraction, did he qualify to go to Choate? There was nothing on the Choate application that asked if the boy was in any part Negro, as it did with Jews. Or Chinese, or Japanese, or Muslim, or whatever else there was, for that matter. Maybe St. John had overlooked his dark skin because he was such a great tennis player. Or maybe they didn't know he was Negro until he showed up. And then it was too late.

Or maybe he wasn't Negro at all. When asked, Davis said he had a pigment problem that made his skin turn dark in the sun. That might be true. Or maybe Davis was trying to avoid being bullied.

I didn't care if Davis was Negro, but Shink and the others did. They gave Davis a hard time. Used the n-word. I told Shink to knock it off, but he wouldn't listen.

Sometimes I wondered how I could be friends with a guy like Shink, who was as bigoted as they came. But he was also a fun guy and a well-liked member of our group. As long as you didn't talk about Negroes, he was okay.

"Shink," I said, "I remember you telling me if a Negro was ever admitted to Choate, you'd find another school. So I guess you don't think Davis is Negro, right?"

"Maybe I'll find out for sure someday," Shink growled.

"Civil War's been over a long time, Shink. Negroes are supposed to have the same rights we do. Hasn't worked out that way, though. Many Negroes served in the Great War. Doesn't that count for something?"

"Not to me. They should go back to where they came from—Africa."

Ahead, I saw a group of Negro men walking on the side of the road. Laborers, I guessed. Weary looking. Guess they worked all day in the rain. Now they had to walk home in it.

"Hey, Shink," I said, "I'm going to give these guys a ride. You don't mind, do you?"

"Keep going," Shink said, putting his hand on my shoulder. "I don't want to be in the same car with them."

"They could use some help." I pulled up to the men, who were tired, wet, and dirty. Their shoes were caked in mud.

"Want a ride?" I shouted. "Get in!"

"Sure," one guy said. "Much appreciated."

As they piled in, Shink dove over the seat and sat in the back section. The man I'd spoken to joined us in the front while the other five crowded into the section behind us. Behind them, Shink's head drooped.

"I'm Sargent," the man said. "Thanks for picking us up. Damn wet out there."

"Where you guys headed?"

After I got directions, I decided Shink needed company. I pulled the car to the side of the road. "I'm having trouble steering, men. There's too much weight in the front. Would you mind, all of you, sitting in the back with my friend?" Lem gave me a conspiratorial smile. "He's a good old boy from St. Louis."

Five men clambered into Shink's section. If the passengers were small, four could sit there comfortably, but these were big guys. They were all over Shink. Sat on him, around him, and everywhere else. He couldn't move.

In my mirror, I gleefully viewed Shink's distress. He hung his head and crossed his arms.

"You okay back there, Shink? Making new friends?"

"Got a feeling your friend doesn't take a liking to Negroes," Sargent said.

"No, I guess not. By the time I drop you off, perhaps he'll be more open-minded."

Sargent motioned to turn down a dirt road. "Here we are," he said, a few minutes later. He pointed to a sagging, dilapidated structure.

SCOTT BADLER

Through the windows, I saw people laughing and drinking.
A roadhouse?

"Going to have a drink there. Care to join us?"

"No!" Shink wailed. "We've got to get back to school!"

I laughed at Shink's misery. "Think my buddy prefers studying
for History more than meeting new people. Maybe another time."

"Sure," Sargent said. "This place has great music on Saturday
nights. It jumps. Most people don't know about it. Appreciate
you helping us out. Anyway, some of the best musicians around.
You'd have a great time. It's a black and tan."

"Black and tan?"

"Mixed. Negroes. Whites. And others. We don't, uh…what's
the right word?…*separate*."

"We have a place like that in Pittsburgh," Lem said, "although
I've never been there. The Crawford Grill in the Hill District."

I was curious. I'd never been to a nightclub before, and one
that had live music sounded exciting. "We might take you up on
that. What kind of music is played here? A couple of weeks ago
we had a Negro named Lead Belly at school. Ever hear of him?"

"Sure. Choate had him? That cat has a past. Twice in prison.
Once for murder, another time for assault with intent to commit
murder. Though I'm always suspicious when white folks decide
Negroes are guilty. *Before* the trial. Understand?"

I nodded.

"You know how he got out? He sang a song to the judges,
asking for early release."

"Hope to see you guys soon," Sargent said. "Thanks again for
the ride." He paused. "And for allowing your friend to become
closer to his community members." We both laughed.

Lem and I shook hands with Sargent and waved to his crew. I drove off, but Shink stayed put in the back compartment. I could hear him moaning. His eyes were squeezed shut. He was in utter agony, but well-deserved, I thought.

"Shink!" I yelled. "How you doing back there now?"

No answer.

"I appreciated you being uncomfortable for a few minutes. All that weight in the middle. Mighty dangerous. We could have ended up in a ditch."

"You sure you were having trouble steering?" Shink asked doubtfully.

"Can't be too careful. Especially on a rainy day. Right, Lem?"

"Jack's right, Shink," Lem said. "Thanks for your sacrifice. Wish I had a camera with me so I could have taken a picture of you with your new pals."

"Yeah," I interjected, "so we could blackmail you. Threaten to show the pictures to your father. Probably disown you from the family fortune."

"God damn you, Kennedy."

Lem and I chuckled. Not a word from Shink all the way back. A *sprank?* Sort of.

CHAPTER FORTY

At our next session, we chatted for a few minutes about the weather and the Yankees' current prospects, Lecky suggested it might be helpful to talk further about my relationship with Joe.

"Do you have another memory that stands out?"

"Mom and Dad and Grandma and Grandpa Fitzgerald came to town for his graduation. When he accepted the Harvard Trophy—it's a bronze statue of a football player in a runner's stance—I remember looking at my father. He was beaming with pride and applauding so hard I thought he'd break his hands. I felt sad because I didn't think Dad would ever approve of me like he did Joe."

"I understand how you would feel that way."

"But he's not as bright as they think. Although my grades don't show it, I'm smarter than him. No one understands that. Especially my parents."

"Grades aren't everything," said Lecky. "In what ways do you think you're smarter than Joe?"

"Joe's narrow-minded. Sees things one way. Doesn't look at alternatives. He's knowledgeable, knows the facts, but that's not everything. The scientist Albert Einstein said, 'Imagination is more important than knowledge. For knowledge is limited, whereas imagination encircles the world.' Joe doesn't have much of an imagination. Doesn't see beyond the trees."

"Okay. So, if as you say you're smarter, why haven't you done better at school?"

I looked at the floor.

"Sloppiness, laziness, thoughtlessness?" Lecky said. "The happy-go-lucky attitude? What have you accomplished with all that?"

I didn't have an answer. I shrugged.

"Let's look at a different area. Athletics. Your brother did well in sports at Choate, and I'm aware you've had some health problems. But aside from Choate athletic teams, how do you rate yourself as an athlete?"

I felt everybody overestimated Joe's athletic ability and underestimated mine. In my opinion, I was the better athlete, although it wouldn't show in box scores or write-ups in *The Choate News*. Joe had been on Choate's undefeated football team in 1932. "Joe's got a few pounds on me, and he's a brawler, but I'm quicker, more agile, more coordinated than he is."

"Okay," said Lecky. "What I hear you saying is that you both have your strengths when it comes to athletics. Have you ever thought he might be envious of *your* athletic skills?"

I hadn't thought about it before. "Not really."

Lecky sat back in his chair, looking past me, then back at me. "It's my understanding you started a club at school. Tell me about this club and why you did it—what you hoped to get out of it."

"I thought it would be fun. I didn't know what we were going to do. But we'd have something of our own. Apart from school."

"Okay. Understandable. What do you think you've accomplished by putting together that club?"

"Accomplished? Had a good time, I guess. If that can be considered an accomplishment."

"I'm curious. Why did you do that instead of putting your time and energy into your studies at Choate?"

"I didn't like the headmaster threatening us, or anyone else for that matter."

"Was it you and others?"

"I guess so."

"So you upped the stakes. Challenged him. Used the name he called you as the name of the club."

"That's right."

"Are you proud of doing that?"

"Sort of."

"Why?"

"Well, it wasn't something that Joe ever did," I said.

"You matched him in your own way. You became well-known on campus—for reasons much different than Joe. He won the Harvard Award. Your claim to fame is you started a club called the Muckers. I think you'll agree they are quite different accomplishments."

"Yeah."

"And I don't mean that altogether negatively. Because starting that club shows initiative."

"Thanks."

"Do you think you would have organized the club if Joe hadn't been in the picture?"

It was hard to think of our family without Joe. No Joe, no Muckers? Probably. I hadn't thought about that. "I guess not," I admitted.

"Okay. So you think the school held your brother in high regard and still does. And your father favors him. Would that be fair to say?"

Tears welled up when I said, "Yes. He is the efficient one in the family, and I am the boy who doesn't get things done. If my brother were not so efficient, it would be easier for me to be efficient. He does everything so much better than I do."

Lecky pointed to the Kleenex box. After I'd soiled several tissues, he said, "I understand you feeling that way." He paused. "May I make a suggestion?"

I nodded.

"What Joe does is out of your control. Accomplishments and, for that matter, failures. Because he has failures too. But what you do is something you can control. In fact, that's all you can control. Be as efficient as you can. Get things done. You might find more satisfaction. Consider competing with yourself. The results might surprise you." Lecky stroked his chin. "Jack, you've talked about how he's the star of the family and does everything so well that it can be intimidating."

"Yes, that's true."

"I wonder if you're saying to yourself, 'Why should I even try if he's not only the best, but also the family favorite? I'm only going to end up second best anyway.' "

"Hmmm." Not doing my best because I couldn't measure up to Joe? I never thought about why I hadn't given my best in school. Maybe there was something to that.

"Okay, tell me if this makes any sense." Lecky leaned forward. "If you limit yourself to mediocrity because you think you can't measure up to Joe, you lose out. You don't push yourself. You become disordered, sluggish, and inefficient, as you put it. Perhaps your spelling is an example."

I sighed. "Could be."

"An alternative is to do the opposite. Do your best. Apply yourself to your studies. Get involved in school. But you've avoided going down that road also."

I looked down. I didn't like what I was hearing about myself. Because it was true.

"Do you see the trap you've set for yourself?" Lecky said gently.

"Trap?" What kind of trap was Lecky talking about?

"You believe if you try your best to compete with Joe, you'll come up short. That may or may not be true. You've already told me you believe you're smarter and a better athlete than Joe. I'm not sure why you think you'd lag behind."

I wasn't sure either. Why *had* I taken the easy way out? I was suddenly angry at myself. I ground my teeth.

"In any event, you've avoided doing your best and competing with Joe. And since you have, the result has been the problems we've talked about. Consider whether, by withdrawing from the race, you're avoiding comparison with your brother. Are you on the sidelines because of that? Opting out in other words?"

Was I on the sidelines? I didn't like that image.

"The result," continued Lecky, "is you're damned if you do and damned if you don't. That's the trap."

I couldn't believe I'd trapped myself in the way Lecky described. But he was right. "What should I do?"

"That's up to you, Jack. What do you want to do?"

I slumped.

Lecky sat back in his chair and clasped his hands. "Maybe it's not too late. Still time to extricate yourself from this trap. You're a sixth-former. Finish strong and carry that momentum on to college. Or continue on the current way. But if you do the latter, there will be consequences. How are you going to amount to anything if you have to be thoughtless and sloppy to be true to yourself, to your self-designated role?"

According to Lecky, I'd be under a great handicap in the business world if I persisted with my present course.

"That is true enough," I admitted, although I didn't want to be a businessman.

"Jack, I challenge you to revise your view of yourself." He paused. "If you think it would be beneficial."

The sessions with Lecky reminded me of the Mayo Clinic doctors. They'd probed my body by shoving stuff up my arse. Lecky probed my mind. Had a knack for extracting important information. If you had asked me before the Lecky sessions if subjects like Mother and Joe disturbed me, I would have said no. Or only a little. Clearly, they bothered me and affected me more than I had admitted to myself.

CHAPTER FORTY-ONE

Both Olive and Lem were great at cheering me up while I recuperated yet again at Choate's infirmary. I'd turned the corner on an awful cold, but my nose had become enlarged and red. And I suffered from uncontrollable bouts of sneezing. When I wasn't honking, I coughed.

The three of us relaxed in the sun on the patio behind the infirmary. Winter's snow had melted, and the creek's water surged below the patio. A few patients sat on the stone wall; others lounged on chairs.

By the spring of '35, I had gotten to know many of the doctors and nurses. Since I was nearly finished with school, I hoped this would be my last stay.

A doctor came by. "Jack," he said, "I understand you'll be leaving us tomorrow. Don't take this the wrong way, but please don't come back. We've enjoyed your company over the years, but you've overstayed your welcome. No need to add to your record."

I bolted upright. "Record? What record?"

"For the most time spent at Archbold. Congratulations."

"I'll do my best to stay away," I said, embarrassed at my claim to fame. I didn't want the information to spread. I was about to hit the campaign trail. How could I expect my classmates to vote for a guy who spent half his time in the school hospital?

"If I was going to write your biography," Lem said, "I'd call it, *Jack Kennedy: A Medical Journal.*"

"Not my type of book," I said, turning my head away and coughing several times. The hack finally under control, I said, "Got a better title. *Jack Kennedy: Most Likely to Succeed.*"

"Most likely to succeed," Lem said. "At what? Getting sick? Expelled?"

"The class award. 'Most Likely to Succeed.' "

Did I consider myself most likely to succeed in a class of more than 100 students? No. But I coveted that award. If I won, I'd leave Choate semi-happy. Plus, what better way to stick it to St. John and Maher? Forced to stomach my peers voting me 'Most Likely to Succeed' when the two of them expected me to be a total muck-up.

I could claim some true accomplishments. Maybe the administration didn't value them, but they weren't voting.

I'd overheard classmates say, "Kennedy is Public Enemy Number One." "That's the guy who started the Muckers." "Kennedy's the guy who took on St. John. Almost got him kicked out!"

In my classmates' eyes, I had achieved something. In their view, I had succeeded.

"I'm going for it. Shock St. John and Maher when I win."

"I think you will," Olive said. "I wish I could be here when the votes are counted and see the headmaster's face."

"What about you, Lem? Running for anything?"

" 'Best Natured.' " Lem beamed. "And 'Quietest.' "

" 'Quietest,' eh? Lemmer, I don't think of you as the quiet type. By the way, how do you campaign for the award? Tell them that, if you win, you'll be silent for the rest of the school year? Doubt you could keep that pledge. But if you do win, I'm going to hold you to your campaign promise."

I had thought about running for two different awards, but I reasoned that doing so would split my votes and hurt my chances. Some might vote for me for one office but not the other, and vice versa. Better to focus all my efforts on a single class award. And "Most Likely to Succeed" was the one I most coveted. Not only would I find it satisfying to stick it to the administration, but I'd have also proven Dad wrong about me. He'd be both pleased and surprised.

"Tell us what's best natured about you, Nature Boy?"

"My pleasing personality. Don't you agree, Olive?"

"Yes." Olive nodded. "You're always in a good mood."

"Okay, let the campaign begin," I said. "Once I'm out of Archbold."

Olive sighed. "Jack, after all that's happened, are we still going to the Spring Festival? You're not prohibited because of that Muckers thing, are you?"

"Of course we're going, O. We'll have a great time. I'll have a good laugh as I imagine dancing with you on a fine layer of manure. Can't figure out why St. John disapproved."

"Me neither," Lem said.

"What's the Gilly and Sully musical this year?" I asked.

"Bad news, Ken." Lem rolled his eyes. "It's *Patience*."

"Oh God, we've already seen that," I said, holding my hands to my face in mock horror. He'd forced it on us my first year. "*Patience*? That's the one about the milkmaid. I have no damn patience for *Patience*." I picked up a stone and threw it in the creek. "Can't sit through two hours of that again. Now if the Head had mounted a production of *The Muckers* to honor our contribution to the school, I'd go. Our departed friend A. J. would have done a bang-up job doing the music for it. But A. J.'s gone."

"Attendance is mandatory," Lem said.

"Here's what we do. We sneak out before *Patience* starts, have a little fun, and come back for the dance. That way everybody's happy. They'll never know we left. You in, Lem? Olive?"

"Hold on," Lem said. "Do I need to remind you that if we're caught, we're goners? Permanently. Especially after the Muckers disaster. No second chances."

"Good point, LeMoan. Let's just make sure we don't get caught," I said.

But almost immediately I began having second thoughts. After our "expulsion," I didn't want to put Lem at risk. I gave him an out. "If you don't want to come, I completely understand. Feel free to think about it. You don't need to answer now."

"Can't expel me," Olive said. "I'm in."

Lem winced. "Don't want to miss all the fun."

"Good. Tell Pussy and get her on board with the plan."

Lem's Festival date was Pussy Brooks, a gal from Pittsburgh. They'd been hanging out for close to a year but didn't seem all that serious. I'd written to Lem last year, "I still have your shaving brush, which I shall return when I get back my seer-sucker coat. Have you laid Pussy yet?"

I didn't think he had.

It had crossed my mind several times that Lem might not be interested at all in girls. Our evening in Harlem got me thinking that. The brothel seemed to be the last place in the world he wanted to be. And I was almost positive he hadn't followed through with Eunice. On the other hand, Lem always had a date for the Spring Festival, and seemed to enjoy all the tea dances. But he never expressed even so much as a joking desire to be intimate with any of his dates. Sending me that toilet paper note didn't mean he was homosexual—other boys at Choate did that same sort of thing. Were all of them homosexuals? I didn't think so.

CHAPTER FORTY-TWO

"**L**et's hit the road, Jack," Pete said, revving up his breezer.

We'd slipped away from school and *Patience* and met Pete over on North Elm Street. Pete and Lem had been room-mates a few years earlier. Pete had graduated the year before.

Lem dove into the front seat. Olive, Pussy, and I scrambled into the back. Pete gave Pussy a big smile. He had eyes for her. Lem didn't seem to mind. He and Pussy weren't lovey-dovey. More like friends, it seemed to me.

"Get out of here before they see us," I commanded. "Floor it!"

With the top down and the five of us crammed in, we were quickly on our way. We only had two hours to raise hell while *Patience* had the school stage. I wanted to make the most of the time before we'd slide unnoticed into the dance.

Except for Pete, we were decked out in formal evening wear—Lem and I in white tie and black tails, Olive and Pussy in long silky gowns and high heels.

"Where we headed?" Pete yelled above the din of the open car. Like me, Pete drove fast, roaring around curves and speeding up on the straightaways.

"How about we hit a roadhouse?" I suggested. "There's a good one I know outside of town. Place is different." I'd talked to Lem, but not the others, about going to Sargent's place. I didn't want them making a ruckus.

"Fine by me," Pete said.

"What's a roadhouse?" Olive asked.

"It's a place where the road goes to a house, right, Lem?!" I shouted.

Lem turned to face me. "Exactly right, Ken!"

"O, a roadhouse is a place where there's music and dancing and drinking, but it's nothing elegant."

I directed Pete down a country road where, on each side, vast fields were concealed by dense conifer trees.

When we pulled up to the roadhouse, Olive faced me. "Jack, are you sure this is it? Doesn't look like our kind of place."

I bounded out of the car. "It is tonight. Time for some fun, ladies and gentlemen."

Leading the way, I strode into the roadhouse. The roar of the crowd, the jazz band in full driving throttle, and a wave of tobacco smoke enveloped me. I tingled from head to toe. I loved it. There was action here, and I wanted to be a part of it.

The Saturday night crowd inside was dressed to the nines, a stark contrast to the ramshackle appearance of the roadhouse from the outside. Men in fedoras, jackets, white shirts, and ties. Women had their war paint on, many wearing fur stoles. Behind the horseshoe bar, the bartender, dressed in formal white, mixed a drink, holding the shaker high over his head. The crowd was about three-fourths Negro, the rest white. Nobody was as young as us, and nobody else was in tails and gowns.

Folks stared. We heard murmurings of disapproval.

"Look what walked in."

"This ain't no high-society club."

"You sure you youngins got the right place? No tea dance here."

At the back of the roadhouse, a four-piece band hit its stride, belting out "St. Louis Blues" by Louis Armstrong. The leader played the licorice stick, and a tall thin man caressed his alto gobble-pipe. Behind them, the skin-tickler beat on his white drums next to a guy plucking the thick strings of his standup doghouse.

After twelve years of Prohibition, these people were excited to be drinking and socializing in public instead of carrying on in hard-to-find speakeasies. Folks wanted to let loose.

Sargent held court with several other men and women. I almost didn't recognize him. He and his friends had been in muddy work clothes the day we gave them a ride; now Sargent was dressed in Saturday night finery—jacket, white shirt, and bowler hat.

He smiled, waving us over. "You made it, Jack!" Sargent stood up to greet me, offering me his hand.

"Told you I would. Brought a few friends with me. You remember Lem." I then introduced Pussy, Pete, and Olive.

"Jack, are you trying to make us look bad with your fancy clothes?"

"Nah. We escaped from school, but we have to be back for the big dance in a couple of hours or we'll suffer the consequences. Thought we'd loosen up here, learn a few tricks from you pros, and wow them back at the dance with our new moves." I laughed.

"Jack gave us a lift after a day of clearing out a field," he said to his friends. "We were whipped. Got caught in the rain going home. Glad you didn't bring that other fellow, 'cause I don't think he liked our kind. Join us." He pulled in additional chairs.

We ordered beers, which was the only drink my tender stomach could handle, and one beer was more than enough for me.

"You getting ready to graduate from that Choate school?" Sargent asked. "Hear that place is mighty strict."

"Yes, it is. Not a lot of fun."

"Bet you're itching to get out."

"Bet your ass we are. Right, Lem?"

"A few more weeks!"

Sargent turned serious. "I don't suppose there's any Negroes at your school."

"No, there isn't." I thought of Morton Davis, but as far as I knew, he wasn't Negro.

"And why do you think that is, Jack?"

"I don't know for sure if there is a policy, Sargent, but I don't think St. John wants Negroes at Choate." I'd heard some guys say there weren't any Negroes at Choate because they didn't have the money. Others said Negroes didn't want to attend Choate. But most guys thought St. John just didn't want them.

"I agree with you. Now what about Jewish people at Choate?"

"A few. They ask you if you are of *Hebraic* background before they let you in. Guess they don't want too many."

"Don't seem right to me. Not justice in my book. Tell you something else," Sargent continued. "I've been trying to get out of working in the fields for a while now. No luck. I know the country isn't doing well. Unemployment is high. Lots of breadlines. But when a job does come open that I'm qualified for, they look the other way. Hire a white man instead."

I nodded. Didn't know what to say.

"I don't want to get all serious now, Jack, 'cause you're here to have a good time." Sargent stood and pointed to the band. "Hey, you know this song, 'Minnie the Moocher' by Cab Calloway? Let's help the band out on this one."

I recalled seeing Cab Calloway's name on the Cotton Club marquee in Harlem.

"Hi de hi de hi de hi!" chortled the band leader. He cupped his ear. The crowd echoed the singer's nonsensical phrases. Call and response.

"Hi de hi de hi de hi!" we roared back.

Lem threw back his head and howled. Olive and Pussy tapped their feet and clapped. In the midst of Sargent's friends, Pete laughed and gestured wildly with his hands. We'd been welcomed into the club and Sargent's circle of friends. The evening was taking off, and the roadhouse was hopping.

Sargent said, "What song you want? I'll get the band to knock it out." The man had pull.

That was easy. The Muckers' unofficial theme song. "How about 'Anything Goes'?"

"You got it, Jack." Sargent marched up to the band leader, and the group kicked off the tune.

"Come on, Olive," I said, grabbing her hand, "let's dance."

Olive and I joined a half dozen other couples on the dance floor. Everybody but us was Lindy Hopping, using the dance's signature swing-out to wild abandon—dance moves that surpassed our basic steps.

Sargent and his wife, Augusta, joined us. Despite his burliness, Sargent moved gracefully as he maneuvered Augusta effortlessly and smoothly through the Lindy Hop's partnered, solo, and improvisational steps. I was envious.

"You could use a little help, Jack," Sargent said. "I'll dance with Olive. Augusta, honey, give Jack a few tips so he can impress those damn fools at Choate."

I eased into Augusta's embrace. "Show you how it's done," she said, freeing up my hand. "Now give me a swing-out." She guided me like the pro she was. "Good. Now let me fly a little."

After a few minutes, I had something to add to my repertoire.

I caught Olive's eye. "This guy is good," she said, pointing at Sargent.

"Show us what you learned," Sargent said, returning Olive to me.

Olive and I weren't perfect, stumbling here and there, but we laughed at our mistakes. I loved the bouncy rhythm of the hop and its many variations. I couldn't wait to try out our new steps back at school.

I gave a wave, as Lem and Pussy, and Pete with a gal he'd just met, joined us on the dance floor.

This roadhouse scene was a world away from Choate and our upcoming stodgy formal dance—a liveliness and independence inhabited the club. Black and tan. Black and white. That didn't matter here, unlike everywhere else. Sure, I'd be back at school later, but in a few weeks—as long as we didn't get caught tonight—I'd be a world away from Choate and, I promised myself, at entertaining places like this.

A few more dances, and we went back to the table.

"Whew," Pussy said, "I do believe I got a workout."

"I believe we all have," I said, wiping my brow. "But I could stay all night here. I'd be happy to leave when the sun comes up."

"I'm with you, Jack," Pete said.

"I hate to say it, but we should head back before anybody at school gets suspicious, if they aren't already. Ready, Pete? Take us back so we don't have the honor of getting kicked out a couple of weeks before graduation."

We said our goodbyes. Sargent told us we were welcome anytime.

We were almost out the door when I stopped, having heard the notes of my favorite song, "Love is the Sweetest Thing." The song had been a big hit, and I never tired of the slow, sweet melody.

"I can't leave while they're playing my favorite song. It's my lucky night. One more dance, Olive. For the road."

We returned to the dance floor. While we waltzed, I sang along. Perfect way to end this part of the evening.

CHAPTER FORTY-THREE

"Hell of a time, wasn't it?" I said as we drove back to campus, my arm around Olive's shoulders. Lem was in the back seat with us. Pussy sat close to Pete up front.

"How did you find that place, Jack?" Olive asked. "A club without a name. Never been to anything like that."

"Let's say I've got connections, O. I'll bet your family money that place was a speakeasy when booze was banned. Didn't have a name then, either. Now it's a legal no-name club."

The night had been fun as well as enlightening. I'd learned the Lindy Hop, been to a roadhouse where Negroes and whites mixed, and again learned from Sargent how difficult life was when your skin wasn't white.

Pete gunned the breezer. After the last couple of hours in the warm, smoky roadhouse, the evening air felt great.

Nearing Choate, Pete slowed down, preparing to drop us off. Suddenly, he yelped, "Hey, there's somebody behind us! Think we're being followed!"

"Followed?" Lem turned to see. "By who? Police? G-men?"

"Worse," I said, looking back and seeing the Choate insignia on the car. "Campus Cops."

We'd busted out of campus, but getting back in without getting caught was going to be a lot harder.

"Pete, don't stop!" I shouted. "Keep going! You can lose them out by the farm! Duck down everybody."

Pete accelerated past the school.

"We're on the lam, eh, Lemmer?"

"On the run, Public Enemy Number One. Feels like I'm in a cops and robbers movie."

"Yeah, except it's cops and Muckers."

The cops took up the chase.

Angry for risking expulsion again, I asked myself why I'd taken the chance. Three weeks to graduation and I had put myself and Lem in jeopardy. All I had to do was sit (or sleep) through *Patience* for a couple of hours, then enjoy the dance. And, in less than a month, I'd be enjoying the summer on Cape Cod. Not a care in the world.

When I had planned my escape, I calculated the odds were in my favor. With a large crowd attending *Patience* and the dance, Lem and I wouldn't be missed.

Now, Lem and I weren't going to graduate, and I wasn't going to spend three care-free summer months in Cape Cod unless we could get out of this mess.

Perhaps I enjoyed the challenge, pushing the potential peril to the limit. See how far I could take matters. That's what I'd done with the Muckers. It had also gotten me kicked out, if only for a few hours. Was the same thing happening all over again?

All I knew was I didn't want to be stuck watching that boring play again. Well, I wasn't.

But I didn't want other people to get hurt by what I'd decided to do. Perhaps I hadn't thought about that very much when starting the Muckers. This time, I'd checked with Lem beforehand. He'd known the risk. He'd made his own decision to come along.

For now, I had one thing on my mind: don't get caught. Whatever I needed to do, I'd do it. I couldn't stomach the idea of Lem and I slinking out of school like criminals. That just couldn't happen.

Our only chance to avoid expulsion was to evade the cops and make sure the Head didn't know we'd briefly slipped out of school. If he found out, Lem and I would be expelled for sure, and there was no way the Old Man would intervene. And I wouldn't want him to. This one was on me. And it was on me to get us safely out of this mess with no consequences.

As we screeched around a turn, I thought about some real public enemies—Bonnie and Clyde, John Dillinger, and Baby Face Nelson. They'd been chased by the cops. It hadn't ended well for them.

Pete drove at top speed, slowing down only to careen around stone-fenced bends. I felt like a rag doll as we jostled against one another. Thanks to Pete's daredevil driving and the fact that his car had more horses under the hood than my Choate jalopy, we put some distance between us—enough, in fact, that I considered it safe to holler, "Come and git us, coppers!" Felt good to yell and release some tension.

"Pete," I shouted, "turn into this farmyard, then cut the engine and lights!"

Our hideout. But tonight, we'd have to hide out somewhere else.

Our chances of escaping detection would be better if we hid in the larger adjacent barn. There were more places to hide inside a barn full of animals, and the campus cops would be less inclined to look for us among the pigs, chickens, and goats.

We had one advantage that I couldn't cede, or we were done.

Lem and I hadn't been identified. The cops didn't know we were in the car. Could be anybody. Fortunately, we had taken Pete's car instead of mine. I'm sure St. John knew what kind of car I drove. Since Lem and I were the ones at risk, we had to hide. We could not, under any circumstances, be recognized. Olive would come with us. Pete and Pussy could hold off the cops. Encourage them to leave and look for us elsewhere.

"Lem, Olive, and I are going to hide in the barn. You and Pussy act like snuggle pups," I said. "You've graduated, Pete. Campus Cops can't do anything to you. Give them a hard time."

We scurried into the barn, where we were assaulted by the awful stench of animal shit and dirty straw. We held our noses and hid behind hay bales.

"I can't handle this for very long," Olive said, gagging.

Baa! Baa! Baa! Oink, Oink. Boc boc, boc boc.

We'd disturbed the goats, pigs, and chickens. I hoped the animal racket didn't give us away.

"Looks like we got company," Lem said. "Got to give these pigs credit, though. They keep their living quarters cleaner than you, Jack."

Fortunately, the animals quickly got used to us and just as quickly quieted down.

"Oh, God, I stepped in it," Olive wailed.

"Stepped in the muck," I said. "Sorry about that, O. But now you're officially a Mucker."

"Thanks, Jack," she said, scraping her shoe on a bale of hay. "What an honor."

What to do? Wait the cops out from here in the barn, or make a run for it if they came in?

I felt my way to the barn door, using the hay bales as my guide in the dim light. One bale was coarse and stringy. And alive. A goat. It bleated and scampered away.

I squinted through a slit in the door. The cops had pulled into the farmyard, parking alongside Pete's car. They left the car running and the lights on, illuminating the barn. One of the cops was our old friend Butter. What a surprise!

The cops approached Pete's car from the driver's side. Pete and Pussy made out, pretending to be oblivious to their new company. Putting on a hell of a performance, if they were acting.

Butter shined his flashlight at Pete and Pussy.

"Excuse me, Sheriff," Pete said, loosening his embrace and pushing away the flashlight. "Kind of busy here. Don't believe it's illegal to kiss your best girl on a Saturday night, now, is it? What brings you out on this nice evening?"

"Do a search," Butter ordered his partner, another graduate cop. "I know there were more than two people in the car." He turned back to Pete. "Driving fast. Any particular reason?"

"What's it to you?" Pete asked curtly. "Wait a minute." Pete grabbed the flashlight from Butter and shined it in Butter's face. "You look familiar. Is that you, Butterworth? It's me. Pete Caesar. Remember? Graduated last year. How the hell are you?"

Faking friendliness, Pete stuck out his hand. Butter weakly shook it. I recalled Lem telling me Pete had bitched about Butter. "Good to see you. I'm a college boy now. Enjoying it, too. But I have only good memories of Choate. Well, mostly. How are things at the old stomping grounds?"

Butter softened. "Oh, hi, Pete. Yeah, sure I remember you," he said unenthusiastically. "It's the night of the Spring Festival. I'm a Campus Cop now." He pointed to his armband. "My job is to make sure nobody sneaks out. Or back in, for that matter. Immediate dismissal. No questions asked. I'm sure you remember the rule."

"I do. I remember the Campus Cops. Didn't like most of them. Acted like they thought they were real cops. Bunch of jackasses if you ask me."

"Well," said Butter, "always a bad apple or two in the barrel, right? Anyway, correct me if I'm wrong, Pete, but weren't there a few more people in your car?"

"Yes, there were. Pussy and I were going to give a brief tour of the campus to a couple of prospective students."

Quick thinking, Pete.

"And?"

"And then some maniac roared up behind us. Scared the hell out of them. When we got far enough away from that car, which by the way was you, they demanded to be let out. Frightened out of their minds. One of them pissed his pants. We dropped them off near the school. I hope you didn't scare them off from enrolling at Choate. They seemed like fine boys to me. Right, Pussy?"

"Right," Pussy said. "But I'm glad they're gone. I prefer being alone with you, Pete." She stroked Pete's hair. "I like it when Pete drives fast. Gets me all hot and bothered."

"See what you did, Butter? You got Pussy all excited. Now tell me why you were driving so fast? That's against the law. Oughta be more careful. Looking for somebody?"

"Might be."

"Who? Bonnie and Clyde? Haven't you heard? Government already got them. And they're dead."

"I know."

Footsteps. The other cop was circling the barn. If he came in and found us, what would we do? Push him into the pig slop, then hightail it out of there before he saw us? Throw him into the pen and let the chickens peck away at him? I tapped Lem and Olive and whispered, "Quiet."

"What are you guys, anyway?" Pussy sneered "Some sort of lawmen at the school? Don't you have something better to do than chase people who aren't even students?"

Butter said, "We're appointed by Headmaster St. John to maintain law and order."

"We'll, you're boring me to death," Pussy said. "So I'm ordering Pete to go find a place where we can have a bit more privacy without a couple of jerks bothering us. Okay with you, honeybunch?"

"Fine by me," Pete said, starting the car. "Good to see ya, Butterworth. Say, do you remember a guy named Jack Kennedy? Do me a favor and say hello if you see him. Thanks. And one other thing."

"Yeah?"

"I just remembered something. I remembered I don't like you," Pete said, throwing the flashlight to the ground. He floored it, tearing out in the opposite direction of the school. Butter bolted for his car.

I turned to Lem and Olive and said quietly, "Hey, guys, Pete took off."

When I looked back, the Choate cop car was roaring away in pursuit.

The Chase, Part II, was on.

But why the hell was Butter chasing after Pete? Did he think he was a real cop? What was he going to do if he ever caught Pete? Arrest him? He couldn't.

"Butter's chasing Pete because he thinks Pete will lead them to the escapees," Lem whispered. "Whoever they are."

"No, Butter doesn't think. Not logically, anyway. 'See car go. Go follow car.' Like a dog. He just wants to chase cars."

"Did the other guy go with him?"

"I'm not sure." I couldn't tell if there were two people in the car, so we had to be careful. "The other cop might still be here. Sniffing around. If he is, he'll keep looking while Butter tries to chase Pete down."

"What do we do now?" Olive said. "We can't stay here all night, Jack. They'll realize you're missing at the dance. You and Lem will be done for. And I'm about to upchuck from this dreadful smell."

"Do you think Pete will come back for us?" Lem asked.

I didn't think Pete would permanently leave us, and the cops had no clue we were hiding in the barn. "He'll be back," I said with as much confidence as I could muster.

"This has been quite the evening," Olive said.

"You got that right, O. Let's just hope it ends well. Because it's not over. We have to get back to the dance, one way or the other, without those damn cops finding us. As of now, they don't know who else was in the car."

"Pete will never give us up," Lem said. "Nor will Pussy."

The animals began mouthing off again, grunting and clucking.

A few minutes later, we saw the headlights of a car. It was headed for the farmyard. Pete or the cops? We held our breaths.

It was Pete's breezer.

We had to split up. I needn't worry about Pete, Olive, and Pussy since they weren't Choate students, but I didn't want to get caught with Lem coming back to school. Less risk for him to go back with the others. I'd get back on my own, but I didn't want them to know that. They'd argue for me to come. No time for discussion.

I pushed Olive toward the door. "Lay on the floor at Pussy's feet and cover yourself with a coat," I ordered. "Lem, you hide in the trunk. I'll be right behind you. Go!"

Olive and Lem dashed for the car, Olive to the passenger side and Lem to the trunk. "Where's Jack?" I heard Pete say.

"He's in the barn," Lem said. "I'll call for him."

"No," Pete snapped. "What if the other cop is still around and hears you call his name? It'll be all over for you guys."

"Right. Well, Jack says to hide me in the trunk."

"My pleasure."

Lem got in the trunk and Pete slammed the door. He dashed back to the driver's seat. As he did, the Choate police car pulled up and stopped. Both cops were in the car. Pete sped away, and the cops took off after Pete. Once more, the chase was on.

Except for my animal friends, I was alone. I crept out of the barn and began making my way back to school. After all the excitement, the solitude was comforting.

Not wanting to be on the main road where cops might see me, I tramped through a wooded area. Who knew how many cops St. John had patrolling for errant students?

As I picked my way through the woody underbrush and rocky terrain, my favorite poet, Robert Frost, and the lines from "Stopping by Woods on a Snowy Evening," reverberated in my mind.

> *The woods are lovely, dark and deep,*
> *But I have promises to keep,*
> *And miles to go before I sleep,*

And miles to go before I sleep.

I tripped over a rock and hit the dirt. A few minutes later, I slammed into a tree. And then I got lost. But I was confident I'd find my way back. My nautical instincts kicked in. I pretended I was sailing back to campus—by land. I trudged for a half hour until I saw the school's lights.

Climbing the stone wall, I beelined for the dining hall, which had been converted into a dance hall. I slipped in the rear entrance and saw couples filling the dance floor. I spied St. John and the prickish Maher keeping tabs from opposite sides of the room.

Keeping to the beat of the rhumba, I approached Olive and Lem. "Mind if I cut in?" I plucked a sliver of hay from Lem's hair.

"Glad you could join us," Lem said. "Any problem finding your way back?"

"Nah," I said. "How about you? Hope your trunk ride wasn't too uncomfortable, Lem."

"Had a wonderful time." Lem smiled. "What's more fun than being locked in the trunk while Pete drives like a madman? But it all worked out. Pete led them on a wild goose chase. He lost them in town, then dropped us off a block from school. We slipped in unnoticed."

Olive removed a stray twig from my hair and a burr off my jacket. "Now you're almost presentable."

Out of the corner of my eye, I saw Smoky fasten the Mucker pin on his date's dress.

"Jack," Olive said, "I lost one of my shoes when I ran from the barn, but my dress is so long I don't think anybody will notice I'm barefoot. Ready to dance and show off our new moves?"

"Sure, but let me see if I can get the band to pick things up. This waltz is too slow."

"You guys are great," I said to the piano player, "but I wonder if you'd do me a favor." I explained how we'd learned the Lindy Hop and we wanted to give it a go. "Could you change the tempo and play "Anything Goes?" Do you know it?"

"That's one of our favorites! Let's go, boys," the band leader said with a wave of his hand to the musicians.

The band kicked off the tune, and Olive and I hit the dance floor. After a few false starts, we found our rhythm. We had it. No stopping us. If you asked me, Olive danced better without shoes. *Bouncin' and boppin'. Rockin' and rollin'.*

Nobody else knew the Lindy Hop. After a minute, Olive and I had the floor to ourselves, and we made the most of it. Our swing-outs were smooth, and I let Olive fly at the right time. We sailed on the open water, the wind at our backs. I had the tiller, guiding Olive effortlessly, as I did the *Victura*.

Everybody stopped to watch, surrounding us as they clapped and cheered us on.

Man, I felt good. I laughed like a laughing hyena. An adrenaline rush like I'd never had before. Olive was also in the moment. Her eyes sparkled and gleamed.

I praised myself for bolting from school. That had been a good decision—so far. If I hadn't slipped out, I would have missed a great dance lesson at the roadhouse and not been able to show off now.

"Johnny be good!" Lem shouted. "Go Johnny, go!"

And I did.

When the tune ended, the band segued smoothly into a faster song that I didn't recognize, but it didn't matter. Our feet flew, our hearts danced.

"Kennedy," St. John said as the evening concluded, "I hope you and your date had a good time. Quite a performance you put on out there. Who taught you to dance like that?"

"The locals," I deadpanned.

St. John glowered. "I see." He pointed his finger. "On another matter of more importance, I don't recall seeing you at *Patience* or until later here at the dance. Can you account for your whereabouts during that time?"

"That Lady Jane is quite the cellist," I said, remembering the opening scene of *Patience,* Act II from a previous year. "This was the best Gilbert and Sullivan production since I've been here." Thank goodness for my damn good memory.

"Could have missed you, I suppose," he answered, scratching his head.

"I'm sure you did."

I wasn't finished. "One more thing."

"And that is?"

"I'd appreciate it if you'd stop reading and intercepting my mail—incoming and outgoing. My sister Kick sent me a telegram, which you or your staff, um, diverted. The cable came to me only after you passed it along to my father. Same goes for the letter I sent to the French Foreign Legion, which you seized."

"I did it for your protection," St. John said with a hard smile. "Mr. Butterworth alerted me regarding the correspondence."

I drew in a breath. So the Head had authorized Butter to read my mail. Was it just me? Or did it include all the Muckers' mail? Or the entire school? No, it wasn't possible to read the correspondence of 500 boys. It was only me.

"I can protect myself," I continued. "But in my view—and I think many others feel the same way—there should be a law against that. I don't think the great majority of citizens want the government, a work supervisor, or a school administrator intercepting their correspondence. I know I don't."

I walked away.

Now I was done.

It had been an interesting and exceptionally good night from the moment we ditched school until right then. Most importantly, another crisis had been averted and we hadn't been identified. I'd made some quick—and, it turned out, correct—decisions when the cops began tailing us. And I'd let St. John know I didn't think it was right to intercept my mail.

CHAPTER FORTY-FOUR

I went home to Bronxville the next weekend. It would be my last time away from Choate before graduating. I was now eighteen.

"You might want to know I'm going to run for a class award," I said, walking into the living room. Dad was reading the newspaper.

Putting down the paper, he said, "That's great, Jack. That shows something. A little late but... Well, that's good to hear. Put yourself out there. As long as you win. Which one?"

"I haven't decided. Thinking of Class Politician."

He frowned. "I like the idea of you thinking about politics, but if I recall, you haven't served on the Student Council. Do you think you have a chance of winning?"

Dad had a point. Still, his doubt hurt. I bit my lower lip.

"Do you have another choice?"

"Most Likely to Succeed."

"Well, I like hearing you say something about succeeding." He threw it back at me. "Do you think you can get the votes to win? Have you succeeded at Choate or shown signs that you will in the future?"

The Old Man didn't wait for an answer, though I didn't have a good one anyway.

"Your marks have been mediocre, though I guess you were successful at starting that Muckers Club. Almost successful at getting expelled, though that's not something to be proud of."

Down to my last two award preferences, I regretted asking him for advice. I was hoping for encouragement, and I wasn't getting any. Just the opposite.

"How about Most Admired or Most Respected?"

"If you think you can win one of those, then go for it." He went back to reading the paper.

I went outside and sat on the steps, staring down at my empty hands. I hadn't gotten what I wanted from my father. Surely not a vote of confidence. Better if I hadn't asked him at all. I picked up the football on one of the steps and passed it back and forth between my hands.

But that was okay. I'd made up my mind.

"Bobby, want to throw the ball around?" I said to my younger brother, who'd come outside.

Bobby attended Bronxville Public School. He'd repeated third grade, but since then he'd been doing fine.

"Sure, Jack. Are you going to Harvard like Joe?" he asked, as we strolled out to the lawn.

"Perhaps. I haven't decided. A few more weeks and I'm done with Choate. Do me a favor, Bobby?"

"What? I'll do it. Anything."

"You haven't heard what I want. What if I asked you to jump off the roof?"

"Well." Bobby smiled. "If it wasn't too high, maybe I would."

"Anyway, I don't know if Dad is planning to send you to Choate, but if he does, make sure to tell me, all right? You are more like me than you are like Joe. You wouldn't like it there. I want to make sure you go somewhere else."

"Okay."

Silently, we tossed the football back and forth for a few minutes. "I have one more thing to do before I graduate," I said, holding the ball. "Win a class award. I'm going to make a run for Most Likely to Succeed."

Bobby tilted his head to the side. "But Kick told me you almost got kicked out."

"Didn't succeed at that, did I?" I laughed. "Before I leave, I want to show the headmaster how wrong he is about me. I'm determined to win this election."

"What can I do to help?"

"Hmm. Would you like to be my campaign manager?"

"Really?" Bobby said, wide-eyed. "A campaign manager. Wow! Sure, what do I do?"

I threw him a tight spiral. "It would be a great help if you wrote a letter saying what an excellent brother I am and why everybody should vote for me."

"I'll do it." Bobby beamed.

Kick pranced down the steps. "Hey, Jack, throw me one," she said, her arms out wide.

She caught my pass and threw it to Bobby. We played catch for a while, then the three of us went into town for ice cream.

After we seated ourselves, Bobby said, "At school, Jack's running for Most Likely to Succeed. Guess who he picked to be his campaign manager?" He didn't wait for an answer. With a huge smile on his face, he pointed a finger at himself.

"That's great, Bobby," said Kick. "I'm sure you'll do a great job."

I asked Kick how school was going.

Spooning out a dollop of ice cream, she frowned and said, "Well, it's all right. It's strict, so it's kind of hard to have fun there." She scowled. "And there's no boys to flirt with."

"Right," I said. "We've got a similar problem at Choate, but we did do something to make the situation better." I told her about the study session with the Lyman Hall girls.

"Gee." Kick brightened. "Maybe I should try the same thing at my school."

"Okay, but don't say you heard it from me."

The next day, Bobby shyly handed me a letter. I wasn't expecting to get it so fast.

All students at your school should know that Jack Kennedy is my brother. He has been a very good brother. He has taught me a lot about sailing. He is the best person and Most Likely to Succeed. Vote for him.

Thanks,

Bob Kennedy

Campaign Manager, Kennedy for Most Likely to Succeed

"That's great, Bobby." I tousled his hair. "Going to show it around school. This should put me over the top."

"Sure. Anytime, Jack." Bobby grinned. "Anything else I can do?"

"Maybe there'll be other campaigns."

Good kid. I knew I could always count on Bobby.

CHAPTER FORTY-FIVE

"I t's our last session, Jack." Lecky smiled warmly. "What do you want to talk about?"

I dove right in and told him I'd thought a lot about our last conversation and about opting out. I had to be honest with myself. It felt comfortable after four years. Maybe too comfortable. "Guess I've gotten used to it, being on the sidelines."

Lecky nodded. "The problem is you can't succeed if you're not participating, can you?"

"No, I guess not."

"And when you opt out, as we've seen, you can't fail. Because you're not in the game. People are afraid to fail, but believe it or not, failing can be productive."

I frowned. "Failing can be productive?"

Lecky spread his hands, explaining, "Yes. Think about it. We all fail sometime or another. If we don't fail, we don't learn. If you only do the things you already know how to do, you'll never learn a new skill. How are you going to learn a new sport, for example, if you don't try it? Or if you don't try your best, nobody will compare you to somebody who's better at it? You'll go nowhere with that line of thinking. How will you ever achieve your goals in life?"

Goals? The honest truth was I didn't have any, although I could say I wanted to have a good time and slide through school. Actually, I'd gotten pretty good at it. But I didn't want to admit that to Lecky.

"You've told me of your interest in history, Jack. I'm also a history buff, so let me tell you about a few well-known people who went on to great things after early disappointments in their lives. Winston Churchill failed the entrance exam to military school twice before he got some tutoring. And young Winston didn't like Latin any more than you did. Did you know he once left a Latin exam almost completely blank except for a few smudges and his name?"

Lecky crossed his legs, then pointed a finger upward. "Or consider Lincoln. He ran for the state legislature and lost. Ran again and won. Won for Congress, but then lost for re-election. Campaigned for the Senate and was defeated. By this time, he could have said, 'Maybe politics isn't for me.' But he persisted. Ran for President of the United States and won. So, a lot of disappointment before his success. And did I mention he also went bankrupt?"

"Really?" I didn't know Churchill and Lincoln had such difficult experiences on their way to becoming important. I'd only heard about their accomplishments—the great things they did. Not the problems and setbacks along the way.

"Afraid to fail," Lecky continued "Sometimes we don't want to participate because we're afraid we'll lose or look foolish. But failure and losing are part of life. Here's another way of looking at it. Don't ask, 'Did I win? Ask, 'Did I give my best effort? Did I try my hardest? If I have, would I be happier with myself even if I didn't win?"

Would I? Possibly.

"Maybe not completely satisfied," Lecky continued. "Your father has put a heavy burden on you to win. To never settle for second place. Maybe Joe feels that pressure too."

I hadn't considered whether the Old Man's pressure to win was difficult for Joe. Not certain I cared, either.

"Sure, we'd all rather be victorious," Lecky said, shaking his fist, "but it's the effort that counts. Don't overlook that aspect. And I'll bet if you put forth your best effort, most of the time you'll come out on top."

I told him how I was going to run for Most Likely to Succeed.

He paused. "That's great, Jack. Whatever you do, give it all you got."

"I will."

"You may or may not find it interesting," Lecky said, "but I have had some experience with failure."

Lecky was about to make some sort of confession. He looked haunted and sad.

"Do you remember our first meeting? You expected to address me as 'Doctor,' and I told you I wasn't a doctor."

"Yes."

"The reason I don't have the title of Doctor is something you may relate to."

"Oh?"

"Remember our talk about active resistance?"

"Uh-huh."

"At our first meeting, we discussed your spelling problems. But active resistance also applies to me. It's something I've struggled with. And still do." Lecky slumped slightly, then looked at me more intently than I could ever recall. "I believe I've resisted, actively, against my own best interests. I never completed my doctoral dissertation." He looked away and then back to me. "Perhaps we have something in common. Perhaps you have taken on the identity of a poor speller, as well as resistance to certain people at Choate. And me? I believed I was not a Doctor of Psychology." Lecky sighed. "And I'm not."

I wanted to console him, as weird as that might seem.

Lecky slumped in his chair. "That's as far as I'll go about my own situation, except to say that because of my resistance to completing the dissertation, the University removed me from the full-time faculty. Schools like Columbia want Ph Ds. So now I'm relegated to teaching a course or two in continuing education. I've taken on clients like yourself to supplement my income. My wife is not happy with our vastly reduced income. Nor am I."

I wanted to help. Strange, because it was Lecky who was supposed to be helping me. "Couldn't you finish it now and get your job back?"

"Thank you for your words of encouragement." He sighed. "It's possible, but very doubtful. They've already filled my position."

"Oh, I'm sorry."

Lecky leaned forward. "Jack, there's a reason I've told you about losing my opportunity. You're young. You'll make mistakes. We all do. But there are big mistakes and little mistakes. The big ones can haunt us forever. Maybe seriously affect or destroy our lives. Prevent us from being successful. Don't let yourself, or your active resistance, get in the way of your own success." Lecky pointed to himself. "As I have."

I was dumbfounded, but I also felt a kind of kinship to him. We were separated by many years, but we had something in common.

"You've been given fair warning," he said, smiling a bit wanly. Standing up, he offered me his hand. "Good luck, Jack."

CHAPTER FORTY-SIX

The Brief board members sat around a long rectangular table. Chesty presided.

"As most of you know, *The Brief* staff coordinates the sixth-form class awards, and I, as editor-in-chief, have ultimate responsibility for ensuring that everything goes smoothly. I expect your complete cooperation. I will be delegating duties shortly." Then he smirked. "I'll be on the ballot for two awards: Most Likely to Succeed and Most Influential. I'm counting on your votes. Okay, back to work."

So Chesty was to be my chief competition. That was going to make things interesting. I sized up his candidacy. He was well-known, had better qualifications than me, and no doubt a higher grade point average than me. I had my work cut out for me.

I decided right there I wouldn't waste any time. I'd begin campaigning immediately. If I planned to outmuscle Mr. Atlas, I had to get an early start.

I had one possible advantage. What I'd learned about myself during my conversations with Lecky might help me win. Made me think a little deeper about why people did certain things— and why they didn't. I told Lecky I was the boy who doesn't get things done. But I didn't think that was quite so accurate anymore.

After all, I had successfully started the Muckers. We'd had a short but successful run. And I had played an important role in having our expulsion rescinded. Word had gotten around about that.

And while it wouldn't translate into votes, because only Lem was privy to our Spring Festival adventure, I was becoming more confident in my abilities. In ways similar to the expulsion mess, I'd taken charge that night and made sound decisions on the fly—in several instances, without a moment's hesitation. Otherwise, we'd have been caught.

Maybe I had a talent for handling myself in difficult and perhaps dangerous situations. When there was a crisis, I seemed to rise to the challenge. That might come in handy later on, I figured.

The boy who doesn't get things done? Not anymore. Now I was going to get something else done. I was going all-out to win that class award.

It was true the award asked voters to consider how successful the candidate might be in the future. Not what they'd done so far.

What did *succeed* mean for the future? Become rich? My family already had a lot of money. I wasn't sure what I wanted to do, what I wanted to succeed at. But I did know I itched to be where the action was. In the middle of it. I didn't know what that meant. But I'd had a taste of it, and I wanted more. If I were in the middle of the action, I'd feel successful.

My campaign strategy was to engage my friends, the former Muckers, to drum up support. I'd contact as many sixth-formers as I could, but having the ex-Muckers talk me up was crucial. If I could get them to persuade their friends to vote for me, I'd have a leg up. And maybe those friends might mention to others their preference for me.

First, I had to make some deals.

I met Rip over at the golf course. I'd overheard him say he was thinking of campaigning for the same award. I needed to get right with him.

"You going to run for a class award?"

Rip putted in. "Thinking of going for Most Likely to Succeed."

"Oh," I said.

"But I'm not sure I will. Not optimistic I'd win."

"Then why don't you run for Most Pessimistic?"

Rip scratched his jaw and looked at me like I was crazy. "Jack, why would I want to win *that* award?" He picked up his ball.

I grinned. "You wouldn't. And I'll make sure you don't win. The Muckers will talk you up as too optimistic. You're sure to lose. That'll be a feather in your cap." I prepared to putt.

Rip laughed at my nutty idea. "But I'll also run for 'Most Generous.' I want to win at least one award."

I made a long putt and watched it go in. "Great. Gotta go. Abyssinia," I said, heading off to class.

"Be seeing you," Rip echoed.

I persuaded another potential competitor to seek a different award, arguing he'd have a better chance at winning "Most Likeable."

We agreed to support each other.

"Deal." We shook hands.

When the candidates were announced, I had one more competitor, John True, or "Pee Wee," as he was known. He played on the Choate football team, was a member of the St. Andrews Society, and was assignment editor for *The Choate News*. A general's son, he planned to go to West Point.

I did some quick calculations. I had twelve solid Mucker votes, and another twenty from fellows I was friendly with.

Chesty could probably count on his Student Council associates, athletic teammates, and most of *The Brief* staff. I didn't think True was that well-liked, but if a few athletes voted for him instead of Chesty, that would help me.

———————

At the next meeting of the ex-Mucks, I cut the Victrola after a few tunes.

I stood up, placing my right hand in my coat pocket. Had to put it somewhere. "As you know, the class awards are coming up. The winners will have their names and awards printed in *The Brief* yearbook. I've talked to a few of you about my candidacy for 'Most Likely to Succeed.' Whether I will succeed in the future nobody knows. But I intend to succeed at winning this election. Chesty and Pee Wee are both worthy opponents." I shook my fist. "But I plan to run, and I intend to win. Will you help me?"

"Yes!" the ex-Muckers cheered.

"Of course," Moe said. "We owe you."

"Yeah. What can we do?" Boogie echoed. "We wouldn't still be in school without you."

I was moved by their show of support. And ready.

I laid out my campaign strategy. "As I see it, the most important step is to contact each classmate." There were 111 students in the Sixth Form. I took out thirteen slips of paper and held them aloft. "I think it would be most effective if each of you, as well as myself, encourage others to support my candidacy."

I passed out the slips of paper. I matched each person in the room with those whom I knew they were friendly with, or who lived in the same corridor.

"I ask each of you to talk with the people on your list about voting for me. Tell them you're voting for me for 'Most Likely to Succeed' and encourage them to do the same. I'm trying to get an idea of how the voting will likely go. So make a note of who they say they're going to vote for. Whether it's me, Mr. Atlas, or Pee Wee. I'll contact the undecideds and follow up with the old Kennedy magic." I laughed. "Whatever that is."

I became serious. "I suppose Chesty is the favorite, but with your help, we're going to kick a little sand in Mr. Atlas's face," I said, referring to the famous print advertisement in which a scrawny fellow has sand kicked in his face by a bully. He bulks up using Atlas's body-building program and becomes the "hero of the beach" after clocking his tormentor.

"I encourage you to trade votes. You know, I'll vote for you for Biggest Heartbreaker or First to Get Married if you vote for Kennedy." I paused. "If they are neutral, offer to forge a tardy slip for them!" I chortled. "That should put them in our column. Well, all right. Enough politics. Let's hear a few more tunes before we're subjected to another St. John sermon."

We stomped along to Benny Goodman's "Stompin' at the Savoy." Then we stomped to chapel.

⟫•⟪

After *The Brief* board meeting ended, Mr. Atlas cornered me. Poking me in the chest, he said, "So one of my staff is running against me."

"Oh yeah? Who's that?" I said, knocking his hand away. Chesty wreaked of Aqua Velva aftershave.

"Kennedy, I don't even know why you're running. I'd be embarrassed if I were you. What have you ever succeeded at?"

He had a point, if you defined success as good grades, scoring touchdowns, and serving on the Student Council. But standing up to the administration might mean a few votes for me. And I knew students would vote for who they liked best. *My educated guess?* More of them liked me than him.

I glared at Chesty, my voice rising. "You don't even know what the award is for. It's not for what you've done here at Choate. It's for what you're going to do after graduation. And there's one thing I'm sure you will have success at: being a jerk."

"Oh yeah?" Chesty sneered. "And what's your plan? A glorious career as business manager for some rag like *Captain Billy's Whiz Bang?* What an honor. Hmmm. That gives me an idea."

"You have an idea?"

"Let's meet up in twenty-five years. Right here at Choate. See who's more successful. Loser has to clean the stables." He stuck out his hand. "Deal?"

"Sure." We shook.

I wasn't really sure about winning the bet. I had no idea what I was going to do with my life, but I was darn sure I'd be successful. Or darn sure I'd get things done.

That week, I campaigned relentlessly, promoting my candidacy with every Sixth-Form classmate. I arrived early and stood outside my classes, talking myself up. "I'd appreciate your vote for 'Most Likely to Succeed.' "

Sometimes I'd campaign by throwing in a snarky remark. "The only thing Chesty is likely to succeed at is having big muscles." Judging from the positive response to my jokes, I concluded that using wit and humor was an excellent way to win people over.

When my friends returned their tally sheets, I calculated the prospective votes. I was somewhat hopeful. I had thirty votes,

Chesty had twenty-nine, and True had ten. That was too close for comfort. That left about forty undecided voters. Not everybody would vote. My "pollsters" reported that many hadn't made up their mind, didn't care, didn't like any of us, or wanted to know how much money their vote was worth.

Were my votes solid? It was hard to say. Perhaps some potential voters had said, "Yeah, you can count on me" but didn't mean it. Maybe they were just being polite or didn't want to be pestered. Or were voting for Chesty or Pee Wee...or not at all.

Chapter Forty-Seven

The Sixth Form assembled in the Speech Room. The thirteen ex-Muckers sat dead center, taking up almost the entire row.

After the Head went over some final details regarding graduation, he said, "Now I'll announce the votes for the class awards."

I stared at the back of Chesty's head. He sat two rows in front of me. He turned around and aimed his finger at me, mouthing, "You're going down, Kennedy." He pointed his thumb south.

The Head read the results of a few of the other contests: Lem won Best-Natured. I gave him a gentle congratulatory punch.

"The winner for Mostly Likely to Succeed..." The Head paused and shook his head.

A good sign. If the Head wasn't happy, then I probably would be.

I held my breath.

"Kennedy, fifty-one votes—"

The Head's reading was drowned out by the ex-Muckers who rose to their feet, chanting *Kennedy! Kennedy! Kennedy!*

I stood up, slightly embarrassed, and gave a half-wave to acknowledge my win and my supporters.

The Head shouted, "Quiet! Order!" Masters converged on us, demanding we sit down. It was a while before order was restored.

"Congratulations," I said to Lem that night in our room. "Mr. Best Natured, Class of '35. And Quietest. Quite a combination of talents."

"That's me," Lem said, grinning. He hooked his thumbs upward.

I'd won easily, fifty-one to fourteen for Chesty and ten for True. Can't always trust the polls. I'd gone the extra step, wooing the undecided voters as well as many who said they were voting for Chesty or True. Maybe I'd swayed a few.

Lem had won Best Natured by only twelve votes.

"You won because a few dolts thought the award was for Best Nature Boy. Mistakenly voted for a guy they thought liked tromping naked in the woods."

"Maybe I do," Lem retorted.

"But you won Quietest by a wide margin. The voters have made it clear they want you to quiet down. Shut the hell up. They've had enough of your screeching laugh echoing throughout campus and destroying their concentration. That includes me."

Lem waved his hand dismissively. "You won because the voters thought you were most likely to succeed at breaking the record for most sick days at Archbold." He laughed. "You certainly succeeded at that!"

Had me there.

"Ready to take the oath of office?"

"What?" Lem said, a question in his eyes. "I didn't know there was one."

"Make it official. Raise your right hand and put your left on this Physics book."

Lem complied, shaking his head.

"Do you, Kirk LeMoyne Billings, also known as Mr. Unattractive, solemnly swear to be good-natured and quiet to the best of your ability?"

"Well, I don't know," Lem stuttered. "I guess."

"Congratulations," I said, offering my hand. "My turn. Swear me in."

He handed me the book, and I raised my right hand.

Lem thought for a moment. "Okay. Do you, John Fitzgerald Kennedy, better known as Ratface, solemnly swear to uphold the office of Most Likely to Succeed and to the best of your ability preserve, protect, and defend the, uh, Choate rule book?"

"I do not."

Lem and I stared at each other.

"Congratulations," Lem said.

We shook hands, then burst out laughing.

After we calmed down, I said, "Well, now, it's time to get serious. Got to put the final touches on the justice essay."

An hour later, I checked my spelling—I now considered myself a decent speller—and reviewed my final draft. I was tempted to put something in about the injustice of our expulsion, but I didn't. I didn't think it was necessary. Also, it might get me into trouble.

Justice is pictured as a lady holding scales in her hand on which is weighed right and wrong. *Always just* is a phrase linked with God. But should this be so? Does God render to everyone his just due?

I compared two boys: one rich, one poor. Was it because of the rich boy's ability that he landed in the lap of luxury? Or was it the poor boy's fault that he was born into squalor? How much greater a chance has a boy born with a silver spoon in his mouth than the boy who from birth is surrounded by rottenness and filth?

Not a square deal.

Justice is not always received from "The Most Just," so how can we poor mortals ever hope to attain it?

Would people living in squalor find solace from the Christian belief that everything will balance out in Heaven? Many will hold on to that hope because there isn't any other choice. If you couldn't get a job, didn't have enough to eat, and there didn't seem to be a way to change your circumstances, you might be more apt to believe things would be better in the hereafter. Hope—the people I'd seen struggling in Harlem—needed it a lot more than I did.

I turned my paper in to Mr. Tinker the next day.

"I enjoyed this topic and writing this essay, Mr. Tinker," I said, handing it to him. I paused. "Although I didn't put everything in the essay I learned about justice."

Mr. Tinker smiled. He understood.

It felt good. I'd tried my best *and* done a good job completing my final assignment before graduation.

CHAPTER FORTY-EIGHT

S itting at my desk, I surveyed the faces in Room 215 for the last time.

Moe and Smoky had their arms around each other's shoulders. Rip dabbed at his eyes. Lem cleaned his nose with a handkerchief.

I stood up. "Congratulations to all those who won class awards. Smoky for 'First to Get Married.' Well done. Let us know the date as soon as possible so we can make plans." Smoky blushed. "Since the Muckers were a club where everybody was president, I'm guessing everybody here will be best men at your wedding. Thirteen best men. Maybe the first time that has ever happened. Cheers also to Rip, Lem, and Moe for their big wins." I clapped my hands, and everybody else joined in.

I started to express my thanks for helping me win, but I got a lump in my throat. I looked down and composed myself. "I, uh, want to thank all of you on my behalf. Your effort is something I deeply appreciate. Without your help, I wouldn't have prevailed. I will always be grateful. And if you ever need a favor, feel free to ask." I grinned. "But don't ask me. Ask my father."

The ex-Mucks hooted and hollered. "Can he get Roosevelt to put my father in his cabinet?" Blambo shouted.

"We'll see what we can do about that, Blambo," I said. "And if any of your schoolwork suffered while you were out campaigning for me, I'll gladly have a talk with your master to give you a break. Not that it would help."

I guessed many of them were thinking, as I was, that we were lucky to have made it through. We'd come within a whisker of being put on a train and scattered to the four winds. Expelled and sent back to Missouri, Maryland, Massachusetts, and wherever. Arriving home, and Mom and Dad ashamed to see us.

But we'd made it. We'd needed a little luck, but I was proud of the successful effort made to thwart the Head's expulsion effort. We'd hung together, allies had been recruited, and a disaster averted.

The church bells chimed.

Chapel… for the final time at Choate.

———➤•◄———

Olive, Lem, Rip, and I gathered at the hideout. Tomorrow we'd graduate. We smiled, lost in our thoughts, realizing this was our last roundup at the old barn. Doubtful I'd come back this way again.

One part of my life was ending and another beginning.

The Old Man was pressuring me to join Joe at Harvard. Lem and Rip were bound for Princeton, and Olive had plans for a modeling career.

I congratulated Rip for winning "Most Generous," and for losing "Most Pessimistic." "Sixteen measly votes. Need to work on your pessimism, Rip."

"I'll try."

"Looks like we made it, Kenadosus," Lem said. "Did you ever think we would?"

"Had my doubts. Anyway, it's over. Four long years. Five for you, Lem."

"Jack, if you had to do it all over again,' Olive chimed in, "would you have started the Muckers? That turned into quite a bit of trouble."

"Yes, it did," I said matter-of-factly. "But I have no regrets. Of course, if we'd gotten our butts kicked out, I guess I would. But we didn't." I reflected on the closeness I felt with the other Muckers. A lot of those guys hadn't been on a first-name basis with each other before the club.

"The entire school knew about the Muckers,' Lem said. "The students who attend after us will take notice. Start their own rebellion."

"We're legendary," I said, half kidding, 'if only in our own minds."

CHAPTER FORTY-NINE

I had a couple of things to take care of the morning before graduation ceremonies.

On the banister a few feet in front of Butter's room, I taped a sheet of paper. In large letters, I'd written "BUTTER BOY." Below it, in letters so small he'd need to come closer to read them, I'd written something else.

"What's this?" I heard Butter say. When I heard him scream, followed by a big thud, I rushed upstairs. Butter was on his back.

"This is the second time I've caught you falling down on the job, Butter. And the last."

Butter groaned and grabbed his butt.

"Should have read the sign," I said, snatching the paper from the railing. "Let's see what it says." Looking down at him, I announced, "Caution: Floor is Slippery When Buttered."

At dinner the night before, I'd grabbed a stick of butter. This morning, I'd spread it in front of his door.

"Well, I always knew you were a slippery guy, Butter. Fortunately, I won't have to worry about you intercepting and reading my mail anymore. You're not only slippery, you're also devious."

"But I was just following orders," he said. He looked almost sorry. And I almost felt sorry for him.

"Maybe it's not always a good idea to follow orders," I said.

I clomped downstairs to get ready for the big day.

"Folks coming?" Lem asked while we washed up in the lavatory.

"No." I winced, swallowing hard. "It's okay. Would have been nice, though."

A half dozen of us crowded into the West Wing corridor bathroom or, what we referred to with our limited French as, *la salle de bain*.

Butch stared at the mirror and picked something from his teeth, looked at it, then ate it. Boogie brushed his teeth and spat over and over. Lem slapped water on his face.

I unscrewed the rectangular bottle of Boots Brilliantine hair oil. An oil-slicked guy graced the label. He had a thick shock of hair, like me. I poured myself an extra generous portion.

Running my hands vigorously through my scalp, I then pulled my mop toward the back of my head. After parting my hair on the left, I combed it back. Looking in the mirror, I admired the extra sheen. Unfortunately, the mortarboard was going to cover my handiwork until graduation was over.

"What do you think, Leem?" I said, pointing to my head.

"Much better, Jack. You were down about a quart."

Somebody hummed "Anything Goes," and we joined in, adding the lyrics.

"It does now!" Rip bellowed.

The noise in the bathroom had never been this loud. Maher wouldn't allow it. He'd shut it down quickly, telling us to do our business and prepare for the school day. But he wasn't around, and he was no longer our housemaster.

"Hey, Rip, looking good," I said. Rip had been smoothing his hair for half an hour.

After donning my billowy gown and mortarboard, I laced up my scuffed black-and-white saddle shoes. I had one appointment to go to before the graduation assembly—an appointment with a mailbox.

I'd decided, after all, not to "edit" a bunch of Choate applications. The risk of getting caught was too great. But I'd doctored the one Choate application I'd been given, and filled it out. The applicant was "Johnny Mucker." I'd made up a North Dakota address for him in. Next to "Is the boy any part *Hebraic?*" I'd crossed off the last word and written "Mucker." Johnny Mucker's answer? "Yes! 100%."

My handiwork, I hoped, would cause a commotion. The Head would have the other applications examined. Maybe worry that more applications had been doctored. Maybe think about getting rid of the qualification and the quota.

I walked a block to North Main Street. "Good luck, Johnny Mucker," I said, "but I don't think they'll take you." I dropped the envelope in the mailbox.

Now, it was time to graduate.

I'd not just made it, but I'd finished strong in all my subjects. My spelling had improved. What Lecky said had made an impression. Though I couldn't take all the credit, I'd been told that *The Brief* had been the most financially prosperous ever produced.

I spied Maher. I offered my hand. Maher hesitated, then offered me his.

"Before I left for good, I wanted to offer my condolences," I said.

Maher let go of my hand. "For what?"

"Your poor showing in the faculty election. The Sixth-Form gave you the fewest number of votes for 'Most Influential,' and you were well back in the pack for 'Sanest.' What do you make of that?"

He waved me off. "The school will be much improved now that you and your fellow troublemakers are leaving."

"I doubt that. Don't you think we brought to Choate...what's that phrase I learned in French? Ah, now I remember, a certain *joie de vivre?*"

"No. I do not. I think quite the opposite. Your disruptive—"

Before he could finish, I started to walk away. Under my breath, I said, "Once a prick, always a prick."

At the ceremony, St. John, as usual, went on too long, but I didn't care. It was the last time I'd have to listen to him.

"Stop squirming," I whispered to Boogie, who was sitting right in front of me. "I'm customizing your chair," I said. I carved *JFKennedy* on his seat-back, having decided that the occasion called for more than just my initials.

When the Head handed me my diploma, he said, "Jack, you made it. Had doubts that you would. Well, see what you can do to make something of yourself."

"I will. And the Sixth-Form thinks I will too."

I walked away and joined Rip and Lem.

"Jack, let's sign graduation photos," Lem said. We exchanged photographs. I wrote: "To Lemmer, the gayest soul I know. In memory of two tense years and in hopes of many more. —Your old pal and supporter, Ken"

Handing him back his photograph, I said, "And thanks for sticking around another year. Don't know if I could have made it without you."

"We almost didn't." Lem grinned. "You can always count on me, Jack. I mean that."

CHAPTER FIFTY

Summer 1935
Hyannis Port, MA

Summers aren't as much fun when you can't sail. And for a few weeks, I couldn't. Nobody could. Nantucket Sound was calm, placid, and boring. With barely a wisp of wind, it was the equivalent of bathtub water. Uncommonly warm too. When I did go out, I wasn't so much sailing as drifting. Drove me crazy.

Before Joe and I would compete a few weeks later in the Edgartown Regatta on Martha's Vineyard, I needed a couple of races under my belt. While I waited for the winds to pick up, I busied myself painting and varnishing the *Victura*. From scratch, I constructed a new tiller, sawing, planing, and lacquering the fine mahogany. Couldn't wait to try out the rehabbed boat.

One day, a brisk wind finally arrived. Plenty of rough whitecaps and fierce rig-straining gusts. Nantucket Sound had come alive. Windswept waters from the Sound roared through the exposed opening in the Hyannis Port breakwater that did little to protect the harbor. Red flag warnings were posted.

A dozen other youthful, oil-skinned skippers, including Joe, assembled at the harbor master's office, where we were shocked by the note tacked to the bulletin board: "No Race Today."

We stared at the sign. No wind for weeks, and when we finally get a blow, the old folks put a kibosh to the race.

Damn elders.

"Oh, well," one skipper said. "Do something else. See ya."

Others turned their backs, but I wasn't going to pack it in. I wagged my finger at Joe. "C'mon, let's have a race of our own. Nobody here to stop us," I said, waving my hand.

"Are you nuts?" Joe said, pointing to the wild seas.

"We've been out in worse weather. What are we, a bunch of sissies?"

Maybe I was nuts but, eager to try out my new tiller, I craved a race.

The only obstacle was a piece of paper tacked onto a bulletin board. I tore it off and stuffed it in my pocket. "Never saw anything about the race being canceled," I said.

Joe and six other skippers took up the challenge.

After I recruited three guys for my crew, I removed the battered tiller and tossed it into the trunk cabin and bolted on the shiny new one. "New tiller, guys," I announced. "Made it myself. We've got an advantage."

I hoisted the sail, which whipped fiercely in the wind. Because it was so blustery, I shortened the sail, so the *Victura* could better withstand heavy gusts. Other skippers boldly, or perhaps naively, carried full sail. The *Victura*, a Wianno Senior, is difficult to capsize, but in high wind using full sail, the risk of tipping too far increases. The result is loss of speed and a good scare.

Squaring the *Victura*, I maneuvered for a spot at the starting line. The new tiller felt great, lighter than the old one, more flexible. The other boats scurried back and forth, zigging and zagging, crowding the starting line. Like a jockey astride his horse at the gate, I was raring to go, waiting for the signal to start.

Too impatient, I overshot the marker.

"Hard-a-lee!" I shouted to my crew. We'd have to come about and get behind the starting line again.

As I sharply swung the *Victura* around, a gust and a wave hit us simultaneously.

Crack!

The tiller snapped right where I'd connected it to the rudder. I held the new tiller like I was holding a sword without a blade. Useless. Who made this thing anyway?

For me, the race had ended before it began. My crew shook their heads, exasperated. "What did you make it out of?" a crewman asked with a smirk. "Cardboard? He got us out here and now this."

Reaching overboard, I operated the rudder by hand, steering the *Victura* into the wind. The boat was out of control; I was in the way of other contestants. I got plenty of dirty looks.

Call it a day? What else could I do? I had been the one who wanted to face the elements. The last thing I wanted to do was go back to the dock. I'd take plenty of ridicule from the crews of the other boats when they got back from the race. "What's the matter, Jack? Didn't see you out there. What are you, a sissy?"

The race started, but the *Victura* wasn't going anywhere.

As they pulled away, the other skippers taunted me, waving their bye-byes.

"Thought you wanted to race," Joe sneered.

"What's a matter? You scared?"

"Quitting before you start, Jack?"

Wait. *The old tiller.*

I dashed into the cubby, retrieved it, unbolted the damaged unit, and swapped the two. *Here we go!*

I looked up to see my competitors halfway to the first course leg. Plenty of ground to make up, but I had time. With my sails trimmed, I had rhythm, momentum, and thrust. I was jacked. The tiller troubles forgotten, I saw the rough weather and the five boats in the distance. I was excited about the challenge.

My plan was to make gradual progress, not attempt any crazy maneuvers, not panic. Stay reefed down.

One at a time. One at a time.

Bucking and bouncing on the rough sea reminded me of a movie of cowboys riding angry broncos. But this was more like riding a bucking bronco on a rollercoaster while somebody spits in your eye. Wet and wild. Crazy.

My crew positioned themselves over the starboard gunwale, the top half of their bodies above the waves, abdomens taut, their backs to the sea. Keep the hull flat and we'd be fine.

The wind became fiercer, pummeling us with ocean spray, but we were making up ground.

After the first buoy, I passed the trailing boat. It was one of the skippers who'd mocked me. I gave him a salute. He dropped his head.

Right hand on the tiller, I gave a forward motion. My crew whooped.

Full speed ahead, but I was tiring, my strength sapped by the pull of the tiller against the strong current.

Passing two more boats, we were within inches of the second-place boat when a sudden gust jolted both of us. They weren't ready for it; they were carrying full sail, and their crew was unceremoniously dumped in the Sound. The Race Committee, which had come out in an unofficial capacity, motored over to pick them up.

Seconds later, a familiar sound.

Crack! This time from above. *Goddamn it!*

The gaff, upon which the top of the mainsail was attached, had broken, and a pole swung loose. The mainsail was now secured by only three corners instead of four. That gave us a smaller sail area. Like a car missing a spark plug.

The *Victura* was crippled. Sooner or later, the strain would rip the sail. End of game. End of race.

I loved that sail. It had helped me win many a race. If I called it quits, I could save the sail. Could I really win? Chances of victory were slim. I was way behind. But only one way to find out for sure.

Go for it.

The wind increased and the ocean poured in. As the cockpit filled, the water came up to my ankles. The crew bailed furiously.

I looked up. The rope edging on the sail was threadbare; the mainsail was going. But when? I prayed for the sail to hold until the end of the race.

Ahead, I spied the leader.

Joe.

Joe looked back, shocked that I'd caught up. *Didn't expect to see me again, did ya, Joe?* But then he gave me that crooked grin of his, pointing to my damaged rigging.

Yeah, Joe. I know. Still coming after you.

Given my disadvantage, Joe planned on coasting to the finish line a winner.

But what appeared to be a fatal event in a long race might help in a final push. With limited sail area exposed, I was heeling less and going faster. Using the intense wind to my advantage, I was catching up to Joe.

He had his own challenge, struggling to keep his hull at less than forty-five degrees. Water washed into his cockpit, too.

I had time, and my hull was flatter than Joe's.

I found a lane.

I was gaining, but the finish line was only a few hundred yards off, and Joe increased his lead. Doing nothing ensured defeat, so I tried several tactics, one or more of which succeeded.

I surged ahead. Won by half a boat length.

As I passed, Joe looked away.

Back on land, we celebrated, all of us exuberant at successfully taking on the wild conditions. Joe gave me a quick congratulatory slap on the back before walking away.

—⇒·◇·⇐—

"I'll throw you guys a party after the Vineyard races," Dad said, standing above us on the dock.

Joe and I were making preparations for the *Victura*. The next day, we'd be sailing to Martha's Vineyard for the Edgartown Regatta.

"You deserve it," Dad said. "Celebrate Joe's twentieth birthday. And congratulations to you, Jack, for graduating and for winning Most Likely to Succeed." He pointed his finger at me. "But it's up to you to do it now. To succeed. Have fun before school starts."

I'd changed my mind about where I was actually going to school. I'd listed Harvard as my choice in *The Brief*, but I was going to Princeton. I wanted to be with Lem and Rip. Dad had accepted my decision, although not happily.

Dad turned to walk away, then stopped and said, "Oh, and make sure you win."

Joe and I cast off. Sixteen-and-a-half nautical miles across Nantucket Sound to Martha's Vineyard.

I was ready to let loose, free from the Old Man's prying eyes. The Regatta, the high point of the Cape Cod sailing season, was also its premier social event. Nearly two hundred boats prepared to race, and thousands invaded the island to watch the competition and enjoy the beaches, the nightlife—the giant party.

Joe and I still had our problems, but our relationship had improved, and there were fewer altercations. I'd gained his respect. Maybe because he'd gotten wind of the Muckers Affair. What's more, I'd filled out, and now measured six feet. Although Joe was broader, I was now taller by half an inch. And of course, I'd just whipped him in the race.

The next day it was me steering the *Victura* into the open sea. I had been thinking about what Joe had written in my scrapbook. It had caught me by surprise. But I wasn't sure what he meant. "So you think I'm a smoothie," I said.

"Huh?" Joe said while he let out sail.

"What you wrote in my scrapbook. 'To be as much a smoothie as my brother.'" Joe had never expressed any envy or jealousy. Or complimented me.

Joe looked away. "Yeah. So what?"

"What did you mean by that?"

"Got a way about you, that's all," Joe said. He looked slightly embarrassed. Maybe a little envious.

"Like how?" I pressed.

"Oh, how you get along with people. Say the right things. You're not a hothead like me."

We laughed.

"And with the gals. Noticed them eyeing you when we went into Hyannis. Nice-looking ones, too. You know how to chat them up. Make 'em laugh. Comes naturally to you."

"Possibly." Maybe Joe wasn't the best at everything after all, but was he saying he was envious of me? Perhaps Lecky was right…about everything.

Joe finished letting out sail and the *Victura* surged.

I caught a perfect breeze that jettisoned the *Victura* into the North Atlantic. Nothing but the vast ocean as far as the eye could see.

My future seemed just as wide open.

Primary Characters

JOHN ("JACK") FITZGERALD KENNEDY: Pulitzer Prize-winning author, World War II torpedo boat skipper, Congressman and Senator from Massachusetts, became President of the United States in 1961 and was assassinated in 1963.

JOSEPH KENNEDY: Jack's father, a successful businessman, served as Security and Exchange Commission Chairman and Ambassador to Great Britain during the Roosevelt Administration.

JOSEPH KENNEDY, JR: Jack's older brother, was killed while on a bombing mission during World War II.

KIRK ("LEM") LEMOYNE BILLINGS: Jack's BFF and a closeted homosexual, had a room at The White House and was a co-inventor of "Fizzies," in which a tablet; dropped into water, produced a sweet effervescent drink.

DR. GEORGE ST. JOHN: Served as headmaster at the Choate School for forty years.

JOHN J. MAHER: Teacher, football coach, and housemaster at Choate.

Secondary Characters

ROSE KENNEDY: Jack's mother. Her father was once the mayor of Boston. She married Joseph Kennedy, and had nine children. She died at the age of 104.

ROBERT ("BOBBY") KENNEDY: Jack's younger brother ran his campaign for President, and was appointed Attorney General. He led the effort against organized crime, was a key figure in the peaceful solution of the Cuban Missile Crisis, advocated for civil rights, and helped secure the integration of the Universities of Alabama and Mississippi. After JFK's assassination, he won election as a senator from New York, where he raised awareness of poverty and became an outspoken critic of the Vietnam War. While running for President in 1968, he was assassinated in Los Angeles after winning the California primary.

EDWARD ("TED") KENNEDY: The youngest Kennedy sibling served as a U.S. senator from Massachusetts. For almost 47 years in the Senate, he championed economic and social justice. He made many efforts to enact universal health care. In 1969, he pleaded guilty to leaving the scene of a crime after the Chappaquiddick incident resulted in the death of his automobile passenger. In 1980, he failed to wrest the Democratic nomination for President from the incumbent, President Jimmy Carter.

KATHLEEN ("KICK") KENNEDY: Jack's favorite sister died in a plane crash along with her English husband, in 1948.

ROSEMARY KENNEDY: The Kennedys' oldest daughter was intellectually disabled. Due to violent mood swings and erratic behavior, her father had her lobotomized at the age of 23, believing the procedure would calm her down. However, it was botched—she could no longer speak or write intelligibly afterwards, and she spent the rest of her life institutionalized.

EUNICE KENNEDY: Jack's younger sister founded the Special Olympics, a worldwide sports organization for people with intellectual and physical disabilities.

GERTRUDE STEIN: A novelist, playwright, and poet, she is most famous for her quasi-memoir, "The Autobiography of Alice B. Toklas"—Toklas was her lifelong romantic partner—and for hosting a Paris salon at which Ernest Hemingway, Pablo Picasso, F. Scott Fitzgerald, Ezra Pound and others attended.

ALAN ("A.J.") JAY LERNER: Jack's classmate at Choate and Harvard was a lyricist and librettist, famous for his work on "My Fair Lady" and "Camelot."

HUDDIE ("LEADBELLY") WILLIAM LEDBETTER: A folk and blues singer. His best-known songs are "Goodnight Irene" and "Midnight Special."

RALPH ("RIP") HORTON: Jack's close friend at Choate was his roommate at Princeton and helped during his presidential campaign.

CLARA ST. JOHN: Wife of headmaster George St. John.

OLIVE CAWLEY: Jack's first steady girlfriend maintained a friendship with him for life. She became an actress and model and was married to the IBM President.

PRESCOTT LECKY: Jack's therapist was a Psychology lecturer at Columbia, and developed the concept of self-help as a psychotherapy method.

JFK TIMELINE

May 29, 1917: Born in Brookline, Massachusetts.

September 1927: Kennedy family moves to Bronxville, N.Y.

October 1929: Stock market crash triggers the Great Depression.

Fall 1931: Kennedy enrolls in Choate.

June 1935: Kennedy graduates from Choate, ranked 64th in a class of 112.

Fall 1935: Kennedy enrolls in Princeton; he drops out due to illness later that year.

1936: Kennedy attends Harvard University.

Summer 1937: Kennedy and Lem Billings tour Europe.

March 1938: Joseph Kennedy, Sr. is named ambassador to Great Britain.

September 1939: Outbreak of World War II (1939-45) in Europe.

1940: Kennedy writes his senior thesis on English foreign policy prior to World War II.

July 1940: Kennedy's senior thesis on English foreign policy prior to World War II is published as a book called *Why England Slept*.

Summer 1941: Kennedy enters the U.S. armed forces.

December 7, 1941: Japanese bomb Pearl Harbor, compelling the U.S. to enter World War II against Japan and Germany.

1942-43: Kennedy serves on, and then commands, a Motor Torpedo Boat, or "PT Boat," in the South Pacific.

August 2, 1943: Kennedy's PT boat is rammed by a Japanese destroyer. Under his leadership, most of the crew is eventually rescued. Kennedy receives the Purple Heart for his heroics.

Spring 1944: Kennedy enters Boston's Chelsea Naval Hospital with a lower back condition.

August 12, 1944: Joseph Kennedy, Jr. is killed while flying a mission over Europe.

March 1, 1945: Kennedy is discharged from the Navy.

November 1946: Kennedy is elected to the House of Representatives.

Fall 1948: Kennedy is elected to a second term in the House. While on a trip to England, he is diagnosed with Addison's Disease. His condition is kept secret from the public.

1950-1953: Korean War.

February 1950: Wisconsin Senator Joseph McCarthy claims to have a list of Communists employed in the State Department. The era of "McCarthyism" begins.

November 1950: Kennedy is elected to a third term in the House.

November 1952: Kennedy wins election to the United States Senate. In the presidential election, Dwight Eisenhower and his running mate, Richard Nixon, defeat Adlai Stevenson.

September 12, 1953: Kennedy marries Jacqueline Bouvier.

December 2, 1954: Joseph McCarthy is censured by the U.S. Senate. Kennedy abstains from voting on the resolution.

1955-1956: Kennedy "writes" *Profiles in Courage*, a history of heroic American senators. In fact, much of the book work is done by his speechwriter, Theodore Sorensen.

Summer 1956: At the Democratic National Convention, Tennessee Senator Estes Kefauver edges out Kennedy to become Adlai Stevenson's vice-presidential running mate.

November 1956: Eisenhower crushes Stevenson and wins re-election.

1957: *Profiles in Courage* is awarded the Pulitzer Prize.

November 27, 1957: Caroline Bouvier Kennedy, Kennedy's daughter, is born.

November 1958: Kennedy wins re-election to the Senate by a comfortable margin.

July 1960: Kennedy wins the Democratic nomination for president and picks Lyndon Johnson as his running mate.

November 8, 1960: Kennedy defeats Nixon in a closely contested election.

November 25, 1960: John F. Kennedy, Jr is born.

January 20, 1961: Kennedy is sworn in as President of the United States.

March 1961: Kennedy announces the establishment of the Peace Corps.

April 1961: Attempted U.S.-backed invasion of Cuba ends in disaster at the Bay of Pigs.

May, 1961: Alan Shepard becomes the first American in space, and Kennedy challenges the U.S. to put a man on the moon by the end of the decade.

June 1961: Kennedy and Soviet Premier Nikita Khrushchev conduct a summit meeting in Vienna over the status of a divided Berlin.

August 1961: U.S. and Latin American nations join in the «Alliance for Progress.»

March 1962: Kennedy forces the steel industry to eliminate a price increase.

October 16, 1962: The U.S. obtains photos of Soviet missile emplacements in Cuba, bringing about the Cuban Missile Crisis.

October 22, 1962: Kennedy announces a naval quarantine of Cuba.

October 28, 1962: Soviet Union agrees to remove its missiles from Cuba.

June 1963: Kennedy ensures the integration of the Universities of Mississippi and Alabama, and sends to Congress a comprehensive civil rights bill.

June 26, 1963: Speaking in West Berlin, Kennedy demonstrates his solidarity with the city, declaring, "Ich bin ein Berliner" ("I am also a citizen of Berlin").

August 5, 1963: U.S. and Soviet Union agree to a nuclear test-ban treaty.

August, 28, 1963: About 250,000 people travel to Washington D.C. to show their support for civil rights legislation. Martin Luther King, Jr. delivers "I Have a Dream" speech.

Early November, 1963: A coup overthrows the government of South Vietnam. The U.S. has 16,000 military advisors in South Vietnam.

November 22, 1963: Kennedy is assassinated while riding in a motorcade in Dallas, Texas. Lyndon Johnson becomes president

QUESTIONS TO CONSIDER

1. John F. Kennedy is one of the most famous Presidents in American history. In the story, do you see indications he'd become a leader? Are there behaviors/characteristics that you admire? Or disapprove of? Point to examples.

2. Jack faces competing challenges from both his brother and father. How does he meet those challenges? Support your answers with details from the book.

3. Jack rebuffs Lem's sexual overture. Why do you think Lem propositions Jack, and what do you think of how Jack handles the situation?

4. How would you describe the relationship between Jack and Lem (who was his BFF and later had a room at the White House)? What do you think of how he treats Lem and the language he uses in his letters to Lem?

5. In the 1930s, almost nobody admitted their homosexuality and many covered it up by dating/marrying persons of the opposite sex for fear of losing their job or standing in the community. How has that practice changed since then?

6. In the book, Jack is a victim of discrimination. He also rebels against what he sees as repression. What do you think of the strategies he uses to make his points?

7. Jack is frequently ill in the book and throughout his life. Do you think this had an effect on how he lives his life at Choate and afterwards? How so?

8. Is Jack courageous or reckless? There are instances where he challenges authority but also risks his future. Are the two approaches mutually exclusive or can they exist together?

9. Jack is a risk-taker in several instances in the book. What do you think of the risks he took? What makes a risk worth taking?

10. Jack sees a therapist while at Choate. What did you think of the counsel he receives from Prescott Lecky, and do you think it was helpful? How so?

11. Several legendary characters come to Choate while Jack is a student—Leadbelly, Gertrude Stein, and Alan Lerner. Research further what they are known for. Does one interest you more than the others? Why?

12. More than sixty years after his death, America and the world continue to be fascinated by JFK and the Kennedy family. Explore reasons why this is so. What stands out most for you about his life?

FURTHER READING

John F. Kennedy

Jack: The Early Years of John F. Kennedy by Ilene Cooper (New York: Dutton, 2003).

JFK: Reckless Youth by Nigel Hamilton (New York: Random House, 1992).

JFK: Coming of Age in the American Century 1917-1956 by Fredrik Logevall (New York, Random House, 2020).

Live by the Sword: The Secret War Against Castro and the Death of JFK by Gus Russo (Baltimore, Bancroft, 1998).

The Kennedy Family

The Fitzgeralds and the Kennedys by Doris Kearns Goodwin (New York, St. Martins, 1987).

The Kennedy Men: 1901-1963 by Laurence Leamer (New York, Morrow, 2001).

The Kennedy Women by Laurence Leamer (New York, Villard, 1994).

The Nine of Us by Jean Kennedy Smith (New York, HarperCollins, 2016),

Jack and Lem: John F. Kennedy and Lem Billings: The Untold Story of an Extraordinary Friendship by David Pitts (New York, Hachette, 2007).

The Missing Kennedy, Rosemary Kennedy and the Secret Bonds of Four Women by Elizabeth Koehler-Pentacoff (Baltimore, Bancroft, 2015)

Written by John F. Kennedy

Profiles in Courage (New York, Harper, 1955).

Why England Slept (New York, Wilfred Funk, 1940).

A Nation of Immigrants (New York, Harper, 1958).

Historical Fiction

Jack 1939 by Francine Mathews (New York, Riverhead, 2012).

11/22/63 by Stephen King, (New York, Simon & Schuster, 2102).

The Summer I Met Jack by Michelle Gable (New York, St. Martins, 2018).

ACKNOWLEDGEMENTS

I am indebted to many who assisted me in the creation of this book. Those who provided valuable help include my editor, Karen Grove. I am grateful for her masterful touch in shaping the material.

I had many readers volunteer to examine the manuscript. My appreciation goes to Becky Wong, Oliver and Karen Pollak, Bruce Yelaska, as well as the unidentified participants and leaders of the numerous writers' groups and conventions I attended. Thank you for your suggestions even if I didn't take them all.

The staff at the JFK Library in Boston were an enormous help, bringing out box after box of materials and generously answering my questions.

I'm also grateful to Judy Donald, the longtime archivist at Choate Rosemary Hall. She provided valuable insights and guided me to important documents.

And finally, thanks to Bruce Bortz at Bancroft Press, who recognized the potential for a story about young John Kennedy, added his own editing, and made it a reality.

About the Author

S cott Badler has been a newspaper reporter and a regular contributor to such publications as the *Boston Globe*, where many of his humor pieces appeared. In addition to having had published essays about the Kennedys, political history, and satire, he has written two non-fiction books: *What's So Funny About Looking for a Job?* and *Oh Brother, and Other Revelations on Family, Relatives, Pets, and Sex.*

He has taught Humor Writing courses at Harvard and Emerson College.

A native Californian, he was born in Los Angeles but lived in the Greater Boston area for many years, many of them in the district where JFK won his first congressional seat in 1946.

He currently resides in the San Francisco Bay Area.

This is his first novel.